"WE SHOULD START BACK, CARA MIA."

Marco's voice was a low caress; his touch was warm as he slipped his arm around her waist.

The moon was drenching them in silver. Meg was acutely aware of his nearness, of the strange power that flowed between them.

"Ah, Meg!" he whispered close to her ear. She raised her eyes, knowing he would bend his lips to hers.

His kiss was gentle, but it sent a flash of electricity through her, a shock of subtle fire. Astonishment flooded her. So this was what love songs were about! Her body was singing with desire, and she clung to Marco while the moon and stars whirled ecstatically around them....

Finally Marco pulled away. "Forgive me, piccola." His voice was rough. "I had to kiss you...even though we say goodbye."

CATHERINE KAY
is also the author
of SUPERROMANCE #45
DAWN OF PASSION

Robyn Douglas, Ph.D. candidate in ancient languages, was deeply moved by the mysterious desert land. She felt she was home at last—doubly so when she met Sayed al-Rashad, the dizzyingly attractive archaeologist she would be working with.

He obviously didn't share her reaction. Instead he pegged her as a starry-eyed American coed who, like many others before her, would probably fall in love with him to the detriment of their work.

Robyn fought the powerful response she felt whenever Sayed came near her. But she couldn't fight the inner voice that whispered this man was her destiny.

CATHERINE KAY

INTERLUDE

A SUPERROMANCE FROM
WORLDWIDE
TORONTO • NEW YORK • LONDON

For Geraldine and Victor Terry
with love and gratitude

Grateful acknowledgment is made to Kate Simon, for the quotations from her book ITALY: THE PLACES IN BETWEEN, Harper & Row, 1970.

Published September 1983

First printing July 1983

ISBN 0-373-70080-6

Printed in Canada

CHAPTER ONE

THE HEAVY WOODEN SHUTTERS at the hotel window swung wide under Meg's urging hand, and she drew a deep expectant breath. Outside, Venice shone in the shimmering light of sunset. The very air was tinged and permeated with flowing colors. In the brilliant long slanting rays of the sinking sun she saw church domes, green with the patina of age, and a tall golden-crested campanile etched against the glowing sky.

A warm breeze blew gently against Meg's face as she leaned on the broad windowsill to study the scene before her. It was exactly as she'd always pictured it. Suddenly a clamor of bells made her stiffen with surprise, and she listened attentively as the churches of the city called out the Angelus. Across the Grand Canal from where she stood the rich voice of Santa Maria della Salute rumbled around its ancient dome, while from farther away the clear tones of the Campanile of St. Mark's spoke above the mellow bells of San Giorgio. Meg recognized each one of them even though she had never been in Venice before—she knew intuitively how the bells of Venice would sound.

Her eyes misted with tears. It was all so new, yet so familiar. So much the stuff of her dreams! Just then the chug of a motor launch on the canal below disrupted the balmy evening, and the whiff of exhaust fumes reminded her that even dreams were never perfect. With a sigh she turned back to her pleasant bedroom, where her luggage sat unopened on its stand.

The hotel was attractive. She had caught a glimpse of an inviting restaurant off the lobby as she checked in, and she knew that it, too, probably overlooked the Grand Canal.

Hanging up her few things, she showered and put on a robe, all the while trying to avoid the insistent thoughts that tugged at her mind. *Well,* they said, *you're finally here! How long have you wanted to come? It must be at least. . . .*

"A very long time," she said aloud.

Now that you're here, her thoughts continued, *how do you feel?*

"Awful," she whispered, "just awful."

She knew very well that coming here to Europe with this tour was a symbolic and long overdue act of independence. For all of her twenty-five years there had been someone trying to direct the path of her life. First her mother, well-meaning but constantly alarmed at the state of the world and always fearful of change. And then Jim, who had swept her up into his strongly ordered life when she was still in college, had put an engagement ring on her finger and had expected her to follow demurely in his footsteps wherever he decided was best for them to go.

Dear Jim, she thought futilely. Where were all his plans now, all his certainties? Scattered on the slopes of an Idaho mountain with the wreckage of the light plane that had taken his life six months before. And now she'd never know if she would have found the courage to say the painful words, "I love you, but not enough to marry you."

For one distressing moment a picture of Jim's earnest face moved across her mind. Meg sat down hard on the bed and a wave of melancholy flowed over her. *I'm finally here,* she thought, *and when I go out into the beauty of Venice there won't be anyone's hand to take—not Jim's, not anyone's.*

Her private fantasies of the city had never included coming as a twenty-five-year-old single female on a whirlwind tour. Always when she'd thought of this place there had been a sense of presence, of something waiting for her. Was it her own romantic nature that had made a promise to her? Now for the first time a harsh reality was moving into her heart: nothing was waiting. And the only people she knew were the members of her Happiness in Europe Tour—nice, settled tourists complaining about their aching feet and a little bewildered by the speed of their travel schedule.

More than one of her companions had stood close to her in a museum or church these past two weeks and said in a dazed voice, "*Where* did they say this was?" There were so many cities between Copenhagen and Venice!

Meg wasn't one to cry easily, but the sunset glory intensifying outside the wide window hurt her by its very splendor and brought unwilling tears streaming down her face. Every magic stone of Venice seemed touched by loneliness—her own.

If things had been going according to her long-formulated plan, she would be rushing out to find St. Mark's Square, to see and feel everything the first moment she could. But her head ached, so instead she took an aspirin and lay down against the cool soft pillows on her bed....

She woke to a rapid tapping on her door. "It's

dinnertime, dear,'' Mary Lou Nelson called out cheerily before she hurried on down the hall.

Meg liked Mrs. Nelson, a retired schoolteacher whose unflagging enthusiasm was wonderful to behold. But in Venice she needed to be alone, without the presence of her kindly, chirping roommate. When the bus had left Florence that morning Meg had quietly asked the tour director for a single room in Venice and had offered to pay the extra fee to have it. Mrs. Nelson was being a good sport about it.

Meg rushed to change her clothes, then went down to find her tour group, which was having cocktails at little tables overlooking the Grand Canal. Her headache was still with her, and as she sat down, wavy, trembling sensations came and went. The sherry she sipped sent her into a dizzy spin. Her hands were suddenly cold.

''Are you all right?''

Mrs. Nelson and another woman blurred in front of Meg's aching eyes. She clung to the arm of her chair until their concerned faces were clear again. ''I. . .I think I'd better skip dinner. I don't feel well,'' she managed to say.

Mrs. Nelson put a hand on her forehead. ''You're warm—maybe a touch of the pip.''

''It was that shrimp in Verona,'' her friend commiserated. ''Oh, dear, you *are* white!''

Meg was trying desperately to control her heaving stomach. She stood up on uncertain legs. ''I've got to go to bed. . .I'll be okay.''

Mary Lou Nelson saw her to her room and brought Pepto Bismol and Lomotil, then left with assurances that she would look in later. Huge gripes twisted in Meg's belly, and she was well and truly sick at the end of a fast run to the bathroom. Slightly relieved, she drank a bit of the pink liquid and then lay like a statue on the bed, not daring to move for fear it would start all over again.

So here she was in Venice. Weak tears trickled out of her eyes again. She would have to pull herself together and be sensible.

Gentle wafts of warm air flowed over her from the window. Even if she didn't have the strength to stand up she could at least feel the special quality of Italy—a kind of love spell. It was in the faces of the women and in the warmly assessing glances of the men. Even old rotund Italians flirted with their expressive eyes and blew kisses from their graceful fingertips. Well, there were worse places to be sick. Meg willed the tears to stop and mentally began to write a travel article about Italy. Her favorite professor had once told her that a journalist was always a journalist, no matter what the circumstances.

She smiled slightly. If she ever wrote the absolute truth about her tour, with its breakneck pace and near disasters, she would never again be able to face her companions from Happiness in Europe. Since the hopeful little band of Americans first set foot in Copenhagen two weeks before, each day had become a marathon, a total immersion in culture and history—a blur.

Meg had scarcely ever found enough time to write a proper commentary in her travel notebook, and by the time she had crawled wearily into her bed in Florence yesterday, the journal was reading like a teenager's diary, breathless and disconnected:

> Holland...fabulous cheeses, smiling big people, lots of laughter, Rembrandt! Paris...the Louvre...Mona Lisa still smiling mysteriously..

naughty nightclub show with half-naked dancers doing tired routines. Monte Carlo sparkles against a brilliant blue sea. I imagine I can see Italy! Rome: Tour guide has a Rossano Brazzi voice, but there the similarity ends. . . can't wait to discover Venice. I can feel it reaching out to me. . . .

And then this latest hot September day. It had started in Florence with a frantic rush past Michelangelo's *David* and the Duomo, and a tip of the hat to all the glorious Renaissance treasures. Then their group had piled back into the bus and hurtled through the Italian countryside, passing several intriguing hill towns. Not for the first time Meg had questioned the wisdom of traveling in a prepackaged tour.

Lunch had been in Verona at an open air restaurant on the Piazza delle Erbe; then they'd moved onward with brief stops at Vicenza and Padua. Giotto's monumental works in the Scrovegni Chapel deserved more than the fifteen minutes allotted to them. The stunning frescoes should have been savored like a fine wine.

Don't let Venice be like this, Meg prayed to the god of tourists as she stepped back into the bus. The young dark-haired hostess announced, "Venice in forty-five minutes," and gave a rambling history over the loudspeaker while everyone dozed from fatigue and heat. Everyone except Meg. Her eyes had been alert and hungrily watching for the first signs of her dream city. No one on the bus knew what it meant to her to be so close to it.

In a few minutes they were passing a stark industrial area; a sign said Mestre. Then there was the glitter of smooth dappled blue water, a long bridge with traffic speeding across, and a train hooting on its own track alongside the car lanes.

And finally, rising like a fairyland of spires and domes between earth and heaven, glittering and gleaming in the Italian afternoon light. . . there it was!

"And here I am," Meg said under her breath. "Damn. . .damn!" She was restless as she lay in her bed, and didn't dare close her eyes in case the nausea returned. Sleep would be impossible until her stomach decided what it was going to do.

It was so strange to think that Venice was there, just beyond those windows. The low-grade fever that was at work in Meg's body seemed to intensify her emotions, and she couldn't hold back the stream of pictures in her mind—obsessive images that had led her here, to feel and dream and be in love with. . . what? A city? A myth of enchantment and grand passion?

How absurd that she, Meg Brown, would still be held in thrall by a romantic film she had first seen when she was sixteen and still couldn't forget. The movie had been *Summertime*. Meg had thought Rossano Brazzi the most desirable man alive until she realized he was probably by then well past middle age and that the film had been made before she was even born. But what a movie! Nothing had touched her to the core in quite the same way before or since. She had cried as only an adolescent could when Katharine Hepburn did the noble thing and voluntarily left the love of her life.

For all these years a shadow of empathy had lingered in Meg's heart for the tragic screen lovers in their Venetian idyll. Finally she'd had to analyze her intense response to the story. She was certainly no Kate Hepburn, lonely spinster on a trip to Venice caught off guard by the charm of a married Italian male. What was it then?

It wasn't until she was engaged to Jim Reynolds that she finally figured it out: not only had she never experienced that kind of passion, she probably never would. She would most likely live out her life calmly and sensibly, never having the option of embracing romance or walking away from it, as Katharine Hepburn had. With Jim an engagement was the logical step a man took when he'd selected the proper partner for his life. He rarely spoke of love because, as he liked to say with a serious expression on his face, "It was self-evident."

It seemed to Meg now, as she lay on her bed in Venice, that there really was such a thing as Fate, with a capital F. What else would explain her fiancé's sudden death, in the senseless crash that had carried away his boss's hunting party? Or all the coincidences that had piled on top of one another since then? She could almost believe that in spite of herself she was being nudged toward another path.

Her thoughts went back to the decisive night less than a month ago when Ronald Pell had escorted her to the charity ball at the Los Robles Club in Pasadena, her hometown. Pasadena was filled with stately homes where wealthy easterners had once wintered in the agreeable Southern California climate. Lately it had become a business city as well, with a healthy mix of residents from every economic level.

The fine old Los Robles was a remnant of the earlier era. It had tried to turn its ballroom into a bit of Venice that evening, and Meg's eyes had dilated in pleasurable surprise to see huge photo murals that could have come from the picture *Summertime* on the walls. Tables were decorated with tiny flowered gondolas, and a small strolling orchestra in gondolier costumes had played romantic Italian songs.

Ronald worked in her Uncle Frank's prestigious firm of accountants, where Meg was the editor of the monthly newsletter. An ingratiating young man on the rise, he had been eager to escort the boss's niece to this party, where the estimated wealth of the patrons would run into the tens of millions.

It was the first time Meg had been to a party since Jim's death. She hadn't really wanted to go at all, but it was one of those obligatory things that one does when one's uncle *and* boss is a moving force in a city steeped in tradition. Frank Singleton's name was well-known in the higher circles of finance, which made him a figure of some importance.

Once she got there Meg quickly realized that this was the wrong evening for her to be resuming her social life. She just wasn't ready to move into the old rounds as if she were the same Meg who used to be on Jim Reynolds's arm. It was difficult to face the well-meaning sympathy of the people she had known then. And, more honestly, she found that the Italian theme of the ball had a disturbing effect on her ragged emotions.

After an hour of greeting old friends and dancing a little she told Ronald she couldn't stay, that she wasn't feeling well. When he hesitated, she added, "I'll just get a taxi. There's no reason for you to go, too."

She knew that he was mentally weighing the comparative values of being kind to the boss's niece or talking to a few more potential clients. He chose the former, and Meg wished he hadn't. Unexpected and nebulous longings had been stirred in her by the captivating songs of Venice. It was silly, she realized, but she couldn't help it. *Summertime* was still haunting her.

Jim had teased her once when she'd bought a very expensive book full of pictures of Venice. "The city fascinates me," she had told him a little defensively. He had made an amused but skeptical face. "You don't fool me, Meggie." One of his large hands had patted her slightly blushing cheek. "It's that Italian Romeo from the movies who makes those innocent gray eyes of yours go dreamy. Maybe, just maybe, I'll take you there for our honeymoon, so you can see for yourself what's so exciting. I hope it's me," he had laughed and given her one of his playful bear hugs....

The night of the charity ball she'd let Ronald kiss her good-night at the door, didn't invite him in for coffee, and sighed with relief as she shut the door on his poor, dull, inoffensive back.

But Fate wasn't finished with her evening yet. As she turned away from the door she'd heard her dainty Swiss clock begin to chime eleven from its spot above the fake fireplace of her apartment living room. Its pretty face, enameled with delicate wildflower designs, always lifted her spirits, and it did so now.

The clock had been part of her Great-aunt Harriet's modest legacy. Aunt Harriet had traveled widely, and was regarded by Meg's mother as the adventurous one of the family. The dear old lady had always enjoyed Meg's delighted exclamations over her travel souvenirs, and she'd left her a few charming objects of art as well as $2000 when she died. The money had been consigned to a bank account, and there it remained.

After changing out of her evening gown Meg had

wandered about her little apartment restlessly. She was glad she had a domain of her own, free of family scrutiny. The feeling of Italy roamed with her, as if she had stepped into a special atmosphere that wouldn't let her go. It was too simplistic to think she was merely being bothered by an old obsession. The explanation had to be more complex than that.

Abandoning her amateur psychology, she switched on the TV, hoping for some late news. A little reality couldn't hurt.

The usual talk shows were in progress, with the same old guests. And then it happened, as if some mischievous arranger of lives was at work. On the second turn of the dial, color and sound bloomed onto the screen in a familiar, well-loved pattern. Katharine Hepburn sat alone at a table in St. Mark's Square. And nearby, Rossano Brazzi's dark, speculative, romantic eyes were assessing her well-turned ankles and beginning to travel over her body.

Meg stood transfixed. This was too much! A commercial came on and she reached to turn off the set, but she couldn't do it. She had already heard the music of the small orchestra at the *ristorante* and had seen the strutting pigeons. The sound of the bells of St. Mark's flooded into her mind. With a low groan of surrender she sat down on the little couch.

On the side table next to her a fragile jewel-toned Venetian goblet, one of Aunt Harriet's keepsakes, reflected the changing lights of the television image. Meg picked it up and felt an almost tangible vibration from it, warm and cool at once. The commercials ended and *Summertime* returned, and she gave herself up to the pleasure of reliving the story she knew by heart. Her body was immobile on the couch, while all the rest of her—her mind, her emotions, her heart—went to Italy.

Although Meg had seen the movie many times on the late show, she'd never viewed it in quite this state of mind before. A peculiar thing began to happen: not only was she completely absorbed by the story—this time she gradually seemed to become part of the scene. She almost felt as if she could turn around and see other people outside the camera's vision, as if she could enter into that life. She'd had an urgent desire to walk into her own adventure in Venice—out past Florian's, past the basilica, under the magical archways and into the narrow paved walkways along the labyrinth of canals....

Meg could almost hear Jim's voice. "It would be strange living with all that water," he had commented after the one occasion when they had seen the film together, at a festival of old movies. "It's pretty, all right. A nice place to visit."

She remembered the way Jim had looked when she first met him, the tall blond quarterback who had just made the winning touchdown in the first game of the season for the private college they'd both attended. He had smiled at her over the heads of a cluster of admiring fans and had said, "What are you doing tonight, pretty girl?"

"Our little Meg's snagged The Great One," her friends and sorority sisters had laughed indulgently. She had thought that some kind of lucky star had touched her.

There was no doubt that she *was* a lucky girl. Who would have predicted that Meg Brown, with her long soft swirl of honey brown hair, irrepressibly curly no matter what the current fashion; with her big dove-gray eyes behind her reading glasses, would have impressed

Jim Reynolds? He had been pursued by some of the campus beauties, but he had decided on Meg for the partner in his dream-building project.

Jim had laid out his life early; it was to be "the good life." That meant being a successful consulting engineer, marrying a girl who would mother him as well as the children he would give her, joining the best country club in town and a beach club for the summers. His wife would make charming appearances at business affairs and be grateful for his efforts to provide for her. The children would get good educations; he would spend his weekends comfortably watching sports on a big-screen TV, and he would go hunting with the men in his firm.

Intrigued by the bright energy of his sparkling blue eyes, Meg had been drawn into his dream, too. Only gradually did she become aware that his plans left no room for any of hers. Yet he was so enthusiastic, and he loved her. His "book mouse," he teasingly called her.

Meg's widowed mother was fond of her handsome future son-in-law, and even Uncle Frank approved. "One less female in the family to worry about," he'd once said, perfectly soberly.

Meg felt a familiar tightening deep within her body, an unsatisfied longing. Jim's lovemaking had not been expert; it had been quick and energetic. She had refused to go all the way with him, and he'd respected her principles. That was what he wanted in a wife.

But it wasn't only her principles that had held her in check. If he had been more romantic, more persuasive. . .if they had just been *right* for each other! She had reluctantly come to realize that he wouldn't arouse her to a rapturous fulfillment.

After they both graduated Jim had accepted a

scholarship to MIT for two years of advanced engineering training. He already had a job commitment in Pasadena, and his future looked bright and solid.

Meg had majored in English, for books were her first love. She wanted to do graduate work in journalism, but Jim begrudged her those ambitious plans. He had wanted her to marry him right away so that they could go to Boston together while he studied. She could get a job and support them, and then later, if she still wanted to study journalism, he'd be happy to let her do it. He felt it was a fair offer.

But Meg had known that, once she fell into Jim's prefabricated plans for their lives, there would never be another chance for her to study. For the first time she opposed his wishes. He went to Boston alone and she stayed in Southern California.

Meg's next two years were filled with cozy seminars in the homes of certain of her favorite professors; with classes in writing, layout, drawing, and design; with letters from Jim about his progress at MIT; with brief reunions when he visited California. Several of the magazine articles she wrote were published, too. If Meg nurtured a dream for herself it was to be on the editorial staff of a good magazine, or to work for one of the interesting new publishing houses on the West Coast. In the meantime when she finished graduate school she appreciated Uncle Frank's offer of a job in his office. She was put in charge of the company newsletter, *The Ledger*, where her journalism and art training would be well used. The first several issues received lots of positive comments.

When Jim finally finished his own schooling and returned home for good, something inside Meg kept making excuses about why they should wait just a little longer before they married. Jim never understood; he called her resistance "the matrimonial jitters" and tried to kid her out of it. The week before the plane crash she made the decision to call it off. But she never got the chance.

And now Jim was gone; that was a fact. She was glad she hadn't hurt him with her rejection. She missed his steady companionship, even if he hadn't been the right man to marry.

Somewhere, she found herself thinking, there must be a man with deep feelings, capable of exciting love within her. Someone with a mind full of ideas and an appreciation for the beauties of life. Someone who wouldn't think her impractical for reading Browning's poetry and loving Debussy.

Meg gave a cynical chuckle, which disturbed the tenuous balance in her stomach. Maybe she was as stereotyped in her own dreams as Jim had been in his. Who was she to expect some superfate to hand out gifts to her specifications?

"Who do you think you are, Meg Brown?" she whispered to the darkness of her Venice room.

She slept fitfully and woke up in the middle of the night with the vague feeling that Aunt Harriet had invaded her rest and given her a message. The spry and vital old lady had been running lightly ahead of her, looking back over her shoulder and laughing ironically. "Don't settle for someone else's souvenirs, my girl," she called out. "I'm sorry I left mine for you. . .you need to get your own!"

With that Meg was fully awake again. Even if the dream had been a fever-induced figment of her mind it brought everything rushing back into focus, especially the feeling that had engulfed her after the charity ball. Venice had still been clinging to her, and she couldn't shake off its spell. What was it trying to tell her?

She had driven her old subcompact car to work through heavy traffic, dismally aware that she could see no flash of water flying from the stroke of a gondola oar, nor was she passing the warm ocher reflections of Venetian palaces rippling on smooth canals. No caressing male Italian voice spoke to her, and no pigeons bustled around her feet.

All the way to the office she had driven automatically, while inside she was reaching a daring conclusion. She simply had to find out about this crazy fixation of hers. She had to expose it to the light of day, to reality, and lay it to rest once and for all. If she didn't, the rest of her life would contain a nagging question and no answers.

She had Aunt Harriet's legacy. It might be enough and to spare once she paid her rent ahead and bought a few necessities for the trip. The newsletter was already laid out for the next two issues. She didn't care how scandalized Uncle Frank would be or how her mother would worry.

She reined in her excitement and tried to think logically. Even in her present state of euphoria she wouldn't put all her eggs in one basket and buy a ticket to Venice alone. Recently she had met a woman who worked for a travel agency in town, and they had spent most of a luncheon given for one of the women in the office just talking about Europe. There had been one tour in particular, Meg remembered, that included Venice and wasn't too expensive.

Downstairs in her office building was a photo studio that developed passport pictures instantly. It took Meg all of three minutes to get them. As soon as she reached her desk she called the bank to find out the balance in her savings account. She had exactly $2,831, a sum that made her feel rich.

Her next call had been to the travel agency. "You're just about the last person we can book," her friend's pleasant voice informed her. "But are you sure you want to go so soon? The tour leaves in ten days."

Ten days. It wasn't much time, but there wasn't another tour like it at that bargain price until the following spring, and that was too long to wait. During lunch hour Meg transferred the money from her savings account to her checking account, then drove home to retrieve her birth certificate. Fifteen minutes later she was at the main post office filling out a rush application for a passport. That done, she stopped at the travel agency and paid for the trip. It was the largest check she had ever written. Aunt Harriet's money was going to just cover her expenses, with a little left over.

At her desk again she reassured herself that even if she left for several weeks, *The Ledger* would go out on schedule. Now that everything was falling into place so neatly she began to relax and appreciate what she was about to do.

The boy from the mailroom interrupted her and dropped a packet of mail on her desk, including the latest issue of *Au Courant* magazine. She had submitted an article to the magazine several weeks ago, something she had worked on in her spare time. It was about the renewed interest in Greene & Greene architecture in Southern California, those beautiful old dark wood bungalows with the broad verandahs and the masterfully designed interior paneling and motifs.

Meg thumbed quickly through the magazine looking for the architecture section. If they bought her story she would be published in one of the newest and trendiest magazines in America. She visualized her article, "The Revival of Craftsmanship in California," with her name, Margaret Brown. How she could use some extra money now! And what a door *Au Courant* might open for her. Perhaps she could leave the tiresome, dry *Ledger* behind her and work in a way she had always wanted to.

With an editor's instinct she glanced at the architecture page. It was well presented, all about some international design competition. There were photos of the semifinalists, architects from Japan, the United States, Italy, Germany, and Sweden. From the small composite picture it was impossible to tell whether the Italians were handsome, and she laughed at herself for even caring.

The finalists had each submitted preliminary plans for a yet-to-be-named institute for the study of Renaissance art and culture, to be built on a hilltop near Malibu. The winner would be the architect whose final design best expressed the donor's vision for the institute.

Meg was intrigued. The donor was a man named Roscoe Veitch, whose lifelong ambition had been to establish a cultural landmark. He was a newcomer to the world of art and scholarship.

She ran her eyes down the copy. The writing bordered on supercilious at times: "The new institute will be founded on a base of Veitch cement brought to Malibu in Veitch trucks." Meg felt sorry for the multimillionaire. How he made his money had nothing to do with his artistic and humanitarian urges. She drew in her breath as she read the prize: $500,000. An unheard-of amount. Who *was* this Mr. Veitch? One of those architects was going to be rich. She rather hoped it would be an Italian.

Looking through the rest of her mail, Meg was excited to find an envelope with the bright blue *Au Courant* logo. Inside was a check for $300 and a short note:

Dear Meg,
We enjoyed your Greene & Greene piece and would very much like to see more of your work. Your article will be in the December issue.
Best of luck!
Maude Draper, Senior Editor

It had been a day for surprises and changes. *Yes, Maude Draper,* she had said to herself jubilantly, *you'll be seeing lots more of my work...but after I get back from Venice!*

That afternoon Meg asked to see Uncle Frank, a man who cared very much about the formalities and rules of life. He had been a widower for many years and was childless. Meg couldn't even remember her Aunt Lucy, and she thought it unlikely that he would ever marry again. He seemed happy in his small but elegant town house with its Persian rugs and solid mahogany furniture, with his taciturn houseman to care for him and his men's club downtown as his haven.

All of this he justified as necessary spending. But what was an unjustifiable expenditure, Meg had learned, was paying his niece an adequate salary.

"Everyone has to prove his own worth," he was fond of saying.

If she was ever going to do something extravagant and purely for her own enjoyment it wouldn't be on the salary she got from Frank Singleton & Associates. By the time she entered her uncle's silent well-appointed office that afternoon she had decided that she'd be looking for another job as soon as she returned from her trip.

As she told him about her plans for Europe Uncle Frank sat back in his dark leather chair with a growing expression of disapproval on his face. She hurried to assure him that *The Ledger* was ready for the printer two issues in advance and that if she stayed she would only be planning further ahead.

He showed no sign at first that he had heard what she was saying. With his usual conservative approach he spoke of untrustworthy foreigners, of deceitful males intent on coming to this country by female help, of the possible theft of her money, her passport.

"Three weeks isn't very long," she said in a small but quietly defiant voice. "I'm not going around the world. I only want a short vacation like everybody else."

"You haven't worked here for a full year, Margaret. New staff aren't entitled to vacations until that time. Holidays cost the firm money and...."

"I don't want a paid vacation, only a leave of absence." She looked up into his serious face, the face of a man who cared for her but couldn't express it. "Do you realize, Uncle Frank, that I've had no change at all since Jim died...and even before, for that matter?" She pulled out her last argument: "Jim always promised me a trip for our honeymoon. I think he'd want me to go."

"All right," he said with a resigned sigh, "go ahead

and get it out of your system. We can fill in while you're gone. I just don't see why a trip to Hearst Castle wouldn't do as well. At least the water would be clean, and you could bring your mother with you."

Meg dissolved in smiles and gave him a grateful peck on his dignified cheek. She knew he felt obligated to bluster and object.

Next on her list was telling her mother. When she phoned she got the predictable reaction.

"Oh, my! Do you *really* want to go all alone, Meg, dear? Such a tragedy you and Jim couldn't have gone together." Her voice cracked with feeling.

Meg didn't want to hear the usual eulogy to Jim just then.

"Just wish me well, mother," she said gently, ending the conversation.

THE HOTEL ROOM was going slowly around in circles, and Meg reached over for another dose of Pepto Bismol. A hint of predawn light was showing outside her windows, but she couldn't have gotten out of bed to watch the sunrise over Venice if her life depended on it.

Was this her punishment for wanting to come too badly, she wondered, and then canceled that thought as unworthy. Her last thought before she finally drifted off to sleep was that maybe she could get a piece of Venetian glass to go with Aunt Harriet's goblet. Her first souvenir.

CHAPTER TWO

WHEN MEG LIFTED HER HEAD from the pillow the next morning her whole body ached and trembled from the effort. Even the weak tea Mary Lou Nelson brought her made her stomach lurch. Her legs were made of rubber and any motion brought dizziness.

The hotel doctor, a suavely courteous man, recommended several days of rest, and he left some pills for her. The chambermaid sympathized in soft Italian clucking sounds, and late in the afternoon Mrs. Nelson returned to tell tales of gondola rides, fabulous glass factories on the island of Murano, the amazing interior of St. Mark's Basilica, the art treasures of the Accademia....

By the time she finished her excited account Meg's spirits had touched bottom. The first of her two allotted days in Venice was almost over. The next afternoon at one o'clock the tour group would take the train to Milano, and from there they'd travel by plane to Geneva—and she hadn't seen anything of Venice but her hotel room. It wasn't fair! A weak anger against fate moved in her solar plexus.

Mrs. Nelson left and Meg slept again. At dusk she was wakened by a phone call from the tour leader. "My dear," the older woman said in a practical voice, "you obviously aren't able to travel yet. The hotel has agreed to give you two more days, at your own expense, of course." She would leave train and plane tickets at the hotel desk, she said, adding, "By the time you arrive in Geneva we'll be ready to leave for London and home."

Meg barely had the strength to reply. "Thanks," she whispered.

"I'm sorry, but it's the best we can do. You'll get only a quick look at Geneva, and the plane connection will be tight. But surely you'll be better in two days."

"I'm sure I will," Meg agreed shakily and hung up the phone. At least she had two more days in Venice. Maybe tomorrow she would be strong enough to get out. She could lie back in a gondola and have the gondolier take her everywhere. She wouldn't have to walk. Coupled with that thought was a vision of the last of her spending money flying rapidly away from her. Why couldn't she have caught this cursed stomach bug in France or somewhere else—any place but Venice!

That night she forced herself to eat some clear soup with tortellini—tiny twists of pasta. The room-service waiter was helpful and brought her a dish of melba toast as well.

She hadn't been nauseated for most of the day and she found she could stand up without dropping to the floor from weakness. She pulled a chair to the window and sat for a long time listening to the sounds of Venice—bits of music, laughter, shouting, boats' horns, church bells, pigeons cooing in their rooftop perches.

By morning she was stronger. After a breakfast of more melba toast and tea she went to the lobby to say goodbye to Mary Lou Nelson and the others, who were gathered around their luggage waiting to be checked out. They were going to see the Lido that morning before taking the train to Milan. Their bags would be taken directly to the train station.

Then they were gone, and Meg was truly alone in Venice. The man at the desk handed her her envelope of travel tickets and asked about her health. "Better, thanks," she said. "I just need some time to rest."

The man looked distressed. "*Signorina*, I regret to say..." he started. "If it were up to me...." He swallowed uncomfortably and made a wide gesture with one hand. "As you can see, this is a busy time for the hotel—for all hotels in Venice. I regret...you can only keep your room until two o'clock today. We have prior reservations that cannot be canceled. There is nothing I can do." He shrugged his shoulders helplessly.

Meg drew an uneven breath. "But the leader of our tour promised me two more days. I've not yet recovered from my illness."

An older man was called over. He, too, was regretful but firm. "An unfortunate misunderstanding," he said, and suggested that she go to the nearest tourist office, which was just off St. Mark's Square, a short walk. "They will make calls to find a place for you."

Meg's knees suddenly went weak. She couldn't think of packing right now. She walked slowly out onto the hotel dining terrace, which was serving late breakfast. The setting was perfect for a movie; even in her misery she could appreciate that. Across the Grand Canal the rounded bulk of the church of Santa Maria della Salute, built in gratitude for the end of a terrible plague, stood firm and solid. Tables on the terrace were spread with pink linen cloths and cool-looking silver. Geraniums and oleanders bloomed in big terra-cotta pots along the iron railing at the end of the dining area.

Meg sat down at a table and ordered, bemused by the view before her. All kinds of boats were moving on the sunlit surface of the canal. A few gondolas waited for fares in front of the terrace, swaying against their mooring ropes. Their black polished sides gleamed, and the sun glittered from their high golden prows, just like the photographs she had pored over for years and years.

The coffee gave her a lift. She postponed as long as she could the inevitable effort to find the tourist office, but at last she started out. The narrow walkway from the hotel door led to a wider lane and she turned right, following the small map the concierge had given her.

She found the office tucked away between shops that beckoned with Venetian glass and displays of jewelry and fine shoes. A young man at the office was polite but not very hopeful. "An unusual late-summer season," he said. It had something to do with the relative value of the dollar and the lira stimulating tourism that year. He promised to try to find a room for her, suggesting that she come back in two hours.

"But I have to know before noon—before your office closes for siesta."

"Come at eleven-thirty. It is all I can do," he said and turned to answer the telephone.

On trembling legs Meg kept moving toward St. Mark's Square. She couldn't leave Venice without going there, at the very least. If there was no hotel room available she would have to take the train to Milan with the tour at one o'clock, sick or not. Alternate waves of hot and cold shivered over her but she was determined to find the square.

When at last she passed through the arcades at the end of the walkway she stopped, forgetting her protesting body. The immense and beautiful paved area of the square stretched out before her, and her feet refused to move until she had taken her fill of the sight. At the opposite end, the face of the Basilica of St. Mark shone with rainbow mosaics. Jewellike domes and arches gleamed against the deep blue sky. Two bright flags rippled from the tops of their tall poles and to her right the great Campanile soared upward to its blue-and-gold pyramidal apex.

On either side of the vast oblong space arcades gave shade to shops, and to the left the clock tower stood over its deep archway, its two bronze Saracen figures waiting with their hammers to strike the hour. Morning activity filled the square. Queues of tourists were waiting with guides in front of the basilica and along the intricately carved facade of the Doges' Palace.

Meg moved slowly into the crowded piazza. She didn't need a guidebook to know that the bustling restaurants on opposite sides of the square were Quadri's and Florian's. In both restaurants waiters were moving among the clutter of yellow outdoor chairs and tables, preparing for the lunchtime customers. Florian's had been there since the eighteenth century. Even Lord Byron had written about sitting there with his friends and enjoying the atmosphere.

It was near here that Kate Hepburn had sat at her little table, not knowing that destiny was about to set Rossano Brazzi in her path. For Meg that was irresistible. If everything worked the way it should, and her strength held out, she knew she would end up this morning at Florian's, if just for a little while.

Pigeons strutted and cooed, moving just a little out of the way of human feet. Hawkers with tiny movable stands sold twists of newspaper filled with grain for the birds. Meg spent one hundred lire for one of the packets, a transaction followed by the bright eyes of the knowing birds. All at once she was surrounded by whirring wings, and her arms and shoulders were weighted down with iridescent feathered bodies. Cool pink claws bit gently into her arms and swift beaks pecked the grain from her outstretched palm.

In a moment the grain was gone and the birds gradually deserted her for new donors. Meg began to set one careful foot ahead of the next as she moved toward the basilica, like a pilgrim at the end of a long journey. She had to see it.

Inside, the cool domes echoed to the sound of many voices. The stone floor waved and rippled where the winter floods of long centuries had caused part of it to sink a little. Meg moved about slowly, looking up at the mosaic of the domes and pausing in front of the Pala d'Oro, the golden altar screen. A sense of peace filtered into her heart, easing the ache of frustration. There was no way in the world she would see all she wanted to of Venice.

People flowed around her in the vast beauty of the basilica, disorienting her slightly. She was starting to feel uncomfortably weak again, and knew she should rest for a while. Outside once more, she walked across the piazza until she reached the sea of tables belonging to Florian's. She had to find a place to sit down. One table near the front was unoccupied and she claimed it, feeling very much like her movie heroine—sad and lonely. *How ridiculous,* she thought, and scolded herself for still seeking out the mood of the old film.

The bronze Saracen clock began to strike the hour,

and the strong resonance made the pigeons fly up from the pavement in a flurry of flapping sounds. Eleven o'clock. She had thirty minutes to herself at Florian's before she returned to the travel agent. She smiled at the sheer beauty of the scene around her. She didn't need a movie to tell her about the magic of Italy. It was here, pouring down like sunlight. The very taste of romance caressed her in the soft air.

A waiter came and she ordered coffee and a plain roll—anything to give her a reason to sit for a while. She pulled an empty chair nearer and put her heavy handbag on it. The bright sun was comforting and warm.

While she sipped her coffee she became absorbed with the pageant of people moving around the square. It was like having a front-row seat at a play, with the whole piazza as the backdrop. What had someone written about this place.... "St. Mark's Square is the living room of Europe." It was said that if a person sat here long enough he would eventually meet everyone he knew.

A boyish voice spoke close to her. "*Signorina*, polish shoes, *per favore*? I do good." Wide brown eyes looked into hers from a cherubic face.

Turning in her chair, Meg stretched out her foot to show him that her shoes were made of cloth, not leather. "I'm sorry—*mi dispiace*," she said at his desolate expression.

"It's okay." His big smile suddenly beamed at her, and then the boy moved away. The tables around her were starting to fill up. People were moving and jostling close to her, but Meg hardly noticed them. Just then the waiter came with the check. *"Il conto, signorina."*

She turned to get her handbag; the waiter seemed anxious for her to settle her account and free up the table for a larger party that was waiting. But her bag wasn't on the chair. She looked down at the pavement by her feet. Surely it must have fallen off by accident. But it hadn't—it was gone.

An icy lump formed in her stomach. "My handbag," she said through stiff lips. "It was on this chair. I think it's been stolen!" She could barely say the words.

The waiter bent to look under the table, then straightened up with a worried look. "You saw nothing?"

"No, I was talking to the boy who shines shoes."

"Maledizione!" he swore. "*Orribile!* I regret, but we call the *polizia subito*—right away. Maybe you get a check cash at your hotel to pay *il conto*?"

Meg's stunned brain was waking up to her awful situation. "But all my money and checks were in my handbag. What am I going to do? My passport is gone—everything!"

"*Calma, signorina.* I will call the *pol—*"

"What is the trouble, Giorgio?" A deep smooth male voice cut across his words.

Meg looked up to see a tall man standing beside her. Perhaps in his mid-thirties, he had the assurance and poise of vital maturity. His finely cut face was dominated by golden brown eyes and a handsome Italian nose. His strong wavy black hair was elegantly tinged with silver at the tip of each sideburn. His lips curved in a slight smile while Meg stared.

Although she knew he might be just another opportunistic male ready to play on the distress of a tourist, another part of her recognized the personification of her romantic fantasies. There he stood, in flesh and blood and a well-tailored suit. His immaculate white shirt was open at the neck to show a paisley silk scarf knotted under the collar and fastened with a gold stick pin.

"What is the trouble, Giorgio?" he repeated.

"The *signorina* has been robbed of her handbag, Signor Montevalde, only moments ago...taking money, *passaporto... terribile!*"

The dream man spoke directly to her. "Did you see the thief?"

A shiver fluttered through her and her voice was unsteady. "No, I never saw anything."

"Hmm. Giorgio, you were about to call the *polizia*...." As the waiter hurried off he pulled out a chair and sat down. "I am deeply sorry, *signorina*, that you have been made so unhappy in my city." He reached out and put his tanned long fingers over hers. "Something can be done." His warm hand curled protectively. "*Poverina*, your hand is like ice. Are you all right?"

Meg's body responded to the comforting touch with a swift rush of heat, which tinged her cheeks with red. "I...I've been sick for a few days. The...this is my first day out. My tour had to leave without me and now I've lost everything, even the medicine the doctor gave me...and my air ticket, too!" Her voice was rising with her distress.

His hand tightened gently on hers and he answered in that honey-smooth voice that went straight to her nerve endings. "You must not worry. I am Marco Montevalde, and I feel it a matter of the honor of Venezia to assist you." His charming accent wove fascination into even his commonplace words. "And what is your name, *signorina*?"

She swam back from bemusement to reality. "I'm

Meg Brown, Signor Monte. . .Montevalde. My home is California." She cleared her throat and tried unsuccessfully to release her hand from his. "You are being so kind, but I mustn't impose on you. I'll find the American Express."

A look of knowing amusement started in the depths of his eyes. "Do not be upset, *piccola*. You do not impose. It is my pleasure to be of service." He let go of her hand to rest his fingers very gently on her forehead. "You have still some fever, I think. You should have stayed in bed another day."

Her attempt at courage wilted at his compassionate gesture. When she could speak again she said, "I expected to have two days, but my. . .my hotel told me I must leave today because they had prior reservations. I'm late returning to the tourist office. They're trying to find a room for me somewhere. . . . But now I don't even have a passport and I can't check into a new hotel without one." Meg was just starting to realize the full extent of her loss, and in her weakened state she felt like a homeless waif adrift in a storm with only this man to save her. She could hardly believe she had just confided her woes to this stranger, and worse, that she'd had such an overwhelming desire to do so. What was wrong with her?

Marco Montevalde's brows were drawn into a frown. "We will see about your situation. Ah!" Giorgio had returned.

"The *polizia* will come soon," the waiter announced proudly.

"*Bene.* Now bring for Signorina Brown a small glass of sherry. All of this has been a shock for her. And Giorgio. . . please assure her of my respectability." A laugh moved beneath his last words.

Giorgio's wide grin showed several gold teeth. "*Rispettabilità? Dio!* Conte Marco. . . ." His voice faded under Marco Montevalde's sharp glance, and he turned to Meg. "*Signor* Marco is a citizen of Venezia most well-known. I, myself, am knowing him for a lot of years. His family is old here and he is a man of good business."

Two men were hurrying toward the table, one of them dressed in the fine caped uniform and Napoleonic hat of the local *guarda* or police. The other was a slight serious-faced man in a business suit.

"Marco," the latter said with a laugh, "when I heard your name mentioned I thought I'd better come, too." He turned to Meg. "This is the unfortunate lady?" His expression was warmly sympathetic.

"Signorina Meg Brown, may I introduce my friend, Giulio Prati, *agente investigativo*—detective, I believe you say."

Signor Prati bowed and introduced in turn *Poliziotto* Santini, the uniformed man. Meg smiled at the kind faces, and when the two policemen sat down at the table, she described the circumstances of the theft. She couldn't help feeling conspicuous as she sat with the three attentive men, especially with the one who looked so much like a musical-comedy character, cape and all. He had extracted a notebook from some inner pocket and was taking notes dictated in Italian by Detective Prati.

Giorgio was hovering nearby to refill her glass, but she had sipped less than half of what she had and already felt light-headed. The men spoke in Italian for a few moments while she sat there helplessly. She was hedged in by all this masculinity and she wasn't quite sure she liked it. If only her face weren't so hot, and if only the waves of dizziness would stop. She had trouble thinking straight.

"Please excuse me," Marco Montevalde said. "Wait here, *signorina*, while I go to make a call to your hotel."

As the policeman began questioning the waiters and others at nearby tables, Signor Prati smiled at Meg and tried to occupy her with conversation about her travel plans. She responded as well as she could, considering the fact that her attention was riveted on one subject: Marco Montevalde. He was too near to her dream, a fact that was terribly disconcerting. Every time his eyes had met hers she responded. *Like a silly adolescent,* she thought angrily. *I'm acting helpless and I'm not.*

When he returned he had good news. "Your hotel has reconsidered and will have a room for you for two more days. I have also called the American Express. They will see to renewing your checks if you bring them the proper information this afternoon or tomorrow." He looked intently at her. "You do not look well, *signorina*. I think we must get you to your hotel for some rest. Your passport will take a little time to renew, but Detective Prati will assist you."

"But how will I catch up with my tour?" Meg suddenly pictured herself missing her flight from Geneva. If she couldn't cancel her tour flight and get credit for it in time, she would lose more money buying a new ticket home. She could imagine having to wire Uncle Frank for emergency money. His I-told-you-so attitude would be too much to think about.

Marco was speaking. "You will have to see what can be arranged with your tour. If necessary you could go directly home from Milano." He smiled. "A few more days in Venezia . . . would that be so bad?"

She shook her head. "It's really Venice that I came to see. It's just that—"

Signor Prati murmured sympathetically. "*Si, si.* You are now alone in our city. I understand. It would please my wife and me if you would visit us for dinner, Signorina Brown. My wife Adella would want to hear about Hollywood. She thinks California is a kind of paradise."

Meg liked Signor Prati. His dark blue eyes held a combination of warmth and sharp intelligence. "You are very generous," she told him gratefully, "and if I'm better in the next day or two I will accept with pleasure." The sun seemed very penetrating, yet she was shivering. "I've got to get back to my hotel now." She stood up, but had to hold on to the table for support. Marco was quickly at her side, his arm steadying her and his body offering its strength.

"Are you able to walk?" he asked.

"Yes, of course." Actually, she wasn't too sure.

Detective Prati said goodbye, assuring her he would start the necessary action to have her passport renewed, and Marco began to walk with her across the piazza toward the hotel. She had to lean heavily on him, she found, and the warmth of his muscular body, added to the clean scent of his cologne, gave her a searing sense of excitement, even through the wavering haze of her perceptions. How strange it all was!

When they came to the long narrow passage that led to the hotel he lifted her quickly in his arms and carried her to the entrance. Setting her down, he held her against him for a moment while she found her balance.

Then he pulled open the big door and went with her to the desk.

"Ah, *buon giorno*, Signor Montevalde." The clerk was eager to please. "A room is just ready for Signorina Brown. We have had to change locations, I am afraid," he apologized to Meg. "The maids have moved your luggage." He held out her new key.

Marco insisted on seeing her to her room, which turned out to be very small and on the top floor, with a view only of rooftops. She didn't mind. The smooth bed looked so inviting, and the tiled bathroom that she glimpsed through a partly opened door promised an easing shower.

She turned to thank her rescuer, only to find him using the telephone. Rapid Italian crackled into the mouthpiece and then he hung up. "The *dottore* of the hotel will attend you very soon. Now, is there anything you need?"

She shook her head.

"Then rest. You must not worry." He took her hand, holding it in the warmth of his own. How long had she known him—an hour? Her nerves buzzed with unwilling excitement.

Meg had a powerful urge to engage him in conversation—anything to make him stay a few moments longer. Her common sense warred with her desires.

Marco Montevalde was still holding her hand. He looked concerned and questioning, and she couldn't take her eyes away from his. She felt almost desperate to commit the whole of him to memory. Their gazes held, and a small spark seemed to catch fire in the depths of his smoky topaz eyes.

Meg's heart was beating erratically, not only from illness. She dragged her eyes from his, only to see more clearly the firm and sensitive line of his lips. Now her hand was being raised, and those lips were touching her fingers gently, softly, leaving a warm tingle on her skin. A swift glow of pleasure sped through her. No one had ever kissed her hand before, except as a joke. None of the men she knew had even pretended such old-world courtesy. Her dream momentarily flooded reality again.

"You will hear from Giulio Prati tomorrow. It has been my pleasure to serve you, Signorina Brown." He released her hand. "Rest well." He left with swift steps, closing the door behind him with an imperceptible click.

Meg sat down heavily on the bed, her eyes fixed on the doorknob, with its little hanging sign that said *non disturbare*. Her dream had left and probably wasn't coming back.

CHAPTER THREE

WITHIN HALF AN HOUR the hotel doctor had come and gone. Meg bathed quickly and climbed into the freshly made bed. At her most imaginative she could not have made up a fantasy like this one. She dozed off with the mellow voice of Marco Montevalde drifting through her dreams.

She woke to a light rap on her door and saw that the day had turned to early evening. Pulling her robe around her, she went with wavering steps to the door, where a bellboy held out a beautiful little glass vase filled with ferns and three red roses. He gave her a brilliant smile and ran off.

The vase was of Venetian glass—red with flecks of gold suspended like minute clouds within the glass. Meg set it on her bedside table and removed the small bisque-toned envelope that accompanied the flowers. Her name was written on it in a firm attractive black script. The crisp little card inside was engraved "Marco Montevalde," with the name centered beneath an embossed crest. The same handwriting said, "From Venezia. Be well and be happy."

Meg took the card to the window to see the crest better. It showed a mountain peak with two gryphonlike figures on either side of it. She carefully put it back into its gold-tasseled envelope and tucked it into the side pocket of her large suitcase. Surely his card held nothing but a sincere and friendly sentiment. Her mind was racing with instructions to herself: she should leave a small note of thanks for him with Signor Prati. She should let Signor Montevalde know that she was a woman of some courtesy and experience herself, and not a typical inept tourist—not a naive American.

But never to see Marco Montevalde again! To be so close and then find that the dream looked and felt real, but wasn't.... That was hard to accept, and an aching misery spread through her. What did she expect, anyway—an invitation to ride in his magical gondola into the sunset? No. His note was entirely correct for the situation.

Yet it was hard to give up her speculations about him and what his life must be like. Was there a woman in his life? Thinking about how she must have appeared to him made her squirm with embarrassment. She *had* seemed like a ninny, she was sure of it. *It was only because I was sick,* she excused herself. *I wouldn't have shivered and flushed at his touch otherwise.*

Then another thought came uninvited—wasn't it wonderful to be treated with such concern? How nice to have her hand kissed—by a man who ignored no detail in making sure that she was cared for. In the stillness of the darkening room she sank into a half-waking state of romantic imagining—then opened her eyes abruptly to stop the flow of provocative pictures. She would *hate* having an affair like that, with a total stranger, far from home. God only knew how many vulnerable women Marco Montevalde must have enjoyed.

A tiny irrepressible voice said, *Maybe those women of his enjoyed it, too, and he's not just the stereotypical*

Romeo. It wasn't his fault he was Italian and handsome.

Anyway, it was all academic. She wouldn't be seeing him. After more tossing and turning she finally fell asleep and stayed there until morning.

Meg felt better when she woke—a little weak in the knees, but on the mend. She still didn't feel hungry, and her reflection in the mirror showed a fragile look unlike her usual bloom. However, things seemed more possible than they had yesterday. She would have to hurry with her business—contact Signor Prati, see about her passport and her air ticket—so that there would be time left to her to enjoy Venice.

Downstairs on the breakfast terrace she ate without appetite, only because she thought she should. She was carrying a small straw purse from Florence, and she was grateful that the bill for breakfast didn't have to be paid on the spot. When she went to the front desk to leave her key the concierge greeted her with a too-familiar hangdog face.

"*Signorina*—we regret...."

"I can guess: You have no room for me; there are prior reservations, and I must leave," she finished for him.

He raised his shoulders with expressive pathos. "*Signorina, per favore*, tell to Signor Montevalde that we would not inconvenience a friend of his unless the situation was *imperativo, urgente*—you understand?"

She didn't understand, but the distress in the man's eyes spoke of his honesty. It wasn't his fault. "All right." She turned away and went to stand near a large window where she could see the Grand Canal. She was back where she started: no money, no passport, no tour. She could have wept there on the spot, but didn't.

Briefly she considered finding Signor Montevalde. No doubt he would help, and it would be a good reason to see him again. The thought was an enticing one.

She gave herself a mental shake. What had happened to Meg Brown, efficient professional, independent thinker? She was the last person in the world to be chasing after a man.

"Signorina Brown?" The desk clerk's raised voice made her turn around, and as she did so her heart gave a wild leap.

Marco Montevalde stood there smiling. He looked startlingly handsome as he came toward her, like some modern-day genie who had materialized from thin air. His dark hair and gleaming eyes were highlighted by his tan suit and beige silk shirt. Then her hand was in his, and he was bending to put a light kiss on it. The scent of his cologne was like a memory of excitement, and a vital energy flowed from him.

"I seem to have come at the right moment, once more, hmm?"

She nodded, struggling for composure. "I wasn't going to trouble you again."

"That would have been unkind, *piccola*. I do not like unfinished business. I came to help you and I see I am needed."

"I'm very glad you're here." She couldn't let her foolish response to him cause problems. "I'm sorry, I'm not usually in difficulties. And thank you for the roses. They cheered me up—until just a few minutes ago."

"Your face is still pale—and no wonder, with your room again taken from you. I have just spoken to the manager and the situation is truly beyond their control. A large tour group is arriving momentarily somewhat ahead of schedule. But I have a solution." His hand gently took her elbow. "We will go now to do something about your traveler's checks. You have the numbers? Then we will have coffee at Florian's or wherever you wish, and I will tell you about my idea."

They were near the desk by now, and Marco looked at the clerk from his superior height. "You will have the maid pack for Signorina Brown," he said, as if such service were expected. "She will return later for her luggage."

Marco Montevalde was good at getting things done. In a single brief visit to the American Express office Meg was given new checks. "Now," Marco said, "we will rest at Florian's while I tell you what our Detective Prati has found out."

His smooth competence was having a healing effect on her, but more than that, she was reveling secretly in this morning interlude with him. When she returned to California she would have a special memory—of being in Venice with this quintessential Italian man, attentive, warm, and as unnervingly good-looking as anything ever sculptured by Michelangelo.

He leaned back comfortably in his chair, his eyes thoughtful and preoccupied for a few minutes after they had ordered. Then his attention returned to her swiftly, along with a smile that melted her reservations and made her tingle down to her fingertips. There was something so intimate about the way his heavily lidded eyes looked at her.

"It is a shame it is not nighttime," he said softly. Meg drew a quick breath, fearing the direction of his thoughts. *Here it comes,* she said to herself, *the Italian line.*

He noticed her reaction with a little quirk of his lips. "*Si*, because if it were, you would be able to see in your mind's eye the story I am about to tell you." He made a gesture with one hand that included the whole of the piazza. "If I am to be your tour guide, for lack of a better one, you must be attentive when I speak about the history of this place."

She felt her face color slightly, a result of her mistaken opinion of his motives. "Tell me."

"It was nighttime here in the Piazza San Marco, in the heat of the summer of 1902. The band was playing a waltz or a march—as was usual—when everyone in the crowd heard something very strange: a groaning, crumbling sound. And when they looked up at the Campanile they all screamed in horror, for it was trembling. The square was emptied immediately. After all, when a 325-foot tower announces that it is ill, one doesn't stand around asking questions.

"The tower groaned and cried out all through the night, while the citizens of Venezia shivered in their beds, waiting for the worst. The next morning shortly after nine it happened—the venerable Campanile of San Marco collapsed upon itself, leaving a mountain of fine red bricks and dust where the noble tower had stood for so many centuries."

Meg found his voice hypnotic. She was like a child at the knees of a storyteller, listening to marvelous things. He moved his hands expressively as he indicated the crash of the tower, watching for her reaction.

"But what is that tall brick tower we're looking at right now?" she had to ask.

"Ah, that is yet another story. Ten years later, on San Marco's Day, to be exact, our new Campanile was dedicated with full pomp and honors. It was rebuilt exactly like the old one. Think of it, Signorina Brown—the original tower had withstood earthquakes and lightning bolts, and had become a symbol of the power of San Marco himself to preserve our city. And so, on that April morning in 1912, Venezia wished to tell all of Italy that the guardian bell tower was once again taking up its high duties. Two thousand four hundred seventy-nine carrier pigeons, each with the message tied to its leg, were released, to bring the word to the many cities of this land. My father was a little boy at the time, and he never forgot that morning—the cries of the citizens, the sound of the wings as the birds ascended to the bright spring sky with their glorious message."

"How wonderful!" Meg exclaimed.

Marco reached to give her hand a quick squeeze and then stood up. "Since I have now given you something to think about as you sit in this ancient place, you will be well occupied while I make a brief telephone call. I won't be more than five minutes."

She wanted to say, *Don't leave—don't break the spell,* but she managed to hold herself back in time.

When he returned he was all business. "I promised to give you news of your handbag, didn't I? I spoke to Signor Prati earlier today, and he believes it is most probably at the bottom of the Canale Grande by now. He has contacted the proper authorities at the American Consulate in Milano and the renewal of your passport is in process. He will vouch for your identity, since you are unable to go in person at this time."

"How very kind of him," Meg said somewhat stiffly.

She was startled by Marco's abrupt change from storyteller to helpful stranger. "I didn't know that the police would do that for you."

"They don't as a rule, but we are friends, and our Signor Prati is more than just an ordinary detective," he said quietly. "Now for the best news." He suddenly broke into a boyish grin. "A good friend of mine owns an apartment that is seldom used by him. It is part of the very old Palazzo Specchiato. Roughly translated, its name means great house of mirrors and reflections, which you will understand when you see it."

Meg's warning signals were going off. She wasn't sure what he was really proposing.

"My friend—I have known him since we were small children—has already agreed that you may stay there for as long as needed without expense. I placed a call to the Specchiato just now."

"You...you already arranged it?" she asked incredulously. "But—"

"The apartment is very modern and is cared for by a maid who lives there. She is an excellent cook and can look after you. All very respectable, I assure you. Palazzo Specchiato is an architectural gem and may even have a ghost or two. For centuries it was one of the great houses of Venezia, but lately it has not had the care that such a landmark deserves. You will find it far more interesting than any hotel."

He held up a hand to stop her from interrupting. "You mustn't make conditions, *signorina*. May I call you Meg? I am aware that you are American and proper and full of pride, but my friend will be insulted if you refuse his offer. Besides, Lucia will be delighted to have someone to serve."

He waited with slightly lifted brows while she debated. But the outcome was certain, and after a few feeble objections she agreed. She would love to stay on in Venice at a wonderful old palazzo. What a fascinating opportunity. Melodramatically she pictured herself lying languidly in a luxurious palace, while a maid brought her trays of food and she took copious notes for a dazzling article on the real Venice behind the ancient facades.

And she would be able to see Marco again. . . maybe. She hugged that hope to her.

He gave her hand a light kiss, sending her nerves into turmoil. "I will escort you there and see that you are settled in. But first we must check with Giulio Prati. . . and take care of one other item of business."

They left Florian's, and he led her across the piazza, under the clock tower and into a winding walkway lined with shops. Jewelry and glass glittered in the window displays. Silk blouses and scarves, hand-knit sweaters and stoles, elegant shoes beckoned temptingly. It was a fairyland of beautiful things, from lamps to art, from gloves to lacy negligees and amazingly skimpy bikinis. Marco drew her into a small store where multicolored silk scarves were displayed like huge blossoms tucked into the handles of finely crafted leather handbags. The dignified, elderly proprietor obviously recognized Marco, and greeted him effusively.

"I am looking for a particular handbag," Marco informed the man. His own manner showed friendliness mixed with an expectation of good service. By now Meg was certain that her rescuer was a man of aristocratic status.

She was also certain what he had in mind. She moved

toward the door of the shop, but Marco reached out a long arm to detain her.

"I'm *not* going to get a bag," she announced, trying to move past him. But his hand on her arm was firm.

"*I* am buying a handbag, *piccola*, and you have nothing to do with it. If you will be patient with me, we can go very soon."

So she had made another mistake! Maybe he was getting a gift for someone else, and she had misunderstood his intentions once again.... He took his time looking at the merchandise, finally selecting a golden beige leather purse of moderate size. It had beautiful stitching, and little golden tassels on its zipper pulls. The color and the style would go with many things.

Marco went to a display of scarves and pulled out one in a gray-and-gold design. He ignored her presence as he paid for the items, the total of which came to more than Meg would ever dream of paying for such things. What was on his mind—another woman? His wife? He'd never said he was single.

The scarf and bag were folded in tissue and put into a charmingly dignified paper wrapping. After handing the package to Marco, the proprietor showed them to the door, thanking them profusely.

Outside again, Marco walked Meg to a tiny campo with a single old olive tree in its center and a circular stone bench around the gnarled gray trunk. "You need to rest before we continue," he said, sitting down beside her. With a fluid motion he pulled off the wrapping, removed the price tags, and placed the new handbag on Meg's lap. "You will put the contents of your tiny purse into this one, *signorina*—without argument or resistance, do you understand?" His face was stern and his voice commanding. Meg failed to locate the slightest humor in it.

She had a momentary impulse to rebel, but the delight she felt at receiving this lovely gift swamped the voice that warned her to be careful. "I don't know how to thank you, Signor Montevalde," she said awkwardly, beginning to transfer her things. She savored the rich leather odor and the velvety feel of the new bag, even as she heard the echo of a childhood warning from her mother: "Never take gifts from strange men."

She looked up to find him smiling. "I have found the way to turn you to my will. I must be harsh and cruel, hmm?" He gave a little laugh. He was the very essence of masculine charm, she thought.

Meg blinked against the light of his smile and a shiver, almost of fear, went over her. He was again the man of her dreams, almost irresistible. It was an intolerable feeling, one that she tried at once to change so that she could regain her balance with this man...this stranger.

Marco Montevalde was saying gently, "Now I have paid the debts of Venezia. You have back what was taken. The scarf is for a souvenir and because the spray will be damp on your hair when you take the obligatory tourist's boat trip to the islands later."

Meg thought she heard Aunt Harriet's laughter from some deep place in her mind. She was beginning to collect her own souvenirs all right, but she wasn't sure whether to smile or sigh....

They went next to the office of Signor Prati. It would take a bit more time to obtain a new passport, since she would not be applying in person at the American Consulate in Milano, he said. Now she must sign certain papers before a notary, have the police photographer take her picture, and later sign the new passport in Signor Prati's presence. It could all be done at the office with no difficulties.

In eloquent words of textbook English the detective expressed his regret at the inconvenience to her. However, he smiled with delight when Marco described the arrangements for accommodation. "*Va bene*, Marco," he said. "Then there shall be no problems about finding a hotel. Your friend is most generous to offer his apartment."

The men chatted together like old friends, and in the course of the conversation Meg learned that Marco was leaving for Rome the next day.

"And how is the new project?" Signor Prati asked.

"I'm sending out the final design proposal when I get to Roma." Marco turned to Meg. "I am an architect, *signorina*, and as Giulio knows, I am at work on a large project which, if accepted, will be most helpful to me."

Signor Prati laughed. "I have no doubt of your success, Marco. I only await the time of celebration." To Meg he said, "Since you will be alone in Venezia for several days, I hope you will accept my earlier invitation to join my family for dinner. . .tomorrow, perhaps?"

"I'd love to come," she replied. His sincerely smiling face helped to ease her tension. It would be fun to dine with an Italian family, to join into the Venetian lifestyle if only for an evening.

"Then I will be in touch about the time."

Marco stood up. "We still have to collect the *signorina*'s luggage. Then I will see that she is settled at the apartment in the Specchiato."

Signor Prati's eyebrows shot up and a broad grin

creased his face. "Ah, the Specchiato! It is good to have such friends, is it not?" Meg thought she saw him wink at Marco, and she felt a new pang of worry. What was so amusing about the Specchiato?

They left with Signor Prati's assurances that the police had not stopped searching for her stolen property. Then Marco, in his efficient way, whisked Meg the short distance back to the hotel, where they claimed her luggage. He hired a *facchino pubblico*, a public porter, who loaded her things onto his wheeled cart.

Clutching her new handbag, Meg stood to one side and watched. Her life was being quite well arranged for her by Marco Montevalde.

CHAPTER FOUR

"WE WILL WALK to the palazzo—only a short distance," Marco said. "That way, when you feel well enough to explore in the days ahead, you will be more oriented to the peculiarities of my city." He pulled up short and called to the porter to stop. "But I have been inconsiderate, Meg. Do you feel able to walk farther?"

"I'm good for one more walk if it's not too long. Then I absolutely have to rest." The trip to the hotel had made her legs feel like water, but Marco was so full of vigor that just being with him made her feel stronger than she really was.

"You are not a complainer, my friend. I like that." He took the vase of roses, which she held in one hand, and wedged it upright between her cases on the push-cart. Then he turned to offer her his arm. The porter smiled and said something in the rapid Venetian dialect, which Marco translated. "He says his cart is now as fine as a gondola with flowers at its prow."

Meg took Marco's arm, discovering that his muscles were warm and taut under the smooth silk of his suit. His body seemed to send out signals of masculine strength and protectiveness, as well as an unsettlingly pleasant sexual force. Meg found it exciting to be walking so close to him.

She tried not to think about the fact, or to make any

kind of analysis about what was happening to her. She only wanted to enjoy walking with him through the narrow lanes and over the arched bridges.

They came to a wider canal. Marco warned her not to use the word canal for anything except the Grand Canal and a few of the largest waterways. The rest were properly called *rii*, and one of them alone was a *rio*. At the end of this particular *rio* she could see the Grand Canal, busy with traffic. Their little procession turned and headed toward it.

The *facchino*'s cart rumbled over the paving stones, with Marco and Meg close behind. Just before reaching the Grand Canal they came to a wide area of smooth pavement in front of a building that was decorated with patterns of mosaic. Tiny tiles of blue, purple, and scarlet were interspersed with golden ones. The sun glittered on them and shone on a heavy old door of dark weathered wood, bound with iron and studded with huge round-headed nails. Near the door a lamp hung from an ornate holder, and a massive iron gryphon acted as a knocker.

Marco pulled some keys from his pocket and went up several worn stone steps to the door. It swung inward easily and the *facchino* put the luggage inside. While Marco was paying the man, Meg stood in the entranceway, overwhelmed by what she saw.

Rising from the marble pavement were high columns of pink marble, supporting a slender balcony that ran along the four walls of the spacious hall. In the shadows beneath the arches of the colonnades were several closed doors with frescoes painted around them in soft muted colors.

An old stone well, beautifully carved with figures of

cherubs and fruit, stood in the center of the room. A heavy wrought-iron arch over the top held a chain whose nether end was lost in the depths of the well.

Meg's eyes followed the towering sweep of the walls upward to a high stained glass ceiling, which glowed in the filtered light of the sun. She looked again at the colonnades and realized with surprise that the arches and balcony on one wall weren't real at all, but painted in trompe l'oeil, that clever technique of perspective perfected by the Italian masters. The observer's eye was fooled into believing that a roundness of form and a depth existed where actually the wall was flat. In the middle of the deceptive wall there was even a false door, but it exactly matched the real doors behind the other balcony sections.

"Interesting, isn't it?" Marco's voice pulled her from her fascinated observations. "It is believed that much of the painting here was done by Tiepolo's students and some by the master himself." He touched a switch by one of the doors and a big Venetian chandelier came to life above them. Its lights were concealed in clusters of pale-toned glass flowers and gold-flecked leaves. The reflections cast prismatic streaks of color over the smooth marble pavement of the room.

Marco picked up the suitcases and moved across the hall to a broad marble staircase with intricately carved balustrades, which led upward from beneath one section of the real colonnades. They climbed the echoing steps, coming out onto the wide balcony. Meg looked down at the hall where she had just stood, and felt like Alice in Wonderland.

Behind them a small staircase led upward again and seemed to stop abruptly at a tiny balcony with a low door. She was about to continue her climb when Marco touched her arm to stop her. "That leads to an unused wing of the palazzo. Through here—" he pointed to a closed door next to them "—and down several hallways is the grand reception salon, completely lined with fine mirrors. The old merchant who built this place had an exquisite jewel collection and many rare art objects, collected from his travels. He liked to display them in the mirrored room, for the sheer pleasure of seeing them reflected to infinity."

He turned Meg gently toward another closed door, high and carved, and took out a second key. "The apartment is here. My friend has given me a set of keys, since he is rarely in residence and I sometimes have need of a hideaway. He has converted much of the original banquet hall into self-contained and quite civilized living quarters."

He pushed open the heavy door and stood aside for Meg to enter, smiling at her wide-eyed perusal of the hallway before them. "Later I will explain the building in its entirety, but you can see from the mosaics and frescoes that this palazzo was once very prosperous and full of life. I sometimes wonder how the old aristocratic walls feel with hardly a soul around to admire them.

"Downstairs are the boat landings, the original offices of the old merchant prince, and various storage areas. On this floor begins the true living area, safely above the dampness." He looked around at the cracked plaster of the painted walls. "So much needs repair. The building stretches back to the next *rio* and has numerous bedrooms and sitting rooms and servants' quarters, as you would expect. The kitchen is at the rear and has been partly modernized.

"The apartment also has its own small kitchen, and three bedrooms, a living room, and a dining room that overlooks the rooftops of other palazzi." He smiled. "Feel free to explore. There really aren't any ghosts, I assure you. And the owner is only too glad to have his home appreciated. He has grown used to my speculations on its architectural history. He plans to give the palazzo in historic trust to the city of Venezia very soon, keeping only the apartment for himself."

As Marco talked he opened another door and swung it wide, waiting for Meg to enter. The room she stepped into was in startling contrast to the highly elaborate Renaissance decor of the halls she had just walked through. Instead of marble floors, she was standing on warm wheat-colored carpeting, deep piled and luxurious. Modern furniture upholstered in fine linen in understated tones of browns, blues and greens picked up the colors in the Persian rug that lay in front of a grand marble mantel. The legs of the chairs and couches were made of natural, oiled woods, with here and there a glint of chrome.

The windows along one wall were obviously original ones, many hundred years old. Rather than clear glass panes there were clusters of thick round medallions that produced multiple tones of filtered light, adding a touch of antique charm in this gracious contemporary room. Bookshelves lined a second wall, and several dark and dignified oil portraits hung on the remaining spaces. Sleek steel lamps with long curving necks had been carefully placed about the room to highlight the owner's collection of small carvings and glassware on the occasional tables, and soft natural-fiber cushions were stacked in welcoming arrangements near the fireplace. Everything proclaimed comfort and taste.

An inner door opened quietly and a plump middle-aged woman in a dark dress and white apron came to greet them. "*Benvenuto*, Signor Marco!" Her wide smile fixed on Meg. "So. . .this is the *poverina* who has the illness and troubles. It is good you come. Lucia will care for you. I am good cook and you will put something under the skin on those pretty bones."

Marco laughed. "Let me get a word in, *cara* Lucia. This is Signorina Meg Brown. See that she rests until I pick her up at six o'clock for dinner." He left with a wave of his hand and no further explanations.

So she would be seeing him again! Mixed signals of fatigue and excitement rattled along Meg's nervous system.

Lucia took over right away and offered help in unpacking, which Meg happily accepted. Never in her life had she been so taken care of, but now, even if it was for a few days only, she decided to enjoy it. There would be no way of stopping Lucia, anyway, she sensed.

Handsomely carved antique furniture stood on soft gray blue carpeting in the bedroom she was taken to. The windows looked out over uneven roofs and the great bulbous chimney pots so typical of Venice. Shutters and windows were open to the balmy warm afternoon air, and in the distance over the rooftops Meg could just see the blue-and-gold tip of the Campanile of St. Mark's. She set her glass vase on the leather-topped bedside table. Her roses had survived their perilous journey through the city.

"You rest, *signorina*. I bring the tea." Lucia went purposefully out the door.

The small exquisite bathroom beckoned her to take a hot bath. Its tiles and tufted rugs repeated the blue of the bedroom carpet, and thick blue towels hung on brass towel heaters, inviting use.

Meg bathed happily, then wrapped herself in her shell-pink peignoir. Lucia had brought a tray of tea, tiny cakes and sandwiches, which she'd left on the bedside table.

The bedroom had many little treasures. Part of one wall was hung with shelves on which stood small Etruscan clay figures. Another section of shelves was reserved for books, several of them in English, she noted. There was a travel book on Italy that Meg had almost bought at home when she'd purchased her Italian phrase book. It was Kate Simon's *Italy, the Places in Between*.

Lifting the volume from the shelf, she settled herself cozily on the bed with pillows at her back and Lucia's tray on her lap. A sigh of pleasure escaped her lips. Venice wasn't a lost cause, after all. Here she was, in a fine old palazzo, being waited on hand and foot. And Marco Montevalde was taking her to dinner! Outside the windows the air was ringing with the sound of bells, the voices of Venice, proclaiming the hour. How incredibly fortunate she was that she could stay longer in this city of her heart—not as an ordinary tourist, but like this! *If Uncle Frank could see me now,* she thought with a smile.

Meg sipped her tea as she turned the pages of the travel book. Finally her eye was caught by a chapter near the end. "For Women," it was headed. Italics underneath the title said, "particularly for those old enough to have been bitten by a film called *Summertime*." Her teacup clattered back in its saucer.

Her attention riveted to the page, Meg read on. The text began, "Intoxicated by the mists of Venetian canals, her American guardedness lying at her feet like discarded robes, our heroine was ready for Italian love."

There was a description of the "soft spoken persuasive charm whose smooth energy is endless"—the Italian male. His various approaches to women were enumerated in florid detail. The author used the words "*Summertime* syndrome" to describe the urge to go to Venice that overcomes women who dream of romance. Meg felt her stomach tighten. An embarrassed heat flooded through her body; it wasn't fever.

"Are you looking for a hotel room?" the chapter went on with relentless irony. "He offers to take you to a good inexpensive *albergo*, centrally located, clean and respectably run by good friends. Be prepared, if you accept his company and advice, to share the bed with him...."

Meg found it hard to continue, but a horrible fascination urged her eyes to read. There were a few profound Italian male convictions, the author noted: "One assumes that foreign ladies, English and American particularly, find all Italians irresistible." The horrid words "sexual malnutrition" stopped her cold.

Not sexual deprivation, Meg thought defensively. Her own *Summertime* syndrome was more like romantic malnutrition.

Suddenly she could imagine streams of women converging on Venice, sitting hopefully at Florian's, waiting for the grand passion to walk up smiling.... A sentence leaped out at her: "The *Summertime* mirage is still pursued—now timidly, now boldly—by a good number of women."

She shut the book with a snap and threw it toward the foot of the bed. Surely Marco's eyes had been straightforward in their gaze. They'd been tinged once in a while by amusement and a kind of pleasant male protectiveness, but nothing more menacing than that. Yet his eyes were also full of vital masculine power, enough to make a woman wonder how it would feel if he were to love her. What would it be like to experience those firm lips in a lover's kiss, to be held tightly against that strong and elegant breast?

"But handsome, energetic men all have some of that power," Meg said aloud, ending the one-way conversation with a sharply whispered, "Damn!"

She returned the book to its shelf. The most annoying thing was that her obsessive dream of Venice wasn't hers alone, but had been shared by many a lonely heart. She felt duped by the whole romantic packaging.

She wandered about the room, analyzing Marco. He couldn't be one of those hard-up womanizers the author was writing about. Deep down she felt offended to have her dream reduced to the level of cold emotional thirst—and her hero degraded to a dime-a-dozen Romeo. She wasn't going to stand for it, either. If there was any problem, she knew she could handle it. Meantime, she would enjoy what the gods seemed to have given to her—more time in Venice and a delightful male escort for this one night.

Meg smiled. This *would* be something to remember—if she didn't get involved. "So help me, Katharine Hepburn, I won't!" she said firmly to her reflection in the dressing-table mirror. Chances were excellent that she wouldn't be seeing Marco Montevalde after tonight, since he was about to leave for Rome. She would be safely back with her tour group before he returned.

She dressed carefully in her old but nice street-length dresden-blue dress. The color complemented her eyes, and the soft jersey material draped gracefully over her figure. She put on a little more makeup than usual in an effort to look healthier than she felt. Marco shouldn't feel sorry for her or obligated in any way to take care of her, her pride said. Her tan pumps didn't clash too much with her new bag and silk scarf, but she hoped she would have a chance to buy a matching pair of shoes before she had to leave Venice.

A knock came on the door and she answered, to find Lucia there with a tall gray-haired man carrying a small black case. "Dottor Norelli, *signorina*," she said. "He has come to examine your health."

The tall doctor smiled pleasantly and moved with purpose into the room. "Signorina Brown, it is my pleasure. I am Franco Norelli, family physician to Signor Marco. He tells me you have had a distressing time since your arrival in Venezia."

His series of brief questions drew an admission from her that any sustained effort brought on a severe trembling in her limbs. "Hmm," he remarked, "you must not rush your strength, *signorina*. Do not attempt strenuous sight-seeing until your body readjusts itself."

He patted her cheek with a fatherly hand. "You are fortunate that Signor Marco interests himself in your welfare. His kindness is well-known." He reached into his bag for a bottle of pills. "Merely a homeopathic tonic," he smiled. "For energy." With the bottle was his card in case she needed anything further. He left with a bow, formally kissing the air just above her fingers.

When he'd gone Meg sat down at the dressing table to smooth her hair. She felt very pampered. Marco certainly had thought of everything.

It was almost six o'clock. The long twilight would soon start spreading over Venice, bringing the glowing orange colors of golden mist so dear to artists. Lucia bustled in with a soft knitted shawl in sky blue and admonitions not to get chilled in the night air, or too tired.

"But the air is so warm and soothing," Meg protested.

"In the boat of Signor Marco it can be very damp on the way to Torcello."

"Is that where we're going—Torcello?"

"*Si*—you will enjoy." The housekeeper smiled.

Marco arrived promptly at six. Meg heard his key in the door, and then he was striding toward her. *"Buona sera,"* he said in a low and gentle voice. "How lovely you look in those tones of blue. I met Dottor Norelli at the water steps outside. He told me I mustn't tire you, but we can have a few quiet hours on Torcello. By his permission, of course."

He took her arm solicitously and escorted her outside. A shiny white motor boat awaited them at the landing. The polished dark wood and blue-vinyl-upholstered seats looked immaculately cared for.

Marco lifted her easily, holding her for a moment in his arms before settling her into her seat. Meg's heart lurched alarmingly out of rhythm. She was surprised at the intensity of her reaction to him. He was holding out a delicate corsage of miniature pink roses in a cluster of lacy ferns. He smiled as she reached to take them, and her words of thanks were an uncontrolled whisper, not the way she wanted them to be.

Marco threaded the sleek launch through a maze of canals, coming out finally into an expanse of water dotted with low islands, some close and some far away. The late-afternoon colors had turned the whole lagoon of Venice into a smooth mirror of blue and gold.

Meg drew in a blissful breath. "It's like being part of the sunset itself—moving right into the heart of it," she said, and wondered if he would think her silly for saying something that bordered on the poetic. Jim had usually laughed at such statements.

"Be happy, *piccola*." His voice was gentle. "I think you haven't been truly happy enough in your life. Let beauty heal your heart." The words enfolded her with comfort, yet their very perceptiveness caused a flow of apprehension in her.

CHAPTER FIVE

MARCO AIMED THE BOAT across the lagoon, cutting the water cleanly and leaving behind a feathery wake of shimmering foam. Islands came close and receded again, and he called out their names: San Michele, the cemetery of Venice, with high walls and tall cypresses; Murano, the island of the glassmakers; Burano, the island of the fishermen and lace makers. Some miles beyond, after they had passed several flat islets covered with coarse scrub grass, was the island of Torcello.

The golden light was in full splendor when Marco tied up the boat at Torcello and they climbed out onto the island. There was a strange feeling, Meg decided, as if ghosts lingered in the silent deserted place.

Marco took her hand in his as they proceeded to the central piazza, which was grass grown. They visited the very ancient Byzantine cathedral with its curving apse and bishop's throne. A few other visitors were talking in low voices in other parts of the cool stone building. The marvelous mosaic of the Last Judgment, done in shades of brown and beige on the back wall, held Meg fascinated. The dreadful scenes of punishment and suffering must have over the centuries helped naughty children to mend their ways and be good. Her heart twisted as she looked up at the great Teotaca Madonna, whose mosaic tears had hung on her thin cheeks for hundreds of years.

Outside again, they continued along a path through cultivated fields to a small cluster of buildings. Hardly anything remained of what had once been a busy and populous community. Artichokes, grapes, orchards, and little farms spread over the flat land.

Marco explained that Torcello had been the first area settled when, long ago, desperate mainland people fled from the northern tribes to the safety of these islands. Now Torcello was nearly deserted, ruined by malaria many centuries in the past. This "mother of Venice" now lay in melancholy dishabille, while the daughter had gone on to acquire magnificent raiment.

They came to a small inn, the Locanda Cipriani. Marco led Meg through the building and onto a terrace, where ancient Byzantine pillars held up a beautiful grapevine, and where people were sitting enjoying their wine in the soft light of sunset.

Seated at a small table, Meg savored the taste of her sweet vermouth over ice with a twist of lemon and a bit of soda, a drink he had ordered for her. The headwaiter seemed to be a friend of his, just as the waiter at Florian's had been.

"Everyone knows you." There was a question in her voice.

"A man who was born and brought up in Venezia and whose family for generations has belonged to the city must have a few friends, hmm?" He answered her question with another one and continued to smile at her.

Meg tensed inside. She *had* to ask a few things, but not obviously. Her curiosity was building. Who was this man, sitting as close as if he had long been intimate with her? Everything she'd observed about him indicated he was a solid citizen, but there was the awful *Summertime* syndrome buzzing in the back of her mind. "I don't know anything at all about you, Signor Marco, and you know little about me," she began, letting the rest of her thought dangle unspoken.

His topaz eyes reflected some of the sunset light in their depths, giving him the look of a medieval nobleman. "So. . . it is time to satisfy curiosities. I am willing. But first, let me tell you, I perhaps know more about you than you think." He leaned back and sipped his drink. His finely drawn hand reached out for some olives from the *appertivo* tray, and she noticed that he wore a gold ring with the same crest that was on his calling card. He chewed on the olives unhurriedly and, for Meg, frustratingly.

Bright glints of humor sparked and glittered in his eyes. "Little Meg, I know you are sweet and puzzled. Venice is like a big dream in which you now move." His hand came to rest gently on hers. "I know that you have not experienced all that a woman hopes for. Your eyes tell me that you are brave and highly intelligent, and when not wasted by sickness, very capable. I also know that Meg Brown is searching for something beyond what she has known of life, and freedom to be an individual. I know that you have never fully known a man's love. Perhaps only the love of your childhood boy companions."

He paused and gave her a steady look that made a connection with her heart and caused its beat to speed up. "I am sure that you have never been kissed with real passion, although you have dreamed of it."

She opened her mouth to object, but his raised hand asked for silence. "I know your age, twenty-five; your mother is alive and lives with her sister. Your father is dead and you work in your uncle's office. You have a degree in journalism, and your fiancé died in the crash of a small plane...was it six months ago? A hunting party, I understand."

Meg flushed. "How have you found out about my life, Signor Montevalde?" She was compelled to be formal with him. "Is this a usual thing in Italy?" She had a hard time keeping her voice steady and was glad for the bite of irony in it.

"Do not glare at me, *piccola*. Giulio Prati had to check on you in the course of getting your passport. He told me. The rest is based on my own observation."

His eyes challenged hers. But those other intimate things he had said were too much, were none of his business. "In my country men do not intrude where they are not invited," she said. "You have decided a lot of things about me in your own mind. You could be wrong."

He chuckled deep in his throat. "Don't scratch me, little cat. I'm sorry. I admit I went too close to your secrets. In your country perhaps men do not intrude because they do not care enough about a woman." His expression became serious. "It must have been very painful to lose your fiancé so suddenly. But now you will make a career for yourself and go on with your life, *è vero*?"

Meg still simmered. "I am already a journalist, and my work has been published in several magazines." She lapsed into silence, sipping at her vermouth.

Marco was quiet also, then said softly, "And what have you observed about Marco Montevalde?"

She gave him a swift cool glance. "I see a very experienced man who is kind to women but tends to think of them as unstable, vulnerable, and easily affected emotionally. A man who is sure of himself. . . almost close to arrogant."

She drew a shaky breath. The impact of what she was saying to him suddenly hit her, and she felt disgustingly ungrateful. Here she sat, at his expense, wearing his roses and staying in the lovely palazzo he had found for her.

"I see also a talented and intelligent person whose instincts appear to be considerate. He is well liked and respected." The ire went out of her. "I just can't make judgments on a life that I know nothing about, and I won't comment further."

Still, it was annoying that he had read her so clearly. Had he also seen the mixture of fear and deep attraction that was warming within her?

He was watching her intently. No flicker of response to her insults showed. His lips were set in a strong but gentle line. If she could put a name to his expression it would be kindness. "I'm sorry," she said sincerely. "Please forgive me. You've been very helpful and I had no right to say anything. I guess I didn't want to be thought so transparent—so naive about life."

A smile came to his lips, so vitally attractive that she blinked. "And how do you want to appear, my Meg—a worldly woman?"

"No, not really. Just. . . not stupid."

He threw back his head and laughed at that, the mellow sound making heads turn at other tables. He leaned closer. "It's not naive to be sweet, *piccola*, or even to dream."

She managed a wavery smile in return. He could unsteady her so easily. "*Piccola.* That means little one, doesn't it?"

"Yes, does it bother you?"

"Forse che si," she quoted from her Italian study list, *"forse che no."*

"Perhaps yes, perhaps no. Then shall I not use it any more?"

Meg shook her head. "Say whatever you wish if you honestly feel like it."

He gave her a serious look. "Then I feel like saying that you underrate yourself, *piccola*." He emphasized the word. "You are very charming and quite beautiful, and you have a wistful natural quality that makes a man want to care for you, to protect, to think how you might be made happy."

She smiled wryly. "I am a self-sufficient woman, Signor Marco, and I accept myself as I am. But thanks for the compliments. They're pleasant to hear."

Dinner came just then, to her relief. It was served beautifully, and the food and wine were perfection. Marco proceeded to tell her about the history of the small inn where they sat, about the Cipriani family and Arrigo Cipriani, who had developed the famous Harry's Bar, the Locanda, and even a fine hotel of first class in Venice proper.

As she ate, Meg looked out at the blooming garden and enjoyed the sound of Marco's smooth, resonant voice. At least she could sit here for a short while in her fool's paradise pretending that he was truly interested in her, that she could come close to him and his life. She heard only part of what he was saying, more about the brave story of Signor Cipriani, who had been helped to start his bar by an American named Harry, proving that there can be trust between good people.

I shouldn't have come with him this evening, she told

herself eventually. *It's a good thing he's going to Rome.* This was too bittersweet, too much like a play staged in the most romantic of settings. And she was too much of a natural actress, ready to play the tempting role of beloved. She was embarrassed with herself and no better than those silly ladies infected by the "syndrome."

She should be taking mental notes at least, about the interesting things Marco was telling her. What kind of half-witted journalist was she to let good material slip by her?

Marco was asking her a question, which she missed completely. "You were very far away, Meg. What is it, *cara*?"

She turned her eyes to meet the deep fascination of his and made a swift and unalterable decision. "There's a lot you still don't know about me." She smiled and his face relaxed a little. "Maybe I should tell you why I'm in Venice."

His eyes did not lessen their intent gaze.

"A long time ago, when I was sixteen, to be exact, I saw the film *Summertime*."

He nodded. "I know the film. A most beautiful treatment of my city and a poignant love story, as I recall."

"Yes. I think that I fell in love with Venice that day. Afterward I bought books with pictures of the city and dreamed myself into them. I got so that I could almost feel the stones and smell the air. My fiancé intended to bring me here on our honeymoon, just to please me."

Marco's expression changed and he reached out to touch her hand. "Do not tell me if it is painful."

"No, it helps to tell it, because I've just begun to understand some things much better. . . ." She hesitated, reaffirmed her decision, and plunged on with the matter-of-fact narrative. "This afternoon at the Specchiato I read a chapter from a travel book that was in my room. It was about Italy, and it described what is called the *Summertime* syndrome. It said that many female tourists come to Venice hoping to replay a story like the one in the film. Suddenly I felt very foolish. Was I so fascinated by Venice itself, or was it some adolescent romantic yearning that I hadn't quite acknowledged to myself?"

She had Marco's undivided attention and felt a pang of regret for what she was about to say to him. "After my fiancé's death I became restless. I wasn't satisfied with working for my uncle—I plan to advance my career in journalism. And then one night a month ago I attended a charity ball with a man I know. The whole ballroom was decorated with huge photographs of Venice, and there was concertina music playing. Later that evening when I couldn't sleep I turned on the television, and what should be playing but *Summertime*!"

By a frustrated wave of her hand she hoped to convince Marco of her confused state at the time. "It was too much of a coincidence. Even more so that I had recently heard about an inexpensive European tour that included Venice. I felt impelled to go. . . ."

Marco murmured something in Italian.

"My family thought I was rash. My uncle warned me about having my passport stolen, and my mother worried that I would meet unscrupulous men." She laughed again, trying to sound genuinely amused. "You can imagine how I felt, being sick and unable to see the city I had dreamed about. . . and to have my uncle's prophecy come true! It seemed a most unkind fate. I tottered out to see St. Mark's Square, at least . . . and everything else happened. . . ."

"You said you have understood some things. What are they, Meg?" Marco's voice had a caressing vibration that almost destroyed her resolve to cut through any sentiment between them.

"You know what happened in the piazza. I learned then that dreams come true in unusual ways. I learned that there is no special romantic place—people are people everywhere and it's no more romantic in Venice than anywhere else." The lie stuck in her throat and she swallowed hard, reaching to take a sip of the ruby wine left in her glass. The very taste of it was compounded of romance and she felt desolate.

Summoning a bright smile, she said in a grateful voice, "I was so fortunate to meet you and Signor Prati. My illness was a blessing in disguise and so was the theft. They allowed me to catch a real glimpse of your wonderful city, and even more, to learn about the generosity and kindness of Italian gentlemen."

Marco had leaned back in his chair and his eyes were in shadow. His lips, set in a straight line, had a rather controlled and almost stern expression. Meg had a few more things to say, and she forced herself to continue, "I'll always be grateful to you and Signor Prati—and to Venice. I'll go home happily now and take up my life where I left off. I guess I had to come here to get my heart and my head straight about the future. It's all falling into place for me at last." She gave another light laugh. "Wish me luck!"

Marco's lips twitched into a mirthless smile. *"Buona fortuna,"* he said softly.

They sat in silence for a few moments while Meg

fought down the shivery feeling in her body. A trio of strolling musicians was moving among the tables. Marco waved them over and spoke in Italian to them, discreetly slipping them a few bills. With wide smiles they broke into a familiar tune—the theme music from *Summertime*. A special something in their version of the music was the essence of Italy.

Marco said slowly, "I am glad that you are happy, Meg. I understand you more now, I think. You should be good at your chosen profession. I notice that you are very aware, very observant—even if you don't speak of things directly."

"Maybe I'll write about Venice. Would your friend mind if I mentioned his palazzo?"

"Probably not. It is well-known in architectural circles. But I wish to change the subject. Why haven't you asked me more about myself? I am most willing to confess everything about my life." Little sparks of amusement lighted his eyes and put a lift on the corners of his expressive lips. Meg had to look away from his face. His attractiveness was the enemy that threatened to break down her protective veneer. She could feel the tremors of nervous energy darting through her body, and it made her angry.

"I would like to hear about your life. . .of course," she said.

He told her then about his youth in Venice and how he had ridden his horse on a deserted area of the Lido. His childhood sounded happy and sunlit, marred by the early death of his mother during the stillbirth of an infant brother. Marco's father had continued an active but lonely life until his death a few years ago.

"My parents truly loved each other," he said with a

vulnerable, reminiscent look on his face. "My father did not remarry, and I have not married as yet. Perhaps I have my own dream. Perhaps I am afraid no woman will be to me as my mother was to my father."

Meg couldn't think of anything to say and kept silent.

"Don't you want to wish me luck also?" he asked suddenly.

"Auguri," she responded, not at all at ease.

"You sound like a charming cynic."

"Not really, but such a romance is not a usual thing."

"Undoubtedly you are correct."

He had agreed too easily to suit Meg. However he went on with his story. He had become the head of his family. His father had a twin brother, younger by only minutes, named Claudio. Claudio had died ten years before, doing rescue work after a terrible earthquake in Southern Italy. He'd been a doctor and had left a widow and two children behind. "Ugo and Teresa are my young cousins, now in their early twenties. I feel very much like their father, since there is no other mature male in the immediate family. My Uncle Claudio's widow, Bianca, is living in Firenze, where her own family has a small ancestral house and she can live modestly with great style. She is a most attractive woman still, the very essence of femininity, although not capable of handling the affairs of Ugo, her son. Ugo's problems fall to me to deal with," he said ruefully. He smiled when he spoke of Teresa, describing her as a sweet girl with good sense. She was just finishing her college studies at Bologna, with a degree in music.

"I speak freely to you, *piccola*, the way a man on a train speaks to a woman he expects never to see again. You see, you find me at a most tenuous point in my life, with great hopes and great burdens, and no assurance that the future will go one way or the other. And so I sit here with you, a most dear stranger to my life, and tell you everything that I tell no one else."

Marco's story unfolded uncomfortably: Ugo, the male cousin, had already gone through the small inheritance left by his father and felt he deserved more. He had always been angry that Marco wouldn't give him the money to buy a Ferrari. He was in a stage that many young men go through, obsessed with speed. One night a few years before, he had borrowed one of the luxury sports cars of a friend and had taken a girl riding. They were in Cortina on a ski holiday and the roads were icy and dangerous. He crashed the car on a hairpin turn and the girl was badly injured.

"She spent a year in the hospital and is now home with permanent injuries to her spine. She will not regain the use of her legs," Marco said soberly.

"How terrible!" Meg could see his distress.

"*Si*, but that is not all. He had been driving without a license. It had been suspended because of numerous arrests, and the girl's parents are suing for a very large amount of money. I pity them. In their grief they seek revenge. Whatever the outcome of the lawsuit, I am the head of this family and responsible for Ugo's debts. The girl will have to have nursing care for the rest of her life, and I am happy to pay for that. But the family wants far more."

"I'm so sorry!" Meg exclaimed. She felt so inadequate. What were her little romantic ups and downs compared to this deep problem?

"My family funds are protected under my father's will and only a portion of them can be used. There is very little money left in the small estate of Ugo's father. I send my dear Aunt Bianca what I can for her needs, and I have advised Teresa never to lend Ugo money from her part of the inheritance. My own personal funds come from my work as an architect. I have a business with two partners in Roma, and at present I am working independently on a project which, if it is accepted by a wealthy American client, will bring me a considerable sum of money. This could pay the demands of the girl's parents. Otherwise, my business funds would be terribly depleted, and I would have to borrow from my partners, which I have no intention of doing. A matter of pride. Perhaps that is being only a typical Italian to your mind, my friend, but it is what I am."

Meg didn't quite know how to sympathize with him, but she longed to reach out and touch his hand. She didn't, however. "Something like this shouldn't happen to a man like you," she said at last.

Marco gave a complicated smile. "Unfortunately, Ugo was not yet of age when this happened. The attorneys for the girl's family realize that Ugo's mother has no source of money and that I am concerned with protecting her from further stress. The lawsuit has dragged on for four years. Very trying for all of us—except, apparently, for Ugo himself, who behaves as if nothing has happened." He sighed.

"But I should not have burdened you with this. You were most polite to listen. Thank you, *cara*." He took a deep breath. "Anyway, I do have this prospect in my business that may solve many things. I am not begrudging the money to the poor girl. Her life has been disastrously affected. As for Ugo...I don't know. He is unrepentant."

Meg searched for comforting words, but they all had too intimate an overtone. She looked down at her wristwatch. It was almost eleven.

Marco noticed her movement. "We should start back." He signaled for the waiter. "My train leaves very soon for Roma."

"Tonight?" She couldn't keep the disappointment from her voice.

"*Si*—so that I can sleep and have the full day tomorrow for my work."

They walked out onto a flat paved area that led toward the boat landing. The sound of the music in the Locanda carried far in the quiet night. The moon drenched everything in its silvery glitter.

Meg was acutely aware of Marco's nearness. She let her hand hang freely at her side, then realized she hoped he would take it in his own. Immediately she raised it and held onto her purse, as casually as the awkward motion would allow.

Then she felt his warm touch on her arm, and his hand slid gently around her waist to turn her toward him. "Dance with me, *cara*. I need to dance." His voice was low and close to her ear. The magic light of the moon folded them into a dream. There was never a doubt in her mind that she would obey him as he pulled her into the steps of the waltz that was being played at the Locanda Cipriani.

Meg let him lead her across a sea of thick moonlight. His strong body supported her, and her head moved irresistibly close to him, until it nestled against the firm expanse of his shoulder. Her hand, held against his breast, tingled with the energy that flowed from him. The music drew them into its rhythm and then came to an end. They swayed slowly to a stop and stood still, caught in the strange power of the moment.

Reluctantly Meg moved her head from his shoulder. She knew she must pull away even though her whole body cried out to stay where it was. She began to lean back against his confining arm, but it tightened around her waist. She raised her eyes to look at him and with a soft groan he bent his lips to hers.

The touch of his mouth was gentle, but it sent a flash of electricity along her lips, like a sudden shock of amazing and subtle fire. His urging warmth pressed her mouth open. She could feel her lips trembling against his, and for an instant she regretted that he could feel her excitement.

Then all thought stopped. A sensation of bliss was exploding in small exquisite bursts down the length of her spine and reverberating through her body. Never in her most vivid dreams had she been able to imagine such a sense of perfect attunement to another being, such anticipation and desire for more. No kiss from Jim or any other man had been like this.

So this was what love songs were about! Astonishment flooded her. Her body was singing with its own desires, and she clung to Marco while the moon and stars whirled in ecstatic joy around them.

Finally, after a long and almost unbearable exploration of her lips, Marco raised his head. His eyes—different now—looked down into hers, and his fingers traced the lines of her face, barely touching it.

"Forgive me, little Meg." His voice was low and very rough. "I could no more *not* kiss you than I could stop breathing." His hand smoothed her hair. "This is goodbye, *piccola dolce*. Tomorrow I will be in Roma, and after that you will be on your way back to your familiar life. This will be an amusing tale to tell your friends, hmm?"

She still looked up at him, but now a cold weight was pressing against her breast, deep inside her. She felt him release her and saw a kind of pain in his eyes. Moving away from the sphere of his comfort, she began to walk unsteadily toward the boat, his steps not far behind hers. She didn't want to think.

Silently they reached the landing. Marco helped her into the boat and then sent the smooth prow dashing into the moon-bright water, leaving a path of sparkled foam in their wake. Meg huddled on the blue cushioned seat.

Marco concentrated on driving the launch, standing with graceful balance at the wheel, his tall figure swaying with the motion of the boat. With horrible desolation Meg acknowledged to herself that he *was* the man of her dreams. Her fantasy had just played itself out, but one thing was wrong: he was leaving her after just one kiss. There wouldn't be more, and she wouldn't even have Kate Hepburn's memories of love. Furthermore, to him she was just a sweet young thing. That thought simmered under the spell of the kiss, which was still with her.

She just *couldn't* imagine that she loved him! She was too sensible to fall into the trap laid by an accomplished Italian lover. How could she know whether all those things he'd told her about himself were true? The fact was she couldn't.

The kiss means nothing to him, she thought, *and that's good.* He must never know how deeply he had touched her. She had nothing to do with his life.

That last thought brought a clenching misery into her stomach, and she thought she might be ill all over again. She closed her eyes and concentrated on breathing steadily. *Marco Montevalde is not the beginning or the end of everything.*

They were sweeping through the canals now, sending wavelets against the wet stone of the old buildings, little floods over water steps and under the grilled gateways of landings. Marco had cut the motor. They cruised into the *rio* in front of the Specchiato and came to a stop.

He leaped out and extended a hand, pulling her up swiftly onto the stone quay. His polite touch at her elbow guided her to the great wooden door. He used his key and opened it for her, then his hand tightened for a moment on her arm. "Will you forget me, *piccola*, in the busy world of your California?"

She dragged up a reasonably natural laugh. "Of course not. Who could forget Marco Montevalde?" She smiled and put out her hand. "There are no words to tell you how grateful I am for your kindness." A lump stuck in her throat, and she had to try hard to sound collected. "I...want you to know that if you are ever in California and my uncle or I can in any way be of help, please call on us. I'll leave the address of the office with Lucia."

"And will there be no more of the dream?" His hand held hers tightly as she tried to draw it from his grasp.

She laughed a little despite the horrid lump. "I've enjoyed finding out just a little about your wonderful city." She tugged at her hand, but he kept it, raising it to his lips.

"*Arrivederci, piccola. Felicità*...be happy." For a timeless moment his eyes held hers, and then he was looking at her trembling lips. She was sure he would kiss her again, but he drew in a sharp breath, turned swiftly and walked away.

The boat vanished down the *rio*, leaving resonant echoes in the silence. He was in a hurry to catch the train to Rome. His mind was already busy with his own life. She could stop wondering now.

Meg walked up the stairs to the apartment with knees that barely supported her and sat down on one of the soft chairs in the living room. *"Il salotto,"* she recited dully, having learned by rote the Italian names for the rooms of a house. She had an empty, awful feeling. With hesitant fingers she touched her sensitized lips. "*Il bacio*—the kiss," she said in a barely audible voice.

Would Marco have stayed if she had leaned forward to welcome that second kiss? At least he hadn't discovered that she didn't have the strength to refuse him.

"Well," she whispered to herself, "you *would* come to Venice. You were obsessed with it, so you got all kinds of unexpected things—including Marco. Oh, God. . . ." Her voice faltered to silence. She stood up and went to her room. While she made ready for bed the inner dialogue continued:

Now what, Meg? You know you've been an idiot.

But I won't be unsatisfied now. I will have been to Venice. Things are bound to look different once I get home.

Is that so! Any reminder of Venice will give you a giant heartache. You'll hear Marco's voice for the rest of your life.

Nonsense! I'm a liberated woman. Sexual fascination comes and goes. Just as soon as I get busy in a good job I'll be able to forget him. I was just a pleasant interlude for him, nice to kiss under the moonlight. He obliged my fantasy. . . .

And don't you think he saw how undone you were by his slightest touch? You did kiss him back, didn't you? He probably thinks you're able to handle yourself. Aren't you? Well—aren't you?

"I don't know," she said into the stillness of the room. But she was sure of one thing: she had to get out of this place before she lost all touch with reality.

Resolutely she set herself to the task of going to sleep, playing every mind game she knew. She imagined she was walking into her apartment at home and tried to picture everything clearly, every little thing. But all she could see was Aunt Harriet's Venetian goblet and the TV set where, if she switched it on, *Summertime* would be playing.

Finally she gave up and climbed out of bed, pacing restlessly around the apartment. After a while she slipped into her robe, went out into the shadowy corridor and down the marble steps to the balcony overlooking the entrance hall.

Moonlight filtered through the stained glass skylight. The old house seemed to be breathing. Little creaks sounded here and there in the shadows. Meg looked down into the hall with its trompe l'oeil painted walls, which even in the semidarkness still fooled the eye. Soundless whispers of presences from the distant past moved around her—men in robes of velvet and fur, women with pearls sewn around the necks of satin gowns and on close-fitting caps. They had loved and wept, had been born and had died in this great house.

What was she doing here among them? They weren't unfriendly ghosts—just surprised and aloof. What could you possibly know of us, young woman, they seemed to say. Meg stayed a long time at the balustrade of the balcony, absorbing the feeling of the old house. She mustn't forget. Wasn't she planning to write something terrific for *Au Courant* magazine, after all?

A sudden sound that could almost have been the breaking string of some musical instrument sent her scurrying back to the apartment, where she locked the door and rushed to bed. At last she slept.

CHAPTER SIX

MORNING WAS LONG GONE by the time Meg opened her eyes. Her little travel clock said one o'clock, and the sunlight that streamed down from the windows onto her bedclothes confirmed it. Another day almost gone before it had started. But the day was hers entirely, and she could do with it as she wished. It was a heady thought. Her list of things to see in Venice was endless. She had every intention of making the most of her time, no matter how she felt.

She hopped out of bed as if she were in normal condition and nearly fell on her face. Dr. Norelli's tonic tablets weren't working any miracles, but her appetite was returning with a vengeance. She slipped into her robe and eased herself toward the kitchen, expecting to see Lucia's cheery face. Instead she found two notes on the kitchen table, one saying that Lucia was out shopping and had left food prepared for her, and the second saying that Signor Prati would be honored if she would dine with him and his wife that evening. A gondola would be sent to pick her up at 6:30.

There was no doubt in Meg's mind that this would be a combined business and pleasure engagement. She could be receiving her passport tonight, which made it more certain that she would be leaving Venice on schedule. The thought wasn't entirely welcome, no matter what she might have decided last night.

Fresh rolls, an assortment of cheeses, preserves, and a cup of black coffee cleared her head of its fuzziness. She dressed for the hot humid day, checked the money in her purse, consulted her tiny folded map of the city, and with more resolve than energy, stepped forth from the Palazzo Specchiato. On her way out she peered down into the ancient well in the entrance hall. She couldn't resist looking into its cool mysterious depths.

She hurried to open the heavy door and was at last on her way to find a gondola of her own. No matter what it cost, she was going to be taken the length of the Grand Canal, and then some! She was going to be the complete tourist—hear the lap of the gondola oar in the water, see the Ca' d'Oro, the Rialto Bridge, stare back at the bold eyes of the Italian men, greet children...in short, do every trite thing that pleased her. It was her day, and as long as her body held out she was going to soak herself in the spirit of Venice. *Without Marco Montevalde,* she thought firmly. She pretended that she had never met the man.

She aimed herself in the general direction of the gondola pool near St. Mark's. There, a dozen boats rocked slowly at their moorings. One gondolier, with a fast patter of enticing words, stepped forth from an animated group of men. "Gondola, lady? Best tour in Venezia! Ponte dei Sospiri, Santa Maria della Salute, Ca' Rezzonico...you Americano? Lots to see...."

She held up her hand to stop him. "Take me everywhere," she laughed, "starting with the Grand Canal."

He grinned widely. "Two-hour special! Not so cheap,

but best in Venezia! I know what lady want to see!" He didn't wait for her to answer, but quickly took her elbow and helped her into his sleek black boat.

He was a wiry short man in his forties, wearing the black-and-white striped cotton shirt that Meg knew was authentic, not like the pseudogondolier costumes at the country-club ball last month. She was suddenly feeling better than she had for days. She didn't need a romantic man to make her happy in Venice, and she would most likely forget Marco in a short time. It was happening already. "Tell me what you love the most in Venice," she asked the gondolier.

He kissed his clustered fingertips. "Ah, but that would take more than hours, *signorina*. My name is Alfredo and my heart is in every *rio*, every stone. But I take you to see many of them. Tomorrow you come and I take you to see more."

But there won't be a tomorrow, she almost said.

Alfredo pushed off from the mooring with a strong surge of his pole and deftly worked the gondola out of the pool. "You like old things?" he asked after he had maneuvered them through a zigzag of *rii* and into the Grand Canal. Meg nodded, craning her neck to see the facade of the Doges' Palace behind them. Alfredo's voice rose above the chugging sounds of water taxis and slow moving water buses—the *vaporetti*.

She was finally doing it, she thought gleefully, and tried to block out everything that didn't belong to her enjoyment of Venice. She had her thin pocket camera ready, at last indulging her dream of taking her own pictures of her beloved city. Alfredo was good enough to slow down or even stop when she wanted more time for a good shot or needed to change her film.

He proudly pointed out palaces on either side of the Grand Canal. "Ca' Rezzonico, the home of Robert Browning. . . Palazzo Mocenigo, where Lord Byron stayed with his ladies. . . ." He chuckled naughtily. Alfredo turned the gondola into the smaller waterways, moving past charming little campos and churches, and streams of people who were walking the narrow lanes beside the water. They reentered the Grand Canal right in front of the magnificent Byzantine face of the Ca' d'Oro.

Between points of interest Alfredo told Meg all about his family trade as *gondolieri* and about their passion for their home city. "My brother went to Florida in the *Stati Uniti*, but he was not happy. He make lots of money and come back to his gondola. For me, I will never leave," he said earnestly.

They ended their two-hour tour at the place where they had started, the gondola pool behind the piazza. Meg's mind was racing with ideas. Tonight, after her dinner with Detective Prati's family, she was not going to bed until she had made notes for at least three articles on Venice: "What can happen when everything goes wrong in a foreign city, and you haven't a friend in the world. The *Summertime* Syndrome—its care and feeding." And something more free flowing and serious. She didn't have a title for it yet, but it had to do with the intangible mood of Venice, the way the past and present overlapped constantly; the mysterious pull the city exerted on the heart of a woman. That piece would take time and deep contemplation.

Alfredo helped her out of his bobbing craft and she paid him without haggling, adding as large a tip as she could afford.

"You come again tonight, *signorina*," he said smiling. "My brother take you for special romantic gondola ride—especially for lovers. You bring someone."

"I'm sorry, I won't be able to." She reached to shake his hand and started back to the Specchiato. Did every Venetian man have romance on his mind, just as the travel book suggested? Best to take it all with a large grain of salt and write a lighthearted article about it.

Meg browsed and window-shopped her way home, stopping in one appealing little store in particular to purchase two silk scarves for her mother and aunt. Extravagantly, she bought a soft knitted triangular stole for herself in clear blue, and matched it with a string of Venetian-glass beads.

It was four o'clock when she let herself into the palazzo, feeling a sense of belonging and knowing how absurd it was. She stood in the entrance hall, now completely familiar to her, and savored the aura and mood of the place.

I don't ever want to go home, she thought. Yet once she had her passport in hand she would have to go. That was hard fact. What she wouldn't give to be some magazine's Venetian correspondent, permanently on duty here.

She felt restless waiting for the dinner hour and Detective Prati's gondola. Lucia was still out, but the refrigerator was filled with fresh fruits and cheeses, substituting for the lunch Meg never ate. She stood at the doorway to the apartment as she enjoyed the tasty wedges of a fresh peach, gazing down the darkened hallway beyond. She couldn't help wondering about the rest of the Specchiato.

When she'd finished eating she found a little pad and

pencil for quick sketches, then started to explore. If the downstairs hall was any example, the palazzo must be incredible. Marco had said it was permitted, and there was so much of it to see. Still, she felt a bit awkward as she started down deserted hallways and approached closed doors.

Just as she reached out toward a tarnished metal latch a large black-and-white cat brushed against her leg. Meg jumped in guilty reflex. One of Lucia's cats, she supposed. Wasn't Venice famous for its love of cats?

The first room was large and dark, with white shrouds over chairs and tables, and dusty crystal chandeliers giving off weak light into the gloomy space. The floor was parquetry patterned, probably oak, and several Oriental rugs were rolled up along one wall. Heavy torn velvet curtains hung at the tall windows. The air was stale. If the owner was a wealthy man he certainly wasn't spending his money to keep the place up.

Meg moved through a connecting door into a second shrouded room. Little skittering sounds told of the presence of mice not used to being disturbed, except, perhaps, by the cat. She was about to turn back when she remembered Marco's comments about the room of mirrors, the prize of the old merchant-prince who had built the palazzo. Figuring that it must be nearby, she proceeded through a series of gray, dusty, humid rooms, flicking on the wall switch in each and seeing only more dreariness.

She was about to turn back when she saw a glow at the top of a narrow stairway. Curious, she climbed the curving stone steps, instinctively trying not to make a sound and feeling somehow as if she were about to discover something she wasn't supposed to see. *The usual dramatic Meg,* she thought and purposely set her feet down firmly on each step. It was time to stop making more out of simple things than was healthy for a woman of her age and experience.

At the top of the stairs was a door, partly open. She peered around it before stepping out onto a tiny half circle of balcony high above the floor of a very large room. It was the room of mirrors! Three of the enormous Venetian-glass chandeliers were lighted, allowing a clear view of the breathtaking room.

Had the Hall of Mirrors at Versailles been modeled after this one? This was surely older by at least a century. Tall mirrored panels, dappled with age, lined the walls of the cavernous oblong room. Even the frescoed ceiling was edged with mirrors set into squares of plaster coffering. Meg could see how in the centuries before electricity they must have reflected the light from the hundreds of candles in the chandeliers.

She leaned lightly against the turned-wood balustrade and started to sketch the room from her vantage point. Each mirror was framed with elaborately painted wood moldings. She tried to capture the unearthly fragility of the effect, as if the room floated in some more subtle dimension, where reality and fantasy blurred. . . .

A sound drew her eyes away from the details of the glass panels to the floor directly beneath her balcony. Carefully she leaned a little farther over the railing to see what was happening. She wouldn't have been surprised to see some old caretaker on his rounds, or another cat.

Instead she saw two men—one, carrying a small framed painting, walking quickly toward the other, who had just opened a door. They both disappeared from view beneath the balcony, but Meg didn't dare lean out farther to see where they'd gone. The hair was standing up on the back of her neck. Something surreptitious was happening in the room of mirrors, she knew instinctively, and she mustn't be seen. She pulled back against the wall of the balcony and listened to the voices of the men. Speaking in Italian, they sounded hurried and querulous. Then the door closed and the room was silent again.

Meg stood rooted to the spot for several minutes, until she was sure that the men were gone. Then she did something that went against every bit of common sense she'd been born with—she went down to the mirrored room. She had to see it for herself, to prove that she was just being silly.

Finding a door that led into the hall was easy. At one end of the room at the bottom of the stairs was a narrow panel with a latch, which she tried tentatively. The panel opened into a kind of pass-pantry that continued through into the great room. She pushed at the door a little, just enough to see for herself that the room was empty. Then she ventured into it, with her breath in check and her footsteps soundless.

Somehow, she didn't want to look directly into the mirrors all around her. They carried a feeling of being laden with more faces and images from the past. It was like being in a timeless place where, if the music suddenly struck up a Mozart or Vivaldi theme, people would magically materialize out of the dusty air, dancing.

Meg's eyes moved quickly around the room. Beneath the little balcony where there should have been a door—where the two men had entered just a while before—there was nothing but a solid wall with tall thin panels of mirror and decorative molding around them.

She mentally shook herself. Surely she had seen it with her own eyes—the door opening and then shutting again. *It's a secret doorway,* she said to herself, remembering all the Nancy Drew mystery stories she had read as a child. The hairs stood up at the back of her neck for a second time.

As if to force herself to be sensible she deliberately took out her pencil and made several quick sketches of the room. Then, because she was still not satisfied, she turned around and did a careful drawing of the mysterious wall where the men had come and gone. When she thought she heard the muffled sound of voices coming from behind it, she hurried out of the room.

Within minutes she was back in the apartment, sitting at the dressing table with her hairbrush in hand and studying the drawings that lay on the table in front of her. It was none of her business what anyone was doing here. Someone could ask the same about her.

Still, it was intriguing how the two men could have disappeared behind that solid-looking wall of mirrors. . . .

SIGNOR PRATI had said he would send a gondola for her at 6:30. Meg spent the next hour dressing carefully and bringing her mind back to the concerns of a tourist. She used her small travel iron to freshen up her blue cotton skirt and white ruffled gauze blouse. Then she lifted the blue stole from its tissue wrappings. It went well with her skirt and with the long chain of peacock blue Venetian-glass beads.

Lucia complimented her. "You will like the family of Giulio Prati and they will like you."

"You know them?"

"*Certamente.* My second cousin has work for Signorina Adella many years. When they need help for parties, I go."

"Does everyone know everyone else in Venice?" Meg laughed.

"Not everyone," Lucia grinned back, "but more than you think. Signor Prati is respected. He is a childhood friend of Signor Marco."

"And does he know the owner of the Specchiato, as well?"

Lucia didn't answer, but bustled to the windows that overlooked the front of the palazzo. "Ah! Luigi comes for you." She snorted in laughter. "He will make Italian eyes at you, but it mean nothing. He is a good man and brother to Giorgio, the waiter at Florian's."

She waved out the open window. "*Ciao*, Luigi! *Aspetti un momento!* I tell him to wait. Have good time."

Meg went downstairs, smiling at Lucia's exuberance. Luigi helped her into his shining gondola with the grace of a courtier. *"Buona sera, bella signorina."* His dark eyes admired her boldly. "I am to take you to the home of my friend Signor Prati. He is tell to me to take care of the *signorina* or he throw me in jail." He laughed happily at his own joke.

They set off down a winding way, threading through *rii* that Meg hadn't seen before. Smells of cooking wafted from high windows, voices called out to one another, while snatches of music came and went on the currents of the warm air of evening.

They came to a grilled water gate, which Luigi pushed open, sliding his gondola smoothly into the dark area under the building. In a niche above the entrance stood a lovely ceramic figure of the Madonna, surrounded by Della Robbia type tiles. "*Casa* Madonna," Luigi said. He reached up to pull a chain that hung by a narrow stone quay. A faint ringing echoed somewhere over the slap-slap of the water against the walls.

A door opened above, and a light slanted down a stone stairway. Signor Prati hastened toward them, smiling. Luigi steadied the boat, taking care not to scrape its well-tended sides against the stone. Signor Prati held out a helping hand to Meg and she stepped onto the small wet footholds in the stone.

"*Ciao*, Luigi—*grazie tanto*. Welcome, Signorina Brown."

Meg turned to wave at Luigi, who bowed and blew her a kiss before he backed his gondola expertly into the *rio* again.

Signor Prati's hand guided her up the inner stairs. The door led into a small hall, and from there another door opened into a comfortably furnished room. A woman rose from a plump sofa, setting aside some embroidery that she had been working on.

She was small and graceful, with huge brown eyes and dark curling hair cut close to her head in pixie fashion. Signor Prati introduced her as his wife.

Adella Prati had a whimsical manner, warm and welcoming, and Meg quickly felt at ease. Adella bombarded her with questions about "'ollywood" almost immediately, while Signor Prati looked on indulgently.

Meg couldn't help noticing the high ceiling of the room, which was painted with festoons of glowing flowers held by fat and smiling angels.

"This house is one of the older ones," her host remarked, noticing her glance. "It has been in my family for some generations. It is nothing of the grandness of the Specchiato, of course."

"I love it," Adella said earnestly in her charmingly accented English. "Houses that have been lived in and loved gain a special—how do you say it—benevolence. That is the right word, isn't it, Giulio?" He nodded and put an affectionate arm around her.

They took Meg on a tour of the house, which rose another two stories. The whole place had been lovingly cared for and the furnishings were old and beautiful. In one room, curled in sleep, was their four-year-old son, Roberto.

On a wall in the study hung an unusual tapestry made of many separate embroidered pieces sewn together. Each of the great cities of Italy was represented, with its coat of arms as well as the flowers and birds of the region. The overall pattern they made was delightful. "My wife's design and work," Signor Prati said with pride.

Meg was impressed with the careful blending of soft colors and the expert craftsmanship. She turned to Adella with words of praise. "I am a journalist at home. I have had some articles published, and I've wanted to write about unusual things in Italy. I'd love to write about you and this special artwork."

Signor Prati pulled open a desk drawer and took out some color photos. They showed stages of the designing of several tapestry projects, and Adella at work. "You may have these," he offered, looking very pleased. "There are slides as well."

"How did you start making tapestries?" Meg asked.

"My grandmother taught me to sew," Adella replied. "But I didn't start embroidering until I married Giulio and came here. That wall always bothered me, you see.'' She laughed. ''It has a secret panel from long ago, and whenever I saw it I imagined things coming out of it. Night-dream people, you know.''

Giulio chuckled. ''She was like a hypnotized person. I would find her here staring at the wall.''

''So I decided to cover it. If I couldn't see it I was not bothered. I made the tapestry—it was my first. Since then I have made others for friends, and now I hire a family who are expert embroiderers to help me.''

''Decorators from as far as Firenze have asked Adella for special hangings,'' Giulio added, giving her a loving smile.

A picture of the mysterious panel at the Specchiato came into Meg's mind. ''Do these old houses commonly have secret passages?''

Her host gave her a keen glance. ''*Si*, it is often the case.''

Just then a soft-spoken maid called them to dinner. The dining room was lovely, with a ceiling of carved and painted wood. They ate at an old oak table, polished to a satin sheen, and sat on chairs upholstered with embroidered cushions, also Adella's work.

The food was delicious and varied. Meg learned to her surprise that Adella had done most of the cooking. ''Foods are like colors,'' the woman said seriously. ''Their flavors blend in harmony if they are understood, making a meal wonderful to enjoy.''

Over cups of irresistibly fragrant espresso Signor Prati asked how Meg was enjoying the Specchiato. Adella bubbled up with, ''Poor Marco—he wants to renovate it. . . . And he has such good ideas. . . .'' She stopped talking as she met her husband's eyes. ''Oh,'' she said faintly.

"Marco would do a fine job," Giulio finished for her. "Let us hope that the financial situation of the owner allows work to be done." He was quiet for a moment, then went on, "Signorina Meg, you wondered earlier if many of the old buildings here have secret rooms or secret panels. It is true that many do. In the days of power of the Doges, people often had need to escape or hide from political persecution." He gave her a look in which a probing curiosity flickered. "Tell me, have you seen any evidence of such a thing at the Specchiato? The reason I ask is that the owner keeps many treasures there, treasures that have belonged to the family since the days of the prince who built it. The present owner is a cautious man, but my instincts are bothered by the fact that such valuable and ancient things are being kept in a building that is mostly deserted. Those artifacts belong to the history of Venezia and will be put on display in the mirrored hall by the city when it takes possession early next year. . . ."

"I had no idea that there were treasures, apart from the beauties of the palazzo itself," Meg said. Her mind was suddenly alert. Maybe she hadn't been overly suspicious after all, and there *was* something questionable going on at the Specchiato.

"There are pieces of jewelry and other precious works of art." Signor Prati continued, "Fortunately for my nervous system, the Marco Polo Cup is not kept at the Specchiato."

"The Marco Polo Cup?"

"The greatest treasure of them all," Adella put in irrepressibly.

"*Si.* It was given to the original owner of the palazzo, so it is said, by the great Marco himself. It is set with a pearl of awesome beauty—a rare pink pearl that appears to glow by itself. The cup was made with a combination of silver and gold, a process that has been lost to us, and is set with other precious stones. Like the rubies in the Empress Earrings—which, I regret to say, *are* kept at the Specchiato—the stones in the cup are not faceted, but highly polished. Facets on stones are fairly new to history.'' He gave her another penetrating look. ''Are you familiar with jewelry, Signorina Meg?''

''Not very. That is, I don't know about any famous pieces except maybe the British crown jewels.'' She felt a prickle of tension at the back of her neck. Prati's queries had been carefully spaced between casual conversation. She sensed that he was questioning her for a reason. After all, he was a police agent with international connections. All the movies she had seen with secret agents and jewel thieves jumped into her receptive mind.

She remembered as well the mirrored panel and the men disappearing into it. If there was trouble at the Specchiato, then the owner, who was so kindly letting her stay there, should be glad to know what she had seen. Looking into Giulio Prati's canny eyes Meg decided to speak about it. Who better to tell than this respectable detective? ''Earlier today,'' she began, ''I was wandering around in the palazzo outside the apartment area. I happened to look out over a small balcony into the large mirrored room. Two men were there in the hall below. They didn't see me and appeared to be in a hurry. They were carrying something. I think it was a painting.''

''Go on,'' Giulio said. His gaze had turned sharp and cool.

"They went through a door and closed it behind them. I thought perhaps they were workmen." She looked into Signor Prati's concentrating eyes. "I was curious, of course, so I went down to the room after the men had gone. The place where the door had been was—seemed to be—a solid panel of mirror. There was no sign of a door. I had my sketching material with me so I made some drawings of the area. I. . . I wasn't sure I had seen correctly. I *have* been ill, and I didn't trust my own eyes at that point."

"Bravo!" he exclaimed. "You may have done us a considerable service, *signorina*. It is the first time I have had more than my own nervous feelings to go on. I know that the owner of the Specchiato is worried, and I have heard stories circulating that something is not correct about the treasures of the old place. Only rumors, but ones that have circulated since earlier this year."

"Giulio gets a second sight—you say *hunch*—about trouble, you understand?" Adella interjected. "That is why he is so good at his work."

The detective blew his wife a kiss. "Adella is my best promoter," he laughed. "Maybe you have heard that we are having much difficulties with the theft of Italian art masterpieces. Unfortunately, there are collectors, wealthy people, who want to own precious and famous things. They take pleasure in secretly obtaining objects of high value, and some of them are willing to pay amazing prices. The works of art simply disappear. Sometimes they are held in secret bank vaults for years before they are one day presented for sale by a discreet art agent." He sighed. "The international police spend much time on this business, and much frustration." He looked directly at Meg. "You will keep this to yourself, please. And you will keep your eyes in your head and report to me if you hear or see anything further at the Specchiato. I would like to see your sketches, *per favore*."

"Of course," Meg said. "May I ask a question of my own? What are the Empress Earrings?"

"A pair of perfect rubies once owned by Theodora, Empress of the Holy Roman Empire. There was a fabulous necklace to go with them, but that was lost during the Second World War, when it was taken from a museum in Rome. Probably it is safely in the hands of one of those wealthy collectors now, but no longer available to the world to appreciate."

"Then the earrings must be priceless!"

"Indeed." Prati steered the conversation away from treasures at that point and began to discuss an unforeseen delay in getting her passport. Somehow, the computer in the USA had become confused in its numbers. "It will have to be reprocessed. I regret, my friend, but you may not be able to leave Venice for a few days yet. I am sure you will have the apartment at your disposal for as long as necessary. The owner is not presently in Venice."

Meg's heart gave a lurch. Maybe she wouldn't have to go before Marco returned. Maybe.... But she couldn't stay on in the palazzo like the Man Who Came to Dinner—a semipermanent guest when she had only been invited for a couple of days. A day or two more might not matter, however. She would leave a gift for the owner and something special for Lucia. She relished the idea of spending a little more time in Venice.

The Pratis sent her home with warm declarations of friendship, and Adella promised to call her for lunch to explain more about her tapestry making. Meg took slides as well as prints of Adella's work, at Giulio's encouragement.

When he handed her into Luigi's waiting gondola he said quietly, "If you wish me to notify your tour in Geneva that you have arranged your own passage home, I would be happy to do it for you. It is no inconvenience. And please—anything that is unusual at the Specchiato . . . let me know immediately."

CHAPTER SEVEN

MEG BLAMED HER WAKEFULNESS on the delicious espresso she had drunk with such gusto. Unfortunately, insomnia wasn't what she wished for. It forced her to be alone with too many thoughts, and her emotions weren't up to it at the moment. She made a halfhearted attempt to jot down notes for her Venice articles as she had promised herself, but stopped after a few minutes. Marco, fabulous jewels, mysteries, Marco—she was too distracted by the images clamoring in her head.

Signor Prati had opened up the possibility that she would see Marco again—would be here when he returned from Rome. She wasn't sure she had the strength to spend another evening with him, listening to his velvet voice speaking beautiful words to her and knowing that he saw straight into the secret places of her heart.

His kiss was something she would never forget. She had complimented herself on getting safely through the evening on Torcello without making a complete fool of herself. A flare of excitement shot down the length of her spine, making her uncomfortably aware of his long-term effect on her. Part of her prayed that she would have her passport in hand and be well on her way before Marco returned. The other part was careening madly on another path of imagery.

Meg put down her pen and got up from the desk in

the living room, where she'd been trying to work. She decided to distract herself with a careful perusal of the bookshelves. The Specchiato's owner had an interesting taste in books as well as in objets d'art. He apparently knew English very well, since he had a well-worn book of Shakespeare's plays and sonnets and a fine leather-bound set of Gibbon's *Decline and Fall of the Roman Empire*.

She ran her fingers over the faded gilding on the cover of an old leather folder lying on its side. Carefully opening the loose-leaf volume, she noted the title: *I quattro libri dell' architettura*. The author was Andrea Palladio, a name she recognized from her art studies, and the date in Roman numerals was MDLXX—1570. Palladio was the great sixteenth-century architect who started the revival of classical styles in Italy. This was possibly a rare first edition. The large heavy pages contained sharply defined woodcuts depicting Roman temples and other classical buildings. Very carefully Meg returned the folder to its position on the shelf. Her host was certainly eclectic in his tastes, literate, an admirer of fine things. But she couldn't reconcile those attributes with the run-down condition of his palazzo.

She prepared for bed, knowing it was futile, but going through the motions anyway. When she emerged from the bathroom after a long relaxing soak in the tub she curled up on a couch close to the tall windows of the living room, tucked her robe cozily around her and tried to read Act I of Shakespeare's *The Tempest*. Soon the words started to swim before her eyes, and the fatigue of the long day finally caught up with her. The book slipped from her lap and landed with a thud on the floor.

Meg jerked awake. The book was being returned to

her lap by a hand that belonged to a grinning tanned face. "Who are you?" she said quickly, pulling her robe tighter.

"And who are *you*?" The man's English was heavily accented. He appeared to be in his early twenties.

"Margaret Brown, *signore*," she said with authority. "And I think you are in the wrong place." As soon as she'd spoken she realized with a jolt that *this* might be the owner of the Specchiato, newly returned from his travels.

"I most certainly am in the right place. My family's apartments, to be exact."

Oh, God! she thought, and suddenly she was furious with Marco. He must have known that the owner might return.

"You won't mind if I pour myself a drink?" he said ironically, opening the antique cabinet that held a setup for a bar.

Meg stood up. "*Signore*, this situation is very awkward for me. You see, Marco Montevalde said I could stay here while I recovered from a slight illness, and that he had obtained permission from you. I'm terribly sorry...."

The well-dressed young man draped himself almost languidly on one of the large, cushioned chairs and looked at her through the amber glow of his highball glass. "Marco never asks my permission for anything. My cousin thinks very little of my opinion."

"Your...your cousin?" she almost demanded. Her mind began to calculate rapidly. "Marco Montevalde? So this is *his* apartment?" She was afraid to hear the answer.

"*Si*, of course. Did he neglect to tell you? You must be a shy one for him to lie about it." He smiled like a naughty satyr, as if Meg's discomfort gave him great pleasure.

A bright red flush streamed over her face. This was outrageous! "Who else has a key to these rooms?"

"Just the family and a few charming ladies. Marco isn't easy to live with...but you'll find that out." He chuckled at her expression.

"You have jumped to the wrong conclusion, *signore*! I have only a slight acquaintance with your cousin. He is not even here; he's in Rome. I may have been wrong to accept his help, but I see nothing amusing about deception!"

He raised his eyebrows skeptically. "Don't you want to know my name? I have been thoughtless. I am Ugo—the other Montevalde about whom you have probably heard so much." He spoke with heavy sarcasm and drained his glass.

Ugo's eyes were a light clear blue, and his hair was curly and sun bleached. Despite his handsome appearance, Meg could feel the disturbance in his character, and was uncomfortable even being in the same room with him. She began to understand Marco's worry. But that didn't change the fact that Marco himself had lied about his ownership of the Specchiato. Why had he done so? She would never have accepted an invitation to stay at the apartment of a man who had, in a manner of speaking, picked her up in St. Mark's Square.

"You don't look very healthy, *signorina*. Maybe you need a drink." Ugo's eyes wandered over her summer-thin robe and looked up again with an innocent look that was meant to appear helpful.

"No, thanks. Has my being here changed some plans of yours?" She had a suspicion that it had.

"Oh, I forgot. Angela is standing in the hall downstairs, waiting for me to bring her up. I had to check if Marco was here first, you see. He hates to have me entertain my girl friends when he is in residence," he said with bitterness. He got up and poured another drink straight from the bottle of bourbon.

"Aren't you going to rejoin your young lady?"

"Oh, she'll go away in a few minutes if I don't come back. Angela is nothing special. I want to know about *you* much more."

Meg felt her temper rising dangerously. "Someone should say something to the poor woman. That's very rude of you."

"Didn't Marco tell you? That is how I am." Ugo lowered his eyebrows. "You tell her, then. It won't be the first time she sees another female in the palazzo."

Meg reached for her blue stole and draped it around her shoulders. With a sharp look at Marco's cousin she headed toward the apartment door. Downstairs she found a pathetic young woman—she must have been only sixteen or seventeen—sitting on the edge of the old well. It wasn't until Meg walked up to her that she realized neither of them could understand the other.

The young woman rose at the sight of Meg, and her eyes widened with apprehension. Meg found some Italian words as fast as she could. "Angela? *Signor Ugo non può...non può uscire.*" She hoped she had said that the unpleasant man upstairs wasn't coming down. Anyway, the poor girl understood—perhaps more than was the truth of the matter, since she took a long look at Meg, turned, and fled toward the door.

Returning quickly up the stairs, Meg confronted Ugo, who was just walking out of her bedroom. "She's gone.

I'm sure she thought I was your new companion for the night. I feel sorry for her."

Ugo looked up with a semiglazed expression. "If we feel sorry for everything that is pitiful we have nothing to spare for ourselves, *non è vero*? I was looking for aspirin. I see you have Marco's bed."

"Signor Ugo, I don't like you very much, I have to be honest," she said firmly. "With that in mind, I would like you to leave me alone and go on about your business."

He stared briefly at her flashing gray eyes and seemed to lose his pose of grandeur. "If you think you interest me, you are wrong. I like my women young and agreeable." He was beginning to slur his words, which made his heavily accented English hard to follow. "I am going to my room now. My headache is a bad one tonight." He gestured with his glass toward a door at the far end of the living room. "Marco thinks I am in Trieste for a week. I would appreciate it if he did not know I am in Venezia. You'll do that for me? Then I will not have more unpleasantness with my cousin. I shall be gone in the morning."

He walked to the door and opened it, leaving Meg standing in the middle of the living room wondering if she should somehow protect herself from this cousin of Marco's. She carefully locked the door of her bedroom as she retired.

Of course she didn't fall asleep right away. Instead she stared at the moonlight patterns on the ceiling above her bed—Marco's bed—not able to relax until she could make some sense of her situation. Marco had lied to her about his palazzo. Had he lied about other things? Had Ugo been lying about the many women in Marco's life, or was he simply being vindictive? Perhaps she should leave the Specchiato in the morning and throw herself on the Pratis' generosity, begging them to take her in as a boarder for the time it would take to get her passport.

She felt like a complete idiot. Since the moment she'd arrived in Venice she had appeared for all the world like an incompetent, gullible, fragile, pitiful American tourist, no different from the ones described in the travel book. And her biggest mistake had been to let herself be taken over by Marco Montevalde. She should have dragged herself to the train station that day to meet her tour.

Almost anything would have been preferable to *this*!

SHE WOKE THE NEXT MORNING to hear raised voices coming from the living room, and then the angry slam of a distant door. Her first thought was that Ugo had retrieved his girl friend during the night and they were fighting. Meg wanted nothing to do with it.

After a few minutes of silence there was a gentle rap at her bedroom door and a woman's voice called her name. "Signorina Brown, I am sorry to disturb you, but I must speak with you at once."

It was not the girl from last night. Meg tied her robe about her and unlocked the door, to find a petite honey-haired young woman standing there. "Please excuse me, but I am Teresa Montevalde, the sister of Ugo. I must apologize for his intrusion on your peace." She extended a friendly hand to Meg, looking at her with warm dark eyes that echoed the sincerity of her words.

"Please don't apologize," Meg said. "I am the stranger, not your brother." It was easy to like Teresa Montevalde.

"No," the woman said in a rush, "he had no business

to be here at all. Marco expects him to be looking for work in Trieste, where he will be far away from the influence of. . . of certain persons here in Venezia. And I will make sure he does not come uninvited again. But now I must beg a favor for myself." She smiled in hesitation.

"Marco said that he had a friend staying here whose passport had been stolen. He made you sound quite proper and dignified. He said that you might not mind my occupying the other bedroom . . . actually, he thought you would be gone by now. But I see you are not." She spoke almost breathlessly and grinned—very much like her brother, but a world apart in every other way.

"I'm planning to leave this morning," Meg said.

"Oh!" Teresa exclaimed, gesturing with her hands. "I didn't mean to suggest—"

"It's not that. I was intending to leave. There seems to have been a misunderstanding about some things, and I want to be gone before Signor Montevalde returns, that's all. It has nothing to do with you."

Teresa's face showed immediate distress. "Then I shall feel most guilty. Besides, where will you stay? Do you have a hotel room, or other friends in Venezia?"

Meg couldn't lie to her. "Not really. I would just rather be elsewhere."

"Did my cousin Marco intimidate you? He does that sometimes and doesn't realize it."

Meg gave up with a small laugh. "It's nothing like that. I am being too sensitive."

"You *must* stay. I am visiting my fiancé today, but I am mostly free if you wish a guide to the city."

"Thanks, I'd like to see things with another woman. . . window shopping and just browsing. And I honestly didn't have another place to stay. I was thinking about asking Signor Prati and his wife to take in a boarder."

"Oh, Giulio!" The young woman grinned again. "Such a serious man and so secretive! But, *signorina*, I insist. For the honor of the house of Montevalde you must stay here!" Her voice was urgent like a child's, although she appeared to be just a few years younger than Meg. "That's settled, then. Have you explored the palazzo yet? It's quite a relic from the past. May I call you Meg?"

Like a collapsing rag doll Teresa sat down on a plump love seat and laughed at herself. "There I go, assuming you want to hear everything I say. Forgive me. I'll go and put my things in the other room while you dress. Lucia made some coffee and fresh rolls. Then we can decide what to do with the day. Marco said you were ill. Do you feel well enough to go out? You have good color in your face. . . ."

"But you were going to see your fiancé," Meg interjected.

"Not until this afternoon. Right now Enzo is meeting with a very important art critic who might want to write an article about his sculptures for a European magazine. Enzo shares a studio with another sculptor on the island of Burano. He feels it's bad luck for me to be there when he is showing his work. Personally, I think luck has nothing to do with it. Enzo's work is brilliant." Teresa breezed out of the room and closed the door behind her.

Meg stood looking at the door, a smile on her face. What a refreshing change from Ugo—and, for that matter, from Marco. She dressed quickly and joined Teresa in the kitchen. Coffee was waiting, pungently aromatic, and Lucia's mouth-watering rolls.

"I just finished my studies at the University of Bologna," Teresa bubbled. "I'll be looking in Venezia for a teaching job—maybe tutoring children in the joys of piano playing." She made a face. "I spent a year in New York studying at a conservatory, but I had to come back here to Italy."

"For your fiancé?"

"Si," she smiled meaningfully. "For Enzo and for Venezia. I love my city very much."

"I can understand why. I think I love it, too. And this palazzo. I'm very grateful to your cousin for allowing me to see it like this. Not many tourists are so privileged." She knew how stiff she was sounding.

"That's all you are, a tourist?" Teresa asked pointedly.

"That's all, a tourist in distress who was rescued by two kind gentlemen in St. Mark's Square."

"I don't think I believe you, Meg. Once I have decided that someone is a friend, that's what he or she is, and you are no longer just a tourist. Now, let me show you around my family's ancestral home."

As they strolled through the musty, moody hallways that Meg had ventured into previously, she had to ask, "Are there any workmen presently in the Specchiato?"

"No, and I wish there were. The palazzo would be so beautiful if it were cared for and restored. Why do you ask?"

"Yesterday as I wandered around a bit I imagined I heard noises."

"Most likely tiny four-footed workmen! We have too many of those." Teresa opened one door after the next until Meg was totally lost. They stopped in a room with a high domed ceiling, richly decorated with ornamental plaster and more trompe l'oeil paintings—fat cherubs with musical instruments in their plump little hands. "The music room. They say that Antonio Vivaldi gave concerts here in the eighteenth century. Did you see the room of mirrors yesterday?"

"For a minute. I tried to make sketches of the artwork around the panels."

"Marco would appreciate that. The original plans of the palazzo have been lost, and Marco makes it his hobby to do detailed studies of every room. He has even found a secret corridor or two behind these walls."

Meg was intrigued but said nothing more. Teresa pointed out her favorite pieces of decoration in several more of the reception rooms, and then they were standing in the mirrored room. "Marco has a very big new project...he told you about that, didn't he? We hope it will pay off Ugo's lawsuit, with money left over to renovate at least this one magnificent room. Then he plans to give the Specchiato to the city as a cultural landmark. He will keep the family apartments permanently, but the treasures of the Montevalde family will be on display in this room. The proceeds from tourist fees will pay for renovation of the entire palazzo. It is the only way Marco can envision the preservation of our family home. Venezia has little money to spend on palazzi, not while it worries about raising enough to keep the entire city from sinking on its wooden pylons. This is Marco's way of expressing our gratitude to the city we love. And then...there will always be the Marco Polo Cup," she said proudly.

"I've heard of it."

"We have a fine fifteenth-century painting showing the cup being presented to the Holy Virgin, in an allegory that was commissioned by an ancestor of mine. I can't show you the cup itself—it is kept in a vault at a bank—but I can show you the other Montevalde valuables that are here."

Meg almost wished Teresa weren't being so very kind and trusting. It was only making the thought of leaving Venice harder to bear.

Teresa didn't stop for long in the great and dazzling room, but continued past the place where Meg had seen the men disappear, and out the opposite door. Near the end of a long corridor she put out her hand to stop Meg. "They're here, behind this wall."

She smiled at Meg's dubious look. "Marco rediscovered a cleverly hidden storage room several years ago. He has made part of it into a vault. Ugo and I used to hide in the little anteroom as children when we played games with some of our friends, but we stopped using it when Marco found out about us."

She turned a decorative plaster scroll on the wall and a richly painted panel swung inward with a long sigh. A light automatically clicked on, revealing a fair-sized room and, at the far wall, the massive metal door to a vault, which looked as imposing as a bank's.

Teresa stepped up to it and turned a series of dials, then pulled the heavy handle downward to open the vault. "I always feel very important when I do this," she said. "Marco has entrusted me with the combination. He knows I have the deepest respect for the Montevalde heritage. It is a problem for Ugo, though. Marco has no trust in him, and for good cause. Therefore, he has not been given access to the vault."

They stepped inside the cool steel-lined chamber, which was as large as a small bedroom. Dozens of paintings in heavy gilt frames were stacked against one wall, and a low table was piled with tarnished silver chalices and candelabra. Crates were stacked in other corners of the vault, with tendrils of wood shavings showing between the slats.

"Don't be afraid to touch anything," Teresa laughed. "It won't break."

"I wouldn't dare. I'll just stand here and admire."

"If you wish. But let me show you the painting I was telling you about." She started dragging out some of the heavy paintings until she had the right one. Then she returned the others to their positions against the wall. Meg caught glimpses of aristocratic faces of noblemen and noblewomen. Montevaldes, no doubt.

"Close your eyes, Meg. Now—open them." Teresa's expectant face showed above the dark painting she held as Meg opened her eyes.

"Is *that* the cup?" she asked in awe.

"That is it. See how the artist showed the great pearl with its fine pink luminosity? Almost like a Vermeer with the treatment of light."

"Did you study art, too?"

"In self-defense. Enzo expects me to know about his world. But see. . . that is one of my ancestors presenting the cup to the Holy Mother. Probably to atone for his sins, which must have been many."

"Is the cup well-known?"

"Only in certain circles. It has never been on display and won't be until Marco presents it to the city as part of his gift of the Specchiato. It was photographed once for an art book. We have a copy of it at the apartment. The cup is supposed to have been given to Marco Polo by Kublai Khan himself, and then into the hands of a doge of Venezia who was related to the Montevalde family. But all we can be sure about is that it *is* from the Orient and it *is* a treasure."

"If it's anything like the painting, it's fabulous!" Meg said.

"There is much more here. Are you interested?" Teresa asked. Seeing Meg's rapturous expression, she turned around again. "Let's see. . . ." In one corner was a small safe, which Teresa opened quickly. She reached inside for several velvet and leather jeweler's boxes, opening them one at a time to show Meg. There were rubies, pearls, sapphires—the glitter of gold and pavé diamonds set into elaborate brooches and tiaras. "They can never be sold," Teresa said as she rested a heavy sapphire and diamond necklace in Meg's hands. "That is a very rigid part of the Montevalde inheritance. Cousin Marco would not dishonor his trust by selling them, even today when there is such need for money."

She started returning the jewels to their boxes, taking the necklace carefully from Meg's nervous hands. "Don't tell Marco that we amused ourselves with the family jewelry. He wouldn't understand the need women have for fantasy. I sometimes imagine I am a *dogaressa*, or at least a *principessa*."

Teresa returned the boxes to the small safe and then drew forth an ornate red-and-gold jewel box. "I want you to see my favorites. They have a history that goes back to Constantinople and the Empress Theodora."

Almost reverently she lifted the lid of the box. In an instant the look of pleasure faded from her face and she went white. "*Madonna mia!* One of the Empress Earrings is gone! Where is the other!" She felt around in the velvet lining, then snapped the box shut. Her expression was thunderous. *"Madonna mia!"* she repeated, seeming paralyzed for a moment. "Who would...?" She looked beseechingly at Meg. "Why...? I'm the only other one who knows the combination to the vault. How could this happen? Surely not at night, because we have a watchman who sleeps in an alcove next to the vault room. He would have heard something...."

"What are you going to do?" Meg asked lamely.

"Something...I don't know yet." She returned the box to the safe, and they hurriedly left the vault. Back in the apartment, Teresa placed a telephone call to Ugo. There was an odd look on her face when she hung up. "He is coming over when he can, he says. He laughed at me for alarming people."

"I'm so sorry," Meg said inadequately.

"Ugo must know something about this—I'm sure of it! But how, I don't know. I have to go to my room to be alone until he comes. I must think about what this means and what to do about it."

As Teresa shut the door of her room, Meg wondered if she should call Detective Prati. She decided against it for the time being. There might be a simple explanation. For her to go behind Teresa's back right now might be considered meddling.

She paced restlessly for a while, then searched Marco's bookshelves until she found a heavy book on the art treasures of Venice. It was written in Italian, but the photographs spoke for themselves, especially, *"Il calice di Marco Polo."* She preferred the Italian word for chalice to the simple English translation of cup, since the object was far beyond that prosaic description. It was designed simply with pure, clean lines and no handles. Around its golden bowl were three bands of decoration, the top and bottom ones encrusted with tiny beads of lapis, coral, and smoothly polished precious stones, forming two serpentine patterns with fine twisted threads of gold.

The central band contained the great pink pearl, glowing with a soft light of its own. It was nested inside an open lotus, whose many graceful petals appeared to have been formed out of the same mysterious gold-silver metal as the cup itself. No wonder Giulio Prati was interested in protecting it!

An hour passed before Ugo presented himself at the door. He walked jauntily inside as if nothing were amiss. Teresa reappeared, having composed herself, and half dragged him out the door toward the vault room, insisting that Meg come too as a witness. Meg stood back while Teresa went straight to the small safe and took out the earring box. Ugo smiled as she placed it defiantly into his waiting hands.

He lifted the lid slightly, then all the way. "Look," he said in English to Meg. "This proves that little Teresa is having another fantasy dream of dragons and perils, just as she did when she was a child." He removed the contents of the jewel box with exaggerated care. "*Guarda!* See—one earring...two earrings! Count them, Teresa. Now, let us not speak of this further. Our guest from America will have the mistaken idea that Italians are too emotional." He grinned at Meg, a smile she didn't return. But she did let her eyes rest for a moment on the two perfectly matched blood-red rubies in their settings of large luminous pearls.

Teresa said nothing, but touched both earrings as if to verify their reality. Ugo laughed at her. "One...two," he counted, and returned them to the box. "By the way, Signorina Brown, they are rare pigeon's blood rubies."

Teresa's eyes met Meg's. Who was telling the truth now? Meg hadn't actually seen the single earring when Teresa opened the box earlier. She couldn't swear that there had been only one and not two. She distrusted Ugo completely, but she still didn't know if she should tell Giulio Prati about this episode.

"Teresa is so worried about the sacred family jewels that she imagines the worst. Do not worry, little one," he said and patted Teresa gently on the cheek. "Everything is perfectly safe and will be until Marco makes the presentation to the city. There will be no loss of honor, and Empress Theodora's earrings are intact. *Dio mio*, what foolishness!"

He strolled out of the vault. *"Ciao,"* he tossed back and was gone.

Teresa's face was as red as the rubies. "He did something, I will swear—but what?" She looked utterly frustrated and turned around with a sigh. "We have time to catch the regular boat out to the islands. We can be tourists together. By the time we arrive at Burano, Enzo will be finished with his art critic and I will be in a better state of mind. Enzo says I have been working too hard lately." She looked suddenly at Meg. "You asked if there were workmen here. Why? Did you see them?" Her voice was tinged with urgency.

Meg debated with herself. She didn't want to be a part of anything more that involved the Montevalde family. She had the strong feeling that she was standing at the edge of a maelstrom, and with a small step in the wrong direction she would be drawn irrevocably into it.

"I heard noises and I thought I saw something, but I can't be sure," she hedged. Lying wasn't something she relished.

"People? Men?" Teresa pressed.

Meg nodded reluctantly. "Two, I think."

Teresa's face changed. "Can you find your own way back to the apartment? I have to run a short errand. Then I will come back and we will go out to the islands. I'll only be a few minutes. And wear something to protect from the dampness."

Meg watched her walk rapidly down the corridor and disappear through a door. The simple occurrence of a stolen purse in St. Mark's Square was turning into something far more complicated on several fronts, with the delay of her passport, the peculiar behavior of Ugo, the questionable disappearance of the earring.... Did she really have a choice about becoming involved?

Right now the journalist in her was awakening from its dreamy preoccupations. Back in her bedroom, she opened her sketch book to the drawings of the mirrored room. She made notes in the margins about the exact location of the hidden door, and wrote a quick paragraph about her observations of the two men. *For whatever good that will do,* she said to herself and closed the notebook. She would give the pages to Detective Prati and try to forget about it after that.

She glanced at her watch. It was ten-thirty. Ironically she congratulated herself for not having had a single nervous tremor about Marco for the past three hours.

CHAPTER EIGHT

When Teresa returned she said little about the incident of the earring, passing it off as one of Ugo's pranks. "I used to think he would drive me crazy when I was a little girl. He would do such awful things!" she laughed. "But I *am* concerned that he may have obtained the combination to the vault."

The two women left the Specchiato together and walked at a leisurely pace along the back lanes of Venice toward the place where the water bus would pick up its island-bound passengers. The day was hot and humid, with high wispy clouds and very little breeze. After a few minutes Teresa stopped and hailed a *traghetto*, a kind of public gondola that carried several standing passengers at once. There wasn't a tourist among them, and Meg enjoyed the feeling of doing something very Venetian.

As they were standing on the boat to the island, watching it pull away from the landing, Teresa said, "I have asked our night watchman, Ernesto, to be more alert. I do not want to bother Marco: he has enough to worry about right now. It was nothing, really nothing." The tension in her voice was in contrast to her words. "It is better you forget about what happened."

"I will," Meg promised, knowing she would never be able to.

A wind had come up, stirring the surface of the water on the lagoon. It looked so different from the night she had gone to Torcello with Marco.

"I really need you with me today," Teresa said suddenly. "Enzo is a moody artist, and I know he is going to give me another of his lectures about why we must postpone our marriage date. I have failed to convince him that I am a grown woman who can work and support us while he develops his reputation as a sculptor—the best one in Italy, I think."

"And you feel that if I'm with you he won't give his lecture?" Meg could sympathize. Hadn't she heard enough lectures from Jim about all sorts of things?

"He is very private, Meg. Painfully proud and completely stubborn. He will marry only when he is able to support a wife, he says. I find his old-fashioned attitude tiresome, but I love him with all my heart. Stay close to me, Meg. I do need you," she begged with a delightful sparkle in her soft brown eyes.

Meg turned her attention to the lagoon. By day it seemed quite busy and almost commonplace, not veiled by the liquid amber light of sunset. She wished Marco had taken her to Torcello in the honest hours of the day, when it would have been easier to stay clearheaded.

As they neared Burano Teresa took her hand and squeezed it. "Every time I see Enzo it feels like the first time. Is love supposed to be so exciting, Meg?"

"All the books about romance say so," she said evasively.

"But haven't you felt that way?"

Meg's eyes quickly blurred with tears.

Teresa saw them. "Oh, I'm so sorry! How rude of me...."

Meg dredged up a weak smile. "I lost my fiancé several months ago," she said for lack of a better excuse.

"And your love for him was strong...?"

She didn't reply, but clenched her fists until her fingernails dug painfully into her palms. How could she say, *it's Marco Montevalde! He is the cause of my tears, no one else.*

The water bus pulled into its mooring place near a broad paved area and let out its several dozen passengers. Meg admired the hodgepodge of small buildings that clustered around the little square, almost like a miniature village. Many of them were brightly painted in primary colors. Tourists were already crowding around tables set up in the square, which were tended by women dressed in black. These were the lace makers of Burano, selling the fine lace for which the island was famous.

Teresa guided Meg through a maze of winding lanes and brackish-looking narrow canals, past burly fishermen who were dragging heavy nets from their boats.

"Every island has its own traditions and personality," she said. "In fact, the residents of one small island usually criticize the customs of people on the next island, even if it is only a distance of a kilometer or two."

Burano was almost silent, and the colorfully painted cottages along the canals could have been merely facades for a theatrical performance. Here and there, a woman sat on her doorstep, bent over her lace making.

Teresa stopped and greeted one woman, who broke into a welcoming smile. "This is the place where Enzo has his studio; there is a separate building behind this house." They walked between two bright blue houses toward a large cluttered yard. Stacked near the stone building at the rear was a pile of wood planks, as well as chunks of stone—obviously the debris of two sculptors in residence.

"I will see if he's here," Teresa said, and disappeared into the darkened open doorway of the two-story building. In a minute she came out again, accompanied by a sober-faced young man who had the physical appearance of an athlete. His muscular body was scarcely contained by the faded denim cutoff pants he wore, and his bronzed chest and arms were bare. The residue of white plaster covered his forearms.

Teresa presented him proudly to Meg. "Enzo Arnoldi. . .Meg Brown from the United States." She smiled, but there was a touch of uncertainty in her smile, as if she couldn't count on Enzo to be courteous.

Enzo extended one large hand and his teeth showed brilliant white in a smile of greeting. "What brings you to Burano, *signorina*?" he asked in hesitant English. He was handsome in a certain way, like the heavily muscled Renaissance marble statues of gladiators that Meg had seen during her whirlwind tour of Rome's museums.

"I'm a tourist, but a very enthusiastic one about your beautiful country," she answered. Beneath his dark tousled hair and stubble of beard was a moody face that might have been thoroughly intimidating to some young women. Meg thought that Teresa was the perfect foil for his type of man—gentle and cheerful as a spring breeze, and as stubbornly determined in her own way as he was in his.

"Please," he said with a motion of his arm, "look around the island. I will return Teresa to you in one hour. The people here will be most kind, you will see." It was a dismissal.

Teresa looked sharply at him and said something in

rapid Italian that caused Enzo to revise his statement. "I will talk with Teresa another time, *signorina*. Forgive me. I invite you to see my studio."

Teresa flashed Meg a victorious smile that said, *see, he does not dare lecture me today while you are here.*

Enzo's studio was very warm. The windows were small and a northern skylight lit the high barn of a room. The walls were covered with large sheets of butcher's paper containing sketches for Enzo's work in progress, a massive piece in the style of a Modigliani painting—elongated figures, clean of line, and cool—very cool. It was a Madonna and child, Teresa explained; Enzo was doing a few plaster versions to get a feel for the mood and shape.

"That is not true," he interrupted. "I have no money for good marble. It requires Carrara marble."

Teresa winced at the bitterness in his tone. "Someday you will have a sponsor, and all the marble in the world will be yours," she said calmly.

"I will not be bought by a rich man for his amusement. Plaster, clay, cheap stone . . . these will do for me!"

Teresa put a gentling hand on his tightly clenched fist and he relaxed. "Show Meg the one you are doing for the little girl," she urged.

Enzo removed a cloth from a small piece of black basalt. The stone was carved in the form of a child's hand, holding a tiny bird that was poised to fly. "A little girl on Burano—the daughter of a man who owns several fishing boats—died last winter and the father commissioned Enzo to make a memorial for her grave. He could not pay very much, but Enzo did it from the warmth of his heart." Teresa looked admiringly from Enzo to the stone.

"It is very beautiful," Meg said. The hand looked

poignantly real, and she could feel the love that had flowed from the artist's chisel into the stone. "Did you know the child?"

"*Si*, she liked my studio. She was a good child with dreams in her eyes. Free like the birds." Enzo replaced the cloth and turned away.

Teresa moved closer to him and said something in a low voice. Enzo smiled slightly and gave her a strong embrace. Then he kissed her and let her go.

Meg felt like an intruder, but Teresa quickly took her arm and said, "I will see him another time when he has not so many things worrying his mind."

He bade them both goodbye. Meg could feel the strong pull of emotion that crackled between the two lovers. Why was there always pain, even in the midst of love?

"It wasn't a good day for him. The critic failed to appreciate his work, and I'm sure Enzo growled at him too much. He is an enemy to his own advancement. But I am going to help him. I have many wonderful ideas for showing his work to the public. He won't hear of it, of course. We must first be married, and then I will slowly make my moves. . . ." She laughed. "It is inevitable. He just does not realize it yet!"

They walked back toward the paved square, past a charming old campanile that leaned to one side, and arrived just in time to catch the returning island boat.

Beneath her cheerful, offhand exterior, Teresa was deeply concerned about something, Meg could tell. Whether it was Enzo or Ugo or the incident of the earring, Meg didn't know. Perhaps all three.

When they arrived back at the boat landing at the Fondamente Nuove, Meg was feeling drained. She wasn't sure she had enough energy to go another step.

"Is there a place where we can sit for just a while?" she begged.

"There is a good little *trattoria* around the next corner. Part of your weakness is that I have starved you to death. It is my fault," Teresa replied.

They sat at an outdoor café, watching people crowd past in the congested laneway. A bowl of vegetable soup and two chunky pieces of warm bread brought Meg's energy level back from impossible to possible.

"Lucia bakes better bread," Teresa whispered.

"This is just fine," Meg insisted as she dunked her last piece of bread into the remains of the delicious soup.

"If you are strong enough, would you mind if we stopped at Marco's office on our way home? There may be a message from him."

"I didn't know he had an office in Venice. Just the one in Rome."

"He is a very organized man, Meg. He has his personal office in the palazzo, and this business office as well. But even here, Ugo comes and goes too freely when he wants to beg Marco for money."

Meg was curious. "Doesn't Ugo have a profession, a trade?"

"He was expelled from several fine schools and never stayed long enough to gain any skill. He refuses to do what he calls 'common work.' I just laugh at him and say, 'This is the twentieth century, not the eighteenth.' "

"Isn't it demeaning to him to have to ask for money from his cousin?"

"Not to him. He feels he deserves it. Our poor mother gave up long ago. She lives in Florence, where she imagines that everything is still the way it was when she was a girl. Her attitudes are those of a lady of fashion and style." Teresa grinned and made a face. "Not like me."

They climbed a short flight of marble steps to a building whose paint had been crumbling for such a long time that the facade had a mellow earthy tone. Marco's office was one of several in the old building, all sharing a common receptionist, whose desk was on the first floor.

"It is up the stairs at the top, if you want to see it, Meg. I am going to collect any messages first," Teresa said.

Meg climbed slowly up the long steep flight. She still had no reserve of energy. At the landing she entered a bright sunlit workroom with a long skylight and a drafting table. She had the impulse to touch Marco's pens and notebooks, to put herself in contact with the things his hands had touched. If she imagined that she was getting over the mesmerizing effects of Marco Montevalde, she was mistaken.

She was just brushing her fingers over a large piece of drawing paper when Teresa came in. The Italian woman noticed her quick recoil. "Marco won't mind that we invaded his inner sanctum as long as we don't tell him," she laughed.

"What are these drawings for?" Meg asked. "A renovation of an old palazzo?"

"Oh, I think those are the latest drawings for his big project. Something academic and very much in Renaissance style...for an American client. He is rather secretive about it, even to me."

"It's spectacular," she commented. "Just like those old Italian hill towns, with towers and high walls."

"Marco is very very good at his work. And he *did* leave a message with his secretary. He is returning tomorrow night, ahead of schedule. He said he has finished the project and sent his designs by special courier—"

"Oh, no!" Meg said with a groan. "What if I'm still here and my passport hasn't come? I'm staying in Marco's bedroom! I should find another place."

"There are three bedrooms at the Specchiato apartment. Why are you so upset?" Teresa asked blandly.

"I. . . I hate to be an intruder."

"Three bedrooms for three people. Marco cannot possibly object. Wasn't he the one who brought you there in the first place? He is not a beast, you know! Now, let us go back to the palazzo. Lucia can cook us one of her excellent dinners—*alla Veneziana*."

MEG RETIRED EARLY that night, and on Teresa's insistence, slept in Marco's room. There would be enough time in the morning to move, she said. By then Lucia would have the guest room prepared. "I shall probably be gone when you wake," Teresa had told her during dinner. "I am to spend tomorrow with Enzo. We must make a conclusion to our plans, and I need your prayers that he will choose love above false duty."

Unable to sleep, Meg listened to the ticking of her bedside travel clock. What would it be like when Marco returned, she wondered. She would have done anything to avoid Marco's demanding and penetrating gaze again. *What a coward you are,* she chided herself.

Meg was relieved to hear Adella Prati's cheerful voice on the other end of the telephone the next morning. She wasn't ready to hear Marco's. "I have news," Adella said. "Your passport will be coming perhaps tomorrow or the next day. Since today is Sunday, the mail will not move until tomorrow."

Sunday. Meg hadn't even noticed the passage of the days. At home she was vividly aware of every day, but here she lived as if in a trance.... Adella was inviting her to lunch. "Come to Florian's. I will meet you there, but we will go to another place to eat—one you will like."

"I'll meet you at noon," Meg agreed.

She started out an hour early to walk to St. Mark's Square, so that she would have time to linger before the enticing shop windows. The Italians were adept in displaying things, and a dress in her favorite blue, draped over a Florentined wood chest, caught her eye. On impulse she went inside and tried it on. She was buying it for the warm weather in Pasadena in the early fall, she told herself, and pushed away the thought that Marco might admire her in it—that he might have a last memory of her looking feminine and maybe beautiful. She wanted almost painfully to leave some image of herself that would have a bit of mystery and romance. Something that would make him wonder occasionally what she was doing with her life.

Adella Prati was waiting at Florian's, sitting at a table in the shade and chatting with Giorgio, the waiter. Both of them greeted Meg warmly. Giorgio made complimentary remarks about how being in Venice had made her bloom with beauty. He was devastated that they weren't going to stay at Florian's, but saw them off with bows and flourishing gestures that wove patterns of emotion.

Adella looked lovely in a yellow sun dress, her short compact figure like a cuddly doll's. Her large eyes sparkled, and her vital hair almost vibrated with its springy curls. No wonder Giulio loved her. There was so much that was kind, enthusiastic and happy flowing from her.

They set off from under the arcades of the piazza into the narrow long walkways. Adella, of course, knew where she was going, and soon they came out into a small square that reminded Meg of a stage set. A restaurant occupied one corner of it, and opposite where they stood was the facade of what was obviously a theater.

"This is Campo San Fantin," Adella said, and waved a hand toward the theater. "La Fenice, the grandest theater in Venice. You have read how it burned down and was built again, long ago?"

"I read that in English its name means Phoenix—the mythological bird that rose from its flaming nest to life again."

"*Si*, more beautiful than ever, and la Fenice was the same. Mozart stayed not far from here when he was an old man. Everyone was here one time, it seems!"

Adella led Meg toward the outdoor tables of the restaurant. Its door was shaded by a vine growing over a trellis, and waiters scurried between the white-linen-draped tables with trays of delicious-looking food.

They seated themselves at a sheltered spot against the high wall of a building that marked one side of the square, and perused the menu. The choices were fascinating.

After they ordered, Adella told Meg more about the Fenice Theater. "In the old days it was a regular meeting place. Many patrons with private boxes spent at least an hour there each night—for economical as well as social reasons. It wasn't necessary to light up their home as much during the winter season, you see. The box holders—mostly members of noble families—owned the theater in shares. After the First World War they all turned the theater over to the city to run. Apparently in the old days theatergoers spent much time visiting from box to box instead of paying attention to the performances—even, it is said, on the night of the first performance of Verdi's *La Traviata*. That was a scandal!"

Meg gazed across the square, imagining Venetian society people crowding into the building in their satins and velvets. "I would love to have seen it then, to have mingled with the elegant crowds," she murmured.

"And I, too. Do not be put off by the plain exterior. Inside it is beautiful," Adella said with an understanding smile.

The two women continued to talk about Venetian history over their *trancia di branzino bolleto*, slices of sea bass boiled in wine and herbs, with a salad of sliced *fenocchio*—fennel—and *carciofini*—tiny tender artichokes. Dessert was *macedonia*, a goblet of amazingly delicious cut fruits, laced with liqueur and covered with a mountain of whipped cream. Meg consigned her recently cured stomach to the fates and ate her dessert with relish.

Over coffee Adella's voice became more serious as she talked about Giulio and his work with the international police. She was touchingly proud of his accomplishments and the trust that people had in him. "He had solved some very big cases," she informed Meg. "There are people who steal our beautiful treasures and sell them to collectors. Sometimes they substitute copies for real things and are never found out until it is too late. My Giulio has recovered treasures from as far away as the *Stati Uniti* and Saudi Arabia."

Meg made appropriate sounds of approval.

"Men with great fortunes who collect only for themselves make criminals out of poor or greedy Italians," Adella frowned. "That is why Giulio asked about the Specchiato." She was silent a moment, savoring her espresso. "Marco Montevalde has had a terrible time with his young cousin, Ugo. Did you know that Ugo's father was a twin to Marco's? Marco's father was the elder, so he inherited the family treasures...and a fine palazzo. The brothers loved each other, however, so there was no animosity. And Marco's father was a good overseer of the estate."

"By the way, I met Ugo *and* his sister," Meg said. "And I know that the Specchiato belongs to Marco. It's no longer a secret."

"I am glad you know," Adella stated matter-of-factly. "Giulio told me that Marco feared you would not accept his offer if you thought it was his. Our dashing architect is quite unsure of women's responses sometimes, odd as that must seem."

"I'm very sorry he felt he needed to deceive me. But you were telling me about the family...."

Adella frowned. "*Si*, it is a strange story, one for a fiction tale. Ugo has always been jealous of Marco because only five minutes of time at his father's birth separated him from wealth and from the Specchiato. That is no excuse for his behavior, of course. Because of friendship for Marco, Giulio has pulled him out of many troubles. But now he suspects that Ugo has started to move on the edge of the bigger world of crime."

"I heard about his accident, and the poor girl he injured," Meg commented.

"*Poverina*. Ugo has no conscience about it." Adella

sighed, then switched the subject. "Marco is a wonderful man, is he not? So...." She searched for a word, and not finding one, used the Italian, "so *elegante*." Meg nodded and stared into her coffee cup. "Surely you think he is of the greatest handsomeness?" Adella's eyes were intent.

"Yes, he is like a model for the classic Italian male," Meg admitted.

Adella sat back in her chair and looked at Meg speculatively. Obviously she expected her to say more. But how could she admit that what stood between herself and Marco was a healthy dose of common sense? "I'll never forget him and his kindness to me," she added lamely.

Adella began to smile. "Giulio and I have never seen him so eager to make things better for anyone, than for you. He is usually very much inside himself—too busy with his career to consider marriage." She chuckled. "But do not think that all the mamas in Venezia have not tried to catch him for their daughters...not to mention the divorcées of the jet set and a young widow or two." She looked for the effect her words had had on Meg.

"I can imagine," Meg said, feeling a constriction in her throat. "Hasn't he ever come close?" She tried to keep her voice disinterested.

"Not really. He goes out with a woman a few times and then he disappears into his work again."

"That must be a bit hard on the young women," Meg said crisply.

"It is, I suppose. But most of them just throw themselves at him. A few have not given up—like Antonia Alandi, a contessa. Her father offered to underwrite

Marco's business, but there were too many strings for Marco. . . all named Antonia."

Meg felt a familiar queasiness in the pit of her stomach as Adella went on. "She is a real beauty. Her family is as old in the history of Firenze as Marco's is in Venezia. Many people suppose they will make a match someday. That is why, when Marco took such an interest in you, I wondered. . . . You are so real, Meg, not full of techniques and mannerisms. You are educated and with a career of your own. Marco needs a real person, one who can match his creativeness—"

Seeing the look on Meg's face Adella suddenly broke off. "*Dio mio*, I have talked too much. Giulio tells me to keep out of people's business, but I. . . I like you, Meg. And Marco, too. . . ." She looked guilty, but continued, "And I thought I saw caring in your eyes."

Meg summoned a presentable smile. "Don't worry, Adella. I'm a realist about love." She couldn't believe she was saying those words. "Marco is a very nice man. I'm afraid I am old-fashioned, though. I want what you have—love, a home, children, as well as a career. Marco Montevalde is too strong a mixture for my understanding. Anyway, he was only being friendly to me, nothing more."

Adella nodded. "You do not relish the affairs with men. That does not surprise me. But Marco. . . ." She sighed. "You are right, *amica mia*, perhaps he is of too great an experience in matters of women, but I have always thought that the right woman could engage the whole of his heart and he would become most faithful. Like my Giulio, who was a master of *amore* before I met him." She smiled, a reminiscent look in her lovely eyes. "Is there someone at home...if you will permit more curiosity?"

"Not at present." Briefly Meg told of Jim's death.

As she talked, tears filled Adella's eyes and she stretched out a sympathetic hand to grasp Meg's. "Now I understand, *cara*. You have seemed so...uncertain. Your eyes have in them lost dreams."

Meg's conscience hurt. The lost dreams were of Venice, but Adella must never know the full extent of her foolishness. She only hoped that, when she'd gone, Marco would be enough of a gentleman not to laugh with his friends about the *Summertime* syndrome of the naive American traveler he'd been kind to. She'd been unwise to confide in him.

"Forgive me my silly talk about Marco," Adella said. "He is a good friend to us, and with you I feel a sense of *affinità*. You are someone I wish not to lose."

Meg smiled at the woman's delightfully earnest expression. "I don't want to lose touch, either. You will write me, I hope?"

"*Si*, of course." Adella toyed with her coffee spoon. "I can see that for you Marco appears to be a dominant European male, perhaps with a sophistication, a manner—how do you say it—of sexual expertise. He is a natural charmer, and that is the worst kind. But enough of this." She signaled the waiter and insisted on paying for Meg's lunch. "If you are not tired I would like to show you the Correr Museum."

They entered the Napoleonic building that comprised the south side of St. Mark's Square and contained relics of Venice's glorious past. The costumes of the Venetian noblewomen were exquisite, with their exaggerated high-heeled slippers and rich fabrics. Meg could see at once where Adella took inspiration for some of her designs and textures.

Afterwards, they went by gondola to a small home on a quiet waterway, where several women welcomed Adella warmly. They were at work stitching together one of her tapestry designs; scattered on a large work table were dozens of separately embroidered pieces. Some were already pinned onto the larger design pattern, a colorful panel of birds and flowers, slightly abstract, which reminded Meg of the wall paintings of ancient Crete.

"You are almost right," Adella said when she commented on the fact. "These are adapted from old Etruscan drawings and from some tomb paintings in the south, near Paestum."

As she introduced the women, one of whom was much older than the three others, Adella praised them for their expert needlework. Soon Meg was busily taking pictures of them and their work, and of the two angelic toddlers who clung to their mothers' knees. She jotted down information on the family's history while Adella translated. The grandmother was especially talkative, berating the lack of interest in embroidery among young people today. With Meg's prompting she told about her youth—how she'd been trained in a convent near Naples to embroider altar cloths and vestments. She in turn had trained her three daughters. "Now they are glad," she cackled, shaking an elderly finger at their grinning faces.

"I'm sure an illustrated article will bring you many commissions, Adella," Meg said. "And provide work for others, too. You might become famous."

Adella laughed. "I wonder how Giulio would adjust to that."

"He would be proud. He loves you."

"*Si.* God is good to me, and now, especially, since another small one grows." She blushed and her eyes sparkled. "This one must be a girl. She can carry on my business, and our son can follow his father. Some extra money will be needed to educate our children. Giulio is paid well, but we are not rich."

Before they left, the old woman took her wedding ring and tied it to an embroidery thread. She dangled the ring over Adella's still flat belly and studied the circle made by the motion of the ring. *"Una ragazzina,"* she crowed.

"Of course, a girl!" Adella said through eyes bright with tears.

She and Meg departed with kisses and embraces all around. At the door the grandmother took Meg's hand and spoke to her with a measured tone. Adella translated: "Your heart is in Italy, *signorina*. Venezia has called you from far away to give a gift of love."

She shook her old head and sighed, then raised her wrinkled cheek to Meg and whispered, *"Baci mi, bella giovinetta."* Meg kissed her gently, receiving a hearty kiss in return.

"You have made a conquest of old Franca," Adella laughed when they were once again outside. "You are fated to come back to Venezia, *cara*."

As their gondola neared the Specchiato, Meg felt suddenly cold all over. Marco's white launch was tied up at the water steps. She looked up at the apartment windows as if she expected to see Marco standing there, but of course she saw nothing.

"I will not come inside, Meg," Adella said. "I see Marco has returned."

Meg's heart was beating fast as she turned her gaze from the empty windows. "Adella. . .there's one more thing I forgot to tell you. Something about the Specchiato that your husband might want to know."

Adella's face grew intent, receptive.

"Giulio mentioned the Empress Earrings. Well, I think there is a problem around them."

"What kind of problem?"

"Teresa showed me the treasures in the Specchiato safe, and at the time one of the earrings was missing. But when we looked again later, it was there. At least I *think* it had been gone. Teresa seemed very upset about it. But I never actually saw—"

Adella pressed Meg's hand quickly. "I will tell Giulio."

Meg glanced up at the Specchiato again with trepidation. She was fast losing courage and could hardly whisper her thanks for lunch and the visit.

Adella only smiled at her. "Leave your concerns in Giulio's hands, my friend. . .and I need no thanks for a visit that was entirely my pleasure. Now, *addio*."

She waved as Meg walked up to the entrance door, keys in hand.

CHAPTER NINE

MEG WALKED THROUGH THE LOWER HALL and up the marble stairs numbly, wondering desperately what she would say to Marco when she saw him. Was it necessary to say anything more than, *how nice that you are back from Rome, signore. I trust your trip was a fruitful one?*

She repeated the sentences to herself until she was standing before the closed door of the apartment, shifting her purse and packages and fumbling with the keys. Her hands weren't cooperating, and she dropped the key chain to the floor with a reverberating clatter. On wobbling knees she bent to pick it up, balancing her other possessions as she did so.

When she rose she almost fell against the tall figure of Marco Montevalde, who had opened the door and was watching her predicament. "I thought you had left me, *piccola*. No note of farewell, not a sign that you had ever been here. I was growing quite annoyed with your lack of gratitude," he said lightly as he relieved her of her packages and offered a strong enfolding hand to help her up.

His familiar exciting presence—the cologne, the touch of his hand on hers—deprived her of the little composure she still had. She really did need his assistance to regain her balance on her feet.

"And worst of all, I missed you! That was a surprise

to me!'' He drew her close to him and released her again with a little laugh. ''You almost cost me my concentration, *amica mia*!''

The old feeling toward him was there, undiminished. *Dear God!* And then the memorized sentence tumbled from her lips as she stared up at him: ''How nice that you are back from Rome. . . .''

''Is that all you can say?'' His voice changed and he stepped back from her. ''Forgive me, but Lucia was gone when I returned and I had no way of knowing that you were still in Venezia. I didn't see your luggage. . . .''

''Lucia moved my things to the guest room,'' Meg said automatically, not fully accepting the wonderful words he had greeted her with. ''I knew you would be back today, and I didn't want to impose on your hospitality more than necessary.'' Her lips were working, but she was rooted to the spot, unable to move past him.

''Hardly an imposition.'' His eyes had lost their brightness, and he looked hard at her before speaking again. ''I assume your passport has not arrived. Has Giulio Prati kept you informed?''

''I expect it tomorrow or Tuesday.'' Meg had never felt so awkward with a man in her life. How could he so easily link into her like this, with those invisible coils that robbed her of normal responses?

''I see. Well, you will want to refresh yourself after being out on your errands. I have errands myself.'' He looked intently down at her and returned the packages to her hands, but did not step out of the way to let her walk through the doorway. ''Are you sorry to see me, Meg?''

"Of course not," she managed to whisper, and took a tentative step forward. He moved slightly, but not enough for her to pass without their bodies touching.

"Have dinner with me—we must talk," he said firmly as his arm came out to keep her close.

A bright voice called up the stairway. "No, Marco... Lucia is planning a special dinner for all of us here." Teresa bounded up the last steps and gave her cousin a hug. "I don't want to change your plans, but Lucia would be so hurt if you didn't stay."

"So be it," Marco said, turning away. "I will return in time for Lucia's fine offering."

Meg watched his straight back disappearing down the steps and took a deep breath to restore order to her scattered nerve endings.

"I hope I didn't spoil something," Teresa said earnestly.

"Not at all. I didn't feel well enough to go out tonight anyway. I'm still a little shaky." She dropped her packages on the sofa and sat down. It was best to redirect the conversation. "How was your day with Enzo?"

"I made the mistake of telling him that his *Madonna and Child* were not done in the style that the public will accept right now," Teresa answered. "You can imagine what that did to his humor! *Dio mio!*" She waved her hand in an Italian gesture, as if she had burned herself on something hot. "I think he should make more things like that beautiful little bird in the child's hand—things with warmth and personal meaning, not so abstract."

"Maybe you should be less direct in your criticisms with Enzo," Meg offered.

"I know that now, but how can I take back my words? Oh, Meg, I don't know if I ruined things between us or not! He grew silent and I left." She looked bleak. "I am not a sophisticated woman like my mother. Mother makes a man feel like a king even if he is a poor clown. I have too much self-pride. I cannot tell a man something I don't believe in my heart." She thought for a moment. "But you are correct. I am not subtle enough." A fresh smile eased away the worry lines on her face. "I shall be more subtle from now on! Then Enzo won't know how to deal with me. I shall like that. And I know that one day he will follow my advice without knowing it came from me at all."

Teresa stretched her arms above her head as if a burden had gone from her. "Was Marco angry with me for interrupting him just now? He did not look pleased."

"It wasn't anything you did; it was me," Meg said without thinking.

Teresa regarded her flushed cheeks. "Be careful, Meg. I love my cousin and he is a very fine man. . . but there have been many women chasing after him."

"No need to warn me, Teresa." She felt a rush of defensiveness. "I have no intention of chasing him."

"Don't listen to me," Teresa shrugged apologetically. "Today I am not very good with my words. But Marco is a special man—one to approach with caution." She looked as if she regretted starting the conversation, but went on anyway. "A woman can raise Marco's hopes. He becomes enthusiastic and then he discovers the reality beneath her pretty mask. And so—a door shuts inside of him. Marco has many hidden rooms in his heart—just like the Specchiato. Do you know what I mean?" Her eyes begged Meg to make sense out of the cryptic statements.

"I think I do. And I will take your good advice to

heart. The last thing on my mind is to play games with a man I will probably never see again after tomorrow.''

Meg meant it. Teresa had just given her a little more insight into Marco and his life. In an odd way it was a relief. Things had been put back into some perspective: a kiss in the moonlight in Venice was just that, an encapsulated event that would go on the shelf, labeled *souvenir*. No more, no less. She was going to stop thinking that a romantic Italian male could fit anywhere in her American life-style. It was obviously impossible. Her kind of woman didn't come equipped with keys to open secret doors in complicated men.

Lucia served the many courses of her Venetian cuisine with a flair, and Meg hoped she didn't take the relative silence at the dinner table as criticism of her magnificent cooking. Teresa made small talk and played the good hostess, but Meg picked at the palate-pleasing food and avoided Marco's almost constant gaze. She felt his eyes lingering on her, as if they could reach across the table to touch her face and lips. What was he trying to do? Was it amusement at her discomfort or just calculated sexuality searching for a place to light temporarily?

After dessert and coffee Teresa dabbed at her lips with her pink linen napkin. ''You will have to excuse me tonight. I have an appointment.''

Marco raised his eyes in a question and Teresa said, ''I am to be interviewed by a family that wants a music tutor for their three children. I should be home early.'' She rose and went to the kitchen to thank Lucia for the meal, then left the apartment.

The silence at the table was growing more tangible. Meg sensed Marco's attention still on her, but she ignored it and tried to keep her hands steady as she lifted her cup to her lips. "The coffee is delicious," she commented, feeling she should say something to break the mood. Marco wasn't making it easy for her.

"I agree," he said. "Quite delicious." When he said the word it somehow meant something different. "Would you like to take a walk? Surely you haven't seen Piazza San Marco by moonlight yet, and I have been so busy with my work lately that I have forgotten what it looks like, myself!" He stood up quickly and held her chair for her. "No tourist must miss the Sunday-evening concert there."

"I've heard about it," she replied with a slight smile. She would rather be in a public place with him. She certainly didn't want to spend an intimate evening in the apartment, considering the mood he was in. She didn't trust herself.

"I sense that you are not completely at ease, Meg. Is it the illness, still?" He studied her briefly when she didn't reply at once. "Or did Giulio Prati distress you with something?"

"Neither," she said.

"You will enjoy the concert. It will chase away the shadows I see lingering around your lovely eyes. And don't make that expression at me, *amica*, as if you think I give compliments as easily as I breathe. Your eyes are most eloquent. And your soft, gentle lips. . . I will speak of them another time, when you are not so suspicious." He ended on a laugh.

"Do you always tease women, *signore*?" she asked, trying to seem somewhat knowing and invulnerable.

"Not always. Only when I have hope of seeing the color rise so delicately upon a lovely cheek—as now." He ended the badinage by walking into the kitchen to spread more compliments, this time well-deserved ones for Lucia.

Meg checked her makeup and hair in the mirror of her bathroom. She wanted to make sure there was not the slightest blush on her cheeks. It took two to play, and whatever was on Marco's mind tonight, he wouldn't have a partner for it. The pain that would come afterward simply wasn't worth it; she knew that much about herself and her susceptibility to Marco's presence.

He was waiting for her in the living room. Closing the book he'd been reading, he got to his feet with the swift ease that was so characteristic of him. He took her supple knitted stole and draped it over her shoulders as they moved through the cool downstairs entry hall.

"The evenings can have a touch of chill," he murmured. His voice was gentle. "How happy it makes me to see you here—so different from the pale stranger that I first met in the piazza."

To Meg's surprise a gondola glided out of the shadows just as they stepped from the palazzo. "*Ciao*, Luigi," Marco hailed, and Luigi favored Meg with a heavy conspiratorial wink.

"I have already taken the *bella signorina* to a rendezvous in a hidden *rio*. Now I take her in the moonlight, and I will sing her a love song."

"Luigi brought me to the home of Signor Prati the night I had dinner there," Meg explained. Marco seemed pleased to hear it. He and Meg sat together on the big double seat just in front of Luigi's tuneful activities. His hand found hers, holding it in a warm clasp. She didn't pull away. *Just for this little while,* her mind said beguilingly.

Luigi swept his curved black craft up to the quay at the gondola pool. There was a moment of banter in Italian between the men as Marco paid the fare. Meg turned to thank Luigi for his song.

"For you, *bella mia*, the song is from the heart." He bowed to her, his eyes shining in the reflected light from the dappled water. "But the time I had Pavarotti in my gondola I was afraid to make a sound. He ask me, *'Perche non canta,'* and I could only swallow in the throat. How could I sing to the maestro?"

"What happened?" Meg chuckled.

"Ah, he was *magnifico*! He sang instead." Luigi made wide gestures of pleasure.

Marco led her over a small bridge and along some narrow walkways. Suddenly they were emerging from the arcades into Piazza San Marco. Meg drew in her breath. Soft illumination defined the golden domes of the basilica and the Campanile. The square was filled with people. Little flares from cigarettes lighted up an occasional face in the crowd, and most of the chairs at Quadri's and Florian's were taken.

A large platform stood in the center of the piazza. On it a sizable orchestra was tuning its instruments. Many people were strolling around near the platform, apparently heedless that the concert was about to start. It was like a great party buzzing with guests, all happy and relaxed. Children ran about, playing with yo-yos that lighted up with flashing color as the little spheres ran up and down their strings. The hawkers who sold the toys were doing good business.

Marco's hand urged Meg toward Florian's. Giorgio spotted them right away and seated them at a table that had been reserved, its chairs tilted forward. Around them people were sipping espresso or wine, or enjoying *gelati*, the Italian ice cream. Almost as soon as Meg and Marco took their seats Giorgio was there with cups of espresso and a dish of *pasticcini*—tiny confections and cakes and finger-sized fruit tarts. Meg had that strange feeling again, the feeling that she was outside of her normal self and in a kind of parallel existence. Her reasonable mind was losing its fight.

Marco seemed completely at ease, nodding to people who waved or greeted him. When he looked at Meg the moonlight glittered across his eyes, intensifying the excitement that his closeness was rousing in her.

"Are you happy, *piccola*?" he asked in a caressing tone that started a hot tide flowing through her body.

"It's wonderful!" she admitted.

An indulgent smile moved over his fine lips. "I remember how truly beautiful my city is when I see it through your eyes. You are good for me, Meg. I think I have grown weary with my complex troubles and have neglected important experiences that would help me to a fresh creativeness and perhaps to a personal joy."

His words fell like lead into Meg's heart. So he wanted personal joy—but with whom? Surely not with Meg Brown, who wouldn't even know how to *start* fulfilling his varied needs.

With a kind of desperation she began to talk about her meeting with Adella's embroiderers and how she planned to shape her magazine article.

"To whom will you sell the article?" he asked with interest.

"I hope to sell to *Au Courant*." She watched a flicker of surprise cross his face. "I've already sold one article to them." Her voice was as nonchalant as she could manage. "They requested other material, and Adella's story would be perfect."

"Va bene!" He put his hand briefly over hers. "You have been hiding your light, *piccola*. That magazine wants only very good writing."

"I know," she smiled, feeling suddenly better about things in general.

Just then the orchestra burst into sound. It was a kind of pops concert, with adaptations of musical-comedy numbers mixed with well-loved classics. Meg tried to imprint every moment on her memory. When would she ever find herself in an atmosphere like this, with such a feeling of the past...and with a man like Marco? Her eyes lingered on his face as he listened with closed eyes to the changing patterns of the music. A tiny smile broke the even line of his lips, and he again covered her hand with his. She saw a gleam of topaz from beneath his dark lashes. He had caught her staring.

Blood rushed to her face. The whole situation was so damnably frustrating—a dream without a wakening reality.

The concert ended too soon and Giorgio was saying *arrivederci*. "We will walk home, I think," Marco said. "It is not far and I don't want Luigi's warblings to break the spell of the moon and Venezia, *tesora mia*." They walked silently in the soft night air. Marco reached to take her hand, holding it securely in his until Meg felt it was the most natural thing in the world for him to be doing.

He stopped in the shadows of a crumbling stone bridge and kissed her hand very softly, looking into her eyes for a long moment and saying nothing. He put his thumb beneath her chin to raise it.

Alarms rang in her numbed mind. In spite of her desire to offer her lips to him, a prickling combativeness made her say, "Why didn't you tell me you were the owner of the Specchiato?"

His expression changed. "Why, indeed? Does a good samaritan have to give reasons? It seemed unimportant at the moment to explain the intricacies of my living arrangements. And you might not have accepted had you known. Is that satisfactory?" His eyes were on her lips.

"I just couldn't understand why you wouldn't tell me in the first place. . . unless you had something to hide."

"How American of you, little Meg," he laughed, "and how very logical. You forget that you have already revealed your fantasies to me, so don't play with words. What you really meant was, why didn't I announce my intention to ravish you right then and there—or something of the sort, hmm?"

She drew her hand from his tightening grasp, experiencing a wild urge to slap his face for the crudeness of his answer. But he took her hand again and kissed it. "I apologize," he whispered. "It was not my place to taunt you. And I have no wish to be wounded by a flying hand. I have not been entirely tamed yet and sometimes I overstep. Do you wish to be escorted by someone other than myself, or shall we push on, mindless of the consequences?"

He was enjoying her emotional response. How could he tease her when she was merely attempting to straighten out their situation? He had turned their steps again toward the palazzo. "I'm. . . very tired," she said, hoping that would take care of further conversation. "The day was a long one."

"Were you touring the city with Adella Prati?" The question had no undertones at all.

"We had lunch and went to see her workshop, as I told you. She loves to talk. It makes interviewing so easy."

"I admire Adella very much. And how was your evening with Giulio?"

"Pleasant also. I learned many things about the Specchiato and its treasures. The Marco Polo Cup must be magnificent."

He cocked an inquiring eye at her. "And he told you how much he worries about the safety of the other things?"

"It *does* seem to be on his mind."

"Giulio becomes an old woman about security. What else did he ask you? He is always probing after something."

"He said he thought that—" She quickly remembered Signor Prati's warning not to speak of anything "...he respects you very much," she ended.

"Oh? That is all? Surely Giulio, with his gift of speech, said more than that."

"No," she said firmly. "Why would he say anything more to me? I'm not part of your family."

They had reached the Specchiato, and Marco took her hand to lead her into the entry hall. The only illumination came from the moon above them through the stained glass skylight. Meg was vibrantly aware of his body so near to hers, but tried with an iron will not to care.

How idiotic it would be to pretend that anything could work out between them, how useless. With everything he said he made it more clear that there was an immense chasm between them. Every sign said, *Wrong way. . . do not enter.*

They walked slowly up the marble stairs and came to the balcony that overlooked the hall. As she was about to proceed to the inner door he stopped her, pulling her close to him.

"Have you ever been kissed against a balustrade, like those flirting ladies at masked balls who drew their lovers to them with little signals of the body?"

What could she answer to that, when her own body was in turmoil? She loved the feel of him next to her, the strength of his arm encircling her waist.

"Ah, you don't reply, my lady. I shall have to play the role of smitten *cavalier servente* and press my ardor upon you."

Meg didn't know if he was jesting or serious, but she didn't want to assume the one and have it be the other. She decided to play the game. "A kiss comes with a high price, milord," she said in a dramatic voice, using her hand like a fan.

"Name it," he whispered close to her ear, "and quickly!"

She thought frantically. "The key to your apartment! I know how unseemly it is, but I am shameless!"

She could feel him smiling as he pressed his cheek against hers. "Done." He dropped the keys into her hand and claimed his boon. She caught her breath at the lingering kiss upon her sensitive, unprotected ear. "Tell me, my lady," he said softly, exploring the contours of it with his tongue, "when you have had enough," and he moved his attention to her eyelids and then down the line of her cheek until it came to the very corner of her lips.

She opened her mouth slightly and a little sound escaped her. The insistence of his warm and practiced kiss left her no choice but to find unbearable pleasure in it. She was unwilling to move from his embrace, and found herself kissing him back with a powerful urge to blend her body with his, to be a part of him.

He answered her invitation by drawing her hips tightly against his. Her inner voice was shouting wildly for her to stop and save her pride, but she couldn't.

At last Marco pulled back sharply, as if an invisible force had grabbed him and thrust him away from her. "*I* say enough, Meg," he said roughly and took her by the shoulders with his strong hands. "This should not be a game between us. Forgive me once more." He turned her away from the balustrade and released her. "You have the key. Perhaps you should employ it now."

She could barely hear him, the blood was pounding so loudly in her ears. *The key.* It was in her hand. Steadying herself, she slipped it into the lock and turned it, then walked ahead of him to the door of the apartment. He had left her without possibility of reply, and she felt like a complete fool.

Marco's hand rested lightly at the small of her back, guiding her as they entered. The hand did nothing more, and Meg felt put down by that as well. How perfectly in control he was! *What a master puppeteer,* she thought grimly, feeling her whole body flush with self-reproach.

"This was not quite the celebration I had planned, *piccola*," he said from behind her. She imagined he was smiling at her. "But there will be another day, perhaps—a proper time for pleasure." He withdrew his hand from her back and left her standing at the door to her new room. "Sleep well."

She couldn't tell how he really felt, but she was becoming thoroughly tired of having to wonder about him. There was nothing between them and no reason for her to think he cared for her—at least cared beyond the predictable male-female chemistry that comes from proximity.

She tried to turn off her busy mind as she undressed and selected one of the twin beds—tried to forget that Marco was in the next bedroom. Switching off the lamp on the bedside table, she slipped between the fine embroidered percale sheets. Were they Marco's selection, or had one of his women friends assisted him in the decor of his apartment? *Why should I care,* she wondered. She was disgusted with her persistent curiosity about him.

Sleep evaded her for a long time. She even tried counting heartbeats in order to bore herself with the task and fall asleep, but all that did was make her more aware than ever that Marco had a direct effect on the rate of her heart. She sighed deeply. She needed something to read, something not about Italy or the *Summertime* syndrome. The light went on again and she searched the Florentined bookcase until she found something in English: a collection of poems by Lord Byron, bound in red tooled leather, the way valued books used to be made.

Back in bed, propped against her pillows, she opened the little book at random and let her eyes stop at random. She read the first lines of a stanza, and jumped down to two others on the page, then shut the book with a snap, as if she had to stop the strong force of fate from pursuing her.

How could *those* particular lines be the ones she'd read, out of the thousands in the book?

> Nor yet forget how Venice once was dear,
> The pleasant place of all festivity...
>
> But unto us she hath a spell beyond
> Her name in story....

It had been foolish to pick up Byron in the first place, that prince of romance and dalliance. And what was Marco doing with it, getting pointers on technique? She opened the book again to the first page and read the inscription written in light blue flowing script, a woman's handwriting: *"Caro* Marco...*non dimenticare."* It was signed with the initial "R."

She had intruded where she was not invited. She put the book back into place on the shelf and didn't select another. But the Italian words buzzed in her mind. *Non dimenticare*...do not forget. The meaning was clear enough, yet it hit at some part of Meg's stubborn feminine ego. So there *was* another woman in his life. Adella and Teresa had tried to warn her.

An uncontrollable shiver made its way through her body at the sudden memory of Marco's insistent lips, his enticing voice, the way he knew the smallest places that brought delight to her senses. *That comes from long practice,* she thought cynically as she tried to blot out her desire to replay every touch and whisper.

With the light off once more and her head firmly planted on the pillows Meg made her mind a blank. But no matter how she snuggled into the downy nest of pillows, sleep mocked her. She was still too busy with the two soft words that Marco had spoken on their walk home. *"Tesora mia."* She knew they were an endearment—my treasure, or my darling.

"Damn and hell!" she muttered into her pillows, sitting up abruptly. She should have learned by now that too much coffee had its effects. Giorgio had been alert with refills.... Maybe there was milk in the refrigerator; she could warm a little for herself.

Climbing out of bed Meg put on her sensible nylon tailored robe over the pretty nightgown that had been an extravagance she allowed herself for the trip. She crept past Marco's closed door in her soft slippers, and had started toward the kitchen when a sudden whim took over. She wanted to wander alone in the Specchiato one more time before she left, maybe even write a mood piece one day about the experience. Among the Ghosts of Old Venice, she would call it.

She went on silent hastening feet to the entrance door of the apartment. Leaving the door ajar so that she could reenter easily, she started down the first shadowy hallway toward the interior of the palazzo. The aura of the old building claimed her almost immediately.

Meg knew the layout better now and headed across the wide mezzanine, which led past balconies and doorways and small back stairs. Going through one of the doors she reached another corridor, which made a sharp right angle and ran along the back of the palazzo. Its dusty windows let in an eerie light.

Gently she tried door after door of this wing. Most of them opened into bedrooms and sitting rooms, where pieces of furniture were shrouded under dust sheets like patient ghosts. A gigantic carved bed stood in one room, its embroidered hangings tattered with age. It would take all the skill of an old Franca to mend its silken folds.

Presences seemed to flit ahead of Meg, casting sad looks over their misty shoulders. It was very much the way it had been that evening she had ventured onto the balcony overlooking the entrance hall, only now she wasn't frightened to be sharing this place with them.

Poor Marco! To restore all of this would cost an immense amount of money, and it must hurt terribly to see it slowly falling into decay. After all, this was his heritage. But what if she wrote a series of articles.... Suppose she could excite people enough that they'd make donations for restoration of the palazzo? Would Marco like that or would his ego be damaged?

She shivered suddenly in a cold draft of confusion, realizing how little she understood him, how limited and untrustworthy her perceptions were. She was standing in the midst of a fantasy, this haunted palazzo with its whispers of spent passions, whispers that were part of Marco's very blood.

She felt utterly raw as she reflected on her responses to him. Marco was himself, but he was all of this, too. The mysteries of personality that showed in the depths of his complicated amber eyes gave him a potent fascination, an irresistible charm. He *was* the prince of dreams, no matter if he owned an architectural firm and rode about in modern motor launches and jet planes. And who was *she*?

Standing in the dust-filled room dappled with moonlight she thought how it might feel to be part of Marco's life—to give him the gifts of her efforts, of her love.

"Love..." she said tentatively, and the word seemed to alert the energies of the past to listen. "I love him," she said to them. With a sob heavy in her throat she repeated, "I love him!"

She turned and ran with soft flip-flops of her slippers back toward the reality of her modern bed. The presences were laughing and weeping behind her; she could feel them.

On the way, however, she passed one of the entrance doors to the mirrored room and felt compelled to stop. Something in her made her want to walk in its reflections once more. Without a sound she had turned the gold ormolu handle and pushed open the door.

The great room was silent. The fancifully carved marble pedestals that had once held treasures were empty, like forlorn guardians standing at attention long after the need for them had passed.

While she was walking to the center of the room Meg saw her pale reflection precede her in several of the mirrors. Then she stood still, listening. She hoped she was completely alone, and that the night guard had made his rounds and was snug on his small couch near the hidden vault room.

A moment later she relaxed, letting herself be drawn into the tempting, seductive mood of the room. Who was to know? Echoes of long-ago balls and receptions sang with sad-sweet melodies in her imagination. She'd never been in a place quite like this one, that had the feeling of past and present weaving inside of one another. She had no wish to resist it.

In a flowing motion she kicked off her slippers and unbuttoned her sensible robe, letting it slide from her shoulders to the floor. Her ankle-length nightdress, a deep rose pink, flared around her in long silken folds. The lace top clung to her breasts.

With raised arms Meg began to move on the smooth parquetry floor, her bare feet light, enjoying its coolness. Music of the past whispered in her ears and she was dancing with Marco. He was dressed in dark satin, with white ruffles at his throat and wrists. . . .

She closed her eyes and made a circular path across the room, in a rhythm dictated by the phantom music. Smiling to herself, she opened her eyes again, and wasn't surprised to see another reflection in the room. After all, it was only a dream—and she couldn't stop dancing.

But the second reflection was tall and swift, wonderful and terrifying. Meg found it impossible to turn away from the broken reflections and return to reality. Almost hypnotized, she kept on moving in her dance pattern, watching as the figures of herself and this other merged.

Warm hands grasped her waist. As if from far away she heard a sound come from her throat, and then it was stifled in a kiss, while hands pulled her close to the enfolding strength of a supple male body. He moved effortlessly into the same rhythm of the soundless waltz, swinging her with sure strength in a great circle and then holding her close again.

Their bodies sensed each other perfectly. They danced for what seemed a strange measure of timelessness, and Meg felt the power of his vitality as he moved. Theirs was an instinctive attunement—so very intimate, and so tantalizing.

Finally she felt his arms loosen, his body still. Their silent dance was over. His hands continued to steady her for a moment before they moved caressingly on her bare skin. She lifted her head from his chest, and Marco smiled down at her.

"Did I frighten you, *piccola*? You were so lovely dancing in your flowing dress. . . ." His voice was deep and soft. "I couldn't let you dance alone."

She pulled away from him just enough to see that he wore a satin robe the color of wine. The sleeves of a white silk pajama top showed at his neck and wrists, just as in her fantasy. To have foreseen it all so accurately was too much. It took only a moment for her to retrieve her robe from the floor and quickly put it on again.

Marco laughed and went to pick up her slippers, which were lying yards apart on the wide floor. He bent down to put them on her feet. "You are silent, my Meg," he said. "Am I forgiven for intruding on your privacy?"

She found a small voice with effort. "Yes. . .yes, of course. I. . .couldn't sleep."

He smiled. "I found no sleep, either."

Her eyes were drawn to his, and she saw, deep within them, reflections of the flowing light in the mirrors. An ecstatic shiver of expectancy started through her mind, and she was powerless to stop it. She *did* want him to love her.

He lifted his hand and traced the contour of her face with a delicate caress. "My Meg. . . ." The vibration of his smooth voice stirred responses beyond any touch or kiss. "There is something in my heart that I must say—"

The sound of running footsteps broke the spell. With a crash the night guard flung open one of the doors and burst into the room. *"Chi è la!"* he shouted, sweeping the harsh arc of his flashlight toward them. He came to a sliding halt when he saw Marco and Meg.

Meg put her hand up to block the light, and the guard snapped it off immediately. Marco spoke briefly in Italian. The guard saluted, then quickly nodded to Meg. "*Scusi*, Signor Marco, *signorina*... *buona notte*." He turned away and went on with his rounds.

Marco sighed on a long breath. "Come, *piccoletta*. It must be very late. You need your sleep." His voice was matter-of-fact. The magic had gone and Meg felt suddenly exhausted.

They walked without further words back toward the apartment. She didn't dare ask if they would see each other again before she left, or what he had intended to say to her before the guard came in.

He escorted her to the door of her room, where he said good-night warmly but definitely not romantically, turning away as if there had been no fairy-tale dance or the beginning of tender words. *He is Italian,* she thought with gray spirits. *He can enter into drama and play in it with zest, and then it is over and he is back to his real and practical world.*

She couldn't think anymore about him or the palazzo, or about going home. Especially not about emotions and sudden hopes that glittered in her heart like bright bursts of firework stars, only to die away again as swiftly as they appeared. She must not build on the words Marco spoke, or be weakened by the mesmerizing tones of his beautiful voice.

If she saw him the next day, which was possible, if

only in passing, she wanted his memories of her to be the right ones—memories of a woman in control of herself. And he must never know how close she had come to falling in love.

CHAPTER TEN

THE NEXT MORNING Meg found herself alone in the apartment. Marco was gone, Lucia and Teresa, too, but Teresa had left a note for her.

> Meg, dear, don't worry about me. The family hired me last night at a fair salary, starting today. I think I have the courage to tell Enzo that I can support myself. Don't leave Venice until we can talk... promise! I'll be back this evening.

Meg smiled at Teresa's words. They showed such determination to overcome any problems in her way. *A good example for you, Meg Brown,* she mused.

Knowing what she must do to get herself back home as soon as possible, she called Signor Prati's office, but didn't find him in. His assistant knew about her case and told her to come to the office at 4:00 P.M. The passport would be there.

A second call verified her travel arrangements. She could take the eight o'clock train tomorrow morning to Milan and from there make the one o'clock flight to Los Angeles via Paris.

Meg hung up the phone with a sigh of relief. It was done at last. No more fence-sitting; the die was cast.

She sat alone in the cool *salotto*, looking at every

detail of it with a writer's discernment. If she could come away from this place with good material for Maude Draper's editorial eye, at least part of her Venetian adventure would have been worth it.

When Marco called she was able to match his agreeable tone with a lightness that surprised her. He was asking—no, telling—her to be ready within the hour for a day in the country and a picnic. He wanted her to see the villas along the Brenta River. "I'm at my office catching up with my messages, but I need to relax and celebrate the completion of my design project. I want you to join me."

"I must be back by four o'clock," Meg stated. "I'm picking up my passport at Signor Prati's office." She was pleased with her new steadiness.

"Of course, *piccola*. There will be enough time for my basket of surprises *and* for your business with Giulio Prati," he teased.

Certainly she was capable of having a picnic with Marco Montevalde without falling apart. *At last,* she amended. It would be a wonderful chance to see more of the Italian countryside. And if she allowed anything more than a picnic to take place, she deserved everything that was coming to her! But there was no longer fear of that, thank heavens. She was back at the controls of her life.

She took her time in dressing, knowing exactly how she wanted to appear to him on this last day in Italy. A blue velvet ribbon made a dainty tie to secure her flying honey-colored curls at the nape of her neck. She enjoyed the feel of the new sky blue cotton dress, with its embroidered camisole bodice and smooth full skirt. It made her look terribly feminine and soft, even beautiful, she knew, and she was reasonably sure Marco would say something complimentary, being so very Italian as he was!

Let him remember me like this, she said to herself, not realizing that such a thought showed how vulnerable she still was.

Marco met her at ten o'clock, dressed in unnecessarily handsome casual clothes—navy blue cotton trousers that tied at the waist and a pure white cotton shirt with shoulder tabs and buttoned pockets. By the time he swung his immaculate white motor launch in a wide arc of spray into the *rio* he hadn't yet said anything about her attractive appearance, which was more than a little annoying. He *always* said something, even when Meg knew she didn't look very special.

"Today, as part of your tour package, *signorina*," he said breezily, "we will travel inland from Fusina along the Brenta River and observe the legacy left by the genius of Palladio."

"The architect," she said in an attempt at nonchalance.

"The magnificent brilliant architect," he corrected. "And by the way, I have never seen you more beautiful, *amica mia*."

He aimed the boat across the great S of the Grand Canal and along the Rio Nuovo, leaving Venice behind and heading westward to the mainland, where the Brenta emptied into the Adriatic Sea.

The day was heavy with clouds, sultry and meltingly hot. Meg's curls were sticking to her forehead and her neck in spite of the cooling effect of the boat ride. Marco seemed not to feel the heat at all.

"It's like this before a rain," he shouted over the

whine of the engine. "We'll be at La Mira before it lets loose. Nothing to worry about."

"Where is La Mira?"

"Not far beyond Marghera. The picnic basket at your feet should tell you I have no intention of letting you starve."

Meg was fascinated by the countryside along the banks of the Brenta, a very peaceful waterway. On either side were estates, mostly old and crumbling, but a few that showed they had been cared for. She couldn't see some of them at all because they lay at the end of long private lanes behind high elaborate iron gates.

Marco gestured to one of them, just visible behind a row of cypress trees. "That's a Palladio...under restoration." He drove the launch farther up the Brenta until they passed the town of La Mira. Here the countryside was flat and dotted with villas.

They stopped at last at a landing. High brush and trees allowed a partial view up a long straight path to a distant structure.

"Palladio?" Meg asked, sure that she couldn't go wrong in guessing.

"Unfortunately, no. An interesting imitation by an unknown architect in the eighteenth century. It has always been called the Villa Terza—probably because it was the third attempt on the designer's part to come up with a good copy of a Palladio. It belongs to my family now, and I am employing a village carpenter at very modest wages to help me restore the place in all its eccentricities and affectations. This is my therapy!"

They walked slowly up to the square, two-story, classical-style villa, which was almost choked by climbing vines. Meg examined the Palladian windows and pillars, but didn't know enough to tell that this was an imitation. It looked very much like the drawings in Marco's early edition of Palladio's book.

Marco showed her around the house like a young boy showing his favorite toy. There were signs that workmen occasionally came here: piles of lumber, sacks of cement, wheelbarrows, partially exposed framing where thick walls were being reconstructed. The only part of the villa that was in order at all was a bedroom suite on the second floor, with a high canopy bed, a utilitarian drafting table, a stool and a small couch. There was no telephone because Marco wanted to have one place where the world couldn't reach him, he said.

As he spoke about the house his voice took on that same storyteller's enchantment that it had at Florian's when he'd described the collapse of the Campanile. Meg followed the history of the place, from its shadowy origins in the eighteenth century, through its use as a hideaway for one of Napoleon's high officials and its conversion to a military headquarters during the Second World War.

"By the end of the war it was in sad condition, like today, but my family had no money to spare for its renovation. My father had committed much of the Montevalde fortune to the aid of refugees. The needs of a country house were not important then. But now I feel a great urge to bring it back to life, to treat it like a grand lady who has fallen upon difficult times. I want to stroke her breast, wipe the dust from her lips, make love to her in my own way. That is how I see myself, as the lover for whom she has waited a very long time."

Meg was beginning to understand the ease with which an Italian male could turn every occasion to something vaguely intimate—not suggestive enough to offend, but enough to start a tingle of sensual response in the listener....

But Marco didn't note her wary expression. He led her back outside into the threatening sultry air, intent on showing her where they would have their picnic. He had brought the linen-draped basket with him from the boat. Near the house was a rundown old gazebo, set in the middle of what had once been a formal garden. There had been a huge hedge maze, he explained, and fashionable house parties in the last century had included games where men and women searched for each other in its dead ends and secret places. "I always wondered what it would be like to seek out a woman for whom you felt a passion. She would evade you tantalizingly, until you could not bear it any longer...and then you would find her in the center of the maze." He looked casually in Meg's direction. "In the old days the games became rather naughty ones, I have heard. You must forget the Venice of today and imagine how it was then: there were picnics on the grass, rides through the forests, attendants everywhere to cater to your most fanciful whim."

He paused and started to spread out the array of delicacies that Lucia had prepared for them. He had already made a clear place on the long grass of the gazebo's floor. "Have you read *The Decameron*, Meg?"

She nodded as visions of those centuries-old erotic tales swam across her mind's eye.

"In the summer months the country villas were like scenes from Boccaccio's pen—music, dancing, the play of beckoning eyes. But all that began to die away with the arrival of Napoleon. Just as well, don't you think?" He tilted his head to see her reaction.

What did he expect her to say? "Everything seems to have its natural life span," she evaded rather nicely, but his words were having an uncomfortable effect on her composure. Even the sultry air was doing something to her nerves. She was too well trained in the art of visualization not to be reacting to the images Marco was planting in her mind. Weren't journalists supposed to absorb the total environment of an assignment?

Marco said nothing more about the maze or lovers or passion, but Meg was left feeling that he had begun to weave a spell around her. He smiled at her with his glinting topaz eyes and poured her a glass of white wine. "Will you write about this, *carina*? There are certain Italian traditions that very few tourists ever experience. The picnic in the country is one of them."

Meg tried to keep herself agreeable and, above all, sensible. She smiled at his amusing comments and praised the wine and marinated vegetables, all the while losing ground with her innermost resolves. The eating of their little feast was entirely in Marco's control. He doled out the portions and established which courses came before the next. Meg watched as the picnic became a sensuous ritual and her mask shattered in disarray.

She didn't know if he did it intentionally or if she was so sensitively tuned to him that everything he did had a second meaning. He would hold out a morsel of bread, touching her lips with a barely discernible pressure as he did so. He would brush a mosquito from her cheek and his hand would linger, drawing a line of sensation across her face and ending at her throat. Yet he said nothing; it was as if it hadn't happened.

Thunder started to rumble in the distance and moved quickly nearer, forcing them to gather up their picnic basket and take refuge in the house.

"These summer storms are heavy and sudden. They don't last long," he said. "Now you are forced to hear my best lecture on Palladio."

Lightning blazed a yellowish glare through the windows and the thunder vibrated the building. "It sounds like it's right over our heads," Meg said.

"I propose that we finish our meal in the upstairs suite, since it is the only civilized place in the villa. Perhaps we should light a fire so that we feel less at the mercy of the gods." He picked up the basket. "Coffee will lift the spirits."

"I mustn't be late to Signor Prati's office."

"I promise you a safe return by four o'clock."

But the storm persisted, darkening the sky and making twilight of the early afternoon. There was an ominous feeling in the sudden flashes of light, a shivery electric charge to the air. As they sat on the shaggy white flokati rug before the fire in Marco's bedroom suite, Meg felt more and more isolated from the outside world.

Marco poured the coffee, adding generous amounts of cognac. Meg had never liked the strong bite of the brandy before, but now it seemed delicious, and she even took a second cup that Marco offered.

He was being a gentleman, speaking of the house, his father, his wish to make the Villa Terza into a retreat from the pressures of his life. After a while he set their empty cups aside on the hearth. Without a word he turned to face her, his eyes lighted by the darting brilliance of the crackling fire. Taking her hands in his, he drew her down upon the soft rug until she was lying in his arms.

Then, before Meg understood how it could be happening, they were kissing and Marco was murmuring words of desire against her lips. Instinctively her body moved against his, drawn without effort by the potent energy of his inflaming touch. He was starting to make love to her, coaxing her lips open with his to give entrance to his searching tongue—and her eager mouth welcomed him.

She raised her eyes for a moment to savor his nearness, and found he was watching her with a passionate look that robbed her of any will to stop. He moved his lips over her flushed face, grazing her eyelids with the tip of his tongue, teasing her mouth, and smiling at her response of pleasure.

His hands were gentle yet urgent, stroking her throat, the lines of her shoulders, and deftly working open the tiny blue buttons of her bodice, kissing each newly revealed area of her skin until a low groan came from her throat. She felt drunk with the overwhelming force that was rising deep within her. A new Meg Brown was doing this, delighting in the exquisite sensations, the many small and tantalizing steps that were leading to her complete capitulation.

Beyond thought she clung to him, touching and kissing him, helping him to free her from her confining clothes. Her senses were swimming. She felt him pulling at his own clothing.

"Oh, *cara*, *cara*," he whispered as her hands smoothed their way across his broad hard chest.

With almost unbearable tenderness he began to draw her with him toward the high places of passion. She couldn't stop the dizzying journey, didn't want to. His heart was pounding heavily against her and she wanted to see his face again—that beloved face. Marco's head was bent, his lips and tongue playing deliciously with her breasts, and she looked past his dark hair, up to the ceiling of the room. There, in faded colors, a painted nymph was caught in the arms of a lusty satyr. On her soft face surrender was written.

A flash of cold reality flooded through Meg, and with a distressed groan she pushed at his dark head with her hands. "Stop...oh, Marco...."

Marco pulled back from her. "Have I hurt you?"

Tears of confusion and desire sprang to her eyes and he drew her close again, kissing them away. She felt the heat of his naked body against hers, a new surge of excitement moving between them. She was drowning in his kisses, sinking in the wonder of the sensation. His hand swept along the curve of her hips and began a tender exploration of her thighs, pressing intimately. His hard warmth was urgent against her.

Her eyes flew open again, and the satyr on the ceiling seemed to be leering at the trembling nymph. She couldn't let this happen! Strong and uncontrollable shivers began in her body. "I don't want...Marco..." she stammered. Tears pooled again in her eyes, which begged him to understand.

"Have I gone too fast for you? *Cara mia*, I only wish to make you happy."

Meg pushed herself away from him, not sure what she did want until she heard her own voice speaking in an unfamiliar, thin tone. "Marco, do you love me?"

A look of pain swept over his face, and he held her tightly against his muscular body. "Oh, my little Meg from America! Haven't those words been used too lightly, until they have lost their meaning? And would you believe me if I said them too quickly? Especially now?"

In the silence between them Meg fought with herself. She wanted him so badly. There was a fire in her that only he could create and only he could satisfy. She didn't need to hear him say the special words. . . but somehow she *did*. It would make all the difference. She looked into his deep eyes, so full of passion, and waited. Her body screamed in fury at her for denying it fulfillment.

Marco's voice was low and husky. "All right. I confess my ardor. . . I find you addictive. I find you in my thoughts to the detriment of my work. I find you irresistible. I cannot bear the thought of your leaving. Perhaps I have never defined what love should be. Aren't the things we feel at this moment beyond simple words?" He pressed two fingers lightly to her lips and followed with a hot probing kiss.

"Well?" he asked, sensing the change in her when she didn't respond.

She looked at him as steadily as she could. "I've made a terrible mistake."

He studied her for a long moment, then ran his fingers through his hair, a distracted gesture uncharacteristic of him. "So. . . ." His voice was tight. "The pleasant interlude is over. Your rules are a mystery to me. Does your game always stop at a certain point, leaving your partner begging for more?" His face had taken on a strange hard look and his eyes glinted. Meg couldn't answer him. What could she possibly say?

He got up from the rug and put on his clothes. "I will go check the boat," he said when he'd dressed.

While he was gone, Meg struggled to her feet and pulled on her own badly wrinkled clothes. He returned quickly, to say that the boat had broken loose from its moorings and had been battered against the dock by the suddenly swift waters of the Brenta—enough so that there was a hole in the hull. It would be useless to them. He would have to go on foot to find a telephone in a little *trattoria* about a mile distant.

As she waited for him to come back, Meg had plenty of time to regret what had happened. "How *could* you?" she demanded of her reflection in the mirror of the large marble bathroom. The memory of Marco's touch still sent tremors of pleasure to all parts of her body. She felt like a pathetic sister to those thousands of other women who had walked right into the *Summertime* syndrome with their eyes wide open.

When Marco returned he was soaked to the skin. She watched with distant eyes as he removed his shirt and slacks and dried off unselfconsciously in front of her. She hated the perfection of his tanned, lean body—and she hated her own weakness.

He opened the carved double doors of an old oak armoire and pulled some dry clothing from it. Meg's eyes lighted for a revealing instant on the colorful line of women's dresses that were also hanging in the wardrobe. Even a negligee! She might have suspected that she wasn't the first woman to share the delights of Marco's flokati rug, his considerable charm.

"You will be rescued in about an hour when my office assistant comes for us in his car. He was the only one I could reach," he said at last.

Sitting stiffly on the small couch, Meg simply nodded. The air between them grew thicker with each passing minute.

The rain was slackening. The thunder had rolled past and was making low noises somewhere to the south of them. When the car arrived they left the villa, separated from each other by a million miles.

The drive back was more than unpleasant. Meg had a violent headache behind her eyes and spent the whole time composing speeches to Marco. She wanted him to know where he had been mistaken about her, why she resented his casual use of her, why she could never be just one of many women in a man's black book....

But it was Marco who spoke first, depriving her of the advantage of the first strike. While they stood at the Venice parking garage waiting for a water taxi to take them into the city, he turned to her and said, "Is it merely a problem of American puritanism? Was I supposed to beg?"

"You couldn't be further from the truth," she shot back bitterly.

"Meg, listen to me! I don't want it to be this way. What happened at Villa Terza was the most natural thing that can happen between a man and a woman who are drawn to one another."

"If it feels good, do it? Is that what lovemaking means to you?" Anger was choking her voice. What a typical male justification of lust.

"Then you really don't understand me at all, do you?" he asked.

She didn't look up to meet his intent gaze. "Only too well," she said through the constriction in her throat. "You used your very advanced powers of persuasion on me, and I believed you for a little while. Frankly, I feel used!"

Marco said nothing more to her until they reached the Specchiato.

"Listen to me, Meg." He stopped her from passing

into the entrance gates. "I will not be placed in the role of seducer of young maidens. You knew exactly what to expect and you knew how to tease me with your appearance of naiveté. I found you very accomplished—very good at playing the wide-eyed innocent who needed protection. We Italians have a word for artifice: *malizietta*. Think about that when you meet other men. At least be fair to my successors!"

He jammed his key into the lock and threw the door open for her. "Sleep well," he rasped and started to walk away.

"You're not . . . ?"

"I'm not spending the night at the Specchiato. I have other arrangements."

"I'll be gone in the morning. I'll leave the keys with Lucia."

"Don't talk to strangers on the train," he said bitingly and was gone.

WITH THOSE UGLY WORDS it was ended. Meg finished packing as fast as she could, not caring if her things would wrinkle. Why should she care? She tore out the pages from her sketch book and put them into an envelope for Signor Prati. He could do with them as he wished. She had no business toying with petty intrigues of decadent Venetian families.

Thank goodness she had had the foresight to arrange for her tickets home. One more day in this place would be far too long!

Her watch said five o'clock. She called Signor Prati's office with apologies for her lateness. She had needed a few minutes to herself before she ventured out into the world of men again. When she left the palazzo she was looking as if the incident at the Villa Terza had never happened. She was growing adept at denial.... But that was a necessary part of maintaining her grip on sanity right now. She had an almost passionate haste to be finished with Venice, to put it behind her and start life where she had left off.

She walked quickly in the direction of the office of police. When she arrived Giulio Prati was surprised to see her in such a state of urgency. "Is there a problem other than a passport with which I could help you?" he asked solicitously.

"No," Meg said, sorry that she was so transparent. She would have to concentrate on steadying her nerves. "Thank you, *signore*. I've come to the end of my stay in Venice, and now I'm eager to return home."

A frown of concern creased his face. "Adella felt that you were enjoying your time in our city. Was it always your intention to leave so precipitously?"

"I...have a personal situation that cannot be resolved except by leaving." That probably wasn't the best thing to have said to this man whose business was curiosity.

"Oh? May I ask if it concerns my friend Marco? If it does, I shall have words to say to him for causing you distress." His eyes were warm with the best of masculine protectiveness.

"No, please. There is nothing to be said." She certainly didn't want to air her linen in front of Giulio Prati. "I'm only sorry that I won't be seeing Adella again. But I have the photos of her work, and I'm going to write an article about the tapestries very soon. Tell her how very much I enjoyed knowing her, will you?"

"Si." Prati looked at Meg for a moment as if to

assure himself that she was all right, then he showed her the new passport. "We, too, will be sorry not to see you again, very sorry. But that is your decision. Adella will be happy if you write to her. Will you be at this address when you return home?"

She nodded as she signed her name on the passport, then had a sudden thought. "Don't tell Signor Montevalde my address, please. It will make it easier for everyone if he doesn't contact me."

"If you request it, you have my word. May I ask if you were planning to leave with me certain drawings you made at the Specchiato?"

"I have them here." She handed him the envelope containing her sketches. "I never spoke of it to anyone."

"And there were no further curious events after that night?" he prodded gently. "Besides, of course, the incident of the Empress Earrings? Adella informed me of the confusion around them."

"That was all. Ugo was rather cruel to suggest that Teresa only imagined one of the ruby earrings had been taken. But I can't be sure that it was." Meg still had a feeling of apprehension about Ugo.

Signor Prati's eyebrows shot up with interest. "And now everything is as it was...the earrings are in the vault at the palazzo?" he asked smoothly.

"As far as I know. I saw them there, anyway. Teresa thinks that Ugo was trying to play on her nerves by temporarily taking one and then returning it. She's not happy at the thought that he may have the combination to the vault."

"I see. Maybe your ill-fated tour to Venice has been of great benefit to more people than you think," he said cryptically. "Please remember only the pleasant hours here and forget any others." He extended his hand to her.

"I plan to. Especially those I spent with you and Adella. And thanks for all you did to help me."

"Addio."

"Addio," she repeated and left his office with a heavy feeling in her heart.

THE TICKET AGENCY was just closing when Meg arrived, but when she quickly explained her need for haste the man relented and let her inside. At least something was going right, she thought, as he handed her the packet of tickets.

"These are for tomorrow...you're sure?" she demanded. Too many mishaps had occurred. She wasn't going to take anything on faith.

"Absolutely, *signorina*," the clerk said. "The eight o'clock express train to Milano and the one o'clock flight via Paris to Los Angeles. Confirmed."

She gave him the last of her traveler's checks to pay for the tickets. Fortunately, the agency had credited her with her tour fare so she had to pay only the difference between that and her new flight. But still it took the last of her money. She blessed Maude Draper at *Au Courant* for being so prompt with her three-hundred-dollar payment. Without that money.... Meg didn't even want to think of the problems she would be in right now.

THE TELEPHONE RANG several times that evening as she sat on the couch near the tall windows in the living room. She let it ring, until eventually it stopped altogether. There was nothing Marco could say that would alter the situation, and if he wanted her to admit that she had been wrong, he would be disappointed. Words were deceitful things, anyway. They could be twisted and shaped to say what they didn't mean. Meg knew that much from her journalism training.

She brought herself to an upright position at the sound of a key in the door. Teresa walked in and looked at her questioningly. "Something is wrong?" She went directly to Meg with her arms outstretched.

"I'm leaving in the morning. It's all arranged."

"You can't leave! I won't let you, Meg! It is Marco, isn't it?"

Meg pulled back from Teresa's warm embrace. Her own feelings were enough on edge; she couldn't take much more emotion.

Teresa sat down next to her on the couch. "I went to his office just now to pick up something I had left there and I saw him, working furiously at his drafting table. I asked him about your day at La Mira and he wouldn't talk about it. Meg, I didn't know...are you and Marco...?"

"Lovers?" she said acidly. Teresa's eyes were wide. "That is not the word I would use to describe us. We are so far from being lovers, it's laughable. In fact, I plan never to see him again until hell freezes over!" She knew she sounded extreme, but the words just tumbled out, to Teresa's apparent horror.

"But Enzo and I have arguments all the time, and it is never serious. What happened?"

"This is quite serious. A breach of trust, a grand delusion, a folly of vast dimensions. Oh, Teresa, I'm sorry! Maybe Marco *does* have good qualities—I'm sure he does. But I resent the fact that one man's Romeo complex will interfere with my friendship with you and Adella Prati! It isn't fair! And I hate to leave you just when you need support.'' Meg's tears were near the surface and she stopped.

''When are you leaving?'' Teresa asked softly.

''The express train at eight o'clock. I'll slip out quietly and not disturb you.''

''That is not the way of a friend. I will go with you to the station. You will need a good meal first before your very long day. Now, you look tired, Meg. Why not go to sleep. I will wake you at six. I won't try to convince you to stay longer with us. . .or to argue that Marco does not play Romeo. I can see in your eyes that it would do no good.''

They gave each other a brief hug and said good-night. Meg had a feeling of great loss. *Damn Marco Montevalde,* she wept to herself. *Damn him!* She climbed into bed and made a conscious attempt to blot out everything from her overheated brain. Emotionally wrung dry, she fell into a troubled sleep.

Some time later, in the middle of the night, she felt a solid weight on the bed near her legs, and she woke to a feeling of disorientation.

''Shh,'' a man's voice said, and she bolted upright. *Marco!* She pulled the covers up to her chin, gathering her wits as fast as she could. How dare he come into her bedroom!

A hand reached out to pull the covers away, groping in the darkness. Meg scrambled to the opposite side of the bed and stood up. She searched around wildly for something hard and heavy to fend him off.

Rough laughter rumbled from the man's throat and

Meg knew at once that it wasn't Marco. "Get out of here!" she hissed. "I'll call Signor Montevalde...the police!"

"I *am* Signor Montevalde!" He laughed again. "You don't have to call me!" He fell back onto the bed, laughing hysterically. Meg smelled the sickening odor of stale alcohol.

"Ugo—get out! If Marco knew you were here you would be in real trouble!" Meg wasn't afraid now. He was obviously drunk and nearly incoherent, but he had to go. She rang the call bell for Lucia and turned on the bedside light, then picked up her robe from the nearby chair.

"I have a message for you...." Ugo leaned forward with a deadly glare in his eyes. "Get out of Venice and don't talk to any more police." His words were slurred and measured. "Don't come back...and don't draw any more pictures!" He staggered to his feet and swayed toward her.

Lucia appeared in the doorway just then with a look of disgust on her face. "Oh, *signorina*, how sorry I am. He will leave here *subito*—now!" Even though Ugo was taller than she, the housekeeper half pulled and half carried him out of the room. Ugo was mumbling drunken words in Italian, but he didn't resist Lucia.

Meg heard the front door close and the latch thud into place. The older woman hurried back to apologize again. "He means nothing. He drinks too much and then...." She gestured with her hands. "He can sleep in the watchman's room."

After saying good-night, Lucia returned to her own bedroom. But just then Teresa hurried into Meg's room.

"Do not think that all Montevaldes are boorish and cruel," she said quietly. "Ugo and Marco are two completely different people."

With a hand on her shoulder Meg escorted her gently to the doorway. "It doesn't matter. I have no illusions one way or the other. I'm just sorry for the disturbance." She moved to shut the door, but Teresa didn't budge.

"Don't do this, Meg." Her face was anguished. "Don't become bitter. And don't leave our lives as suddenly as you came into them. I will write to you about all of us and I want you to write to me. You must!"

Meg sighed in defeat. Of course she couldn't leave Teresa like this. What rudeness! "In the morning I'll give you my address—but you must keep it in confidence."

"Until you tell me otherwise," Teresa smiled. She quickly kissed Meg's cheek, then left the room.

Meg couldn't get to sleep, left as she had been with Ugo's disturbing words. She stared at the shadowy ceiling thinking about the loose threads, the mismanaged relationships she had gathered in her short time in Venice. How did Ugo know she had seen the police, and how did he know about her sketches of the mirrored room? She had never been threatened before in her life and it left her with a cold feeling of fear.

TERESA WAS SILENT the next morning as they drank their cups of strong coffee and picked at their sweet rolls. There was nothing more to say about her departure, so Meg tried to speak of other things, like her hope that the Specchiato would one day be restored as it deserved.

As they were leaving, the palazzo bell rang several

times. Teresa went down to answer it and returned quickly with a long cardboard box.

"Something for you—from Ugo," she said, a question on her face.

Meg pulled the ribbon from the florist box and found a dozen red roses and a note.

"Ugo's usual apology when he has been bad," Teresa clucked.

Meg read the note:

I beg forgiveness for my condition last night. But my advice is still good—go home. It is where you belong. I say this for your benefit only. You are a nice woman, and Italy will hurt you if you stay. I wish you well,

Ugo

"Keep the roses," Meg said to Teresa. "I'm so sorry to be leaving you like this."

"I will be all right. Now, we must go. No matter what my personal wish, I would not be the cause of your missing the train." She put a sympathetic arm around Meg's waist, then picked up one of her suitcases.

CHAPTER ELEVEN

To Meg it seemed like no time before she was back home. Her mother, tearful and relieved, met her at Los Angeles International Airport. Meg assured her that all was well and that she was planning to go in to work the following day. She certainly didn't want to stay in her empty, silent apartment, nursing her jet lag and brooding. Work was the best medicine in the world.

Uncle Frank welcomed her with a long list of particulars for her to take care of right away. He had already hired a young college graduate to be her assistant. He wanted her to redesign *The Ledger*, expanding it to eight pages. The new format would include more photos and more in-depth interviews with leading tax experts in the city.

Meg was amazed at how quickly she was able to get back into the routine of work. She stayed on at the office most evenings, poring over pictures and artwork, and crawled home too tired to think of anything but sleep. Her ploy worked well for two weeks; then she had a fit of conscience about Adella Pratti and the article she'd planned to write. What kind of friend was she to shut out everything having to do with Venice?

With an effort of will she sat down one weekend and recreated on paper her meeting with Adella and the women who sewed for her. Carefully she steered her mind through the shoals of painful memory, staying far away from Marco.

The query letter she wrote to Maude Draper at *Au Courant* was sharp, factual and enticing, she thought. She included photos of some of Adella's most interesting designs and stressed how unique that kind of needlework was to the spirit of Italy. Meg put the letter into the mailbox at the corner on her way to work the next morning.

Within a week an envelope with the now-familiar *Au Courant* logo was dropped onto her desk by the mail clerk. Meg held it for a moment without opening it, then smiled at her cowardice. Her major life decisions seemed to be punctuated by letters from Maude Draper, whose name appeared just below the logo. To Meg's delight, her proposal for the article had been accepted. Maude's letter also included the magic word "job." "...entry level staff writing, but room to prove what you can do. Interested?"

An hour later Meg found herself sitting in Uncle Frank's office with a short, carefully worded letter of resignation in her hands. "I'm very sorry," she said in a professional voice, "but I've had a once-in-a-lifetime offer, and I've decided to take it. I know the new editor will do just fine in my place—she's quite competent."

"This isn't a complaint about your salary, is it, Meg? I told you that when you'd been here a year we would review it." Her uncle looked at her with shrewd eyes.

"It isn't just the pay," she explained. "I've been given a chance to move up in my field—to *Au Courant* magazine." The name felt good as she said it.

"As much as it goes against my grain to admit defeat, I must. Go on, Meg, try your wings. Just give us a week here to make the transition, will you?"

Meg had a request of her own to make. "If anyone tries to get in touch with me—from Italy—don't give out my address or the name of the magazine, all right?"

Her uncle lowered his brows and cleared his throat. "If you remember, my girl, I warned you about foreign travel." He smiled and stood up, putting an avuncular arm on her shoulder. "Good luck, honey—I mean it from my heart. I'm proud of you, Meg."

She left his office feeling a rush of warmth for him. Once back at her own desk she made a call to Maude Draper, setting up an appointment for later that afternoon. The address was on Sunset Boulevard, at the edge of Beverly Hills. A fashionable location.

Maude greeted her like an old friend. The woman was in her forties, tough but good-natured, with a narrow, clever-looking face. She was dressed in a khaki split skirt, a brightly patterned East Indian belt and a tan man-tailored silk blouse. Gold in profusion adorned her wrists, throat, ears and fingers.

Meg was quickly swept into Maude Draper's aura of positive thinking. She listened with her heart in her throat to the words, "I'd like to try you out for a few weeks here, see what you can come up with for us. You know the kind of things we like—nothing ordinary, nothing static. We're an upbeat outfit, and my gut feeling is that you'll do okay here. I'll pay you enough to keep the wolf from the door for the trial period, and after that we negotiate."

Maude took her by the shoulders and turned her around slowly. "First things first, though. You've got to start *looking* like *Au Courant*, as well as writing for it."

Meg nodded. She would have agreed to almost anything at that moment.

"I want you to get your wild head of curls down to my salon on Wilshire double quick, and tell Raoul I sent you. He knows what I like. Then get a couple of casual outfits—some slacks and a suit—and a dinner dress at Celine's. And check the blouses at Gucci's. I can't have you looking like you just climbed out of the old sorority house, can I?"

"But. . . I can't afford all this!"

"Who said anything about paying for it? This is all part of the job, Meg. Consider it your uniform. I've got a big fat budget item labeled "business expenses: clothes and accessories." The one thing that's okay is your handbag. Where did you get it?"

"In Venice. I was in Italy on my vacation."

"Terrific! And Meg, honey. . . don't take my bark too seriously. Everyone'll tell you I'm basically harmless. Just give me some fabulous writing, and you'll see only the pussycat side of me." She pulled an angelic face, then her sharp features erupted into warm laughter. "Honest!"

Meg walked out of Maude's office feeling the best she had since leaving Venice. Maude's assistant, a tall and polished redhead named Charlene, escorted her back to the reception area, where she announced that she would go with Meg on her beauty rounds. "Maude comes on strong and then apologizes every time," she confided. "But she's in deadly earnest about the *Au Courant* look. Every one on our staff who has any contact with the public buys clothes on Rodeo Drive, believe it or not." Charlene's emerald silk dress with its assymetrical neckline went well with her blunt 1920s haircut. Meg decided she was experiencing culture shock already.

"Lead the way before I wake up," she grinned.

At the salon Raoul himself took charge of Meg, nodding distractedly as she told him what she wanted. Feeling like a prisoner in her pink smock and towels, Meg looked pleadingly at Charlene, who merely shrugged and smiled.

With flashing scissors, Raoul set to work on her newly shampooed hair. Off came two inches of her honey-colored curls; he was adamant about that. What was left he proceeded to brush back into a very chic French roll that spiraled up the back of her head. He showed her how to shape the hairdo herself, then explained how she could leave it loose for casual occasions.

Meg emerged looking sleek and cool—and definitely attractive, she had to admit. Having her hair swept back did interesting things to her eyes, and brought her cheekbones into prominence. Raoul had swirled a partial side bang on her forehead, an artistic touch that added a little softness.

She thanked him with enthusiasm and offered him a tip, which he refused with offended dignity.

At Celine's, Gucci's and two other places on Rodeo Drive Meg discovered that all she had to say was, "This, this, and that," and it was hers. Charlene stayed with her, urging her to select certain items she was sure Maude would approve of.

A few hours later Meg walked out of the last shop, carrying a number of elegant zippered bags. The salesclerks in every store had been extraordinarily helpful and pleasant. Her spree hadn't been the intimidating experience she might have expected.

In the weeks that followed Maude drove her hard, demanding better and better writing and being ruthless with her blue pencil. Meg polished up an article she had begun earlier in the year about the similarities between animals and their owners.

Maude liked it, drew her out about her ideas, and then changed direction 180 degrees. Meg's new assignment was to write about the most "in" pets of the international social set. When she started to explain that she didn't know how to get that kind of information, Maude insisted that she *did*. "Start with the celebrity veterinarians and go from there," she ordered.

Meg discovered aptitudes in herself she hadn't known existed. She was becoming good at interviewing people about the most off-the-wall subjects, and was doing her best to discover that special tone and style of writing that *Au Courant* was known for. The experience wasn't without some pain, but Maude provided an occasional "bravo!" As for her new look, Meg was learning not to be surprised whenever she passed a mirror.

She still went weak when the thought of Marco came unexpectedly to mind. The first autumn thunderstorm brought back the events at the Villa Terza with agonizing clarity. Once, in an elevator, a man was wearing Marco's brand of cologne, and tears welled up in Meg's eyes. In this respect she was still a victim of her tenuous emotions, hardly the sophisticated Southern California bachelor girl.

A scattering of casual dates with men who knew only the "*Au Courant*" Meg Brown turned out to be depressingly predictable. She grew tired of sushi restaurants, of modern-jazz combos at little clubs, of the obligatory groping at the door of her apartment. Her last date, a stockbroker friend of Charlene's, had resented her refusal. "What are you saving it for?" he had fired at her before he strode back to his silver Porsche.

But Meg was still wounded. Time wasn't improving the ache in her breast or the need to feel Marco's electrifying touch on her skin. She dreaded going to sleep each night because Marco was a painfully persistent visitor to her dreams, and she often woke up shaken by the urgency of his kisses. She had to work it out with herself, she knew. Meanwhile she still jumped at the sound of a foreign accent, and had that split second of hesitation as she opened her mailbox. All in all, even with her wonderful job at *Au Courant*, she was anything but peaceful and content.

In late November she was made a full-time member of the staff, one of the special-assignment writers. The salary negotiations turned out to be a simple dialogue, with Maude saying, "How about such and such per month?" and Meg replying, "Fine." The amount was more than Uncle Frank would have given her if she'd stayed with *The Ledger* for years.

Meg's one connection to Venice was with Teresa. At first the Italian woman said nothing about Marco in her letters, writing mostly about her problems with Enzo. Then, two letters in a row, she included a second sealed envelope, addressed in Marco's distinctive handwriting. Each time, an agony of longing and regret overwhelmed Meg, but she refused to open them. Instead she held them close for a long moment, savoring the nearness of his energy. Then she carefully put them into a larger envelope and returned them to Teresa, with a note that said, "Please don't send me any letters but your own."

A quick response came back:

> Dearest Meg, I beg you not to turn my cousin away. His family problems are grave—much worse than you think. Ugo's vendetta has led to something far more severe, but I am too ashamed to speak of it. Believe me, dear Meg, Marco is a good man! He is in danger of losing the heritage that is rightfully his...I cannot say more....

Was this Marco's idea, to play on her sympathies with melodramatic stories? No doubt Ugo *was* spiteful, but why should she care about the personal problems of a man she hoped never to see again? A forlorn thought prodded at Meg's stubborn mind: Teresa was so certain that he was a man of honor and sensitivity....

Teresa's next letter, which came early in December, rambled on about her fears that she and Enzo would never marry. He still refused to have his wife support him.

> He will hear nothing. Oh, Meg, if only the Holy Mother in heaven would find a way for him to receive an important commission. Anything! We are both so miserable!
>
> I have enclosed photographs of Enzo's latest works—some of his smaller pieces. I especially like the classical figure, which a friend of my mother commissioned him to do. In spite of Enzo's modernistic soul he has made a beautiful sculpture of a

child playing a lute—just like a Veronese painting! Write me soon....

Christmas came, with Uncle Frank hosting his usual elaborate family supper. The California weather was sparkling and balmy, yet Meg felt strangely cheerless. Even her relatives' warmly sincere toast to her future at *Au Courant* didn't lighten her mood. She raised her Venetian-glass goblet anyway, with all the zest she could muster.

After dinner, while her mother, aunt and uncle reminisced about Christmases past, she brooded unobtrusively. Three months ago she'd had a tiresome job and had imagined herself in love. Today she was on her way in a fabulous career and her heart felt like ice.

Her mother turned sentimental eyes toward her. "It must be doubly hard for you to celebrate a family occasion, dear, what with Jim gone...."

"What...? Oh...yes, mother." She saw the others exchange knowing looks, and tried not to squirm. *Dear God, it isn't that at all,* she cried to herself. How eager she was to get back to the solitude of her little apartment! She wished she had a story to be working on. However, Maude had given her a Christmas gift—no work during the holiday week.

Later that night she gave in and allowed herself to wonder what Christmas would be like in Venice. Teresa had written recently that the weather was frigid and windy and there was always a fire roaring in the fireplace of the Specchiato's apartment. Every letter from her friend brought too many images to Meg's mind. She still felt a stab of excitement whenever an

Italian postmark appeared in her mailbox. Those envelopes held the fleeting familiar fragrance of Italy.

Meg refused a date for New Year's Eve, and celebrated that occasion with a few private and painful tears. Teresa's holiday greetings had included a Polaroid shot of Marco, Enzo and herself standing in front of the Specchiato doors. Meg had understood Teresa's motives and smiled wryly at her determination. She went to sleep New Year's Eve with the photo on the bedside table, propped against Marco's vase.

After Christmas she submerged herself in her work again, but she also wrote a long letter to the Pratis. Poor Adella would be wondering if her article had ever been written, and now Meg could tell her what Maude was planning for it. Some time that summer *Au Courant* was going to devote an entire issue to Italy. Not every story was scheduled as yet, but Adella's was definitely going to be one of them.

Maude was being secretive about plans for the Italian issue. She sometimes left cryptic memos on the desks of her feature writers, demanding information about the wine season in the Veneto region, or the piazzas of central Italy.

Meg worked on a series of local fashion articles and on Adella's story until early March, when one of Maude's memos came across her desk:

> Set up interview with Roscoe Veitch. Get background on his new institute for Renaissance studies. Must have this for Italian issue. Roscoe's a sweetheart! Be sure to get latest data about the architecture competition....

The woman who answered the telephone at Veitch's office sounded very welcoming and set up a luncheon interview at his Malibu home. Meg did a little digging in the local library to discover just who Roscoe Veitch was. By the time she'd finished she was looking forward to meeting this colorful old-timer who had started as a wildcatter in the oil fields of the Oklahoma panhandle and had made a fortune in cement and trucking since then. If she couldn't get a great story out of him and his architectural competition, she didn't deserve to be on the *Au Courant* payroll.

She was met at the door of the Veitch estate by a large white-haired man with a weathered face. "Welcome to my little place!" he boomed, extending a beefy hand. It was Mr. Veitch himself.

"Rosebud's back in the kitchen fixin' us something good for lunch. She told me to keep you away for a while. . . get the institute out of my system before we sit down to eat. After nearly fifty years, Rosebud knows me pretty well!"

He walked her to the edge of the broad front terrace. "There it is, honey!" he said in a pleased voice. "My institute'll stand right over there, on the best piece of real estate I could find."

Meg followed the sweep of his hand to a plateau across a small canyon. "On the top there'll be the main buildings and down the hill is gonna be a park, kind of a replica of the Tivoli Gardens. . . you know, that little bit of paradise outside of Rome. You ever been to Italy?"

She nodded. "Last year. . . on a tour. We didn't have time to see Tivoli."

"Well, don't miss it next time you go. Or better yet, watch what I do with this raw acreage. I'm doin' it for

Rosebud. Gosh, I love that woman! I want to do somethin' real special for her, too. But I haven't made up my mind what yet." He looked at Meg and grinned. "I suppose you think I'm just a country boy with no business dreamin' big dreams. Leave that to the Ivy League fellas, right?"

Meg sensed he was testing her, but she had to answer him honestly. "Mr. Veitch—"

"Roscoe, honey. Just plain Roscoe," he interrupted.

"Well. . . Roscoe," she said and smiled. "You're far from being a simple country boy, from what I hear. You probably know how to leave the Ivy League boys choking in your dust."

"Is that flattery, little lady?" he demanded.

"*Au Courant* wouldn't have sent me out here to interview a man who had nothing to say about a lot of things." She took out her notebook and pen to emphasize her point. "I think you're a lot sharper than most men *because* of how you started out, not in spite of it."

"Maude Draper sent me the right gal, didn't she?" he laughed. "Okay, listen to this." He began to describe every detail of his dream for an institute of Renaissance studies. The idea for the architectural competition had come to him after he had taken a long hard look at the latest styles of academic buildings—and had been disappointed. "People need to get inspiration from the environment," Roscoe mused loudly. "If I was a scholar I couldn't learn worth beans in some ugly mountain of cement, steel and smoked glass. Even if cement means a lot to me. But I'm damned if a whole lot of it belongs on the outside of my institute!" He laughed heartily and checked his watch. "Uh, oh! Rosebud'll be wonderin' where we are!"

Rosebud Veitch turned out to be a motherly no-nonsense woman who knew her rambunctious husband only too well. She greeted Meg with a hug, apologizing for her wet hands. "Maria's day off in the kitchen... but it feels good to get back to basics once in a while. I suppose Roscoe's been talking your head off about his institute while you scarcely got a word in edgewise!"

"Not at all," Meg protested. "I'm fascinated by everything. It's just incredible that one man could do so much to forward a cultural institute—a real gift to the world—and not have any of the usual committees and advisors."

"Now wait a minute!" Roscoe thundered. "I've got Rosebud! She's all the committee I need. If my Rosie says I'm way off base on an idea, I listen."

He seated Meg on a wide enclosed verandah, which overlooked the Pacific Ocean on one side and the site of the institute on the other. "Rosie's the one who arranged for a roomful of experts to go over the entries and tell me how sound they were. I don't pretend to be an engineer. But when it comes to picking out the winner, good design is simple to spot, and that job I'll reserve for myself! I don't care if the winner's got credentials from here to Borneo! He's got to be my kind of person with my kind of vision."

Rosebud silenced her husband with a steaming plate of chili, then started a conversation of her own. Meg soon found herself on the wrong end of the interview. By the time her visit was over Rosebud knew everything—almost—about her, from her teenage infatuation with Italy, her unhappy engagement, and her trip to Venice to her present situation. Marco's name was never mentioned, but the talk of Italy started the old dull heartache and brought memories of him flooding back to her.

When she absolutely had to leave, Roscoe saw her to her car. "I'm a stubborn old coot, Meg. Put that in your story if you want to. I'm proud as hell of what I do, and it's the last time in my life I'll have a chance to do something really big. I know that and my doctors know that. Hope to see you again real soon, girl. You can tell Maude I don't want anyone else doin' our story but you. I'll expect you at the mayor's cocktail party Friday. A bunch of my finalists'll be there." He winked. "I'm gonna do this thing right. Got to stir up a little media interest—for Sunday, when I announce my winner."

Meg left with the feeling that she had known Roscoe and Rosebud all her life. But she still didn't know exactly how Roscoe was running his architectural contest. She sensed that the old fox was telling her only what he wanted her to know—no more, no less. She wasn't even certain exactly why he was building this grand institute of his. Some journalist she was!

THE NEXT FRIDAY Meg was once again in Malibu, on the site of the institute-to-be. She spent the whole morning on assignment with one of *Au Courant*'s staff photographers, Snapper Medwin, the easy-going but meticulous sidekick she had acquired at Maude's request. The two of them trudged over the Malibu hills while he lived up to his nickname, taking pictures from every possible angle—behind boulders, through artistically bare branches of shrubs, with the ocean as backdrop—utilizing the full limit of Snapper's prolific artistic sensibilities.

"We can't possibly use a single more photo," Meg complained at last. She was looking distractedly at the workers who were busy setting up several ornate medieval-looking tents at the center of the building site. The bright canvas flaps blew in the steady ocean breeze, and Meg hugged herself against the early spring coolness.

"Mine is not to reason why," Snapper said amiably. "If Maude wants to pay for the film, I'll do the rest. You should know how she is by now. A thousand shots make her a lot sweeter to deal with than a hundred!"

The lovely tents and the buffet tables inside were for Roscoe's ground breaking, two days hence. With the finalists being introduced at the mayor's party that afternoon, Roscoe wasn't giving himself much time to choose the winner. Meg dearly hoped he knew what he was doing.

"Tell me that's your last shot, Snap! And don't forget you're going to have to be with me at the cocktail party this afternoon at three o'clock. I've got a lot of things to go over with Maude before lunch. Most of the finalists are coming in today."

"Okay—that's all, honey," Snapper said. "Let's get back to the office."

Like an old pro Meg maneuvered her car around the looping curves of unpaved road leading to the busy Pacific Coast Highway. The sweep of hills, stretching down to the cliffs below, was covered with homes, swimming pools, green lawns, trees and flowers. The film colony had made Malibu famous. The nearby Getty Museum was drawing serious tourists as well, and now, in a few years, Roscoe's Renaissance institute would probably be the crown jewel, focusing world attention on the hills of Malibu.

Meg had to smile at the way her career had suddenly opened up. Six months ago the most she had hoped for was some humble reporting position, an article now and then, and perhaps some research work. And here she was, driving a sporty company car and definitely on her way up. Even Uncle Frank was impressed.

"You look awfully cheerful for someone who has to attend one of the mayor's bashes," Snapper commented. He gave her one of his attractive smiles. "How about dinner after the chores are done? I know a good new fish place." He looked hopeful.

Meg's nerves tensed. This wasn't the first time he had asked her out. In a way he reminded her of Jim—a kind of all-American young man with the added quality of a creative sensitivity. He had won some respected photo prizes.

"Well, how about it?" he asked again.

Meg had pretty much stopped dating altogether these last months. Opportunities hadn't been lacking, but the memories just wouldn't go away. The thought of even a good-night kiss from a man was distasteful, because it wouldn't be Marco's lips on hers. Six months hadn't been long enough to erase the hurt, no matter how she tried to forget him. Her frequent correspondence with Teresa only kept the longing alive in that stubborn corner of herself that couldn't let him go completely.

Snapper was waiting for her answer. "Okay," she finally said, "just a friendly dinner. I'm not ready for more than that."

He gave her a penetrating look. "Whatever you say, m'dear. I'll even let you cry on my shoulder."

She gave his hand a quick pat and laughed lightly, then changed the subject. "Sometime before the cocktail party I have to find a few minutes to bone up on the finalists. I don't even know who they are, or where they're from. Maude's going to brief me. She's the only one Roscoe is talking to nowadays about his secret plans."

As Meg pulled the car into her assigned space in the parking garage Snapper looked at her seriously. "Listen, if it makes you uncomfortable to go out tonight, I understand."

"No, I'm looking forward to it, honest. And don't worry that I have some deep dark past. I shouldn't have indicated that I do."

CHAPTER TWELVE

MEG HAD ABANDONED THE IDEA of lunch, the scheduling was just too tight. Instead, she took a few minutes to tend to her appearance. The dust of Malibu was still on her shoes, and the ocean air had probably done awful things to her hair.

She rushed up to the top floor of the *Au Courant* complex and into the luxurious women's lounge. First she freshened her makeup. Then with a few flicks of her brush she smoothed her hair into its sophisticated setting again.

In the wall of mirrors she presented a charming picture, even if she did still find it hard to recognize this new face and sleekly defined figure. Her wheat-colored silk suit was a creation of François Vitelli, the French-Italian boy wonder whose designs were starting to make stiff competition in fashion circles. *Au Courant* had run an article about him recently, and in gratitude he had sent Maude this suit. Fortunately for Meg, Maude hated it and had passed it down to her, since they were the same size. Meg loved the soft ruffles of the off-white blouse and the loose drape of the suit jacket.

She reached into her purse for a little packet of tissue paper and unwrapped a cluster of velvet violets for her rolled collar. Aunt Harriet's alexandrite pendant and fine gold chain were there, too. The round-cut stone glowed with fire against the V of her creamy throat. With that as a finishing touch she felt ready for the afternoon's fete.

Her watch said 11:45 as she strode confidently into the elegant reception foyer and headed for the big double opaque glass doors that led to Maude's executive suite. As she pressed against the right-hand door someone else approached from the other side.

Meg's momentum made the man step back to let her pass. The silvery tint of the glass made him a blur, but she realized she had been discourteous. She turned with an apology on her lips and stopped short. Her heart lurched.

Marco Montevalde stood looking down at her with a slight polite smile.

"Oh!" she gasped. "Wh...what are you doing here?"

Now that Meg was facing him fully his expression changed to recognition. "I might ask you the same, Signorina Meg Brown. It *is* you, is it not?"

The deep tones of his voice started an uncontrollable reflex in her solar plexus. The reality of him—the dream that never stopped haunting her—was overwhelming. She wanted to throw herself into his arms.

"Y...yes. I work here." She gave a tiny cough, trying to open her tense throat. "I'm just surprised to see you, Signor Montevalde." Her mind was racing. Had Teresa broken her promise? No, Marco seemed as surprised as she was. But Teresa must have known he was coming to *Au Courant* and they might meet. Wily Teresa!

His eyes were cool and intent. "*E vero?* Surely you know that *Au Courant* is featuring the architectural contest for the Veitch Institute for Renaissance Studies?"

"Of course, but...I've...."

"I am one of the finalists, *signorina*. No doubt you recall that I am an architect and that I was preparing a proposal for a large project?" He stepped back and looked at her with a tight smile. "You have changed."

His eyes narrowed. "Tell me, Signorina Brown, why you left me without a word...why you have returned my letters unopened! A poor return for the courtesies I showed you in my city and my home." His voice had a hard cold edge.

"P...please, Marco. I was certain you would have forgotten me by now. I...I wasn't ungrateful, and I left a thank-you note for you and Lucia."

"Dannazione!" he exploded. "A polite little thank-you note! I demand an explanation!" The words hissed from between his clenched teeth.

Meg reeled back from the force of his emotion but his hand shot out, grasping her arm. His fingers dug into the tender flesh beneath her silk sleeve.

"So that's where you are, Meg," Maude's strong voice drawled from across the broad antechamber of the suite. She stood in the open door of her private office. "Signor Montevalde, you seem to know my most valued assistant, Meg Brown."

Marco froze. He turned, shifting his hand to Meg's other elbow. "We became friends in Italy, but I did not at once recognize Signorina Brown. There has been a change—a most delightful change." His smile was suddenly full of charisma. Meg wished he wouldn't smile like that.

"Hmm," Maude remarked. "Well, this *is* interesting." She gave Marco a warm smile. "I was just about to order lunch for Meg and me. Since the two of you are friends, why not join us? Especially in view of the plans for the ceremonies at your palazzo—there's still so much to arrange before you get swept up in Roscoe Veitch's awards activities. How about it?"

"*Piacere*—my pleasure," Marco said with a slight bow.

Maude, her eyes bright with speculation, led them through her office and out onto the glassed-in terrace, where a table was ready. Fuchsias bloomed from huge hanging baskets, and topiary boxwood cut into fanciful shapes decorated the corners. Maude went to the small rattan bar and poured drinks, phoned for an extra lunch and busied herself with getting another place setting from the drawers of the bar. Meanwhile Meg huddled in one of the cushioned wicker chairs with her glass of sherry, and Marco stood with his gin and tonic looking out over the city.

Maude caught Meg's forlorn eyes and then gazed at the broad stiff back of Marco Montevalde. She pursed her lips in a silent whistle, then went to stand beside him. To Meg's further discomfort Maude started questioning him in her usual blunt manner about how he and Meg had met in Italy. He sketched a picture of what had happened, ending with the remark that his cousin Teresa had been quite unhappy to have Meg leave. "Signorina Brown left a number of loose ends behind her in her hasty departure." He smiled noncommittally.

Maude, her eyes more keen than ever, invited her guests to the lunch table. After a waiter had served the plates of salad and fruit she fixed Meg with a playful glance, under which curiosity and iron determination were mixed. "You were naughty not to tell me that you knew this gorgeous man."

Meg's stomach tightened, and she considered making a quick suicidal dash through the pebbly glass screen. "It didn't seem important," she heard her own voice saying on a flat note.

"Not important! Great heavens, Meg! I've been racking my brains for the right person to do advance coordinating in Venice, and here you are, right under my nose—capable and a friend of the family as well! This story is going to be the very centerpiece of the Italian issue. Think of it. . . the Montevalde family graciously turns over its incredibly beautiful palazzo to the public and *Au Courant* gets the exclusive right to the first story about it. The paintings, the jewels, the Marco Polo Cup—everything! And you sit here like a shy violet when you have all the qualifications I've been looking for."

Marco nodded and smiled at Meg, but not with his eyes. "Most fortunate," he said crisply.

Maude took over the conversation. There would be a gala showing of the newest Italian designs by François Vitelli himself. "We're even toying with the idea of having a tableau showing Marco Polo presenting his jeweled cup to the Doge of Venice." She waved an impatient hand. "It's going to be absolutely splendid!"

"I trust the beautiful people who attend will make contributions toward the restoration of the Specchiato," Meg said somewhat sharply.

"Of course, of course. That's the whole point of the gala," Maude scolded, then put a hand lightly on Marco's. "If you win the Veitch prize, Signor Montevalde, then you can use some of that money to fix the palazzo yourself, right?"

"Please, God," he said in a rich velvety tone. "The city will give special protection and guards for the treasure. The mirrored ballroom will at least be restored before the presentation—*if* I am the winner. If not. . . ." He shrugged.

His eyes caught Meg's for a second, and she felt a stab of pain. Was he remembering their midnight dance in the mirrored room?

Maude flew along on a river of words again. "I'll send Snapper and some of our best people with you, Meg. You won't be like a little lost lamb, believe me. François is difficult, but he likes women—a bit unusual for a man in his profession. If he raises a fuss just let it blow over and do what you think is right. I'm putting you in full charge until I get there a few days before the actual bash. You'll be more like a coordinator; the social part, with invitations and all that, will be taken care of."

Maude was like a steamroller, flattening even a hint of protest, and Meg was silent for most of the lunch, cringing at Maude's expansive plans for her. So Marco was one of Roscoe's finalists! Why hadn't she put two and two together and figured that out? Marco must think her a perfect fool, on top of everything else. But why had he encouraged Maude to assign her to the Venice story? She struggled to keep her eyes away from him. She hadn't forgotten the fine line of his lips or the autocratic tilt of his head, and she hated herself for trembling at the very sight of him.

The discussion moved to the qualifications of the other finalists. Marco withheld his own opinions and merely nodded. Then, finally, it was two o'clock and Marco rose, explaining that he had to return to his hotel to dress for the mayor's party. He bowed over Maude's hand and then Meg's. The butterfly touch of his firm lips sent heat surging through Meg's body. Nothing had changed in her involuntary responses to him.

Maude sat quietly for a moment after the outer door had closed behind him. Meg's heart didn't just feel like lead; it *was* lead—a real weight. She mustn't start to cry, or she'd be a mess for the mayor's reception.

Maude took her hand in a hard grip. "Don't cry over men, baby," she growled. "So he got to you—it's not the end of the world." She put a gentle hand to Meg's hot cheek. "But wow, he *is* a hunk of man! Who knows. . . if you do a really fine job, he might—"

"Don't, Maude," Meg whispered. "I've been enough of an idiot, and I don't think I can do what you want—go to Italy and all."

"Nonsense!" She got up and paced with quick stabs of her stiletto heels on the terrace floor. "This is your big chance, honey. For your career. . . if you don't want *him*. But if I were you, I'd fight for him. I saw how he looked at you."

"All Italian men look at women," Meg said drearily.

Maude barked a laugh. "Okay, okay. I guess he is a bit big league for a beginner like you. It would take quite a woman to tie up that elegant devil." She watched with a shrewd gleam while Meg took the offered bait.

A flash of competitive anger flooded through her, then a horrid reality took over. What did it matter? She probably could have him for a night without any trouble—or for many nights. But she would have only part of him—an uncertain paradise with no real clue to when it might end.

"Honey, were the two of you lovers in Italy—is that what it's about?"

"No, but we came...too close for my self-respect." Meg turned her head away.

Maude made a strangled sound and said, "This is the twentieth century. He probably thought nothing of it, except if you turned him down. That might have been a new experience for him."

Meg decided to be frank. "You may think I'm silly," she began, "but I went to Italy on the strength of a fascination." The story of her *Summertime* obsession spilled out to Maude's sympathetic ear. "You see," she concluded, "Marco seemed to step right out of my fantasy. But you're right—I'm not cut out to deal with him."

"I suppose you were nice and honest and told him about this *Summertime* thing?"

"I'm afraid so."

"Lord!" Maude remarked to the city view. "Well, my girl, he was probably giving you a little bit of the dream to take home with you. I can't say it wouldn't have been a temptation. Did he try to get in touch with you?"

"I...sent his letters back unopened."

Maude stared. "Weren't you even curious?"

"Of course! But I couldn't have him think...."

"And you love him." Maude touched her hand lightly. "Poor kid. But you are friends with Teresa, his cousin?"

Meg nodded. "We still correspond."

"Nothing could be better! Now listen to me, Meg. Whatever you believe Marco Montevalde thinks of you, you've got a chance to show him a new Meg Brown.

You can do the job—help make his palazzo come to life—do something for the city that you love. Keep Teresa for a friend. And then. . . just be pleasantly cool to Marco." She sighed. "I don't want you to throw away such a boost to your career. You're talented, my dear, and if nothing else develops, you can leave him with the memory of a fine capable woman. What do you say?"

Meg's thoughts ran around frantically. Even if it hurt, she wanted to go back to Venice, to the Specchiato and Teresa and Adella—and to Marco. Maybe she *could* help him. That would be her payment for the kindness he said she had not appreciated. "Standing on pride gets to be uncomfortable," she said at last. "I'll get over Marco Montevalde. . . and I do want to go back to Venice, even if it hurts. I'll try to do a good job. I really want to!"

"Okay!" Maude pulled her into a hug. "Now, we've got business to talk about."

THE MAYOR'S COCKTAIL PARTY was being held in a hotel garden in the center of Beverly Hills. Meg and Snapper presented their credentials at the entrance to the main reception area. Once inside, they were immediately surrounded by people who had been told that *Au Courant* was covering the event.

Being among the architectural finalists and their associates and publicity agents was more like being at a theatrical press conference than a formal social event. The male foreign contestants were full of suave compliments for Meg, the *Au Courant* rep. A big hearty German offered to drive her home, with dinner included. She could have her choice of Ma Maison or Scandia.

The Dane sidled up to her and suggested a cozy lunch, so he could fill her in on his background. *How can this woman be best appealed to,* their eyes said. It was the closest Meg had ever come to being a celebrity, and she didn't like it one bit.

She felt as if she was in a knot, dreading and yet wanting to see Marco. Then she found him, flanked by two lovely women, a real blonde and a counterfeit one. "Oh—here they are, the people from *Au Courant*," the latter said vivaciously.

Marco came forward somewhat stiffly and introduced the women—Contessa Antonia Alandi and Mrs. Bette Slocum. Meg tried to control her expression. This must be the countess—the one interested in Marco—whom Adella Prati had described. She was a real beauty, with silken blond hair pulled into a knot and large blue eyes.

Meg was already acquainted with the other face and the too-blond hair. Bette Slocum's jet-set life was well documented in society columns around the world. Her scarlet-nailed hand rested on Marco's arm, and Meg was reminded of a large capricious cat.

Snapper went to work with his camera, and there was some polite jostling between the women to pose as close to Marco as possible. Every move of his graceful body and turn of his fine head was a disturbance to Meg, though she dutifully took notes and asked a few seemingly interested questions. In a way she was glad to be seeing Marco in this situation—his normal environment. He was the very picture of the society architect. It was obvious that she had no place in his life, none at all. *Then why are you having such a hard time keeping your hands from shaking,* her inner voice demanded.

Bette Slocum placed herself in Meg's path as Marco moved off to meet the mayor. "I must check to see that my name is spelled correctly," the woman said. Meg took note of the spelling under her probing eyes. "Aren't you the sick little tourist who Marco rescued last year in Venice? Ugo Montevalde told me all about you. What a clever boy he is! Marco doesn't appreciate how much Ugo cares about the palazzo and its fabulous treasures."

Before Meg could reply, Bette Slocum's harsh voice pressed on, "Ugo didn't say you were a reporter for *Au Courant*."

"I wasn't at that time, Mrs. Slocum. I got this job after I returned home." Meg suddenly realized she had an active feeling of dislike for this hard-eyed woman.

She felt a light touch on her shoulder. "Meg is more than a reporter, Bette," Maude's voice said from behind. "She's now a feature editor, in charge of the Specchiato project." Maude quickly introduced herself to the Contessa Alandi, who had moved close to them in the crowded room. Then she linked arms with Bette Slocum, and they both headed in Marco's direction.

Standing with the countess, Meg asked the first trivial question she could think of: "How long will you be in California?"

The Italian woman shrugged her slender shoulders. "I simply had to come to meet the American tycoon who is doing this delightful Renaissance institute. And to help my darling Marco, of course," she smiled patronizingly. Meg made a pretense of taking notes.

"I have not yet met Signor Veitch, but I like tycoons. They know what they want." She gave Meg a shrewd look. "You know the man?"

"Yes. I'm working with him for the special edition of *Au Courant*. He is a remarkable gentleman."

"I see. You are of influence, then?" She favored Meg with a deliberate smile. "Surely you can use your position to sway the granting of the prize. Marco should be the one to win. Who but an Italian in love with the beauty of his own heritage should win, eh?"

Meg bit back a sharp retort. "I'm only slightly acquainted with Signor Montevalde."

"Oh," the countess purred with a tiny commiserating smile. "In that case you are not of much use—or do I mean to say help? Will you indicate to me Signor Veitch, *per favore*?"

Meg complied, pointing him out across the room, where he was standing beside his wife. Rosebud was resplendent in huge baroque pearls, and diamonds that sparkled on her bosom, which was covered in rose pink tulle.

Marco could have his countess, Meg muttered to herself. If she ruined things for him by pressuring Roscoe, he deserved it.

She turned away to look for Snapper. A warm hand closed on her arm and her body automatically grew rigid. Without looking up she knew who it was.

"I want you to meet me after this is over, *signorina*," Marco's voice growled. "We will go somewhere to talk."

"I'm afraid that's impossible." Meg gave a tug to free her arm, but wasn't successful. "I have a date."

"Break it." His fingers closed tightly.

"I won't. We have nothing to say."

"I disagree." Marco gave her arm an angry shake. "Your superior, Signorina Maude Draper, insists on appointing you to be in charge of the Specchiato celebration. So, my cold little *piccione*, we had better come to a working truce. Nothing more. I will meet you by the entrance door at six o'clock." Before she could say anything he had left her and was making his way toward the Veitches.

"Hey," Snapper said as he loped toward her. "Come on, I've got some more architectural egos lined up. You look funny. . . everything okay?"

"I'm fine."

She worked hard, concentrating on her interviews and notes, yet still feeling the tantalizing bonds of energy and response that bound her to Marco against her will. She was disgusted with her own frailty. Even his rough touch on her arm became a thing to recall with excitement.

Roscoe's voice sounded close by; he had discovered her. "There's my darlin'," he boomed. Meg found herself being heartily embraced by him and Rosebud in turn. Released from Rosebud's perfumed hug, Meg looked up to find Marco's amber eyes fixed on her. She felt them probing her defenses.

While Snapper was arranging a group picture with quick efficiency, Roscoe leaned close to Marco and lowered his voice to a fraction of its usual pitch. "We've got to have a talk soon. Why don't you bring Meg out to the house for breakfast tomorrow? About seven-thirty, and just keep it quiet. I'm not supposed to be hobnobbing with a finalist, I guess. But I've got a few questions, and I want to hear about your palace. They tell me it's falling into the cana. . . er. . . it could use some repairs. I'm thinking about giving a jag of money for Venice restorations and I need your views. These fund-raising committees never tell me the straight stuff—always hedging or saying what they think I want to hear. How about it?"

Meg desperately wanted to ease out of the invitation. "Roscoe...I've got to be at work in the morning."

"We won't take no for an answer, honey," Rosebud said in an iron-sweet voice. "Roscoe will make it okay with Maude, won't you, darlin'?"

"Sure thing. See you kids at seven-thirty. Don't be late." He turned to greet some waiting friends, and Bette Slocum appeared to tug Marco away in another direction.

"Whew," Snapper said under his breath. "*He's* the one you met in Italy?"

She hesitated. "Yes."

"Definitely old-world. I don't think I'd like to cross him. Gets what he wants, I'll bet."

"I guess so...come on, there's more to do."

BY SIX O'CLOCK Meg was truly weary, her notebook crammed with names and life histories of the finalists, as well as tidbits of her own observations. The guests had gone, the mayor's staff and security agents dispersed, and now the waiters were cleaning up the debris. Meg hoped Roscoe had achieved the kind of publicity he wanted and laid solid groundwork for a broad acceptance of his new institute by the powers-that-be in the Los Angeles area.

There was the uncomfortable question of Marco hanging like a dark cloud over Meg's plans to leave the hotel. He was somewhere outside waiting for her, she suspected. Snapper was packing up his camera equipment. They had already matched up his film roll and picture numbers with her notations of names. Finally there was nothing left to do before they left.

Together they went out into the gold red twilight, where a vivid sunset was softening into muted tones. Meg was taking deep breaths and holding them, involuntarily preparing for an assault on her composure. No one rose authoritatively from a lobby chair to stop them, and they continued out into the plant-filled patio entrance. Maybe Marco had given up; her irrational heart lurched in disappointment, and the pulse in her throat beat unevenly.

She walked with Snapper around a splashing fountain, and a man came quietly from behind a big tubbed oleander plant to stand in their path.

"I have waited," Marco said in a dark tone, "even though I knew you would make efforts to avoid me. We must speak."

"Won't tomorrow on the way to Roscoe's breakfast be enough time?" she asked without looking into his demanding eyes. "I told you I had a date tonight."

"It will not."

Snapper shifted from one foot to the other. "Listen, Meg," he said softly, "I'll be going home. Maybe you should find out what Mr. Montevalde wants. Business comes first, you know." He gave her a quirk of a smile. "It's okay about tonight." He nodded to Marco and got a curt "good-night" in return, then ambled off, leaving Meg pinned by the cold fire of Marco's gaze.

"I see some garden chairs over there. Shall we sit down?" His hand curved heavily on her arm, urging her toward the white iron seats. She sat down on a bench, clutching her purse defensively as he pulled a chair forward to sit facing her.

He was silent for a moment. In the dusk his face looked haggard. Long lines etched the sides of his mouth. "I want an explanation," he said at last in a cold voice, "...about a number of things. Whatever personal there is between us aside, what did you tell Giulio Prati about the Specchiato?"

It was the last thing she expected him to say. "Didn't he tell you? He's *your* boyhood friend!" A ridiculous feeling of guilt rose in Meg, for no good reason.

"He said you had done sketches of certain panels in the mirrored room...hidden doorways. Why?"

"I don't know. Curiosity, I guess. It was so odd."

"And you said nothing at all to me. Do you not find that even more odd?"

She had nothing to say to that. It was all she could do to be so near to him and have him chastising her for something as unimportant as her sketches.

"Hmm," he said at length. "And then I come here and find the gentle young woman I knew in Venezia not what she appeared at all, but a sophisticated fashion-polished woman mingling with the rich and in a position of influence—even to be given the management of the Specchiato celebrations. As you say—odd."

Meg bristled and sat up straight. It was too much. "I was as surprised as you when Maude Draper gave me the job. I've told her I don't want it, but she insists. I suppose you think I'm incapable of doing it and will muddle up your big event!"

"I have begun to wonder how experienced you are in more ways than one." His tone was icy. "I find you full of contradictions. In Italy you told me of no job like this one."

"That was true, but I was planning to try for one at *Au Courant*...."

"So," he remarked. "I find also that your uncle, for whom you worked previously, is a man of wealth. Why were you traveling as you were? I thought you had limited means."

"I *did*. My uncle believes in work, not in relationships, and I used a tiny inheritance to come to Italy. Anyway, it is none of your business how I got there, and I resent your implications." She made a move to rise, but he put a threatening hand on her knee.

"Not yet, *signorina*."

Meg sat back down, too tired to fight him. Somehow, as angry as she felt, she was powerless to leave.

"I didn't think about your literary work to any extent, so it was only after you suddenly changed in your attitude toward me—when we were at La Mira—that I came to wonder what your true motives had been. Were you really sick after those first days, or did you play on my good nature in order to obtain more than a simple story about Italy? Perhaps you wanted a story about a family in some distress...my own?"

She shook her head mutely and he plunged on. "I wondered why you were so permissive with your body, and why you pretended friendship with Teresa, who trusts you." He leaned forward and took her by the shoulders. "Was your touching story of the old film and your love for Italy just a way to enjoy a brief *avventura* and advance your standing with your editor? I demand to know!"

He released her with a shake. "I am not a man who is given to meaningless sexual encounters." The harshness in his voice struck hard at her heart and she stood up, indignation flaring through her pain.

"I think you're crazy!" She didn't care who heard her. "I thought your family were wonderfully kind, and I love Teresa. If you are so jaded as to think I was using you for a story, then any explanations I give would be useless. And I *had* to stay longer in Venice, because my passport was delayed. As for...what happened at your villa...I was a fool, but not completely. It was time to end my dream, to wake up to the fact that your little play of romance was designed to satisfy a naive American woman." She looked at him from gleaming eyes. "I suppose I should thank you for waking me up."

He stood up, his hands clenched into tight fists at his sides. "And that was why I wrote to you, I suppose... to see how naive you were! *Per Dio!* Why didn't you answer me instead of returning my letters?"

Meg straightened her spine, suddenly relishing the chance to hurt him as he had hurt her. A door was closing between herself and Marco, and she was pushing it shut. "I sent them back because there was no possible reason to keep up a connection with you, *signore*. As you say, our real lives are far different and each of us wants different things. As for Teresa, our friendship has nothing to do with you."

She wanted to end the conversation right there, but he drew breath to speak again. "At least we will have no illusions anymore. I am convinced that you are no longer the vulnerable innocent I thought you to be."

Meg's temper was flaring dangerously. "If you had thought me vulnerable and innocent, just why were you taking advantage of me at your villa? Picnic indeed!" Something like pain twitched across his features, and she felt perversely pleased. One last thrust was irresistible: "I suppose I don't understand the Italian male's code of honor. And please—never insult me again with a condescending analysis of my motives!"

"You think that I. . .that I intended to use your innocence? *Dio mio!*"

"You wouldn't be the first man in the world to act that way." She turned away from his glaring intensity. Anything to break the unwelcome control he had over her emotions.

But he whirled her back with a heavy hand. "I do not use vulnerability for my own pleasure, *signorina*!" he said darkly. "And when you responded warmly, I thought—" He broke off abruptly and dropped his hands. "Never mind what I thought."

"It was difficult to know *what* you thought," Meg whispered.

"*Si*, we are as we are, *non è vero*?" He sighed, but did not move away as she expected. "I will not interfere with your doing your job for *Au Courant* in Italy. If Maude Draper thinks you are capable of doing this job, I will accept her judgment." He raised a hand to softly trace the curve of her cheek.

What colossal nerve, Meg thought, but stood her ground to show him that his gesture meant absolutely nothing to her.

"Moreover, Teresa's mother, Bianca, is coming from Firenze to help with the invitations and planning." His hand cupped her chin gently so that she couldn't look away. "Let us act in a mature way now, Meg Brown. I suggest we call a truce and get our work done. This will mean a great deal to both of us. I suppose you have not lost your love for Venezia, hmm?"

She was seething. How could she be reacting this way to the touch of his hand? How could she let him persuade her to his point of view while he patronized her with his deep beguiling voice? Had she lost all control of her senses?

But she *was* in control. She would do this job and show him. *And torture yourself with the bittersweet reality of being near him in the Specchiato again,* the troublesome voice of reason said to her.

"I'm perfectly willing to work with you, Signor Montevalde." She forced a tight proud smile to her lips. "As you say, it is childish to be disturbed over the sexual mores of a different culture. I think you will be pleased with my work. And nothing will change my love for Venice," she ended rather lamely.

"*Va bene*, it is agreed." He looked down at her, his eyes exploring her lips—insolently, she thought. For a breath-catching moment she was sure he would try to kiss her, but the moment passed and he stepped away.

"If there is a restaurant nearby, I would be glad to take you for coffee, to discuss some of the plans. I must be at an appointment by eight o'clock, however."

Meg was proud of the even voice with which she replied. "Thanks, but I have a date myself, as I told you. We can discuss anything important on the way out to Malibu in the morning."

"Ah, yes—our breakfast. I like that man and his wife, too. They are honest and loving. A rarity today."

"We should leave the city about an hour ahead of time. Morning traffic is heavy. I have a car, and I can pick you up at your hotel."

"I, too, have a car. And if I pick you up you will have

a little longer to sleep, since you will be out late tonight. With the photographer, is that not right?"

It was none of his business. "I enjoy his company," she said. "He has won several important prizes for his work."

"*Eccellente.* I must make his acquaintance further. Shall we say six-thirty, then?"

She wrote down her address hastily, starting to explain where it was.

"Don't trouble," Marco said crisply. "I shall find you." His words made her shiver. He was right—something of him would always find her. *"Buona sera,"* he almost whispered. "And for convenience I think we cannot remain so formal. Let it be Meg and Marco again, eh?"

CHAPTER THIRTEEN

THE TELEPHONE WAS RINGING as Meg opened her apartment door. It was Snapper. "That guy looked a little intense," he said. "You okay? I got worried."

"We straightened things out. But... I'm terribly tired, Snap. Would you mind awfully if—"

"That's the reason I called. I thought you might want to cancel tonight."

"Yes," she wavered, "I want to stay in tonight. It's not you...."

There was a silence and then Snapper said, "Okay, honey, think nothing of it."

THE NEXT MORNING Marco arrived exactly on time. Meg saw a sleek convertible slide up to the curb in front of her apartment complex and knew immediately that it was he. She went out onto her tiny balcony and waved so that he wouldn't think of coming up. Somehow she didn't want him to come anywhere near her personal life. Far better to keep him separate in every way.

At least she knew she looked smooth and stylish, in a straight sheath of creamy raw silk with matching low-heeled pumps, and at her throat, a dawn-pink scarf fastened by a tiny sparkling pin shaped like a turtle. All at once she realized she was using the handbag that Marco had given her. It was too late to change.

Marco gave her an appraising glance and helped her into the car. Meg was ready with directions on her lips, but something about his manner and expression stopped her. He drove swiftly, surely, as if he had lived with the intricacies of Los Angeles freeways all his life.

When they moved onto the Coast Highway heading north toward Malibu, he made the first attempt at any real conversation between them. It was all business. Meg found it hard to focus her attention on his words as she looked over at his strong hands resting so easily on the wheel. The dark hairs on his wrists showed beneath the cuffs of his copper-toned silk shirt. The gleam of a gold watch when he turned the wheel, the movement of his long legs beneath his dark slacks as he braked the car—all contributed to upsetting her concentration.

Marco was outlining the work that would have to be done to get the Specchiato in order for the presentation ceremonies. "It's a help that you are familiar with the place. I don't need to waste time trying to describe it." He gave an exasperated sigh. "The problem is, how much money can I spend to revitalize the main rooms? Venezia will expect the Montevalde family to have some honor, after all."

How much your pride shows, signore, she thought.

"There are some fine artisans—friends of mine—who have offered to work for low wages and even to donate their free time in order to prepare. I would like to present the palazzo to the city in perfect condition, but that is not possible, unless by good fortune I should win the prize from Roscoe Veitch."

Meg stayed silent, wondering if he was probing at her sympathy so that she'd put in a good word for him to

Roscoe. Was that the reason for his one-way conversation? In truth, she couldn't imagine him asking anybody for help or influence. But what did she really know of him, this complicated man whose eyes gave mixed signals of irritation, pleasantness and something deeper and more disturbing.

It was the pleasant Marco who was engaging her in talk now, discussing the bedrooms and suites to be used as dressing rooms for François Vitelli's models and for the musicians. A few people could perhaps stay at the palazzo, furniture could be brought out of storage, and, Marco said hopefully, several bathrooms unused since his grandfather's time could be updated.

"You know that I am keeping the family apartment as part of the agreement with the city. But if the rest could only be beautifully furnished! Bianca, my aunt, has friends with attics full of antique furniture. They may be persuaded to give some of it to the restoration."

Meg started visualizing the renovated palazzo, catching his enthusiasm. "Even a good cleaning would help," she said, and he laughed.

"At least that can be done." He talked about the need for a press area, as well as a place for the film crew to store their equipment, then explained a bit about the guest list. "I gather that you will coordinate all of this—keeping an eye on everything." He smiled warmly at her. "You will do well. You have a Botticelli face and people will adore you."

Meg's fears flared, but she fought them down again. *I'll be damned if I'm going to let him reel me in with flattery! But I swear I'm going to do a first-rate job of the Venice project!*

THE OCEAN was a smooth blue mirror, with gulls and pelicans skimming its surface. "Almost as lovely as Italy," Marco remarked with a little smile. He and Meg wound up the curving roads above Malibu and drove through the high gates of Roscoe's property, taking the narrow road up to the house that aptly bore the name Hilltop.

Breakfast was set by the huge oval pool, surrounded by a balustrade and Italianate statuary interspersed with tall cypress trees. "I feel at home," Marco announced graciously.

Rosebud, in her rose-sprigged hostess coat, beamed with pleasure. Meg watched as her hostess visibly capitulated to his charm.

Under Rosebud's watchful eyes Marco ate heartily of the eggs and hominy. Roscoe generally monopolized the conversation, talking about his plans for the institute. "In a month we'll be having a wedding anniversary," he added. His smile was expansive. "I've been studyin' what to give my darlin' girl here." His face softened, and the two older people exchanged a loving look, so sincere and unselfconscious that Meg felt moistness in her own eyes. This wouldn't be an appropriate time to look at Marco.

"Since I married her," Roscoe said in his big voice, "I've never had a day of unhappiness. We've had our spats all right, and sometimes I think she's the worst aggravation that the Lord could visit on a man, and she feels the same about me—" he grinned and she laughed back "—but all the time we're happy underneath because we love each other and we're so damned lucky to be together." He took a gulp of coffee to cover the roughness of emotion that had come into his voice.

Rosebud put her hand into the big hard-working palm that he extended to her. "Isn't that a pretty hand?" He smoothed his thumb over the delicate veins and age spots and over the nails painted strawberry pink. "I've got an idea, and maybe you can help."

Meg saw that Marco's expression was gentle, and he was indeed paying attention. He had told the truth when he said he liked this odd couple.

"Let me explain," Roscoe said. "When Rosebud came to stay with her aunt in my Oklahoma hometown I thought she was the sweetest thing in the whole world. Her family had passed on and she only had this old aunt, and no money at all. I was working my guts out in the oil fields. We boys'd go to the Bluebird Tavern on weekends and whoop it up. Rosie got a job playin' the piano and singin' there. She was a real lady—wouldn't stand for any rough stuff, and if anyone would try to lay a hand on her she'd stop playin' and singin' and just look at the damn fool until he noticed how everybody saw how stupid he was."

He smiled at her again, and she dropped her eyes like a young girl. "Well, I fell in love—but hell, I didn't have two nickels to rub together and she was a lady, not from the rocky side of the tracks like me." He massaged his big nose reminiscently. "I didn't even dare talk to her, but I'd hang around places where I thought she'd be. At night her aunt would come to the tavern to walk her home. I used to follow at a distance to see they got back all right."

He looked at Marco with serious eyes, as if he knew another man might understand. "I don't like to hear an old man ramble any more than you do. But the point to my story is this: When I read the life of the Italian poet

Dante some years ago. . . ." He paused slightly, appreciating the incongruity of his statement. ". . . I realized that Dante had hung around to see his lady Beatrice just like I used to do with Rosie.

"One night Rosebud invited me to escort her and her aunt to church the next Sunday. I went, and well. . . I couldn't ask her to marry me with nothin', so I began to hustle. Pretty soon I knew a lot about makin' money, and as quick as I got enough to buy a new Model T and good clothes on my back—some money in the bank and good prospects—I married her.

"I took her to Europe for a honeymoon and that's when Italy hit us hard. We've never forgotten. Every time we go back we fall more in love with your country, its art, and all that beauty." He leaned back, his eyes shrewd but kindly.

"Believe it or not, we took some art courses together, and I started collectin' things. Even made good friends with a scholar at Padua, Sergio Masini. A hell of a good man. Got me all fired up about the Renaissance. Made a reader out of me!"

"Masini!" Marco snapped to attention. "You knew him? He was my teacher at Padua University. It was he who started my interest in architecture."

"I'll be damned," Roscoe grinned. "He was the one who gave me the idea for my institute—a long time ago."

"I saw him recently." Marco's voice was keen. "He's nearly eighty-five and very frail, but full of life yet."

"That clinches it," Roscoe muttered. He raised his eyes to Rosebud. "Wouldn't you say that clinches it?"

"I'd say so, honey." She smiled warmly at Marco and winked at Meg.

Marco has won the prize, Meg thought, then realized he had probably missed the meaning of Roscoe's American slang.

Roscoe returned to his earlier point. "We were talking about an anniversary gift. It occurred to me that I'd like to have a sculpture made—a memorial to the love that Rosie and I have shared for the last fifty years." He laughed at his wife's surprised expression. "I'd like to put it in the courtyard of the institute, and I want it to be of Dante and his Beatrice—but made to look a little like us. Younger, of course."

"Oh, Roscoe," Rosebud said softly, "I'd just love that!"

"My problem is, who can I get to do something in the style of that period? Most things look like trash today." Roscoe looked straight at Marco. "I thought you might have some suggestions." He leaned back, waiting.

Meg's thoughts flew to Enzo and Teresa. If Enzo did this sculpture his name would be known immediately.

Marco smiled. "I've got the very man for you. A young sculptor in Venice—very good and very temperamental. He would be ideal. . . if he'd do it."

"Bravo," Roscoe crowed. "You sure he's not a modern type? I want realism and I'm willin' to pay for it."

"He's the fiancé of my cousin Teresa. She would be the best one to persuade him. He, too, refuses to get married until he is able to support her."

"That can be fixed."

"He's proud, too," Meg warned. "But his work is beautiful. I have some pictures from his studio. I'll get them to you."

"Couldn't be better!" Roscoe boomed.

Rosebud looked interestedly from Marco to Meg. "So you two met in Venice," she cooed. "How romantic."

"Not too romantic," Meg said quickly. "I got sick and my tour had to leave without me. I was sitting at Florian's feeling absolutely awful when my purse was stolen—passport, checks, everything." She smiled tentatively at Marco. "Just when I was desperate Marco came to my rescue." She glossed over her time at the Specchiato, mentioning her acquaintance with his cousins, and managing to sound appreciative of his help. "That's why Maude offered me the coordinating job for *Au Courant*'s coverage of the ceremonies at the Specchiato. I was already familiar with it."

"Always said that Maude's nobody's fool," Roscoe commented with a smug smile to a low-flying gull.

After breakfast they strolled around the extensive gardens. Roscoe took Meg's arm, while Rosebud engaged Marco in conversation about Italy.

"Hmm," Roscoe said softly. "What's between you two? I don't need glasses to see that what looks cool only covers up what's hot." He peered into her eyes, and she felt her face flush with color. "Aha!" he chided. "You'll be glad to know I've chosen Marco for the prize. It takes an Italian to know about Renaissance design. I imagine you'd agree." He put a hand on her shoulder. "Now, Meg. . . you've got to keep your pretty little mouth shut until day after tomorrow at the ground breaking—understand?"

"I promise."

Walking to the car, Rosebud in turn slipped her arm into Meg's and gave her a conspiratorial smile.

On the drive back to Meg's apartment Marco commented on the Veitches' beautiful love story. Meg cynically wondered if he could really understand that kind of love. Was his heart capable of such devotion?

When he helped her from the car he bowed over her hand, not quite touching her fingers with his lips. The complete Italian gentleman. His cool politeness stabbed her, making her suddenly miserable.

An hour later she was at the *Au Courant* offices. "Well?" Maude Draper called out as Meg walked past her door. Maude's bright eyes took in her false expression of cheeriness. "Come in," she ordered.

Meg sank down in a chair opposite the desk, and Maude shoved papers around in an exasperated way. "How was breakfast?"

"Fine. Rosebud cooked it herself."

"I take it you've collected wads of human interest on the homey life of a zillionaire?"

"The funny thing is, it *is* homey. They're really dears, both of them."

"I gather that doesn't go for Conte Marco Montevalde. . . ."

"You could say that. Maude, couldn't you please put someone else on this assignment? He'd probably be relieved."

"That's good—he's not indifferent."

"Yes, he is. . . with irritation simmering down somewhere underneath it all. It's going to be terrible going back into the Specchiato—"

"Shut up, Meg, you're babbling." Maude flashed a smile of kindly irony. "You're going to do this job or I'm going to fire you—take your pick."

Meg smiled inwardly. She really needed Maude's incisive commentary to keep her feet planted on earth.

She quickly filled Maude in on Roscoe's desire to have himself and Rosebud immortalized in marble, "kind of like Dante and Beatrice," and the possibility of Enzo being the fortunate sculptor.

"Phew!" Maude exclaimed, her gaze flying upward. "How could those two look anything like Dante and Beatrice? But it's rather sweet. Good luck to your Enzo fellow. I hope he's up to it."

"It could change his life."

"One more thing. Have you any inkling about the prize—who will win?" Maude's look was sharp and penetrating, and Meg felt her own eyes waver nervously.

"So!" she exploded. "You do know! All right, Topsy, you can tell me. It won't go any further."

"I promised Roscoe."

"While I send reporters scouting around the finalists, wasting time and money, you're sitting on top of the secret! It's Marco, isn't it?" Meg tried to hold a blank expression and failed. "Okay, don't say anything. Does he know yet?"

Meg gave a slight shake of her head and Maude grinned. "That's good. He deserves it. He's really a fine gentleman, Meg." She snorted, seeing Meg's closed face. "Great jumping Jove—if I were a little younger I'd be tempted to try my wiles on him. Now get out of here and go write your stuff!"

THE DAY OF THE GREAT announcement and ground breaking was bright and brisk, perfect March weather. The huge tents, medieval pennants flapping in the wind, gave shelter to a horde of caterers and waiters dressed in tights and jerkins. Roscoe had set the scene well.

The place was soon a crush of eager guests snacking

from the trays of appetizers and sipping champagne. Meg recognized many faces from her social activities with *Au Courant*. A number of old-line philanthropists were here, some of the top fund raisers, and of course, crews from the two major newspapers and television stations. Meg crossed her fingers that Roscoe could carry it all off smoothly.

The finalists arrived in a flotilla of Cadillac limousines, with Roscoe and Rosebud in the lead. Meg and Snapper observed as best they could from a vantage point slightly aside from the mainstream.

From the platform near the tents a clear trumpet note called for attention. Then the costumed trumpeter raised his beribboned instrument and blew another fanfare. Roscoe led the way to the dais. Two gilded spades leaned against a flower-strewn boulder nearby.

Meg saw Marco's tall figure join the ring of finalists, which Roscoe was marshaling into place. What was he thinking right now, she wondered. He looked so serious, almost sad.

Roscoe made a speech, congratulating all the finalists and suggesting that each of them could design a gate along the main road to the institute. The gates would be known by the designers' names.

"It's been an awful job deciding," he told them. "I've asked for lots of opinions these past months from a lot of experts."

He paused and looked around. "I'm going over to get the spades for the ground breaking. I'll keep one and give the other one to the winner. We'll break the ground together." Roscoe put his hands on his hips, took a deep breath and stepped down from the platform to pick up the two shovels.

Then he turned toward Marco and held out one of the gleaming golden spades. "It's yours, Signor Montevalde." Camera crews rushed into place.

Marco's face was expressionless for an instant before it broke into a broad, clear smile. He reached for the spade and stood next to Roscoe. While the trumpeter blew a long blast, they each dug up a shovel full of earth.

A shout went up from the spectators and applause burst out. Meg's eyes blurred with tears. She knew so well what this meant to Marco, but didn't want to care. Contessa Alandi was kissing him and then Bette Slocum, the pushy woman from the cocktail party, was clutching him to her red silk bosom.

Meg turned her head and hastily scrawled several lines of notes. Then she heard a cooing voice calling to her. "Meg, darlin', come over here and join us." Rosebud drew her toward the circle around Roscoe and Marco.

"This is the day!" Roscoe said loudly, giving her a big bear hug. When he let her go she was standing in front of Marco and looking up into his vibrant eyes. She quickly extended her hand.

"Congratulations—I'm so glad you won." Her voice carried her sincerity, and Marco responded with one of his heart stopping smiles. His hand cradled hers gently. People were crowding toward the champagne tables, and he drew her hand through his arm, bringing her close to his side as he walked.

But instead of heading toward the tent he led her toward a nearby stand of tall shrubs and stopped, out of sight of the guests. "Are you truly glad that I have won?" His face had a strange quizzical expression.

"Of course!" What did he expect her to say?

"...and how pleased Teresa will be." She had learned by now not to be drawn into anything remotely intimate with him.

"I will be leaving for Venice tonight. I want to get work started at the Specchiato immediately. There is only six weeks' time for everything." He stopped abruptly and his face became more severe. "I want honesty, Meg. Did you influence Roscoe Veitch's decision in my favor?"

She was startled by the question, and then a rush of irritation brought a crimson glow to her face. "Enough women were working on Roscoe for you without my help. I'm mainly interested in writing a good story."

"I see." He probed at her with his shadowed bronze eyes. "And if I asked what you felt for me last year in Venice, would you say the same? Was it only something for your reporter's notebook?"

Meg said nothing at first. Was he doing a good imitation of a disappointed suitor, or did all Italian interludes include a scene like this? The longer she hesitated, the worse it made things. She was cutting him off, when all she wanted to do was press herself into his arms and beg for his love. *Why am I punishing him when I love him so?* But she couldn't make her lips confess how much she cared. She couldn't trust him not to make a mockery of her words.

He sighed quietly. "Then I will say *arrivederci*, Meg Brown. Perhaps I never knew you—or you me. Perhaps those two people at the Villa Terza never were. Let us leave it at that." He took her hand again. "I am confident that the celebration at the Specchiato will be safe in your competent hands. I have never congratulated you on your success at *Au Courant*. You should be proud."

He lifted her fingers to his lips for a polite kiss and released them immediately. "How soon will I see you in Italy?"

"About a month," she said, noticing with an odd sense of loss that the light kiss held no feeling behind it.

"Bene." He turned away, and she watched his graceful back moving toward the crowded area and the waiting reporters. Despair engulfed her. She had to get home. She had to find Snapper and get out of this place. How awful to have it end like this, with words spoken in cool voices, so remote and so alien. Angry words might have been easier. At least they would have had warmth in them.

CHAPTER FOURTEEN

MEG SAT IN THE CROWDED TRAIN COMPARTMENT alone with her dour thoughts. This trip to Venice wasn't like her first one. There wasn't any of that magic expectancy. Byron's "fairy city of the heart" now had a heavy tinge of painful and unnerving memory, and this long day of travel had taken its toll.

She sighed and tried to concentrate on the outline she was writing—about the history of the Specchiato—to be filled in, hopefully, by Teresa. The swaying motion of the train joggled her hand. She would be glad to see Teresa. *Au Courant* had paid for some international phone calls, and Teresa had been bubbling with news and delight.

"*Cara*, *cara* Meg," her voice had purred across the many miles. "I am so joyful that things go well for Marco." She paused in her urgent flow of words, then said, "You and Marco—you have become all right...together again?"

"We're friendly. Everything is fine," Meg hedged.

"*Bene*. I wish it were as well between Enzo and me." Her voice lost some of its earlier exuberance. "We have had a great and terrible argument. He is *ostinato*! How do you say—with the head of a pig! He refuses to consider doing the commission for the statues of Signor Veitch. I cannot believe it! He stands with the underlip stuck out as far as the baboon and says silly things about prostitution of his art. I tell him a real artist can make something wonderful out of anything." She stopped on a note of futility.

"Maybe I can talk to him," Meg offered.

"I hope so, *cara*, because I am ready to kill him." A sob was audible in her voice.

Meg had tried to sound optimistic. "We'll find a way past him. He'll never win against two strong women." After that they had talked about more practical matters, and Meg learned of the general plans for the festivities at the palazzo. After a few additional calls Meg had decided she might very well be capable of coordinating the job.

Capable was the word that her mother had used. "Our Meg's such a capable young lady now," she had said at the going-away dinner her family had had for her. Meg bore up under the rain of flattery, about how much faith the magazine had in little Meg. But her relatives meant well and the ordeal was soon over.

Meg sighed again and glanced around at her compartment companions. Snapper, looking very young in sleep, was in a corner seat, his precious camera between his knees, and other equipment under his feet and on the seat next to him. Ted Bingham, wedged in among Snapper's things, was being a good sport. He was the layout man, sharp and decisive, with a fine eye for artistic effects.

Patty Stanley, fortyish and a highly trained secretary, sat next to Meg. She usually worked for Maude, but was on loan for this assignment. Patty was holding a book, but hadn't turned a page for a long time. Meg wondered if Venice held any dreams for her. *Everyone can't be such a romantic fool as I am,* she told herself.

Suddenly they were pulling in under the high roofs of the Venice train station. She dragged herself from her obsessive reveries as the train slid to a stop and gave one last shiver. Meg lowered the window and motioned to a porter, who ran toward them with his big cart. The men started passing the luggage out to him.

A familiar figure in a fluffy white sweater and pink skirt was waving frantically from down the platform. "*Cara* Meg! *Benvenuto!*" she called out. It was Teresa.

At last the *Au Courant* group had made their way out of the crowded train, and Meg found herself being hugged tightly by her friend.

She made hasty introductions, then Teresa led the crew toward the water stairs outside the station. Ugo was there waiting in Marco's motor launch, a rather sullen expression on his face. Two gondolas bobbed at their moorings beside the launch, with Luigi standing on the rowing podium of one. He was dressed for the occasion, and his boat was decorated with a red rose in the vase at the prow.

Luigi jumped down to assist Meg into his craft, bowing over her hand like a courtier and drawing an amused look from Snapper. "Venezia will be happy again now that you have come back to us, *signorina*," the gondolier said with a flourish.

The crew loaded their equipment and luggage into the launch, then took the second gondola to the Specchiato. Meg tried not to show the distress in her heart; Marco had not come. She forced herself to smile and listen to Teresa's excited chatter.

By the time the little flotilla reached the Specchiato the spell of Venice had settled over everyone. They approached the huge metal-studded door of the palazzo with wide eyes. Meg herself drew in a sharp breath when she walked into the entrance hall. Spidery scaffolding climbed the walls. The grayed marble of the floor now gleamed with a mellow patina. The iron chain and gears of the well's machinery, previously covered with rust, were painted black, and the wellhead had no more stains on its carved cherubs. Several people high on the scaffolds stopped their work of cleaning the frescoed walls at their arrival. The two groups gazed at each other with curiosity.

The trompe l'oeil wall had been beautifully restored, so that the fake colonnades were even more deceiving to the eye. Sunlight was slanting rich dappled color from the newly cleaned stained glass high above; sounds of voices and hammering made multiple echoes around the room.

"My gosh..." Snapper said inadequately. "If I can only get some of this in color...whew!" He turned in a circle with his head craned upward, and Teresa laughed.

They went up to the apartment, where Lucia in turn folded Meg into an embrace. Meg felt Ugo's eyes on her and a quick shiver ran along her nerves. Under his polite smile he was deeply hostile.

Teresa spoke animatedly about the restoration work being done. "We have made an office for you, Meg. There will be places for everyone to work." She took the tired group on a quick tour of the mirrored room. "You must see the reason for the palazzo's name," she urged brightly.

Meg was amazed at what had already been done in the few weeks since Marco's return. Through their gilded traceries of design, the mirrors glowed. The parquetry floor was polished to a high sheen, and swirls of rose pink showed in the marble squares that edged it. The frescoed ceiling stretched over the room like a tent of color. Tall carved candelabra stood at intervals around the walls, and between them were the elegantly sculpted marble pedestals that had held the treasures of the first Montevalde prince.

Above, in the curve of the ceiling, the Murano-glass chandeliers flashed and sparkled with newly cleaned facets. Some workers were hanging draperies of red-and-gold damask on the tall windows at the end, which opened onto a courtyard below.

Against one end of the room a low stage had been built, and rolls of deep red carpeting were ready to cover it. Meg couldn't keep down the memory of her midnight waltz; however, now everything was bright and clean and the atmosphere of mystery was gone. A twist of pain constricted her heart. She sighed unconsciously, and Teresa looked at her with a quick frown of worry.

Later, when the crew had been seen off to the Regina Hotel, Teresa pulled Meg down on one of the big couches of the apartment, determined to talk. Lucia bustled about with a light supper, which found a small space amid the cluttered paperwork on the table.

"You look so tired, *cara mia*," Teresa said gently.

"Si." Lucia shook her head. "You are even more thin than when you came here with the sickness."

Teresa lifted up one of Meg's arms. "See, you will suddenly appear older if you don't eat more. Is this the style of the *Au Courant* women?" She smiled at Meg's expression. "Enzo says a man doesn't want to squeeze a bag of bones." She laughed, smoothing her dress over her own charmingly dimpled knees.

Lucia supervised Meg's consumption of luscious cream cakes and tea, making sure that she had plenty. But the delicious food sat in Meg's stomach uncomfortably. She was too tense—with memory and expectation. Where was Marco? Finally she had to ask.

"He is in Roma. I expect him by noon tomorrow." Teresa put a warm hand over Meg's tight one. "*Cara* Meg, what has happened? Marco is rushing at the business of fixing the palazzo like a man possessed. He has no smiles for anyone, and Lucia is at the end of her wits to tempt his appetite. He grows thin, too...." She broke off, regarding Meg with a soft questioning gaze.

Meg fought to keep tears away from her eyes. "It is all the pressure, I'm sure."

Teresa smiled, unconvinced. "Hmm. Well...Lucia has brought your bags to your old bedroom. My mother will arrive tomorrow and she will share my room." She stopped at the sight of Meg's protesting face.

"I can't stay here, Teresa! I'm going to the Regina with the others. This is your family's place. I won't displace your mother. I couldn't—"

Teresa leaped up and stamped her foot, her riot of curls almost shooting electric sparks. "Nonsense! Meg, you must stay here! What do you think to do? Haven't I looked forward to having my friend with me?"

"But Marco...where will he be?"

"In his own room—*Sant' Agnese* give me patience!"

"There is Ugo, too," Meg enumerated and stood up to make her point.

"*Dio mio*, I want no room for him! He sleeps in the old rooms of the Specchiato if he wishes, or with his rude friends in the city."

Meg knew she was beaten. "All right. I just didn't want to cause trouble."

"Trouble? You give it now. I have one piece of good news for you if you will sit down again."

Meg listened intently to Teresa's breathless account of the troublesome lawsuit. "The judge was a compassionate man," she said. "He agrees that Marco should not suffer too much for Ugo's mistake. Marco promised to continue to pay for the cost of the poor girl's medical care, but there was no punishing settlement beyond that amount. Isn't it wonderful?"

"I'm happy for Marco," Meg said.

"For two days we were all filled with joy, and then another problem, far worse in its implications, appeared." Teresa looked darkly around the room, as if expecting to be overheard. "I fear that the good God delivers us from one curse only to bring another. My brother—my own flesh—is so jealous of Marco's position as head of the family that he has invented a black scheme to take it from him." She stared at Meg, her eyes reflecting deep sorrow.

"What could be so terrible?" Meg asked. "Marco is a very intelligent man and Ugo is only—"

"Ugo is seeking proof that our father was the first-born twin, not Marco's."

Meg didn't understand immediately what Teresa was saying.

"Don't you see, Meg, if our father was born first, then the entire estate of the Montevaldes belongs to Ugo. It is so terrible!" She lowered her head and said in a choked voice, "He has an evil lawyer who would sue Marco for the pleasure of it . . . and for the large purse of money that Ugo will give him if he wins."

"And Marco knows about this, before Ugo has a case against him?"

"Ugo is so filled with anger that he has threatened Marco with the lawsuit even before he has found the proof to set before a judge. He resents Marco for giving away the Specchiato, but he has no understanding of economic realities. This is the cloud of darkness that hangs over our family now, my dear friend. I wanted you to know immediately so that when Marco comes, you—"

"Will have sympathy for him?" Meg smiled. "Teresa, I think Marco is quite able to handle his own troubles."

"You do not feel warmly toward him?"

"I didn't say that. I truly am sorry to hear all of this."

"Then what. . .?"

"Things have happened between Marco and me that have led us to see each other as associates in business, nothing more. I know you hope for a deeper relationship, but that's impossible. There just isn't the compatability. . . ." Meg watched as Teresa's expression changed to painful disbelief.

"I will pray to the Holy Mother, *cara*. It cannot be as you describe to me."

"But it is! I wouldn't have taken this job if there were anything of a personal nature between Marco and me. It would interfere with the project."

"I do not hear these words! This is not my friend speaking! It is only your tiredness. Now, you must rest. Tomorrow we start our work and you will have your happiness back again. I will forget everything you say about Marco." She leaned to kiss Meg's cheek and gave her an affectionate hug.

Meg closed the door to her room gently. She fought back a surge of regret at being here where the memories could so easily overpower her. There was the bedside table where Marco's vase of roses had once stood, fresh and alive with promise. Now the vase was by her bedside at home, and the three red roses were long gone as they should be.

Reluctantly she called the Regina to cancel her room reservation and tell Snapper the new arrangements. Sleep came to her uneasily because she couldn't blot out everything that had happened here in the past. Some time after midnight she heard voices arguing from the direction of Teresa's room. One voice sounded like Ugo's, and she heard her own name spat out in angry Italian.

It would have been far better if she had stayed at the Regina, away from the stresses of the Montevalde family. The Specchiato was not the same place she had known. Always before it had felt beautiful, egocentric, haughty, but harmless. Now there was a vague danger lurking behind its newly cleaned walls. Meg wished Teresa hadn't told her about the latest trouble between Marco and Ugo. She didn't want to feel sympathy for Marco. It would be too easy to step over the line she had drawn between them, and *that* she had to resist at all costs.

MORNING CAME with the bustle of workmen's noises. Lucia brought a tray to her room, and Meg hurried to dress. The weather was sunny, a perfect early May day. It was hard to remember that Venice could sometimes be cold.

She put on a skirt of fine supple wool in a soft blue

lavender that she loved. The matching angora sweater was feather light yet warm and went over a blouse of dull turquoise silk. She grabbed up a chunky pendant of Mexican silver set with turquoise and stepped into plain low-heeled leather pumps that were almost the color of her Venice handbag.

In the mirror of the heavy carved armoire she presented a sleek *Au Courant* image. *Marco will be home this noon,* she thought with a combination of hope and tension. She would *make* things go harmoniously, no matter what he did!

She went downstairs to look for Teresa, who wasn't in the apartment. The workmen gave her low-voiced greetings and assessing glances. Meg wished the male-female game here in Venice were always so harmless.

A commotion seemed to be escalating in the distance. Meg heard Teresa's voice raised in protest, and she hurried along a corridor to the great entrance hall. There, a short man in an overcoat and cavalier-style hat stood surrounded by piles of luggage, large brocade bags stamped with a distinctive gold monogram: F.V.

The youngish visitor looked past Teresa and saw Meg. *"Zut! Zut, zut, zut!"* he exploded and then in English, with a strange accent that was almost French, he announced, "I am Vitelli. I wish to speak with Madame Maude Draper of *Au Courant* immediately." His light blue eyes fastened on Meg's face. "*Alors!* Do you intend to stand in contemplation all day, *mademoiselle*? I wish to go to my rooms and I wish fresh coffee, and then I will discuss with Madame Draper what I will and will not do. She has misrepresented to me what is expected." He strode toward the stairway, his narrow face set and his ornate thin cane whipping about his legs like an angry cat's tail.

"Dio, Dio," Teresa hissed. "It is the couturier from Paris! He is not supposed to be here! He is booked for the Danieli Hotel. What shall we do?" She was desperate, watching the stranger push his way toward the stairs.

Well, Meg thought, *this is it. This was what you didn't want to do, and Maude insisted.* A flash of anger at the situation gave her courage, and she hurried to step in front of François Vitelli. "Eh?" he said conversationally, and came to a halt.

"Monsieur." Meg offered a courteous hand to him. "I am Meg Brown, feature editor in charge of this project. I am also an assistant to Madame Draper, who will not arrive from the United States for several days yet."

He executed a travesty of a kiss in the air above her head. *"Incroyable,"* he remarked acidly, thrashing his cane against the stone wellhead with aggravation. The sound echoed upward, where from the scaffolding several pairs of interested eyes were watching the scene.

"A suite at the Danieli is arranged for you, *monsieur*."

He thumped his cane in a syncopated rhythm: tap-tap...tap...tappety-tap. "I do not like to stay at the Danieli. I wish to stay here in this place, and that is what I will do, *mademoiselle*."

"We must discuss this," Meg said in her most authoritarian voice. "Please come to the Montevalde family apartment for coffee." She turned to Teresa. "This is Signorina Teresa Montevalde, the cousin of Signor Marco—*Conte* Marco," she amended for emphasis.

"*Oui*, I have a slight acquaintance with *monsieur le comte*."

Meg turned to lead the way, not looking back to see if they were following. With relief she heard the patter of Teresa's high heels and the tap of Vitelli's cane behind her.

Lucia took a quick look at Vitelli and without coaching soon presented them with small glasses of an especially fine wine and tiny squares of toast covered with tangy melted cheese. The gentleman swept off his coat and hat. His eyes roamed the room and he gave a slight shudder. "Modernism is an intrusion in this fine old building. I want to see the other, older rooms. I will select one for my use."

"But there are workmen everywhere."

"Have them fix my area immediately."

Teresa looked helpless. "The bathrooms at least are in order."

"*Très bien.* That is my one concession to the present day. It must have been disagreeable in the extreme to exist with commodes and hip baths before the fire, with those endless buckets of hot water." Vitelli scooped up a handful of the toast tidbits and sat down, chewing reflectively. "I will be comfortable here while you are alerting the workmen to my presence. I will choose later."

"I believe you said there was a problem with Maude Draper?" Meg hated to ask.

"A very large problem. Just as I leave for Venice I get mail. On the plane I read it and discover that Madame Draper has suddenly asked that I show something from my fall collection. *Zut!*" he said in displeasure. "I have intended to show several special designs, perhaps, but nevairr my exclusive designs ahead of zee time.'' His accent was growing thicker as his agitation increased. ''I am ready to make an appearance because Madame Draper was helpful to me—but even the prestige of *Au Courant* will not force me to show my fall creations prematurely—to be copied by zee pirates and be on zee racks in every cheap boutique.'' He stopped, red in the face and reduced to angry gesturing.

''I can't think that Maude would ask you to do that. She admires your work so much. Could I see the letter please?'' Meg asked quietly.

He reached with trembling fingers into his coat pocket and extracted an envelope with the familiar blue-and-white logo. Without a word he flung it into her lap. Meg opened it, praying that the little man had been mistaken.

Maude had written that ''the showing of a few of your special designs to the international audience (and in the unique setting of the palazzo) will draw even more excitement about your fall collection. . . .''

Meg looked up into the bright speculative eyes waiting for an answer. ''Monsieur Vitelli, I find nothing in this letter saying that you should show anything from your fall collection.'' With an effort she held his gaze. ''What were you intending to show?''

''*Merde!* I show three gowns from my last year's designs, made up in fabrics that are pure Renaissance in richness.'' He helped himself to more wine.

Meg searched for the right words. ''We have set aside a certain amount of time during the festivities for the presentation of your creations, *monsieur*. The showing of only three gowns will force us to find other attractions, and you will lose the place that would make yours the prime feature of the day."

A short time elapsed before Vitelli opened his mouth to say a single word: "So." His voice had changed to an almost reasonable timbre.

Meg decided to pursue her advantage. "Why are you here so early? The reception is more than a week away."

"*Zut!* You ask questions like a schoolteacher." A hint of a smile bent the corners of his thin stubborn lips. "Suppose I say I wish to take zee small vacation and where better than in Venice, where I have nevairr visited. . . and such a place as this. You object?"

"We will try to make you comfortable," she said dryly, "even though there will be noise and activity around you."

"*Merci.* Now, will you show me the rooms so that I may choose." He rose, flipping crumbs onto the floor.

Teresa gave Meg a dispirited look, and Vitelli broke the silence. "It is too bad I did not see the possibilities sooner of what was here." He fixed admiring eyes on them, a framing hand held out at arm's length. "*Charmante!* I see before me two roses—a red and a pink. Come, show me the palazzo."

He prowled the busy corridors, room after room, with the two women trailing in his wake. Meg was amazed at the high pitch of activity among the workmen. One room was now full of antique furniture, apparently a storage location until other rooms were ready to be furnished.

Vitelli's fancy lit on a bedroom that Meg remembered—the huge room with the antique bed. He was enchanted with the tattered material of the bed curtains, but ordered them to be taken down right away. "With care," he cautioned. "The fabric can be a model for new cloth." He stroked sensitive fingers over the disintegrating weave. "This is at least 150 years old."

He gave orders for a small couch, a writing table and two chairs to be brought from the assortment of antiques in the storage room. Meg remembered how this bedroom used to look, dark and brooding, and now there was carpeting on the floor. The ceiling frescoes and wallpaper looked much fresher, as did the carved marble fireplace. A bathroom gleaming with new fixtures had been made out of a seventeenth-century robing chamber that adjoined the bedroom.

The couturier's luggage was brought up along with his folding work table and art equipment. "In case I am inspired," he told them airily.

In case he is inspired, Meg repeated to herself, and a sudden idea struck her. She remembered the antique clothing she had seen at the Correr Museum when she'd gone there with Adella Prati. Maybe she could persuade Vitelli to design some fashions based on the old costumes. That would be exactly in line with the theme of the celebration.

She and Teresa left him ordering the placement of furniture. *"Dio!"* Teresa said. "What an ego, and yet he is likable." She turned a worried face to Meg. "But he won't show anything new. What can we do? And what will Marco think of a stranger occupying the chief bedroom for a vacation?"

Meg outlined her plan and Teresa crowed, "The very thing! Vitelli is known for his adaptations of classic styles to the present. He only needs to think it is his own idea."

"I will try," Meg said. "But even if he agrees to make the designs, who will sew them in this short time? And how can I get across the idea?"

"Take him to lunch at Florian's—and be sweet. I think he likes you. Then get him to the Correr Museum. It is only a short walk from the piazza. You can do it, Meg!"

"Maybe you should be the one, Teresa." The man was such a simmering, autocratic question mark. "You do a better job of being sweet. I'm just not the type."

"*Che bello pasticcio!* What a mess! It's you he likes. Anyway, I must see that his room is livable. And Mama will be here today, and Marco. There are a million things...and what about Enzo? Maybe you can go with me tomorrow to see him, eh? No, Meg, Vitelli is yours. You are the director for *Au Courant*!"

The difficult little man erupted into the hallway where they were standing. "I am hungry," he announced with a satisfied look. "And you, Mademoiselle Meg, are lunching with me. We have much to talk of and plans to make."

"Would Florian's be satisfactory?" she ventured.

Before she could truly gather her thoughts Meg found herself seated at Florian's with the orchestra playing, the pigeons strutting and cooing, and Vitelli ordering lunch for her without consultation. Giorgio the waiter hovered solicitously, welcoming her back to Venice.

"Everyone is delighted that Signor Marco won the great prize," he said respectfully. "Have you come here to be with him?" His romantic eyes glistened, and Meg wanted desperately to shut him up. Vitelli's expression was filled with speculative curiosity. Giorgio kept talking, however. "You look so changed, so cool, *signo-*

rina. At first I did not recognize. . . ." Fortunately he was drawn away by a signal from another table.

"You are known in Venice, I gather," Vitelli said. "Are you a special friend of Comte Montevalde? If so, I will not interest myself as much as I would otherwise desire to do."

Meg felt a telltale flush creeping into her face. "We are not special friends," she said crisply. "I was here last year, and my handbag was stolen while I was dining here at Florian's. Signor Montevalde was courteous and helpful. I. . . I met his cousin Teresa and we are close friends."

"Ah." He watched her with eyes that made her uneasy. The conversation was not going in the desired direction. How was she going to get him to the Correr Museum at this rate?

His face softened into a genuine smile, free from the sharpness that seemed habitual. "You are a mystery, *ma petite*. You look like a sophisticated woman of affairs, but I long to put you into one of my romance gowns. Then you would be most beautiful, with the gray eyes and the fine hair shown to advantage. You should be softly draped in muted colors, or fresh and sparkling in white lace with daisies at your waist. No jet-set smoothness for you, *mignonne*, but sweetness that makes your strong intelligence a delightful discovery and not a threat."

What a fine piece of male chauvinism, Meg thought. She felt a little alarmed at the growing warmth of his attentive glances. The endearments he used had a tinge of condescension. He was seeing her as softly feminine and pliant. *Sweeten him up,* Teresa had said—but why couldn't she talk to him honestly? She decided to try.

Taking the precaution of smiling into his eyes, she said, "After lunch I would like us to go to the Correr Museum, just over there." She pointed to the south end of the piazza.

"And what is there that sets such a determined angle to the chin?" Vitelli watched her lazily, sipping at a glass of mineral water that Giorgio had supplied.

"There is some very fine clothing there, from the days of the splendor of Venice—from when it was called *La Serenissima*, the most lovely and serene Venice." Her words, she saw, were having an effect. "I think that you might find some inspiration in them for a few special designs. . . a kind of compliment to Venice, from François Vitelli." She paused. "You might even give the proceeds from your designs to the fund to save Venice. It would make wonderful publicity for you in the press, and would be featured in *Au Courant*."

While she spoke his posture altered from relaxed insouciance to full attention. *"Alors!"* he said suddenly. "Now I see why the estimable sharp-needle Maude Draper has given you charge of this situation." A smile curled the sinuous line of his lips. "You do not answer my compliments with more compliments, but you make me a proposition instead—straightforward, I think you say."

"I am not very skilled at flattery. I'd rather be direct."

A little chuckle puffed his lips. "You won't even give to me a little response when I tell you that I find you *charmante*?"

Meg laughed with him. "No." He pulled a disappointed face, but his eyes were alight with humor. "What do you think of my idea, *monsieur*?"

"I think it is good." His face was completely serious now. "So good, in fact, that I caution you to remember that I have thought of it myself—I alone—an inspiration from my genius." A teasing spark deepened the lines at the corners of his mouth.

"It's yours, all yours," she hastened to affirm.

"*Bien!* Now, how do we accomplish such miracles?"

Meg told him about Adella Prati's sewing ladies, and he gave her a look of congratulations. Over the first course, a salad of sliced fennel, they discussed the possibilities, with Vitelli now more than eager to be inspired by the old costumes.

At one point he switched directions and his questions became personal again. "You do not tell me all I am to understand about Marco Montevalde," he said in a knowing voice.

"I...I don't know what you mean."

"*Ma foi!* But of course you do, *petite*—you are in love with him." The word triggered a rush of blood through her body, and she had no words to reply. "Don't deny it, *ma pauvre*. I have met him before, and he is a man of much attractiveness. You see, Vitelli is not without the eyes to see or the heart to understand." His hand came out to cover her tense little fist. It was a comforting, undemanding touch, and she smiled back at him. He was kind, and she couldn't help leaning closer to him in response to his proffered friendship.

He drew a sharp breath as his hand tightened on hers, and he said close to her ear, "Steady, *petite*, we may have a visitor. The admirable Comte Montevalde walks across the piazza. He has not yet seen...ah...*alors*, he has regarded us...."

Tension flew like wildfire through Meg's veins. Marco had seen her for the first time in more than a month, and in a situation that suggested intimacy. She wanted to vanish from the spot and wake up in her bed in California—anything but this!

Vitelli's eyes held hers and she dared not look away. Pigeons scattered and fluttered—she had to look up. Marco was there, his tall figure outlined against the vivid backdrop of the Basilica of San Marco, and her heart rejoiced in the sight of him, even though his face was set in cold, remote lines. His eyes were dark with a fiery glint that made them seem hard as glass. The sunlight gleamed on his crisp wavy hair.

Without a change of expression he paused a moment and then moved past them. "*Buon giorno*, Signorina Meg—Vitelli." His voice was uninflected—one to be used to salute very casual acquaintances. It was accompanied by the briefest of nods. His straight back disappeared under the arcades of Florian's.

So that was her welcome back to Venice! Vitelli removed his hand from hers. "*Merde!* Now he is convinced of unspeakable intimacy between us. What shall we do, Meg? Shall we give him real cause?" He stopped, seeing her distress. "Tell me," he said quietly, "how did this happen? I shall not repeat your confidence, if given. I am of experience in love, *chérie*."

The strength went out of her. What did it matter? Somehow, she found herself telling this man with the discerning eyes about the *Summertime* dream and what had happened when she came to Venice.

"And what is it that you want, *mon amie*? Is it that Montevalde is an outward image of romance, or do you love him for his true self? Do you even know what that is?"

"I love him," she confessed, no longer surprised at her ability to say the words, "but because I believe that he is kind and good. There is something in him that makes me joyful just to see him, even when he's angry, like today. I. . . want him to be happy."

"Good! Then your Marco is a fortunate man. You must let him know, *chérie*. It does no good for me to know and for him to think whatever it is that he thinks."

"I can't! Our ideas of romance are so different."

"And you will not settle for less than this ideal love?"

"I simply can't. I'm not tough enough to play the romantic game and then go away. It's better to keep my ideal. . . better than a summer love, a taste of romance. The aftermath would be so bitter."

He took up her theme. "Because the only true warmth is in our own self-respect, yes? It is better to love Marco truly, even if you never see him again, rather than leave with him a memory of a weak woman, a plaything?"

"Yes."

"*Eh bien.* You are a woman, Meg, not a girl. Men use *les jeunes filles*, but they love women." His smile was surprisingly tender. "If commitment is what you seek, you are wise. . . but forgive me for not agreeing with your action in this matter. Let us see what can be done. Maybe we can find out what truly exists in the complicated heart of Comte Marco. At least the truth could be healing, eh?"

Giorgio came with more food, and Vitelli reverted to his old, sharp-tongued self, demanding a special sauce for his scampi, saying outrageous things and rapping with his whiplike cane for service. Meg was no longer put off by his facade, however. "You are a very nice man, *monsieur*," she said softly.

"Zut!" he said through a mouthful of herb-scented rice.

A companionable silence accompanied their meal. Afterward they went to the Correr Museum and wandered through the rooms that Napoleon had built. Vitelli was enchanted with the old costumes. He pulled out a small notebook and sketched furiously.

"This *dogaressa*'s cap could become a fad," Vitelli laughed. "I can do these designs—unusual things—if your seamstresses are as good as you promise. Evening necklines with tiny lace ruffs, sleeves stitched with little puffs along them...but we have such a short time. Your women must not only be capable, they must be very fast."

They went immediately to call Adella. Fortunately, she was at home, and within thirty minutes had met them in front of the museum. Adella was very large with the baby she was carrying, but sparkling with energy. "I only pray my little one will wait until the celebration is over," she laughed. She was thrilled with Vitelli's proposal. "Franca will be invoking her saints for the entire time that she is working for you," she said.

Together they went the short distance to Franca's home, where Vitelli was his most agreeable self. He spoke Italian with a strong French accent. "I was born in Roma," he informed them, "but *Maman* was French and Paris is my home."

Franca showed him her best pieces of embroidery, and he was delighted. After much discussion he announced, "I think we can do it." He named a price for their work that made the women's eyes shine with pleasure. "They will work day and night, and so will I," he said to Meg. "It shall be our secret. I shall see that they attend the showing as special guests. They are *artistes*, true *artistes*." He kissed the work-worn hands with genuine feeling. "We shall give Maude Draper a thing or two to think about, eh, my Meg?"

Vitelli insisted on taking Meg and Adella to tea at Quadri's in the piazza, and then Adella left them, filled with French-Italian compliments. As she left she bent to whisper to Meg, "Giulio is upset over something at the Specchiato. Take care, *amica*."

Vitelli escorted Meg back to the palazzo. She was elated with her success, but dreaded seeing Marco again. She sighed heavily and Vitelli gave her cheek a pat. "No sighs, *petite*. The end of this tale is not yet." He leaned forward to give her a gentle kiss. She had to smile at the expression on his face. "Am I always to be the comforting shoulder for weeping? *Hélas!* And now we go to greet the angry master of this place," he said dramatically, leading her through the gryphon-guarded front door.

Somewhere in the vast recesses of the Specchiato Marco was waiting. Meg couldn't meet him a second time on the arm of François Vitelli. She gave him her hand, and he understood perfectly. "Some things must be better done alone, and so I shall go to my room and work while you resolve the conflicts of your heart. Until later. . . ." He walked jauntily up the stairs.

Well, Marco could find her if he wanted her. She had her own work to do for now. She had spent almost a full day already, and she didn't yet know the extent of her responsibilities.

She found Snapper and Ted in a dusty room in the old

servants' wing, where they had been given the wherewithal to establish a darkroom for the development of their black-and-white film. They were top professionals who knew exactly what to do, and Meg was relieved by their assurances that everything was going to be okay.

"No sweat," Snapper said. "I'm going to feel like a native in no time."

No sweat, Meg smiled to herself. She wished she felt as confident.

CHAPTER FIFTEEN

MINUTES LATER Meg stood at the door of the apartment feeling a sharp sense of déjà vu. She knew full well that she would have agreed to anything to get back to this place and Marco.

She entered the front door and looked warily around the living room. The apartment was still in disarray, strewn with invitations, invoices, odds and ends of fabric samples. Teresa looked up from her lapful of papers. "Oh, Meg, I was starting to worry! My mother arrived full of eagerness to meet you, but you had not yet returned."

A smiling woman stood up to greet her. She was perhaps fifty, with silver-tinged auburn hair done up in a soft classic coil—the very picture of gracious femininity. Meg's first impression was of fragility. She couldn't imagine this lady striking out in the modern world without a protective male on her arm.

"I am Bianca Montevalde," she said softly. "I am delighted to meet you."

"A pleasure," Meg answered the warm smile. "I didn't mean to keep you waiting, but François Vitelli—"

"Ah, Vitelli," she interjected easily. "A most demanding man, but a genius, don't you agree? I want him to lend me one of his ensembles for the festivities.

He will suspect that my connection with the wealth and taste of old Italy will be to his advantage." She smiled frankly. "He is a man, is he not?"

"What happened, Meg?" Teresa pressed. "Did you take him to the Correr?"

"Everything went almost too well. He agreed to my idea, and I've already introduced him to Adella Prati and her sewing women. Best of all, he's happy."

"Grazie à Dio!" Teresa laughed and made a face. "If this historic event of Marco's takes place on schedule it will be a miracle!"

Meg didn't want to ask where the great Marco was at this moment. She set to work with Teresa and Bianca, suggesting modifications in the record-keeping system of expenses and guest replies.

"Did you see Marco's message to you?" Bianca asked after a while.

"What message?"

"It was in that pile," Teresa said. "I must have set other papers on top of it. Ah, here it is. Marco is a fine one for instructions."

Meg grew tense at the sight of his scrawled dark handwriting on a piece of parchment memo paper.

Most important that you come to my office in the Specchiato at 6:00 P.M. today.

I shall expect you.

M.

She glanced at her watch. It was already 6:15. "Was there a special problem?"

Bianca shrugged her shoulders. "I suspect he wants a willing slave. These last weeks have been terrible, Teresa tells me, with Marco demanding twenty-five hours a day from every day. We must not let him bully us. I always say that a woman's strength lies in her ability to seem less capable than she is."

"Mother, don't you feel sorry for him?" Teresa argued.

"I am glad I have only just arrived. Don't you agree, Meg?" Bianca's canny feminine eyes looked up for confirmation.

"I don't think one way or the other. But I must find Marco's office. Where is it?"

Teresa pointed. "It is down the first corridor to the end and then down one flight of stairs to the entrance level. Just follow the line of workmen. They have to get Marco's permission for everything." She suppressed a smile.

"I see," Meg said, girding herself. "If his mood is bad he will just have to put up with mine."

On the lower floor of the palazzo the dampness of the canals was more noticeable. She knocked firmly on a large, weathered oak door and was answered from within by a brusque, *"Avanti."*

Marco looked up from the work on his desk. "You are late. I trust it will be the last time. Or is this a vacation for you?"

"Signor Montevalde," she snapped back quickly, "I expect some courtesy. I have had a very long day dealing with a temperamental Frenchman, a houseful of seamstresses, a mountain of untended details...and I am late only because someone else—not myself—lost your *billet doux* beneath the stacks of invitations." She sat down on the chair opposite his desk, trying to regain her composure. It was the worst possible entrance she could have made, but he had goaded her into it.

When she looked at him again he had an infuriating little smile on his lips. "It is all more than you can tolerate, hmm? One bad day and you are at the end of your rope?"

"Not really," she said carefully, refusing to take the bait. "But I must ask for some basic demarcation of duties, some ground rules if this ceremony is to happen on the date you wish."

"What rules would you have me set? For Signor Montevalde, a full day of fighting the inertia of two dozen workmen, all with their own ideas for renovating a centuries-old palazzo. For Signorina Brown, afternoon tea at Florian's with attentive men. . . ."

She stood up to meet his cutting words head on. "You agreed that I would work here in my professional capacity, and I will not accept less than that! If I have misunderstood my contract I am prepared to leave tomorrow."

"Sit down, Meg," he said quietly. "I had no business saying what I did—you are right. But equals should do the same amount of work, don't you agree? I meant nothing beyond that. I am informed that you are staying at the apartment." There was a trace of conciliation in his words.

She sat down slowly. "Teresa insisted. I would rather have stayed with my crew at the Regina."

"With everything pressing upon us it may be best that you are here, *è vero*? Now, tell me about Vitelli."

She sighed. "Vitelli arrived this morning full of demands about his accommodations and his designs. He insists on staying at the palazzo instead of his hotel. . . ."

"And so you offered him a room at the Hotel Specchiato, eh?"

"Not exactly. If I didn't want to risk losing him altogether I had to make some allowances for his eccentricities. . . ."

"Go on. I am eager to know why he is upstairs right now lounging in the *prima* bedchamber of the palazzo."

"Please, Marco!" She noticed his demeanor soften slightly at her use of his given name. "He arrived with only three gowns from his collection, and presented himself as if he deserved a vacation at our expense. But Maude would have my hide if that's all he did. She expects a real show—hundreds of fashion shots, lots of dazzle." By now she was gesticulating like an Italian. "I had to do something fast, so I took him to the Correr Museum and persuaded him to design a special collection based on the Renaissance costumes, which he's doing this very minute, I hope. With any luck the plan will work. . . ."

Marco leaned back in his leather chair. "I am getting a better picture of your abilities. It is often necessary to make compromises to get what we desire." He clasped his hands behind his head and closed his eyes for a moment. "Is there any more I should know about this affair with Vitelli?"

"No, except that he himself chose that bedroom. It seemed best to let him have it, since it was far enough away from the center of activities. This gives him a place to work and soothes his ego. I hope you don't object."

"Why should I object that you are adept at soothing male egos. . .or that this renowned playboy couturier is the first person outside of my family to occupy the master bedroom in the last two hundred years?" His eyes flashed upward. "François Vitelli may draw some inspiration from the fact that most of the Renaissance princes of the house of Montevalde were born in that bed."

"And were you?" she asked impulsively.

"*Si.* I was the first son of a first son. I never thought I would need to prove that point," he added almost to himself. "When I was younger I dreamed that my own son would be born there. But time changes many dreams, does it not?"

Meg cleared her throat. "I'll need to meet the officials of Venice and coordinate our plans with them. Can you arrange that?"

"Will tomorrow be soon enough? You must join my family for dinner tonight. Lucia will be unhappy if you refuse. It is really her invitation I am offering."

"That would be fine...."

"...*Marco*," he prompted. "Dinner is at eight."

"Eight." She stood up and left quickly, brushing past a workman who was on his way to see Marco.

How stupid of her to ask about his family bed, of all things! Meg went rapidly through the busy halls, her mind calculating whether she had won or lost this encounter. It must have taken him years to perfect his masculine technique—first a little acid and punishment, then an abrupt switch to the amused master of the house...ending with a touching reminiscence about his boyhood dreams. And she wished he wouldn't wear that particular brand of cologne!

Suddenly it seemed like yesterday that she'd been with Marco at Villa Terza. She couldn't let all these months of effort be blown away on her first day back at the Specchiato.

Teresa and her mother were gone when Meg returned to the apartment. After a cold shower designed to drive some sense back into her she wrapped herself in her fleecy robe and sat on the edge of her bed. It was imperative that she separate business from everything else and stick to it. *I have to,* she insisted silently.

Just before eight o'clock Meg checked herself in the armoire mirror, satisfied that her pink linen Chanel-style suit looked proper for the occasion. The previous September she had worn a cotton skirt and blouse to dinner at the Specchiato—but circumstances were entirely different now. Her suit was the kind that belonged at business meetings in fine restaurants, worn by women on the way up who wanted to look forceful, businesslike, but completely feminine at the same time.

Nobody was in the living room at the appointed hour. The polished table in the small dining room hadn't been set, either. Just then Teresa popped her head around the corner. "Dinner is in the formal dining room. Did Marco forget to tell you?"

They walked out into the hallway and through tall double doors, entering a room Meg had never seen before. Lit by the subtle glow of candles, the high-ceilinged dining room was decorated in eighteenth-century style. The mood was old-fashioned and romantic.

The "family" consisted of Marco, Ugo, Bianca, Teresa, and François Vitelli. Marco helped Meg into a high-backed petit-point chair between Ugo and Vitelli. *Not exactly an ideal matching of temperaments,* she thought. Vitelli was attired in a *La Bohème* costume—a creamy satin artist's tunic, soft unstructured trousers and supple black leather boots. Ugo was rumpled and careless in a modish sports jacket and slacks, while Marco alone dressed to fit the occasion: topaz-colored dinner jacket over well-fitted darker slacks, with his open-neck shirt softened by a loosely tied silk scarf. In the candlelight he might have been from another century.

Vitelli immediately demanded her attention. "You did not remember my advice," he chided sotto voce from a few inches away. "The pink color suits you, but the cut is too severe." He reached to touch the collar of her suit. "Nevairr linen, remember that. I will find you some special fabrics and create the proper vehicle for your formal occasions."

She smiled noncommittally. Across the table Marco had noticed the exchange. "Signor Vitelli," he said, "are you enlisting amateur models for your show?"

"I was telling Mademoiselle Brown that she does herself a disservice to wear tailored clothes. It takes from her extraordinary feminine charm, don't you agree?"

Marco twirled the stem of his crystal wineglass as he spoke. "I find it impossible to know what suits Signorina Brown."

"Perhaps she needs one of your exquisite creations, François," Bianca said with deference in her voice.

"My feelings exactly," Vitelli said.

Marco turned to a servant who had entered with the soup course. However, the awkward tension around the table left Meg with very little appetite. She could feel Vitelli's admiring glances next to her but she hadn't the heart for bantering. Her alternative for conversation was Ugo, but that was impossible.

Teresa filled in the gaps by talking busily to the table in general about troubles they were having with the postal service, and about the extra caterers who had been hired to assist Lucia. Bianca kept a benign smile on her face through the whole dinner, and Marco for the most part was silent.

By the time the Marsala custard dishes had been cleared away Meg was quite certain she would not be joining the "family" again if she had the choice. She excused herself and said good-night to everyone, maneuvering quickly past Vitelli to avoid a hand kiss or more extravagant compliments. She knew that he had a purpose—playing cupid—but she couldn't carry it off.

Marco's hand detained her at the door. "If you have no other plans," he said with a glance at Vitelli, "Giulio Prati is coming in a little while. I want you to be there, also."

"I have no other plans, except to go to bed at a decent hour tonight."

"And so you shall. My office in half an hour, then?" He bowed and moved away.

"Dio mio!" Teresa said when the women were back in the apartment. "What a dinner! Marco was so rude to Vitelli."

Bianca smiled again. "It is the law of the jungle, darling. With Meg here the men regard one another as rivals."

Meg laughed nervously. "If he was displaying dominant male behavior it was only because of inborn reflexes, having nothing to do with me."

"Vitelli *was* quite attentive," Teresa commented. "Was Marco polite when he saw you earlier?"

"Polite enough," Meg hedged. "We have a working arrangement now."

"*Madonna mia*, Meg!"

GIULIO PRATI WELCOMED MEG with outstretched arms when she reached the doorway of Marco's office thirty minutes later.

"My good friend, how elegant you have grown since I last saw you! Like a butterfly from a cocoon." He embraced her with a peck on each cheek.

"Giulio and I were just speaking of your suspicions about the Specchiato," Marco said.

"The two men and the so-called hidden panel," Giulio explained.

"You know as much as I do, Signor Prati." Suddenly Meg felt on the spot. Their voices were terribly serious.

Marco stepped forward. "If Giulio and I take you to the room of mirrors, would you be willing to stand exactly where you were when you witnessed the two men entering the hidden door?"

"Of course, but—"

"My dear lady, I wish I were free to say more to you, but it is part of an investigation," the detective said apologetically.

"Does it have to do with the missing ruby earring?" she ventured.

Giulio cleared his throat. "It would be best if you did not speculate further on the subject." His face showed concern and a sincere regret that she had made that deduction.

"If you wish," she said.

Marco led them through the palazzo and up a narrow winding staircase once used by servants. Near the great room they stopped. Giulio Prati went inside alone and Meg proceeded up the short flight of steps to the little round balcony where she had stood that day in September. Marco went up with her.

"I was here admiring the paintings on the ceiling," she said loudly enough for Giulio to hear her from his position just below the balcony. "The mirrored room was only partially lit and the balcony was in darkness."

"And where were the men when you first heard them?" Giulio called up from the shadowy room.

"I was leaning forward a little to see where the sounds were coming from. Just about where you are standing, maybe a bit to your right."

"Here?"

"Yes. One man was next to the wall there, and the other was hurrying toward him from that direction."

Meg was concentrating on the questions and didn't realize until it was too late that Marco had come up just behind her. His body pressed lightly against hers, and she felt his hands slip beneath her loose jacket and encircle her waist. His touch was full of heat, possessive and strong, igniting tremors that threatened her equilibrium—except that she was unable to move. He was holding her fast against the low balcony railing.

"Signorina," Giulio continued from below, "and then what did you notice?"

A darkly passionate whisper next to her ear said, "What did you notice, *signorina*? Did you notice this...?" His tongue made hot darting probes around the inside curves of her ear. "Or this...?" His hands slid smoothly up her silk blouse until they were exploring her breasts. Meg felt her nipples tighten and grow hard, and she had no will whatsoever to stop him.

"*Signorina*, are you still there?" Giulio asked.

"Y...yes," she said. "I...." She found her voice again and answered him. "The door closed quickly after them and they were gone." She could think of nothing but the devastating force that flowed between Marco and herself. He was slowly turning her to face him, withdrawing his hands and placing them on either side of her face, very tenderly.

"In this darkness, *cara*," he whispered, "you know I am real. If you cannot be honest with me in the light of day, then perhaps night will give you shelter from your charade." He lifted her face and brushed his lips against hers, back and forth until the heat between them demanded more. The long, slow, penetrating kiss that followed took her breath away.

"Did you think I would let you keep me at arm's length after all the time I have waited for you?" His voice was deep and soft.

Giulio was calling them to come down and join him.

"Silent?" Marco murmured. She could feel him looking at her in the half light. "Silent and innocent and passionate—all at the same time."

She stepped away from him and swayed against the balcony's edge. "We'd better go down now," she said on a whisper of breath. She could barely hear her own voice over the thundering of her heartbeat.

"Of course, *piccola*, I will do as you say. Haven't I always?"

They descended the steps and reentered the mirrored room. Meg was feeling light-headed and flustered, and she saw in a dozen reflections that her hair wasn't in perfect order.

If Giulio noticed anything he said nothing about it, however. "This is a puzzle. We know that the door is here, but we have not found the key to its opening."

"It is not like the other secret door, the one that leads

to the vault room," Marco said calmly. "There doesn't seem to be a pressure point in the ornamental fixture that unlatches the panel for this one."

Giulio nodded his head slowly. "I am worried that one day, with all these workers in the building, someone will accidentally trigger the panel and ruin any fresh evidence that may be behind it. But I have said too much already. Thank you very much, *signorina*. I know I can trust your discretion."

Meg moved her head in affirmation. She still hadn't regained full mastery over her body and thought processes. And what about Marco? He seemed unaffected by their recent potent intimacy. How could he recover so quickly when she was still like this?

There was one obvious explanation: he was playing with her—taking advantage of her in order to show who was more powerful. It was one hell of a game for a full-grown man to be playing! She fumed to herself as Giulio Prati took his leave. It wasn't even a matter of which of them had won this skirmish. There was no game at all, as far as she was concerned.

She looked up at Marco. "If you'll excuse me, I'm very tired. Thank you for a pleasant evening." She didn't care what he was thinking at that moment.

Much later, as she lay in her bed mulling over the disturbing problems of the Montevalde family, she heard Marco cross the living room and shut the door to his bedroom. What a story it would make. But she would never be so cruel as to write about the Montevaldes, as Marco had once accused her of doing. She felt the most sorry for Teresa, who was valiantly trying to hold everything together.

After a while she recognized the little sound that the

liquor cabinet made. So he couldn't sleep, either. Was he reflecting on his sins, worrying about the coming ceremonies. . . or devising a way to block Ugo's dark intentions toward him?

A second door opened, and a conversation started in the living room. Bianca and Marco spoke softly in Italian for a long time. Meg didn't want to listen, but she couldn't help noticing the name *Bette* repeated several times. Was it the same Bette who had dogged Marco's steps in Los Angeles—Bette Slocum? That surely wasn't an Italian name.

The conversation finally drew to a close, and the two bedroom doors shut again, leaving silence. Meg could only guess what it had all been about.

CHAPTER SIXTEEN

LUCIA KNOCKED GENTLY on Meg's door at an early hour. Meg took the large white wicker breakfast tray she carried and placed it on the side table. "Mmm!" she said as she lifted the linen cloth and discovered some warm, fragrant rolls, homemade preserves and dark rich coffee. "How very kind of you to think of me like this." She reached out to squeeze Lucia's hand.

"It was Signor Marco who asked me to bring it, *signorina*. He felt you would be tired from yesterday and in need of a happy waking up. He is a good man, Signor Marco." The housekeeper set about straightening up the room and adjusting the shutters to let in more of the morning sunlight.

"How kind of *him*, then," Meg said briskly.

"*Si*, he thinks of everyone's needs. I am to tell you that you are meeting with a man of the Venezia committee at ten o'clock this morning. His name is Signor Donato. He will be waiting for you in the grand hall of mirrors." She left the room.

Meg savored her coffee and thought about Marco. Lucia had said he was being generous, but maybe he only wanted to be sure that she woke up in time to meet the Venice official. She did appreciate the chance to feel like a princess for a few minutes before venturing forth to the chaos of her assignment, however. She shouldn't be ungrateful.

She surveyed her clothes, which were hanging neatly in the armoire, and chose a cerise silk dress with a matching silk knit sweater. Today she felt like wearing something bright and dashing. She was tired of being taken for a pale flower.

Lucia was clearing away the tray when Meg emerged from the bathroom. "I forget to say that Signorina Teresa has gone to Burano early this morning with Signor Vitelli. Signor Marco told her that you are too busy today to join them." Meg wasn't surprised. Marco obviously needed to feel completely in charge of her affairs. She would have to say something about that.

The telephone rang as she was leaving the room. It was Giulio Prati, inquiring politely after her comfort. After relaying Adella's greetings he arrived at the reason for the call: "I wish to remind you to say nothing about my visit last evening."

A disturbance came on the line, several clicks that momentarily stopped their conversation. "...as I was saying, Signorina Meg, I regret involving you in my investigation, but you possess important knowledge, even though you may not realize it. Take no chances with yourself, please."

"If you mean that my drawings were useful to you, I am glad, but I'm not sure what more I can do...." She had a sudden shivery feeling that a third person was listening to their conversation. "In fact, I really don't know anything at all," she added strongly.

"Do not become alarmed, my friend," Giulio cautioned. "I will speak to you again very soon. Merely keep your eyes open as you go about your duties in the Specchiato. *Ciao.*"

She heard the click as he hung up, and then heard a second click. Somebody else *was* on the line. But no one besides herself and Lucia was in the apartment, and she could hear busy sounds from the kitchen. Were there other extensions to this private number? The line in Marco's office was separate, she knew, with its own number. She was still puzzling over that bit of mystery as she left to meet the man from the Venice committee.

In the mirrored room she was studying the corner where the secret panel was when she heard a throat being cleared behind her. She turned around quickly to find a darkly handsome middle-aged man standing rather too close to her.

"Signorina Brown?" His bright black eyes were clearly pleased with her—and with himself, it seemed.

She managed a businesslike smile and extended her hand to him. "Signor Donato? I am happy to meet you."

"My pleasure entirely," he said admiringly. "I had no idea that a very important American magazine would send us so beautiful a lady—so feminine, so. . . ." He cradled her hand and gave it a lingering kiss.

"I'm honored to be able to work here in your lovely city, *signore*," she said, suppressing a smile. Her perverse mind wondered what he would do if she seized his hand, kissed it and told him that she found him extremely attractive. . . for an official of Venice.

She kept him at a safe distance by offering him the schedule for the ceremonies and leading him at a fast pace around the huge room. She indicated the platform where the fashion models would make their entrance, where the harpsichordists would sit, and how the tableau of the presentation of the Marco Polo Cup would fit into all of it.

Signor Donato soon lost the gleam in his eye and hurriedly started making his own notes. Within half an hour they had exchanged enough information for him to realize that Meg expected the event to come off like clockwork. Venice would oversee the tableau as well as the formal presentation of the Specchiato by Marco, and would host a luncheon during the day. The cocktail reception, decorations, fashion show and photo coverage were up to her.

At the end of their meeting Meg interrupted Signor Donato's flowery compliments by once again offering her hand in a firm and short handshake. "So very kind of you to come, *signore*." He made a small bow of respect and departed.

Meg was pleased with herself. She had half a mind to write to the author of that book about the *Summertime* syndrome and tell her that at least one American woman had her wits about her.

Before she left the room she took another look at the baffling wall. Wouldn't it make a fascinating story if she found the secret mechanism to open it! Just then, Snapper and Ted Bingham entered the room, escorted by Marco, who acknowledged Meg with a tight smile and a nod.

"You should have been with us this morning, Meg," Snapper said enthusiastically. "Mr. Montevalde showed us more rooms than the Biltmore Hotel has! Can you believe there are two ballrooms, a music room, twelve bedrooms if you don't count a whole wing for servants, three sizes of dining rooms depending on how the master feels that day...it's mind boggling!" He swept her into a brotherly hug. "How's my girl?"

"Just fine, Snap. You've certainly got your work cut out for you. But this room is the focal point of our coverage."

"The house of reflections it is, all right. Montevalde was telling us about the first ancestor of his, the one who had the treasures. We're going to have a few hours just before the ceremony to photograph the whole collection, including the Marco Polo Cup. I never thought I'd get a thrill out of hanging around dusty old rooms, but this place is something else. We even got a peek into the secret vault room. Holy Toledo!"

"I know," Meg said quietly.

"I just hope I can get enough available light in some of these rooms—especially the music room—to catch that haunted mood, you know what I mean? I don't want it to look like a stage setting. It's got to hint at all the things that have happened here over the years."

"Watch out, Snap, or you'll end up being a feature writer," she laughed, very much aware when Marco moved closer to her, an intent expression on his face.

"And how was your interview with Signor Donato?" he asked.

"We both found it very educational. I think he had very little idea of my...capabilities at first."

"But you showed him your professional credentials," he finished for her.

"I let him know that I was here on business!"

"The poor man must be devastated."

"I doubt that," she said with a smile. "How many Italian men are truly devastated when their romantic plans are thwarted?"

Marco addressed Snapper. "Did I tell you that the word *specchiato* also has the meaning of upright, honest. . . flawless? Rather a mockery, in a way, since there is so much around this fine old building that is dishonest and flawed."

Snapper looked uncomfortable and turned to leave, but Marco stopped him. "Forgive me, my personal concerns often overflow and affect others not involved. I must get back to the office now. Perhaps we shall all have an opportunity to have a pleasant meal together, eh?" He nodded to everyone and left the room.

"I think I like the guy," Snapper said. "He's a little moody, but okay."

Meg was mulling Marco's words about dishonesty. If they were meant for her, it was a cheap shot.

"By the way, did you know that the Slocum woman is in town?"

"Bette Slocum?"

"I saw her outside the palazzo as I came in. It was her, all right. Blond hair, lots of rings, a voice that would break glass."

"That's all we need," Meg sighed. Whenever she thought of that condescending woman a warning buzzed in her mind. She recalled their strained conversation at the mayor's party. Just how friendly was she with Ugo? And why?

"I know a great place for lunch," Snapper said. "Interested?"

"Just give me a few minutes to check for messages at the apartment, and I'll join you in the downstairs entry hall."

At the door of the apartment Meg met Teresa, who was very downcast. "Enzo was impossible today!"

Vitelli stepped forward in turn, from where he had been contemplating one of the *salotto* windows. "I am shocked. He cuts off his nose to spite his face." He rolled expressive eyes skyward. "I did my best to convince him that a great creative genius must cooperate with the people who have the money. I said, 'Look at Michelangelo! Look at da Vinci! Look at me—Vitelli! It was years before I was free to be Vitelli.' " His broad grin showed his sense of humor about himself and his artistic ego.

"Enzo deserves to be poor," Teresa pouted.

"I told him: 'Enzo, you will lose Teresa, the love of your life, because you refuse a man you consider bourgeois. Now, who is the unprincipled person, eh?' I said, 'If you are as good as you claim, you can make the great passion of Dante and Beatrice flow through your hands to serve the most beautiful love of this modern couple, Monsieur and Madame Veitch.' I left him to think about that. He is no fool." He put a comforting arm around Teresa's shoulder. "You will see. And now I must spend the rest of this day locked in my room with my drawings. My first obligation was to love—my second is to my reputation. Seven days! Madame Prati comes this afternoon with samples of the fabrics of Venice." He kissed their hands and waved an elaborate farewell.

Teresa smiled grimly. "Are you ready for more bad news?"

Meg shrugged her shoulders. "Go ahead."

"Ugo has made his move to attack Marco. My mother will not talk about it, but I must tell you, my good friend."

Ugo again! What a dark force he was. They sat down on one of the couches in the living room.

"I told you that Ugo wants to prove that he has the right to the family title and the palazzo. It sounded so absurd when I first heard about it. But now he has filed a claim in the courts, with evidence that our twin fathers were not properly identified on the birth certificates."

"What evidence?"

"I do not know. His lawyer has a reputation for finding people who will swear to things. I think he gives them money." She put her hands over her face and stifled a sob. "The judge is deciding right now if the donation of the Specchiato should be canceled until after the case is resolved. How could Ugo do this!"

"He must be desperate."

"*Si*, desperate to get his hands on the Montevalde treasures, to sell them for himself, to go against the honor and traditions of our family. Oh, Meg! Everything is so terrible now!"

Meg held her for a long moment, saying nothing. That was what Marco meant when he spoke of dishonesty and flaws—it had nothing to do with her own petty disputes with him. She suddenly felt very small, and a burning tide of shame washed over her. "You shouldn't be alone right now, Teresa. Come to lunch with us. You could use seeing some cheerful faces."

Meg, Teresa and the *Au Courant* crew headed for a charming little restaurant overlooking one of the *rii*. They sat outside, where the early May sun was making a valiant effort to warm the air. Everyone was friendly to Teresa, which helped to lift her from her depression, but Meg was deep in her own thoughts. She wanted desperately to be with Marco, to let him know that it mattered to her what happened to him. How could she ever persuade him that she truly cared about him, and not have him throw it back in her face?

Teresa excused herself early. She had music lessons to give and wouldn't return to the Specchiato until after dinner. Meg herself was too restless to linger with the crew over dessert. All the way back to the palazzo she was like a sleepwalker, readjusting her thoughts about Marco. There seemed no way to clear the air between them.

She was mulling over that point as she entered the downstairs hall. It would be good to get to her office and put her mind on tangible tasks—problems that could be solved by logic.

She was brought up short by Ugo, who was sitting on the curved ledge of the wellhead with a grin on his lips. Meg had to fight down the urge to turn around and leave.

"I have been waiting for you, *signorina*." He jumped to his feet. "Would you care to have a cup of espresso upstairs?"

"I have so much work to do, Ugo. You'll have to excuse me today." It took a supreme effort to be civil to him.

"You must have time for a short talk. Coffee will be good for you. You look very tired." His smile was intense, his eyes boldly fixed on hers. She didn't want him to see her wavering, for she was just the slightest bit afraid of him. But if Lucia were there, what could possibly happen?

"Just for a minute, then," she conceded. Maybe she would find out something from him that might be helpful to Marco. She refused his arm and walked up the steps ahead of him, using her own key at the door of the apartment.

Lucia served them coffee and lemon cookies and returned to the kitchen after giving Meg a look that said, *I'll be close by*. Ugo sat down next to her on the sofa. "Are you happy here?" he asked with a disarmingly innocent smile.

"I have a job to do. Why I'm here has nothing to do with happiness."

There was a heavy silence while they sipped at the dark, bitter brew. "It must be very strange for you to see the things that happen in an old family like mine, hmm?" He watched for a reaction.

"Every family has its problems." She refused to react.

"You are not alarmed with what you have seen?"

"What have I seen?" she threw back at him equally innocently. He would have to come right out with it and stop playing with words.

"I was thinking of your little sketchbook and the pictures you drew of the room of mirrors. Very good pictures, very realistic."

"I have had art training. But when did you see my drawings? I don't remember showing them to you."

He chewed slowly on a crumbling lemon cookie. "One day when you were here last September, I happened to see them on a table."

"In my bedroom."

"*Si.* Are you offended? You cannot expect privacy in such a busy place as this." His pale eyelashes cast odd shadows over his bluish eyes, giving them a not-quite-sane appearance.

"Did you also look at the other sketchbooks in the room?"

His eyes flickered slightly. "Others?"

"Oh, yes. I made dozens of drawings, of many rooms in the Specchiato." She was lying, but somehow she knew that she could distract him by going on the offensive.

"How interesting." His smile was a twisted smirk. "I suppose Teresa has told you about my intention to prove my legal right to my father's inheritance."

"Yes." If he carried the conversation much further she didn't know if she could keep from angering him. "I must be getting to my office now." She leaned forward to set her cup and saucer on the coffee table.

"There is one thing more," he said slowly, moving his body to block her exit from the couch. "You seem to be discreet, and I like that quality in a woman. I want to confide in you, but I do not want what I say repeated to Marco. That would cause unnecessary problems."

"I don't usually reveal confidences," she said, trying to keep her revulsion out of her voice.

"Good. My lawyer wants me to ask if you are willing to give a deposition—a sworn statement."

"About what, for heaven's sake?"

"About slanderous statements my cousin has made. I am finding witnesses who will swear that Marco has systematically maligned me in public. Such slander could prejudice a judge's mind about me when he decides the validity of my claim to the Montevalde title." He had an air of righteous indignation. "I expect to get a statement from a retired Montevalde servant who was present at the birth of my father and his twin. It makes me sick to think of my father being cheated of his position as *conte* because of a small error made by an incompetent midwife. The identity of twins is often confused. Now—when will you be free to meet with my lawyer?'' Ugo's tone was confident.

Meg searched frantically for words. She had to stop his foolishness and yet not make an enemy out of him. ''If I gave a deposition it wouldn't help your case anyway, Ugo. I've never heard Marco slander you, and his observations are always compassionate.''

''Compassionate!'' he spat. ''Of course he made it sound like he cares about me!''

''I think he truly does,'' she said as if speaking to a child.

''He has everyone under his spell!'' He crashed his cup down on the tray. ''But not for long. . . .'' His voice trailed off and he stretched his legs out, reaching into his coat pocket for a cigarette. ''Do not give me your answer now. Think about it. Oh, by the way, did you know that I have hired an architect to redesign this apartment—a good architect?''

''I really must be going,'' she said, eager to get away from his heavy energies.

''It is time a man in my position settles down. I *will* be the Conte Montevalde very soon, you understand.''

''If you say so. Now, please excuse me.'' She stood and pushed past him to the door.

''Consider my proposition, *signorina*. It could mean a handsome sum of money for you if you cooperate.''

Meg walked briskly from the apartment, then almost ran down the marble steps to her office. She'd had an almost overpowering urge to do something radical to the gloating madman on the couch. She felt vaguely sick to her stomach as she opened the creaking door to her dark office, and wrenching tears started down her cheeks. Poor Marco! Poor, poor Marco! What hideous repayment for all the sacrifices he'd made on Ugo's behalf!

For a while she sat weeping, enraged at the injustice of a court system that would even consider such a case. To think of Ugo having the power to stop Marco from presenting the Specchiato to Venice!

Giulio Prati must hear of this immediately, she decided. She picked up the telephone, but stopped in mid-motion. *This* was the extra extension to the apartment telephone number! Whoever had eavesdropped on her conversation with Giulio Prati that morning had probably done so from her office. There was no doubt in her mind that it had been Ugo.

She thought back to her conversation with Signor Prati. What had she said? Carefully she dialed Giulio's number. As the phone rang she heard a familiar click and hung up at once. It was happening again. All the odd bits and pieces of Ugo's peculiar behavior suddenly began to form a coherent picture: the Empress Earrings, the hidden door, even the drunken visit to her bedroom the night before she left Venice last year...Ugo *was* after the Montevalde treasures, but he wasn't waiting for the slow wheels of the law courts to turn. He was going to take what he wanted right now. He had a plan that was still in the process of being executed, and he believed she knew about it.

In spite of the piles of unfinished work on her desk she decided to go right away to Giulio Prati's office. She was beginning to feel paranoid, fearful that things were closing in around her. Hadn't Giulio warned her not to take chances? It was silly to blow the situation up out of proportion, but she would definitely feel better to hear reassurances from Detective Prati's own lips.

His face was grave as Meg sat in his office and related what had happened. She also confessed her suspicions about the telephone and about Ugo's criminal intentions.

"So now you know," he replied when she'd finished. "Unfortunately, Ugo has done nothing about which we can take action. We know he has been systematically removing some of the artwork from the Specchiato, but we have no proof. And none of the items has yet shown up on the international markets. Marco is desperate to bring the matter to a conclusion." He leaned back with a hint of a smile on his lips.

"The difficulty is that there has never been a full inventory of the contents of the palazzo. Certain pieces may be missing, or they may simply be stored in some remote closet. But other pieces—a Caravaggio painting, for example—are no longer hanging on their walls. I never wished for you to become involved, Signorina Meg. I am so very sorry...."

"I *am* involved, whether I want to be or not," she said. "But what will happen next?"

He shrugged. "I wish I knew. I have three men in the palazzo at this moment, pretending to be workmen. I have located a building near the Specchiato and another on one of the outer islands that I believe are used for Ugo's illegal transactions...but the fellow is either very clever or a lucky blunderer. His motives are clear, his access to the Montevalde treasures is obvious. We have but to find him with a Caravaggio in his hands." He gave a short mirthless laugh. "For you, my friend, I can promise that one of my men will try to be near you. I doubt that you are in danger, but it is always best to be careful."

"I'm starting to wish I had never seen the two men go into that invisible door," she said ruefully.

"Feel confident of the support around you. You have Marco very close, do you not? Have you told him the extent of your knowledge about Ugo?" His voice was touchingly concerned.

"No. We have a rather formal relationship. But I think he should be told about Ugo's attempt to buy my testimony. I would be more than happy to give a deposition about *that*—in fact, I insist. Maybe that will help the judge decide to throw the whole thing out."

"Let me take care of it. The judge is a friend of mine." He reached for his telephone. "Your offer alone may turn his decision in Marco's favor."

Meg left feeling better. She had at least done something positive to help Marco. But what would Maude think of the mess her assistant was in? A simple assignment, and this was what she did with it!

She started back to the Specchatio. Maybe everything would be all right after all. Giulio Prati had a firm hand and knew what to do. Marco was aware of what was going on, and Ugo wouldn't dare do anything overt with so many people swarming around the palazzo.

On the way back she stopped in a small campo to buy a bunch of tiny pink roses to brighten up her desk. On impulse she bought a second bunch.

Her first stop inside the palazzo was Marco's office. After knocking she stood outside his door, waiting for him to bark his usual *"Avanti!"* When he didn't, she pushed the door open and went in. There, surrounded by rolls of blueprints and several draftsman's tools, a black-and-white cat was sleeping in a state of confident relaxation in the middle of Marco's desk.

Obviously the master was not in. She found an empty glass on a shelf in the utilitarian bathroom next to the office and arranged one bunch of pink roses in it, then left a little note on a scrap of discarded paper, which she folded like an envelope:

> Please call Giulio Prati. Everything is going to be better.
>
> In friendship,
>
> Meg

She was actually relieved that Marco wasn't there. She hadn't really wanted to face him with her little peace offering, but she did want him to know that beneath all the stress there was goodwill on her side. *More than goodwill,* she sighed in futility, *much more*. But she had to keep the line drawn. What would he think if she cast off her reserve entirely and told him how she really felt? She would never do that, not until that cold day in hell when Marco Montevalde would prove he was capable of constancy, sensitivity, and respect.

Back at her desk she began to tackle the pile of paperwork. The visit to Giulio's office had lifted an invisible load from her mind, and she really did feel better. She knew she had done the right thing to leave the roses on Marco's desk, and she felt as if the careening course of their association would have a chance to stabilize. . . at least enough so that her heart didn't draw into a hard knot every time she came face to face with him. Her own bunch of roses filled her little office with a delightful fragrance, and she soon felt more peaceful.

Patty, Meg's assistant, returned from lunch and worked quietly in one corner amid her own clutter. She was writing all the letters of gratitude to the Venetian officials for their fine hospitality, as well as for allowing the American magazine exclusive coverage of the upcoming event.

In her absorption with her work Meg forgot about time until Patty switched on the lamp at her desk. It was obviously growing late. Both women stretched their cramped shoulder muscles and laughed in mutual sympathy.

Patty was going to have a night out with Snapper and some of the others at Harry's Bar. "Want to join us?" she offered.

Meg declined. She only wanted to get back to the apartment, check with Vitelli and Teresa, kick off her shoes and sink into a deep sleep. Dinner plans could wait.

In her bedroom the first thing she noticed was a silver bud vase that had been placed on her bedside table. In it was a single Murano-glass rose on a long delicate stem, its petals shot with filaments of dusty pink and gold. A small envelope rested against the vase and the note read:

Dare I believe that roses may be without thorns?
In pegno d'amicizia, Marco

P.S. Giulio told me everything. I am in your debt.

She touched the cool perfection of the shimmery rose and smiled. How ironic. For the first time he was making a tentative approach to her, rather than a bitter or headlong one. She wanted to believe that he meant it.

Meg reread the note, searching in spite of her better judgment for something more than the words themselves. *In pegno d'amicizia*... She reached for her Italian phrase book and found the meaning: "as a token of friendship."

She was annoyed with herself for demanding more. Her eyes traveled down the page and stopped at a phrase that made her heart constrict: "*un pegno d'amore*...a love token." Why was she so dissatisfied with her *pegno d'amicizia*? Wasn't it she who held Marco at arm's length? *Face it,* she said wearily to herself, *you're just a mixed-up love-starved American traveler who doesn't know the first thing about orchestrating a real life romance.* Maybe that was why she was a writer. At least she had the power to make what she wrote obey her every wish.

CHAPTER SEVENTEEN

LYING ON HER BED in the darkened room, Meg tried to imagine what it would be like to call this place home. What happiness to think that for the rest of her life she would have Venice—that every time she looked out her living-room windows she would gaze through luminous, centuries-old glass to the limpid waterway below. That she had but to step forth from the great entrance door of the palazzo to find enough beauty to fill her soul forever.

A long sigh followed, and she conceded that it was wonderful simply knowing that a place like this existed. Maybe, some distant day, she would come back to Venice and smile at the child in her that had once held so tightly to her fantasies. She would be a different woman by then, probably a senior writer/editor on *Au Courant* or some other publication, a world traveler who knew that there were plenty of places just as captivating as Venice. She might even be happily married.

Bianca knocked softly, then drifted into Meg's bedroom with a greeting. A waft of fine perfume came with her. She was going to be dining out with friends, she said, and Teresa, too. "A friend of Ugo's is being entertained—Bette Slocum, from California. But Marco has been obstinate about coming. You will not be alone tonight?"

"I have too much work to do to feel alone," Meg smiled. "Have a good time."

"Ciao," said the lilting voice.

Meg had seen enough of the beautiful people—especially Bette Slocum—to last a long time. They weren't any more interesting than regular people, she had decided after her first several assignments for Maude.

She was about to throw on casual clothes, grab some cheese and fresh rolls from Lucia's kitchen and spend the evening in her office, when the buzzer of her little intercom sounded. She pressed the button and Marco's voice crackled over the antiquated communications system, which linked the apartment to his office.

"Are you planning to work tonight?" he asked.

"Yes, did you need me for something?"

"I am feeling restless. How would you like to do something completely different and catch up with your work later? I need a change of atmosphere."

Meg's heart was pounding already. "Have you had dinner? I can find something to eat in the kitchen...."

"No. I have a better idea...a special place you have never been. How soon can you be ready? How about fifteen minutes?"

"I...of course," she stammered. *Of course!*

"I will meet you in the downstairs hall...." The line made a sputtering sound that covered his next words. "Meg...are you still there?"

"I'm still here."

"I just wanted to say thank-you," he said softly, and the crackling connection ended.

Fifteen minutes wasn't time enough to style her hair. The best she could do was to capture the major part of it in a lavender grosgrain ribbon and let the rest frame her face.

Meg's fingers felt clumsy as she worked with her makeup. Her gray eyes were looking very large tonight, she noticed, even without the *Au Courant*-style makeup. She felt like being feminine, damn it, and her taste drew her to select a cocktail length silk chiffon skirt, sea green and cut very full, with a matching long sleeved silk blouse, finely gathered at the low curve of the neckline. Tiny pearl buttons fastened at the bodice front and wrists.

Meg was dressing for herself as much as for Marco. She, too, had a need to get out. She even felt a little reckless.

The woman who looked back at her from the mirror resembled the old Meg Brown, but not exactly. Her eyes—thank heavens—didn't look as wide and eager as they had in the past, or as vulnerable.

Slightly more than fifteen minutes later she had her off-white evening bag in hand and her cozy blue Venetian knit stole over her arm as she hurried down the stairs to the hall. Marco turned at her approach, and a disarming smile spread slowly across his handsome face.

"How very lovely," he said gently. A frisson of pure pleasure left her temporarily without words as he reached to drape the misty blue wrap over her shoulders. He stood close to her for a moment before taking her hand firmly and leading her toward the door.

"Is it far, this place we're going?" she asked.

"As far away as I could take you and still be a gentleman," he said in a tone of exuberance she had never heard before. His hand carried an electrical charge that shot through her body and made her catch her breath with the sheer force of it.

The white motor launch was rocking easily at the little dock. "If the boat looks familiar, that's because it is," he said in answer to her thoughts. "Last year's storm damage to the hull was not terminal." He smiled as he helped her to step inside.

He wouldn't dare take her to the villa at La Mira, she thought giddily. He *had* mentioned taking her to dinner. It really didn't matter where they were going. It was so good—so unexpected—to be with Marco again, away from the Specchiato and its troubles.

"If I said we are going to the birthplace of Romeo and Giulietta, what would you think?" he teased.

"Verona?"

"*Si.* Such a lovely city and not so very far." He started the engine and gunned the boat out into the flow of water traffic, then made a wide right turn onto the Grand Canal. "Do you still feel like a tourist?" Marco shouted above the sound of the engine. "You should be almost a native Veneziana by now." There was no trace of sarcasm in his voice.

"I don't know what I am," she confessed with a laugh, pulling her soft warm stole closer around her.

After a while they came to the broad Piazzale Roma, where Marco moored his boat. It was a short walk to a parking garage and Marco's well-kept but old Mercedes coupe, which had a permanent parking place there.

In a few minutes they had crossed the Ponte della Libertà, racing along the autostrada in the direction of Padua and Verona. "It will not be long, only about 160 kilometers, an hour or so. We will be home at a respectable hour.'' He shot her a boyish glance and revved the engine to a high speed.

It was a lingering dusk, full of bright pinks, purples and golds, giving the shimmering illusion that the distant rolling hills, now deeply shadowed, held mysteries and wonders too magical for mortal men to discover.

''The Euganeian Hills,'' Marco said. ''Many people visit the spas there to take the waters and to bathe. As long ago as the ancient Romans. . . .''

''Does everything in Italy have that aura around it—the sense of yesterday and today all bound together?''

He smiled without taking his eyes from the speeding traffic on the road. ''Not everything, *cara mia*.'' He waited a while before speaking again, then reached out to touch her hand very lightly. ''I like it when we are easy with one another.''

Her fingers stirred with response at the warm contact and he lifted them to his lips for the gentlest of kisses. Meg's mind was already trying to judge exactly what was allowable—her damnable reasoning mind!

''Did you see Verona on your earlier tour?'' he asked as they finally passed beneath the old Roman arches that led to the central city.

"Only for as long as it took me to have lunch in a restaurant and become poisoned from the shrimp. But even then I thought it was a beautiful city.''

''No tourist restaurant for you tonight, *piccola*,'' he laughed.

They had come out into the large parklike expanse of the Piazza Brà, the center of the old city whose origins went back to early Roman times. The broad sidewalks around the square were filled with streams of evening strollers.

"The first breath of summer air has stirred my countrymen," Marco remarked as he swung into one of the rare parking spaces. "We Italians love to walk, to promenade and greet friends. The *passeggiata* is a tradition."

Meg looked about her but saw nothing modern in the buildings that enclosed the square, only that same wonderful familiar sense of antiquity—the high ancient walls on one side of the square, the dark and brooding hulk of the Roman Arena on another. In between, in a colorful profusion of awnings and white-draped tables were the busy restaurants. "One of those?" Meg asked hopefully.

Marco nodded, taking her hand for a dash through the stop-and-start traffic jam. "The one called Tre Corone, there on the right. It means three crowns."

Meg accepted Marco's suggestion that they dine outside to enjoy the activity and the view. Their waiter was attentive to the point of pampering them, and Marco placed the matter of the menu entirely in his able hands.

Through the leisurely dinner of excellent pasta, a vegetable-marinade salad, savory vegetable soup, a poached white fish from nearby Lake Garda and an indescribably good dessert of finely shredded orange peels cooked in sugar, butter and brandy, Meg and Marco talked lightly and easily. Marco seemed to want to avoid anything having to do with the Specchiato or his troubles with Ugo. Instead he commented perceptively about the food, the architecture of northern Italy and the nature of the Italian character.

Very close at hand were touching scenes of human nature. Lovers walked hand in hand in their bubbles of delightful isolation; swaggering young men tried to strike up conversations with groups of coy teenage girls who pretended not to notice them. Middle-aged couples, obviously married and finished with the game, strolled in companionable peace.

"It is indeed a difficult thing that God made male and female," Marco observed as he swirled the golden liquid in his wineglass. "It would have been so much simpler to devise another method of procreation and leave everyone free to develop true and lasting friendships, far from the biological urgencies." He raised a questioning eye to Meg.

She looked out at the passing parade and smiled. "If you took away the biological urgency there would be a terrible gap in people's conversation and activities—that's my humble opinion."

"I think you are right, *amica mia*. And what a waste of human creativity it is—love songs, love poems... paintings and buildings done in the name of love. Lives laid down in the name of the beloved." His eyes had changed their playful gleam and were probing at her for response.

"I will tell you a secret." He leaned closer to her. "You have spared me a similar waste of my artistic impulses, leaving me free to pursue my craft in a more practical manner."

"How have I done that?" she asked in a lighter tone than his, hoping to prevent something awkward.

"Several months ago—in September as it happened—I found myself falling in love with a beauteous American, but she in her baffling wisdom did not allow me to play out my passionate desires. . . ." He raised his wineglass in a silent toast to her. "I think about it now and realize that she was correct. A warm friendship that never burns can last far longer than love, don't you agree?''

''I...I value our friendship, Marco, if that's what you mean.'' What was he up to? He was so adept at seeming sincere, leading her into dead ends and forcing her to say what she didn't want to say.

''Indeed. I can count the ways that your friendship has helped me. Without you I might not have won the competition for the institute, no matter how you deny it. Without you and your offer to give a deposition about Ugo's attempt to bribe you, the judge might have ordered me not to give the Specchiato to Venezia. You have been invaluable to the direction of my life, even without fully realizing it. For that I am eternally grateful.''

His smile, one of alarming intensity, electrified the air between them. He lifted her hand to his lips for a kiss that sent flares of response careering through her nerves. But the gesture only led to a feeling of betrayal and emptiness. There was so much behind his two-edged words. His eyes watched her with apparent amusement as she tried not to rise to his provocation. She could have wept in her yearning for a sincere kiss, a truly loving caress, a gaze that said simply, I love you and will always love you.

He strengthened his grip on her hand. ''I will give you back your lovely hand when you admit that there is something strong between us still.'' His voice was low and demanding.

''I can't,'' she whispered. She drew her hand back firmly and said nothing more, but she felt the disturbing force of Marco's full attention upon her. ''Please don't do this,'' she pleaded softly. ''A real friendship doesn't need to punish. Can't we at least have that?''

His face changed slowly, until his eyes were clear once more, golden and good. "Forgive me, *piccola*. In my search to understand you I seem always to do it the wrong way...would you call it the Italian way, perhaps?" His beseeching expression forced a smile to her lips.

"I don't think all Italians are Romeos, you know," she said.

"And I do not think all American women travelers are confused Puritans with suppressed sexual longings. Now we are equal, hmm?" He made a wry face at her, then grew more serious. "Tell me one thing, my wise friend. What should I do if Ugo really does have a witness who swears there was a mistake at the birth of our fathers? What if it happens to be true?"

Meg reached out instinctively to touch his hand. "Then you will quietly remove yourself from Ugo's life. You have too much to contribute to the world to let one person's obsession affect you."

"I should not fight him? I'm not sure I agree."

"Fight him in the courts, of course. There can be no loss of honor in that."

Marco didn't move his hand from under hers. "Can you comprehend the feeling of responsibility I have for the preservation of the Specchiato and all it stands for?"

"I think I can."

"And still you believe I should release it without struggle?"

"You could spend the rest of your life bound up in Ugo's vengeance and never be free to be the creative artist you're meant to be. That should be your matter of honor, and nothing else," she said seriously.

He looked up at her with warmth radiating from his beautiful eyes. "I am so happy that I was standing in the Piazza San Marco that day when your handbag was taken. Now, shall we go? My watch says we will be home by midnight—a good time for friends to find their beds and be fresh for work in the morning." He brought her comforting hand to his lips for a different kind of kiss and let it go.

How could she continue to doubt him, she wondered. Was the fault entirely hers? She just didn't know. She would never know. It was all too strange, this power he had over her—this enchantment.

They drove back at a leisurely pace along the autostrada, allowing the trucks and honking speeders to pass them by. Marco was talking about the future of the Specchiato. "One way or another, Meg, the palazzo will be restored, no matter what happens. That is my resolve."

"I want to see it when it's finished," she said.

"Perhaps you will."

The night was very clear, with stars growing brighter as they moved farther away from the lights of the city. A crescent moon tinged with buttery warmth seemed to float on its back just above the horizon.

"I want to remember Italy like this," she said almost to herself.

"Will you be returning to California after the ceremony? I never asked."

"If I don't, Maude Draper will have my head on a platter. I'm supposed to be a working woman," she laughed.

Marco said nothing for a long time, and Meg gazed hungrily at the outlines of the Italian countryside, wishing that she *could* stay. How she longed to claim this lovely land as her own by right of love.

A few minutes after they'd passed the sign for Padua, Marco said quietly, "The Villa Terza is over there. It would be easy for the car to find itself upon the side road to La Mira." Another silence. "If we were lovers, Meg, I would take you there."

A flare of excitement and irritation raced through her blood. So, it was still a matter of lovers rather than love. What a universe of difference separated the two words! She burned silently. How bitterly disappointing that all he could offer her was this!

The voice next to her was low and rough. "There was never a shared passion, was there? Was there?" he prodded when she didn't reply.

"No," she lied painfully, "there never was."

After a terrible interval he threw his head back and laughed. "Oh, Signorina Brown. . . !"

"What is so funny?" she demanded.

"You! I expect to see your nose growing just like Pinocchio's! You are not a very good liar. . . ." He pressed the accelerator to the floor, and the car lurched into the fast lane, past a line of slower cars.

Meg sat back in the plush depths of the leather upholstery, speechless with a mixture of anger and humiliation. That he could actually laugh at her efforts to be strong and save them further pain! As if he knew all along that he could arouse her at will! It was too much. . . .

The dark and silent drive ended at the parking garage in the Piazzale Roma, and they exchanged the car for the motor launch. At the door to the apartment Marco put out a hand to stop her.

"Listen to me one more time, *piccola*, because we may never have a moment alone again. Once, long ago, you wanted me to say that I loved you. . . you demanded certain words to make what was between us acceptable. Do not answer, because I am not interested in words. Love is something that I cannot profess with ease, do you understand? I am not sure what such an overwhelming force should feel like, but between us there was once a powerful emotion—a unique emotion. If you will not admit it, then I will. It grieves me to find that such a beautiful feeling has degenerated into these biting confrontations. It makes me angry."

He brought her face up so that she could see the glinting energy of his eyes. "I am a man beset with problems. . . my nerves are stretched to a critical tension. I will not play the bantering suitor or whatever else you seem to need for your delicate sensibilities. And so I wish to say *addio* to anything personal between us. I have not the fortitude for more."

"Marco. . ." she began and was silenced by his sudden hard, powerful claiming of her lips. His arms bound her body to his with a pressure that deprived her of breath as the kiss went endlessly on—invading her defenses, brazenly showing her what she would never again experience, proving in a punishing way that he knew her desires, even if she refused to admit them.

When she found the desperate strength to push him away she saw that his eyes were stony. "I will not intrude again," he said in a voice devoid of feeling, and stood back to let her pass.

Not long afterward Meg lay sleepless in her bed, her heart twisting and agonizing. Was this finally the end of it? The thought came with an odd kind of relief. She felt as if she had been engaged in a battle for the eight months since she'd had the misfortune to order that first cup of coffee at Florian's. It was more like a siege—will opposing will, ego against ego. And yet it had been an undeclared war from the start, each pretending that there was no war at all.

But she *had* won, hadn't she, she asked the silent room during the long empty hours of the night. At least she hadn't succumbed to the dread "syndrome." She should feel proud of herself. But she didn't. Hers was a Pyrrhic victory, with the losses far exceeding the pleasure of having won.

CHAPTER EIGHTEEN

MEG WAS UP EARLY and out of the apartment long before anyone else had stirred. There was a dead feeling inside her where her heart used to be.

She had no appetite for breakfast and didn't even care very much how she looked. She planned to stay in the secluded confines of her office all day, and most of each day until the presentation ceremony. Her clothes showed little relation to the *Au Courant* look, only a comfortable powder blue crew-neck sweater pulled over a pair of faded jeans, which she had thrown into her luggage in case she had to do some of the physical labor herself.

Patty came in later, shamefaced. "I'll work extra late tonight," she said. "We were having such a good time at Harry's Bar that we closed the place up." Italy seemed to have its effects on everybody, even conservative Patty.

Meg forgave her and they dived into the work at hand. At lunchtime Patty offered to go out and bring in some food, but Meg waved her away. "I'm not hungry. You go. Give yourself a break."

As Patty was about to leave she turned back. "You have a visitor, Meg."

Bette Slocum, short blond hair curled close to her head and rings sparkling from her fingers, stood in the doorway. "May I come in?"

Meg nodded, bracing herself for an unwanted conversation.

"I remember you from the mayor's cocktail party last month in Beverly Hills," Bette said patronizingly.

"Are you in Venice for the presentation ceremony?" Meg forced herself to be minimally courteous.

"Didn't you know? I have a special invitation. The Montevalde men are so thoughtful." She sat down on the corner of Meg's desk and crossed her long coltish legs. Her dress was obviously very expensive, but it was still in bad taste, garish, with red and white stripes. Vitelli would have a good laugh.

"Is there anything I can help you with, Mrs. Slocum?" Even if this woman were the special guest of Marco Polo himself Meg wouldn't want to take time with her.

"Well," she looked around the little room conspiratorially, "I had dinner last night with Ugo Montevalde, that charming young man. He told me many intriguing things about the treasures of the palazzo, and he said that you have a special interest in them. I just had to ask you all about them," she said lightly. "I'm a jewelry nut, you know, and you have seen some of the Specchiato gems. What are they like?" She flashed her manicured hands at Meg, showing off the diamonds and emeralds of her rings.

"I saw a few of them last year," Meg said reluctantly, "and they are very nice, but I don't know why Ugo referred you to me."

"He said you could describe the jewels better than a man could."

"Well, I can't. I saw them for a very short time."

"Oh. Well. . .he talked like you knew some of the

secrets of the palazzo, those hidden rooms that everyone says are tucked away behind invisible doors." She gave a little shiver.

Meg began to suspect something. "I think Ugo probably had too much to drink last night, Mrs. Slocum. If anyone knows about hidden doors, it certainly isn't me." This woman was a lot smarter than the twittery female she was pretending to be.

"I had so hoped...you being a reporter...that you might have seen something special that you could tell me in complete confidence. I won't tell a soul until you want me to."

"I'm sorry to disappoint you. You really have the wrong person for this. I'm just here to do the coordinating. If you're looking for thrills, try the Bridge of Sighs or the torture chamber of the inquisitors."

Bette Slocum drew herself up. "That was hardly what I came for and you know it. I hope that the next time we meet you will be more helpful." She slammed out of the office.

How any man could find her attractive was a mystery, Meg decided, and how she was mixed up with Ugo was an ominous one.

The rest of the day passed uneventfully. A quiet dinner with Teresa at a small family *trattoria* gave her just enough time to meet the evening train that was bringing Maude Draper. Meg was pleased to be able to report that the preparations were going well, that the crisis with Vitelli had been averted and turned to something even better than before, and that the *Au Courant* crew were working like demons to get the coverage they wanted.

With Maude's arrival everything revved up to double

speed. Meetings were held at a dizzying frequency for the next several days. If Signor Donato from the Venice committee had thought Meg efficient, the poor man was soon to be overwhelmed by Maude's go-get-em business style. There wasn't any slack time for Meg to worry about the heartache she was carrying around like extra baggage. She hardly had had an opportunity to do more than nod at Marco in passing.

A FEW MORNINGS BEFORE THE GREAT DAY Roscoe and Rosebud Veitch flew into the Aeroporto Marco Polo in their private Lear jet and promptly sent an arrangement of very expensive flowers to Meg at the Specchiato. "We're not here to bother you—only a friendly howdy from Roscoe and Rosebud. See you at the big shindig!" the note said. Bless their hearts, Meg thought, they were the ones she wished she had the extra time to see right now.

At the present time Maude was sitting at what had been Meg's desk and Meg was relegated to a corner table next to Patty. Maude had taken on the *Au Courant* social obligations. She was getting VIP treatment, since the magazine's readers were international and rich, the very people who were in a position to help keep Venice from sinking into the Adriatic. At these parties Maude often had Marco on her arm.

Today, the last but one before the big event, Meg congratulated herself on bringing everything together on schedule. The pace had been a killing one, but the work was nearly done. The mirrored room was set up with dozens of little gilded chairs; the low stage was covered with its carpet, with two broad steps to be used by Vitelli's models. The harpsichords were in place on a dais at the back of the stage—beautiful instruments from the last century, inlaid with satin-textured fine woods.

In the entrance hall long decorated tables were ready for the wines of the Veneto region and for Lucia's appetizers. The serving tables were covered with multiple layers of transparent cloth repeating the soft tones of the frescoes. A nursery's worth of plants—some like small trees—were in place in big molded terra-cotta containers. Around the well were pots of maidenhair fern grouped with blooming begonias. A wide red carpet ran from the entrance door to the stairway and disappeared from view as it continued to the second level. The transformation of the hall was magical.

There was also a special gift for the Specchiato from Roscoe and Rosebud—two authentic Greco-Roman statues, small time-worn marble figures of nymphs. It was an act of generosity that was typical of them. The little nymphs had been placed among the begonias next to the ancient well.

Because it was nearly lunchtime, Maude was getting ready to go out. "One more round of hand kissing and compliments. I don't know if my ego can stand it!" she grumbled happily. "Thank God Marco is always there to fight them off. Doesn't he have eyes you could die for?" She waited a couple of beats for Meg to react, then said, "I've never been one to interfere in boy-girl things, honey, but the tension is getting a little thick around the palazzo, in case you haven't noticed. The two of you are doing the most elaborate dance of avoidance I've ever seen. Care to talk about it?"

Meg shook her head. "We resolved our problems several days ago, and now we just want to forget the past and make the ceremony come off well.'' She didn't look up from the invoices in front of her.

''All neatly tied off and settled, is it? Then I'm a native of Timbuktu! Come off it, Meg. I don't like the help to be dragging. It cuts down on the efficiency.''

Maude's little tirade drew a smile from Meg's lips. ''I'll be fine. And I don't like the accusation that I'm inefficient.''

Maude raised her hands defensively. ''Efficient as a madwoman trying to prove to the world that nothing's wrong with her, that's all! Well, we all have our own ways to cope with romance.'' Maude was baiting her and they both knew it.

''Not romance, Maude. It never was romance.''

''Okay. See you after lunch and whatever else these Italians like to do with their afternoons.'' She waved a cheery farewell, slung her handbag over her shoulder and left.

Patty had heard everything, but, the perfect private secretary as usual, she kept her curiosity from showing. A delivery boy came in and laid a telex envelope on the large desk that Maude had just vacated. Meg picked it up.

> Arriving Venice airport 2:00 P.M. Want to see my favorite niece and have a vacation. Roscoe Veitch has a suite for me at the Danieli. Can you meet me?
>
> Love, Uncle Frank

Patty looked up at Meg's startled face. ''Anything wrong?''

''My Uncle Frank is arriving this afternoon. Roscoe Veitch invited him.''

"Do they know each other?"

"I didn't think so. . . but I guess they do. But there's so much going on, how can I meet him?"

"Send Luigi. He can run the motor launch."

While Patty was gone to find Luigi, the telephone rang. Vitelli was on the other end; he was calling from the home of old Franca. "It is done!" he said triumphantly. *"Fini!"*

"You're a genius," Meg said. It was incredible that he could have accomplished a minicollection in this short a time.

"Not only that, but it is good, more than good. It is *exquise*! A *grand* coup for Vitelli! I wanted you to be the first to know." He hung up without saying goodbye, but that was entirely excusable. Vitelli was amazing. Every day he had visited Franca and her daughters, always with gifts of sewing aids and luxury foodstuffs. They loved him, and had worked around the clock to please him.

At the Specchiato he was domineering and demanding. The servants hated to hear the rhythmic swish of his cane. But he never crossed Marco, treating him instead with cool politeness. His private opinion was to the point: *"Sacrebleu,"* he said to Meg, "the man is a fool not to see a jewel so close to him."

LUIGI BROUGHT UNCLE FRANK directly to the palazzo from the airport. He arrived looking rotund and prosperous and prepared to enjoy himself. Meg's success—and the palazzo—duly impressed him. Maude greeted him in her usual way and sang Meg's praises.

When they were alone again he put his arm around his niece and said, "Well, my girl, you've done very well indeed. Maude Draper has great faith in you."

"Maude's a good friend," she said.

He lowered his voice. "What about this Montevalde? We wouldn't object to a title in the family tree."

Meg let him ramble on about old money and foreign affairs and finally dragged him upstairs to the apartment, where she introduced him to Teresa and Bianca. To her surprise Bianca transformed herself into a middle-aged femme fatale right before their eyes. With fascination Meg watched Bianca's skillful manipulation of her uncle's ego. Soon the two of them were off to the Danieli to see to his reservations and have an early tea.

Meg sighed deeply and caught Teresa's eye. "Your mother is remarkable," she smiled.

"Like a cat with a fresh bowl of cream. Your uncle will be in good hands. But, Meg, I have such news for you!" she said with barely restrained glee. "Enzo has seen your Signor and Signora Veitch this morning. Can you guess what has happened? He loves them! After all his terrible threats and moods, now he acts as if there was never a problem about his taking their commission. He called me to come to Burano as fast as I can!"

"Oh, Teresa, how wonderful! I couldn't be more happy," Meg exclaimed.

"When I think what I went through with him! I expect a very sweet apology, and I want that wonderful old couple to be at our wedding!" She stopped and looked stricken. "But Meg, what about you? You *must* stay here and not go home to California. Why don't you like Marco? I wanted you for my sister. I cannot be fully happy until I know you have found joy for your own heart. . . ."

"Please," Meg said. "Don't speak about it again. It was a pleasant diversion for him for a little while last year, and no harm was done."

"I do not believe that." Teresa looked stormy. "Not when I saw his distress—"

"Please," Meg begged.

"All right. I am sorry, *cara*. I was told that you declined the dinner invitation of the Venezia committee. Was it because you did not want to see Marco, or were you truly too busy to go?"

"Maude is the proper person to attend the dinner. I'm only her assistant now, and yes, I really am too busy to take time out for a social event."

Teresa's face showed what she thought of Meg's answer. "To miss a chance to attend an affair with the top political figures of Venice...I thought you were writing articles about Venetian life, *amica*. This was something not to be missed."

Meg started to walk toward the door. "Congratulate Enzo for me, will you?"

"And now you are the one in my life who is impossible!" Teresa grinned with exasperation.

THE FATIGUE OF THE PAST DAYS was catching up with Meg. Her hands were shaking as she took hold of the doorknob to her office. There was a painful tightness in her breast, and she felt close to tears. It could all be explained, she told herself.

Her desk was a shambles, papers everywhere. She searched the hopeless piles for her clipboard. "Damn," she muttered under her breath. Where could it have gone to? It held all of her last minute reminders.

She suddenly recalled where it was...the mirrored room, probably still on the stage where she'd laid it down this morning while she showed the men where to put the harpsichords.

The corridors of the palazzo had an odd feeling of emptiness in them, like a hush following an intake of breath. The workmen were gone to their well-deserved rest, Marco and Maude were with the Venetian committee, Teresa was probably locked in Enzo's powerful arms this minute, and Uncle Frank was enjoying being looked after by Bianca. The Palazzo Specchiato was poised—elegant and pampered—for its debut tomorrow. Meg couldn't help but liken it to a society woman who throws a grand party, eager to show off her new face-lift. But that wasn't being fair to the dignity of this venerable house.

She felt a tingle of pride as she sped along the beautiful hallways. *I had a part in all of this,* she thought, *and that is something I will take with me for the rest of my life. For a moment I was part of building a bridge of continuity between the past and the future for Venice.* Nothing could take that from her, that intense sense of belonging to something more important than her small self and its emotional concerns. She opened the double doors.

The lights in the huge chandeliers were blazing, a careless oversight by the workmen, Meg noticed. She glanced quickly over the length of the vast room, nodding approval at the placement of the gilt chairs and the scarlet cording that outlined seating areas for the guests. On the stage stood gold-painted pots that would hold tomorrow's fresh arrangements of flowers. The greenery was already in place along the edge of the platform.

Meg quickly located her clipboard near one of the harpsichords, and she couldn't resist touching the old keys lightly with her fingers. The antique sound of the plucked strings made a shiver run down her spine. It fitted perfectly with the mirrored room, too perfectly almost—as if this moment were really part of the distant past, and the first Montevalde prince might stride into his favorite room at any second. The feeling of apprehension stayed with her, not exactly pleasant. The ghosts were crowding her.

She looked around, half expecting to see something—someone else—in the room. Her eyes lighted on the far wall, where the glow from the chandeliers gave a special luminosity to the decorative motifs around the mirrored panels. She started walking toward the wall, and she looked briefly above it, where she imagined she saw something move on the small round balcony.

This would be the last time she'd be alone to examine the mysterious wall and its secrets. After tomorrow she would be flying home to California, where there were no secret panels, no ancient palazzos with compelling histories. She put out her hand to gently stroke the painted design over one panel. The workmanship was exquisite. She ran her fingers over the Della Robbia pattern, having to stand on her toes to reach the very top. As she stretched she put her other hand against the center of the mirror for support.

She felt the mirror start to give way and tried to pull back, but she wasn't fast enough to regain her equilibrium. With the momentum of the pivoting mirror, she pitched forward. During her slow dreamlike fall her mind raced with absolute clarity, knowing that she had found the secret door, that she would have to remember exactly how she had done it, that she should go right away and call Detective Prati. . . .

Her fall was broken by a man's body—Ugo's. He had an astonished expression on his shadowed face. Meg saw a second face behind him—Bette Slocum's. In the second before Ugo roughly seized her arm to pull her completely through the doorway, Meg's efficient mind was telling her to run, get out of here because she had stumbled into something very dangerous. But it was too late. The door swiveled shut behind her, and she had no thought but to stop the extreme pain caused by her arm being twisted cruelly behind her back.

"You'll regret this," Bette hissed, while Ugo forced her to kneel on the dusty floor of the narrow passageway they were in. His flashlight moved crazily over the stone walls. "Well?" Bette said to Ugo angrily.

"What do you want me to do?" he answered weakly, keeping his tight hold on Meg's arm.

"Find something to tie her up with and shove something in her mouth, idiot!" She disappeared down the dark hall and returned with rope. She jerked Meg's head back and slapped her hard on the cheeks. "Open up, dear. This won't hurt. Just for as long as it takes for us to get you safely out of our hair." She jammed a wad of plastic foam into Meg's mouth and waited for her to stop gagging, then tied a scarf over her mouth. Ugo was fumbling with the rope, trying to get her hands together behind her back.

This can't be happening to me, Meg thought wildly. *They're insane!*

"Now, Meg," Bette grimaced poisonously. "Stay there like a good girl while Ugo and I finish our business."

Meg growled at her to show her defiance. Hadn't anyone seen her come into the mirrored room? She fervently regretted ever feeling curiosity about the secret door. Cold and total despair made her whole body start shaking. Every one of the people who could help her were involved with their own activities. She didn't even want to think what would happen now.

Even through the rebellion of her nervous system her journalistic training stayed with her. She would have to mentally record every detail, every word. Kidnapping was a very serious crime, and Meg Brown was going to be a witness with total recall, she vowed grimly. . . total!

For some reason they didn't think to cover her eyes, and she silently watched the activities in the half-dark area behind the hidden panel. There were boxes, lots of them, stacked haphazardly down the corridor as far as she could see. This whole place was some kind of storage room, and now Meg knew absolutely that Ugo was stealing the treasures of the Specchiato.

He grunted as he lifted boxes and carried them down the passageway. Bette had her own flashlight and was taking a swift inventory. After an interminable time during which they seemed not to care that Meg saw what was going on, Bette moved over to her with a question on her lips. "What did you expect to find with all your snooping around? We knew what you were up to! You've put me in a very awkward position—and yourself, I might add. Come on. . . ."

She jerked Meg's elbow upward, and Meg scrambled to her feet, trying not to do something that would provoke her captors any further.

Then other voices approached in the darkness. "The boat is waiting for us," Bette said. "Can you walk okay?"

Meg nodded. Bette sounded solicitous at that moment, even concerned. Probably because the society manners were so deeply engraved in her veneer.

Ugo had joined the voices. There were at least three men and Bette Slocum involved in this, Meg noted carefully. They picked their way along the passage, bending as they went down several short stairways; finally, a narrow and very damp stone tunnel opened into an empty room. They were no longer in the Specchiato, Meg was sure of it. The floors were different, the windows of a more recent style.

No one had said a word. The men opened a large trap door and motioned Bette and Meg down the ladder. At the bottom a black motorboat was rocking gently at its mooring under the building.

It looked evil. Meg's inner voice cried out, *No, I'm not going in that boat!* But the odds against her escaping were growing greater with each passing minute.

She was pushed into the boat and a moment later found herself wedged among the boxes with a tarpaulin thrown over her. The boat started up and roared out into the traffic. Meg was soon feeling queasy from the choppy motion of the swerving craft. It slapped hard against the water, and she knew that they were heading across the lagoon, no longer in the canals.

Once Ugo lifted the suffocating tarp to look at her. "If you had been nicer to me you would not be traveling third class." He grinned at her. "You did great harm to my case against Marco."

"Shut up," Bette snapped. "Put your attention on the problem at hand."

The tarp dropped back over her. She heard the sounds of larger boats, probably the water buses to the islands, and then the boat they were in slowed and they were in calm water again. They were going along a canal. Meg could hear sounds of normal human activity. Evidently no one was paying attention to the little black boat passing by with its special cargo.

Meg's legs had gone to sleep. She ached all over from the rough handling. In all her life she had never been treated this way. But she would remember it all, and when her time came she would see that the world knew about it! Her sense of outrage was growing. And with it came an insistent sense of sympathy for all that Marco had had to endure from his ungrateful cousin. All that he would surely have to endure in the future, unless she could get away from here and tell the police what she knew.

The boat bumped hard against something and the motor was turned off. When the tarp was removed Meg looked around quickly for a landmark but found nothing, only a few low buildings and some scrub growth. It seemed to be a nearly deserted island.

"Out," Bette ordered. Meg stumbled and was picked up carelessly and carried over the shoulder of one of the silent men.

She could smell the rotting wood of the old boat landing. The early-sunset sky was a pale purple, almost surreal. They all proceeded to a small house nearby. The man who carried her set her down on her feet and went back to the boat to unload the boxes with his partner.

Bette took a firm grasp on her arm, guiding her up the broken steps to the old building. Unventilated and close, the place smelled of sweat and sour wine inside. Meg's stomach was near its limit of tolerance. Only her deep anger kept her steady at this point, while she was escorted up a flight of squeaking stairs, pushed into a room and left alone.

None of the adventure movies she had seen had prepared her for this. She stood statuelike in the middle of the little room, at a loss at what to do. Things like this just didn't happen—not to real people.

The footsteps returned, and a flashlight was shone into her face. She blinked, her eyes swimming at the shock of light. Ugo's amused face came into focus.

"Turn that thing off." Bette's voice was edgy. "We aren't playacting, Ugo!" She switched on the bare bulb that hung from the ceiling. "Take the gag out. We have to talk to her. Time is passing."

Meg decided to say nothing unless she had to. The foul taste of the gag made her desperate for some water to rinse her mouth with. She was quick to survey the room. A high dirty window let in only a faint light. The walls were stained with age and water, and a bare iron cot was set near the door. Two straight-back dilapidated chairs completed the decor.

Ugo laughed nervously. "Aren't you going to say something?" His breath reeked of alcohol.

"What do you want me to say?" Meg sat down awkwardly on the cot. She had an odd sense of calm as she surveyed the unsteady faces of Bette and Ugo. "I think you've made a serious mistake."

Ugo looked at Bette. "What do you mean?" he said cautiously.

"I mean I'm furious to be treated like a sack of potatoes and taken against my will. If you don't want me to report this unlawful act to the police I advise you to release me right now." She tried to sound ignorant and outraged.

"What unlawful act?" Bette pressed.

"Abduction, of course. What else do you call it?" *Keep on acting, Meggie,* she urged herself. "I'm not a very good sport when jet-set high jinks include making me very uncomfortable.''

Bette's eyes narrowed. ''You think this is a game for us?''

"Why else would you do something so stupid?'' she replied.

''Don't call me stupid,'' Ugo slurred. ''I'm a lot smarter than Marco. He would have given everything away.''

''Hold your tongue,'' Bette grated.

''Nobody insults me anymore. Let me tell you, Signorina Meg, I am not the younger cousin who has nothing. I have much more than he thinks. Bette is helping me, isn't that so, *cara* Bette?''

''Have you no sense? Leave the room. I will talk to Miss Brown.''

Ugo turned haughtily. ''Don't speak as to a child. I know too much about you.''

''I said, leave us, Ugo. You're drunk. Go see to the boat.''

''No.'' He pushed Bette down into one of the chairs. ''I know what is happening here. You are working with your fellow American to take my money away from me.''

Bette blanched and her eyes grew hard. ''Say nothing more. Don't you have any sense?''

''You need me, Bette,'' he continued as if she hadn't spoken. ''You need my jewels and antiques. Your rich friends need them.'' He was almost babbling.

Bette rose in cold wrath, and her hand shot out in a heavy slap against his face. ''You pig! I'm not going to do business with a drunk who can't keep his mouth shut!''

He rubbed his face. "I can put you in prison for a long time, and your money won't pay the Italian government for your freedom...or the international police, either." He looked around with a sneering smile. "You see, Meg, nobody will insult me anymore."

Bette's face grew ominously calm. "Well, little man, you've done it now. You who are so brilliant. Did you think Miss Brown was deaf? What do we do with her now?"

"Maybe we can give her the Marco Polo Cup to take through customs. Who would suspect her innocent face? She would do this little thing for us." He moved toward Meg, but stumbled against the other chair, cursing loudly as he tried to regain his balance. "Signorina Brown would not refuse ten thousand dollars, would she? Especially with a gun at her pretty head."

Meg's body was in a state of total alarm. She had to get away to tell about this! If she could convince Bette Slocum and Ugo that she was too afraid to betray them, maybe....

She made her voice urgent and trembling. "I hate all of this! Just let me go. I'll go back to California and never think about this place again!" She managed to look thoroughly fearful. It wasn't too difficult. "I beg you!" she said, and desperate tears started from her eyes.

Ugo slapped her hard on the back. "A good try," he laughed. "I made my little joke and now you make yours."

"Let's get on with it, Ugo. You have solved the problem of what to do with her...you and your big mouth. We'll have to get rid of the girl somehow." Bette's tone was flat and weary.

Ugo was still smiling, leering. The empty look behind his eyes made Meg's flesh crawl. He spoke softly. "There are all kinds of ways, eh? The slit throat, the gun shot, poison.... How about that, Bette? You would make a good Borgia."

"Damn it, shut up! This is no matter to be relished. Leave it to the men to decide. I want no part of it." She looked at Meg with a glint of pity. "You were too smart for your own good. Why didn't you just do your little job?"

Ugo interrupted in a conversational voice, "They used to sew up people in bags and dump them into the Bosphorus. No mess, and quiet. *Si*, drowning would be best." His smile was pleasant and completely mad.

"Ugo, stop it!" Bette exploded.

So this is really it, Meg thought, somewhat detached from the reality of the situation. Something irrepressible in her nature had to ask one question, just for her own satisfaction. "Ugo, how did you get the combination to the vault?"

His smile vanished. "That is all you want to know? What a strange female you are. Should I tell her, Bette?"

"Why not?" she shrugged. "But do it on your own time. I haven't the stomach for more right now. I'll be with the men. Miss Brown, it is too bad about all of this. It wasn't to my taste, but we must be practical, mustn't we? *Ciao.*" She left the room.

Ugo was grinning at Meg. "Getting the combination was not a simple matter, since Marco trusted only my sister with it. But I have a good friend, Livio, who has a popular nightclub act on the Lido. I really *am* a genius, you know...." He stared into Meg's eyes.

"I'm sure you are," she said tonelessly. "Go on."

"I invited Teresa to the nightclub for her birthday last year—very special and brotherly. Livio planned to do his magic act first and then demonstrate hypnosis. I told Teresa to be one of the volunteers to be hypnotized and she did. I was counting on her sense of adventure."

"And so your friend hypnotized her, and she gave you the combination. . . ."

"Not quite. Teresa is one of those people who cannot be hypnotized. Livio was prepared to give her posthypnotic suggestions, but she would not go into a trance. The plan did not work. And so I tried a more obvious tactic. I have a second friend who has a love affair with safes, all sizes. In return for a percentage of the profit he came one day to the Specchiato when nobody was watching, and he showed me how to open the vault. After that, I was free to visit the treasures of the Montevalde family and do what I wished, which was to remove certain jewels and paintings and replace them with very good fakes."

"And you hid things in the secret corridor?" If she ever got out of this she wanted to know everything, and Ugo was just drunk and vain enough to want to tell her.

"I was worried when the workmen started renovating the room of the mirrors, and when you seemed to become too interested."

Meg made one last try at using psychology. "Ugo, haven't you any love for your sister or your cousin? Are you willing to do this to Marco, who has helped you so much? Surely you have some wish to live decently with your conscience."

"How naive you are." He came close and caressed her cheek with his hand. "Poor little Signorina

Brown...you could have had very much money, but you chose to act against me. That was not smart." He thrust his face forward. "I do not give a damn for Marco. I hate him. Does that answer your question?" She nodded numbly. "Are you shocked? He gives me a pauper's allowance and acts as if that accident was some stigma on the family. That is no way for an aristocrat like myself to live."

Meg had another question. "What about Bette Slocum?"

"Always the curious journalist, eh? What a morbid last interview." He sat down casually, his legs crossed loosely and his hands folded. "Bette and I are good for each other. She has money and rich friends, and I have fine treasures and a creative mind. We have a good business. There are so many people who will pay high prices, so many who collect...." His tongue was thick, and he seemed to be losing the thread of his thoughts. Maybe she could do something, but what? Her hands were still tied firmly behind her. She refused to believe that the situation was hopeless.

"I understand that you needed money, Ugo," she said, "but what did Bette want?" Maybe if she kept him talking....

"Excitement." He was attentive again. "She has a deal for the Marco Polo Cup. We have a very good copy made from the photographs, but Bette wants the original. I am asking for payment in American dollars—two million."

A hard rapping at the door preceded Bette's tense voice. "The boat is waiting. Hurry!"

"I am not finished, *eccellenza*." Sarcasm dripped from his tone. "I am leaving you to my friends, Signorina Brown. If you had agreed to give me a deposition I would have paid you well, you know. We could have had good times together. But my lawyer has other ways. Once Marco loses his fortune and his title he will not be so attractive to the women, I think. He is really so dull!" Ugo snorted and gave a high laugh, his eyes rolling like a crazed stallion's.

Bette burst into the room and took Ugo's arm. "Now!" she ordered. "The men will do their job and will be gone by midnight to Trieste. It's all settled."

Ugo made a stately bow in front of Meg. Bette avoided her eyes and planted a freezing kiss on Meg's cringing forehead. "I'm so sorry, my dear. You understand my position. It will be quick, I promise. Murder wasn't exactly in my plans, but my clients would have my head if I let you go now. Good names would be dragged in the mud. . . famous curators. . . too many others. . . !"

"Si," Ugo grinned, "Treasures leave Italy with rich tourists, arranged by men of high position. . .*professori, avvocati*, even *commendatori*. A disgrace!" he chuckled nastily. He stood looking at Meg, stripping her naked with his eyes. "It is too bad I have no more time. You should die with a little pleasure."

"Ugo!" Bette choked.

He followed her through the door and turned to blow a kiss. "*Arrivederci.* Wish me luck when we substitute the Marco Polo Cup tomorrow." The door clicked shut and a key turned, and Meg's one burning thought was, *dear God, let me live to tell what I know!*

CHAPTER NINETEEN

MEG LOOKED UP at the dusty window. She longed to see the beautiful world again, the sky and sunset clouds. Surely this stark room would not be the last thing she ever saw. She shivered uncontrollably.

No sound stirred from the room downstairs. Could this whole episode be an example of Ugo's black humor? Were there really no men waiting to kill her? Her mind reached desperately for any possibilities.

The rope around her wrists was cutting deeply into her flesh, and she wavered between weeping and taking action. Finally, with a terrible urge to see the outside world, she struggled to her feet and pushed one of the chairs across the floor until it stood beneath the high window.

Using every unwilling muscle in her aching legs she clambered onto the chair and balanced precariously against the wall. Her head rose just above the sill. How beautiful the muted sunset tones were on the lagoon waters. Gulls flew in wide circles overhead. A man and a boy were fishing from an old quay, well beyond earshot. There was no other activity, no buildings nearby.

She looked straight down. The house was built along a short canal, and water lapped at its foundations. Desperation rose in her heart. She could not die like this.

The black motorboat was taking off from the dock, with Ugo at the wheel. Bette was with him and the boxes were gone. Then the two other men were still here! She could hardly comprehend it. What was she, Meg Brown, doing tied up in a miserable old house thousands of miles from home, waiting for someone other than herself to decide her fate?

Silence settled again, and she heard voices from the room below. She should have been praying with all her might, but instead she thought of Marco with a concentrated love. She thought of Teresa and Maude and Uncle Frank, and even Vitelli. She tried with every power she possessed to send a warning message to their minds.

She was jolted from her thoughts by more sounds. She dropped from the chair with a little thud and waited, terrified of drawing attention. When nobody came up the stairs she went to listen at the door. The men were talking. She heard the words *"a notte calata,"* which sent her mind searching into her memory for a translation. Did it mean after dark? Were they waiting for full darkness to hide them when they carried her body away to sink it into the lagoon waters?

Her strength left her at last, and she cried silently and painfully. She couldn't wipe the tears away, and they ran down her chin into a dark spot on the dusty floor. Why had she come so far to find herself in love so hopelessly? *Maybe it is better that they kill me,* she thought. A saner thought said, *you have to find any means to get away and warn Marco.*

She looked back at the window. If she could climb a little higher, only a foot or two, she could break the window with her head and push herself through it. She could pray that the water below was not too shallow or too deep. If she could somehow swim with her legs as far as the quay she could attract the attention of the fishermen and get help.

She went to work in frantic haste, aware that darkness was almost upon her. With painful contortions of her bound hands she worked with the second chair until it wobbled unsteadily on top of the first one. Kicking off her shoes to get a better purchase, she began to climb up the teetering chair ladder. Her body swayed to find a balance and she almost fell, but finally her head rose above the window again. A precarious step up to the second chair, her last foothold, brought her waist level to the windowsill.

Hastily she pressed her head against one pane of the old glass. Another heavy pressure made it give a little; a long crack slid smoothly across it and then the pane collapsed into fragments, falling with a shimmer into the water below. She held her breath and listened for response from downstairs, but all she heard was the wild pounding of her heart.

Meg gave one last look at the door, this time with a true prayer on her lips. Her head and torso just fitted through the space. She was momentarily paralyzed, looking down at her destination and numb to the pain of the jagged glass edges that tore through her blouse. In the water below she could just make out two motorboats, their engines silent, coasting up to the landing. Several men were in each boat. Her heart sank and she caught her breath in terror.

But there was something familiar about the first man who climbed out of the boats, a taut compact figure. It was Giulio Prati, and, miraculously, he looked up at her. Alarm and concern raced over his features before

Meg, shaken by the sudden realization that rescue was near, lost her delicate balance on the quaking chairs.

There was no way for her to break her fall. For one brief second her eyes held those of Detective Prati. The last thing she saw was frantic activity from the boats, with men leaping ashore. She fell backward heavily, conscious of the impact of her head on the bare plank floor before darkness enclosed her.

A cool touch on her face drew her back to awareness. She was lying on the cot. Blessedly, her hands were free. Her arms ached where the bonds had held her, and Giulio was leaning over her anxiously, applying a large wet handkerchief to her forehead. When he saw her eyes open, a relieved smile softened his face.

Two other men were in the room with him. A small emergency kit was open on the cot and one man was breaking an ampul into a piece of cotton. He held it under her nose. The tangy sting of ammonia cleared her head. "I'm all right," she gasped.

"Calma, calma, signorina," said a deep voice. The man with the cotton came into focus. "You are safe. Lie still." It was a face used to crisis and the exercise of authority.

"Signorina Brown, may I present Comandante Biselli of the special police."

With true Italian gallantry Signor Biselli picked up one of her limp hands and kissed it. Meg managed a weak smile. "And you will be happy to know that we have captured the two men downstairs, some guns, a small amount of heroin and a very large collection of fine art objects. The others involved will be tracked down *subito*."

"Thank God you came... they were going to kill me."

The eyes of the men met in speculation. The third man, introduced as Signor Pelli, brought her a glass of water.

"I examined you a moment ago and I do not think you have broken bones, *signorina*," Giulio said. "But we will find a doctor. How were you able to pile up those chairs and reach the window?"

"Desperation," she said, and began haltingly to tell what had happened in full detail, leaving out nothing that Ugo had said.

"Ah," Comandante Biselli breathed, "and now he wants the Marco Polo Cup. There is no way for Ugo Montevalde and his woman friend to obtain it before it is displayed tomorrow at the ceremonies. Until then the cup will be in its bank vault.... But at the ceremony—that is the moment of vulnerability."

Giulio finished his thought for him. "It will surely be passed then, and that is when we shall capture Ugo, the American woman, and their accomplices. Signorina Brown, we will need your help."

Meg's head was throbbing. "What do you want me to do?"

"For the moment nothing, merely rest. Your friends have missed you, but do not worry. We will tell them at the appropriate time that you are safe."

"We must leave now," Signor Pelli said.

Kindly hands assisted Meg to her feet. To her surprise, she walked without great difficulty down the stairs. Outside, one sturdy police launch was already purring. The other police officers remained on duty in the building.

As they flew across the choppy surface of the lagoon the men briefed Meg on her role for tomorrow. They were returning her secretly to the Specchiato. Only Marco, Teresa, and Lucia would know she was there for now. She need not be afraid. The arrests were expected to be done discreetly.

"We will need you, *signorina*, to be our element of surprise," the *comandante* said, "to make it easier for us to extract the truth from the young man and his American friend."

Meg's mind was on other things, and she listened with only half a thought to the words. *Marco will be safe now. Ugo can't hurt him anymore.* The reality took her breath away, but then her heart tightened again. Marco did not love her, no matter what happened. She sat back desolately in the speeding launch.

Signor Pelli's voice broke into her uncomfortable thoughts, praising her for her resourcefulness. "I can see that you are not a woman to weep and give up."

The *comandante* added, "You have been instrumental in helping justice to work. American women! Ah!" He blew a kiss into the air.

She smiled. They were trying to cheer her up. The launch had turned into the dark *rio* at the rear of the Specchiato and Giulio whispered, "*M'aspetti*—wait." He ran lightly along the quay and through a door, then returned in a moment and beckoned. The men hurried Meg inside and up the service stairs. They went all the way to the top floor, where Meg had never been, and came out at what had to have been the servants' quarters. Sounds of activity came from behind closed doors.

Meg was rushed into an attic room where, surprisingly, some men were tending a very modern-looking communications system. Comandante Biselli smiled. "We have been using this room to pursue our investigations here. . . ."

Giulio Prati took her into an adjoining room with a bed and some comfortable chairs. "Lucia will bring you what you will need for your comfort—and then a good meal. I will notify Marco immediately. He has paced a deep track in the floor of his *salotto*." He bowed over her hand. "I regret that there must be more statements, but not until tomorrow." His eyes were steady, his authority masked in sympathy. But it was authority.

She could imagine Marco's irritation when she, the woman journalist with the questionable motives, publicly disclosed details about the secrets of the Montevalde family. As bad as Ugo was, he was still their relative. She felt awful. How would it affect them all?

Giulio was smiling. "Think only of the ceremony, *cara signorina*. It will be a fine day for Venezia and for this wonderful old house. We will celebrate it by solving a crime. Just think of the excitement when I tell of your courageous escape effort to warn of the terrible plot. . . and I believe you would have accomplished it, too!"

"No, no," she begged almost wildly. "I don't want publicity!"

"Of course," he relented and looked anxious. "A doctor is already on the way. Just to assure us you are fine and to attend to your cuts. You will be safe here and comfortable." He patted her hand warmly.

The door closed and Meg was alone. She felt empty of will, dirty and bedraggled. For a while she just sat on the bed staring into the darkness at the window, feeling nothing. Finally she roused herself and went into the small but adequate bathroom that opened from her room. She stripped off her torn clothes and with a sense of detachment examined the cuts and dried blood that the shards of window glass had left along her waistline. She hadn't felt it happen.

She drew a bath and gingerly submerged herself, trying to cleanse the remembrance of her traumatic experience from her body. Wrapped in a large soft towel she had started to crawl into bed when a soft knock sounded at the door. Lucia entered, set down a small suitcase and held out her arms to Meg.

"Oh, *cara signorina*, we have felt such worry!" Tears stood in her eyes. "Thank the Holy Mother you are safe!" She opened the suitcase and took out Meg's toilet things and robe. "I will stay but a moment." She pressed Meg into a chair. "Now, let me help you with your hair." She took the brush and started to stroke Meg's hair gently.

Lucia's presence was healing, solid, as real as the earth of Italy, and Meg felt close to tears. She touched Lucia's busy hands in a gesture of thanks. "Where is everyone?" she had to ask. "I wish I could tell them all that I'm here."

"*Si*, but we must not. Ugo and that woman must not suspect you have been found. But Teresa has been told, and of course, Signor Marco."

She stopped the motion of the brush and bent closer to Meg. "In all my life I have not seen a man so pained as Signor Marco when he learned of your disappearance. Of course he canceled the dinner with the committee. But it was bad for all of us...the waiting to hear of your safety. And now, *cara*, the doctor is here and I must go." Lucia lightly kissed Meg's cheek. "Very soon I bring a tray with good food for you."

It was after she had seen the doctor, smuggled in by

Prati's men, and had tasted a bit of Lucia's food that the reaction started to settle into Meg's nerves. Bursts of shivering welled up from deep within her. Clad in her robe and nightgown, she huddled under the covers, trying to relax. Lucia had said that Marco was upset. Was it truly for her, or because of the honor of his house?

She sighed and pulled the bedclothes closer. The trembling subsided only after she made a great effort to will it away. Finally she began to doze.

Just as sleep was drawing her deeply into a painless and relieving void, she returned to wakefulness. Someone was in the room with her. She was afraid to open her eyes. Was she going to be killed?

"Grazie a Dio," a soft voice said next to her.

"Marco..." she whispered as she slowly looked up.

"You are safe now." His beautiful eyes were watching her. "Were you hurt? Do you need anything, *cara*?"

She shook her head dumbly. Marco had come to her! He was sitting beside her bed. He was reaching to take her hand, touching her cold fingers with his lips. It was almost more than she could bear to be so close to the warmth of his beloved body and to feel so distant from his heart. She *was* distant from his heart; why else would she feel so desolate?

"I terribly regret that I did not see sooner the danger of the situation, Meg. I am to blame for your suffering."

She listened, removed from him even though he continued to hold her hand. What did he know of her capacity for suffering?

"Ugo and the Slocum woman are downstairs pretending to be concerned. It is all I can do not to...." He left the sentence unfinished. "You are a woman of courage,

Meg, and we are more than grateful. I am honored by your friendship."

Meg glowered inwardly. His impersonal courtesy was a marvel to her. His words had just the right touch of caring. "Thank you," she whispered. Her words sounded as stiff as his. She felt him withdraw even further and saw an odd flash in his dark eyes.

"If there is anything further I can do for your comfort, please tell me." He stood and looked down at her. For a moment she thought he was about to say something personal. "Then I wish you a peaceful evening, Meg. Tomorrow will be a difficult day for all of us, but I have faith in you." With that he turned and walked from the room.

Meg's mind refused to move in orderly channels. *We are more than grateful,* he'd said to her. How nice! How matter-of-fact! This was such a crazy situation. And what was happening downstairs right now? The thought of having Ugo and Bette so near was sickening.

She could picture the scene in the apartment right now, with Ugo and Bette, the proud Marco. . . Teresa, who knew that Meg was safe. . . and Uncle Frank. He should be told that she was rescued. He might be on the phone at that moment breaking the grim news to her mother. *Oh, God!* She'd been stupid not to ask Marco about her uncle. The sight of him had addled her wits!

A knock at the door halted her agitated thoughts. "It is Giulio," the pleasant tenor voice announced discreetly. She went to open the door. Signor Pelli was with him.

Giulio Prati took her hand. "I was sure that you would have questions, *amica mia*, and I am here to bring you news." He smiled and pulled up chairs for everybody. "Maude Draper and the young man with the camera are calling me names of the worst kind for not finding you. They cannot be told yet, but will be as soon as we feel it safe." He pursed his lips in a sympathetic grimace. "I deeply regret that your people have to suffer, but there has to be a genuine distress among your friends. Ugo and the woman possess the sharp perceptions of the guilty, you understand."

"What about my Uncle Frank?"

Smiles flitted over both of the strong male faces before her. "Ah, yes," Giulio said. "It has been necessary to tell him the truth in order to prevent him from alerting your embassy in Rome."

"Thank God!" she breathed.

"Influential people are most difficult to control. I was forced to say something to Signor Vitelli as well, against my judgment. He kept threatening to alert the Sûreté and Interpol, until he was convinced that I am working with Interpol. I told him only that you are safe. I cautioned your uncle to remain silent as well, but I would guess that Bianca Montevalde now knows. Comandante Biselli is speaking to her at this moment about the dangers of the situation."

"Secrets are most difficult to keep, even for the police," Signor Pelli grinned. "But we try."

"We respect your uncle's feelings. We have not given him permission to see you, but he sends his love."

"And how is poor Bianca?" Meg asked. "She must feel so awful about her son. . . ."

"I think you will find her more understanding than you expect," he said soothingly. "She is relieved that Ugo will soon be under protection from himself. And your uncle may supply consolation in her hour of distress." He gave Meg a wide innocent smile, which she answered with one as broad as his own. "*Va bene.* Remember, age is no barrier to romance, and we are in Venezia."

It was almost comical. Uncle Frank in the nets of a beautiful suffering widow. Stuffy, conservative Uncle Frank!

"And now," Giulio said almost apologetically, "the plan for tomorrow. You will be taken to a hidden location above the room of mirrors, where you will be able to watch everything as it unfolds. You deserve the personal satisfaction of witnessing Ugo's attempt to steal the Marco Polo Cup and our quick action to arrest the guilty ones."

"I'm not sure I want to," Meg begged off.

Giulio spoke in measured words. "Surely you will appreciate seeing the inevitable workings of justice. The moment the Marco Polo Cup is substituted, Comandante Biselli will take you to Signor Marco's office for the confrontation with Ugo and the Slocum woman. That should be most effective, since they believe you to be dead."

"They aren't very clever to try to steal a world treasure in front of hundreds of people."

"I agree. Perhaps they relish the danger. A typical twisted response of the egotistic criminal who really suffers from inferiority. It gives them a sense of being above justice," he sighed. "The human mind and heart are so painfully complex, so delicate and easily put off balance."

"Could I ask you how you found the old house on the island? It wasn't just a miracle, was it?" Meg's curiosity spoke.

"Not a miracle. One of my agents was standing at the balcony when you entered the mirrored room to pick up your clipboard. He saw you stumble through the secret door, and he ran down to help you, but it was too late. The door had closed again, but my man heard voices behind it and knew that you were in trouble. Our first suspect was Ugo, naturally."

"But how did you know where they were taking me?"

"We had two locations under investigation, the large empty *casa* at the end of the hidden corridor, which is owned by a Swiss banker in absentia, and the small house on the outer island, which Ugo often visited. There were witnesses who saw a boat leave the docking area of the *casa* next door to the Specchiato. Then logic took us to the second house on the island. Does that satisfy your need for a miracle?" he said with a gleam in his eyes. "And now, my friend, I have a grave apology to make to you."

"For what?"

"For not being honest with you when you were first in Venezia. You see, I delayed your passport myself. There was nothing wrong with the computers, no problem at all. But I needed your intelligent observations in the Specchiato, and I felt that you might possibly stumble upon proof of Ugo's guilt while you were there. Forgive me, please. It was not right of me to involve you that way. But—"

"I understand," she said, not wanting him to apologize further.

"I believe you do, and I am most grateful, *amica*. I was in a very difficult position."

"You gave me more time in Venice, that's all." *Time enough to fall in love with Marco.*

"*Si,*" he smiled warmly. "Do not worry about tomorrow. You will do well."

"I'm not afraid. But the whole affair makes me feel horrid."

As Guilio was leaving with Signor Pelli he turned back for a moment. "Think of it as saving others a great amount of pain. The ordeal will soon be over. Dress for the reception, because you will be able to join it after the unpleasantness is finished. Adella sends her love and sympathy. She is full of admiration for you."

The men left, and Meg spent some time wondering what her life would be like if she had never seen Katharine Hepburn and Rossano Brazzi in *Summertime*.

Prati had taken away Lucia's tray, which Meg had scarcely touched. She still wasn't hungry, and she imagined Maude would be secretly pleased to have her looking so very *Au Courant* and gaunt. She was smiling ironically to herself when her next visitor knocked softly at her door.

Teresa threw herself into Meg's arms. "I had to see you!"

The two friends sat together on the edge of the small bed talking for a long time. "You must recapture the joy of your love for Venezia," Teresa said softly. "After what has happened I pray you do not lose your affection for our family, *amica mia*. I could not endure it, and my poor mother would have great guilt."

"You know I will never lose my love for you, Teresa. . . and your mother mustn't worry."

"*Si*, you are fair in your judgments. You see past the evils of my brother. But what of Marco?"

"I am fair to him, I think," she said and tried for a comfortable smile.

"And how are you fair to him, *cara*? Do you care that he came to your room with wings upon his feet and left with an old man's walk? Something is very wrong with that."

"Marco and I have always had our differences. But he hardly had wings on his feet when he entered this room today. He was polite and no more." As much as she cared for Teresa, this kind of interrogation was unwelcome and tiresome.

"You know very little of the truth about Marco Montevalde, then," she persisted. "You did not see him when he learned of your abduction. Marco wanted to rush to find you with the *polizia*, but Giulio Prati forced him to stay here and play a role. It was terrible, the waiting." She brushed tears from her face. "Meg, I went into your room at the apartment and Marco was there. In his hands was the purse you use so often. *Cara*, he was weeping, holding it close to his breast. He did not hear me and I went away."

Meg shivered and raised reluctant eyes to Teresa. "I'm sorry he was so upset."

"Is that all!"

Meg nodded, her throat too tight for words.

"But he loves you. That was the act of a man in love—deeply in love! I do not know what is between you, but I do see love." She put her hands on Meg's shoulders. "Can't you tell me what is really wrong? I could try to help. . . ."

Where could she start to explain? A picture came into her mind's eye with stunning clarity. It summed up what was wrong. "His idea of love is not mine, Teresa. A man who could feel deeply about one woman does not keep the intimate clothes of other women in his bedroom closet." She was seeing the armoire at the Villa Terza on that shameful day with Marco...all those women's dresses hanging so casually...and the negligee. But as soon as she said it she felt silly.

Teresa just stared at her. "Clothes of women? Where? At the villa?" She dropped her head back and laughed. "After all this time you hold it against Marco that his cousin Teresa left her vacation clothes at the Villa Terza? They were mine, *cara*! Marco has had no women at the villa. It is his special place. You were the first to go there, and probably the last." Her laughter changed quickly to tears. "Oh, Meg!"

Meg's nerves were frayed. "I can't tell you everything else, Teresa, just believe me that there is no hope of our coming together...ever."

"*Assurdita! Nonsenso!* I tell you that a man like Marco does not weep like that except over a woman for whom he feels deeply." She jumped up and paced around the room, then stopped in front of Meg. "Forgive me. You have had enough troubles. You know why I beg so: I love both Marco and you. Please to think about your own heart. It is covered over with unreality. Good night, my crazy sister." She grinned quickly and was gone from the room.

CHAPTER TWENTY

MEG'S BODY FELT HEAVY when she drifted out of sleep the next morning. Her mind was thick with the residue of strange disconnected dreams, and it took a while to realize where she was and why. From somewhere nearby she could hear faint sounds of bustle and preparation. This was the long-awaited day.

Teresa brought up a breakfast tray and stayed to report about the current situation in the Specchiato. "I could have slapped that Slocum woman's evil face as she sat there in the apartment, professing sympathy for us!" Her face glowed with outrage. "She and Ugo made *lagrime di coccodrillo*—crocodile tears. I do not know how Marco could bear it. He is more than a saint."

Meg didn't want Teresa to speak of Marco. The tension of her solar plexus was already overburdened. "I'm worried about my friends. Can't Giulio tell them something about me, anything?"

"Giulio is a tyrant, Meg. Marco had an argument with him about bringing you to a hospital for a more thorough examination. Giulio said you were not enough in need of medical care to take the chance, but Marco was afraid you were hurt more than you appeared. You are all right, aren't you?"

"I'm fine," Meg insisted, "just sore here and there. The doctor assured me I'd be feeling better soon."

"Bene." She smiled. "Vitelli is in a terrible humor. He suspects you are here. He gave me this and ordered me to find a way to get it to you."

Teresa pulled a small cloth jewelry pouch from a pocket of her work pants. Meg took it, and drew out a tiny silver lion of St. Mark, complete with wings and book. It was a pin with a silver guard chain; at the end of the little chain was a long silver straight sewing pin.

Teresa showed her how it should be worn. "On the lap, like this. Do you know, *cara*, that the extra-long sewing pin is the symbol of the couturier? Vitelli has given you the sign of accomplishment, the best praise he knows. I think he would have waited to give it to you—but he wanted to cheer you."

"Tell him I love it." Meg felt a rush of warmth thinking of Vitelli. He was truly a friend.

A tap on the door interrupted them, and Lucia appeared holding a package. Her voice was conspiratorial. "Signor Prati is saying that too much is going and coming up here." She held out her package. "But I must bring this to you. Signor Prati is an old woman. Who would suspect anyone in this attic room!" she grunted.

"What now?" Meg asked with a little smile and reached to take the tissue bundle. She pulled away the scarlet length of ribbon and opened it.

"Madonna mia!" Lucia intoned in a whisper. *"Che bella!"*

From its wrappings Meg lifted a heavily embroidered gown. It was of soft coral silk with embroidery on the sleeves and neckline and around its midcalf hem—flowers of the most alluring pastel colors. The work was exquisite. No one could have done it except Franca and her family.

The card with it was written in elaborate old-fashioned penmanship: *"Signorina* Meg—*con gratitudine e molti baci*." It was signed by Franca and all of her daughters.

Teresa said gently, "They have worked many extra hours to make this for you. Vitelli created the design. They are very grateful to you for giving publicity to their skills. Now they will be contacted for many orders, and they will have money to live better."

Tears flowed into Meg's eyes. "How kind of them—and how wonderful. It's the loveliest dress I've ever seen!"

"They will be watching to see you wear it today."

Meg hesitated. She had planned to stay in the background after the ceremonies. The dress would be like a magnet for attention.

"You will have to wear it because I will not bring any more of your clothes!" Teresa said firmly, sensing Meg's thoughts. "I will not allow you to disappear into the shadows today."

"When Signor Marco sees you...ah!" Lucia clapped her hands. "Now I must go, but I will come back to help you dress."

They left and Meg stood holding the fabulous dress, feeling that she had been lovingly manipulated into something she couldn't go through with. This was a dress made for romance—the very essence of it. She knew Vitelli's clever mind. He was saying to her, *if you can't draw Marco to you in this dress...if you don't become a real Cinderella, wise enough to capture the heart of the prince, then you never will.* Vitelli had done his utmost for her, damn him!

Her fingertips tingled as they touched the dress, drawing into her mind the delicious sensations of romance. It wasn't fair! She said to herself, *you're in all this trouble now because you couldn't stop dreaming impossible dreams.*

No doubt she had gone about everything all wrong. Well, she was tired. There would be no more dreams or pain or wondering. Conte Marco was the heir of a long line of Italian males secure in their power over women—master gamesmen, sophisticated lovers. Their love would never have worked.

She felt absolutely terrible, standing there with the magical embroidered dress in her hands. Couldn't François Vitelli realize that she was unable to play the part that it demanded? Lucia would have to bring her something else to wear.

HOURS DRAGGED BY, but no other visitors came to her room. Meg wished the world would forget her until the whole day was over and done. A small pile of books from the apartment shelves had been left for her pleasure, and she forced herself to read a history of Venice. But her mind wandered. What was Marco doing? Did he even spare her a thought, or was he consumed with the personal triumph that this day meant for him?

At last Lucia appeared, with a small lunch tray and a determination to make Meg beautiful in the new dress. She absolutely refused to bring a more suitable one.

"I don't want to look so...so romantic." She felt herself reddening under Lucia's eyes.

"Just wear the dress, *piccola*," the Italian woman said gently. "It was made with love." She set about preparing steaming black coffee, cheese and rolls. There was a glass of white wine, too. "Signorina Teresa's idea—for your nerves," she said with a knowing smile.

Meg knew she would have to wear the dress. She examined the many tiny grateful stitches that had gone into it. Was there ever a more reluctant Cinderella, she wondered painfully.

She couldn't linger forever over her little lunch, nor could she ignore the fact that the entire Specchiato was buzzing with activity. "When—" she started to ask Lucia.

"Comandante Biselli will be here in a very few minutes. We must hurry."

Lucia eased the dress around Meg's still-sensitive body. A few bruises showed at her wrists from the tight ropes. The sleeves fitted softly over them. The dress hung gracefully and was more than becoming, but her face looked forlorn above the freshness of the pastel colors. Lucia noticed and reached for more makeup, putting a heavier blush of rouge on Meg's cheeks and then tending to her hair.

Meg hadn't had a haircut since Christmas. Lucia pinned the curls into a soft chignon at the nape of her neck. The whole effect was antique and dreamy, and a lump rose in Meg's throat at the sight of herself in the dressing-table mirror.

Lucia gave a last pat to her hair. "It is very difficult for Signor Marco to have this dishonor in his family. What a day for pain and for pride," she said. When Meg dropped her eyes from Lucia's reflection in the old faded mirror, she added, "Ah, *signorina*, what troubles and responsibility he has known. . .the death of his uncle and his father. . .Ugo. . . ."

Meg felt she had to say something. "Signor Marco

has been very kind to me, and I shall always be grateful to him."

Signor Biselli appeared at the door, large and competent. He smiled with pleasure. "Ah, how you have changed since I saw you leaning out of that window on the island. *Che bella signorina!*" He bowed with a gallant flourish. "I am to take you to a hidden passageway that overlooks the room of mirrors. We will not be observed." His easy manner raised Meg's spirits a notch. She thanked Lucia for everything and followed his lead through back stairs that spiraled down inside the palazzo walls. Her hands were damp with nerves.

"Quickly," Signor Biselli whispered. He felt along a wall panel in one corridor and turned a carved rose medallion. A door swung silently inward. He entered ahead of Meg, leading her along a narrow passage, dim and low ceilinged. They stopped at a dead end, where dim light coming through two thin panes of glass gave an eerie illumination to their little space. Meg had to adjust her vision. She realized that she was standing directly over the stage of the room of mirrors, concealed from view by the antique gold patterns on the glass panels.

"This glass appears from the other side to be mirrored," her companion said in a low voice, "but it is not. We are perhaps twenty feet above the floor level of the great room. The first Montevalde prince used to come here to secretly watch his guests admire the treasures."

A hum of human voices overlaid with music rose from the crowded room below. Candelabra were glowing from tall stands and buttery auras of light radiated around the grand chandeliers in the curved ceiling. Meg drew in a trembling breath and felt suddenly cold.

"Are you all right, *signorina*?" Signor Biselli looked at her closely in the half light. She nodded.

"Be calm," he said, "it will soon be finished. No harm will come to anyone. Our people are careful in their duties."

A man and woman were seated at the harpsichords on stage, playing passages of baroque music on the two beautiful instruments, and the room was full of color and movement. Even from her high vantage point Meg could feel the expectancy as the lavishly dressed guests settled into their gilt chairs. Then she saw Marco, standing to one side of the great entrance doors, and her heart melted. How hard the waiting must be, even though he seemed to be concerned with nothing more than graciously greeting his guests. She felt intensely proud of him. He would never know how much.

Signor Biselli touched her shoulder. "We may have action soon. Do you see Ugo Montevalde near the side door?" Meg saw him in conversation with another man. "And do you see the man and woman next to them? *Si?* They are our agents. Others are very near. Let us look for Signora Slocum...ah...she has made quite an effect."

Bette Slocum, bejeweled and gowned in matching sapphire tones, was taking her seat next to Roscoe and Rosebud Veitch. Meg wondered what she must be thinking right now. Was she sorry to have ordered the death of another human being? Was she excited by the danger of her situation and breathless to have the Marco Polo Cup in her guilty hands?

Meg felt anger rising at the sight of the woman. Signor Biselli said quietly, "There is a fine man," and nodded toward Marco, who was making his way to the stage. Spontaneous applause greeted him. Meg yearned to reach out and touch him. How handsome he was, with his dark silk suit and fine white shirt . . . the glint of silver at his temples.

Meg noticed the pedestals supporting clear Lucite cases spaced at intervals along the walls. The old Montevalde prince would have been pleased to see his jewels on display again before the mirrors. Quiet-faced men stood near each pedestal, guardians of the treasures.

A collective "ahh" moved through the audience as a spotlight was switched on and a pedestal on the stage was illuminated. The Marco Polo Cup inside the protective case suddenly glowed with life. The great pink pearl emanated its own peculiar energy of mystery. Marco smiled at the effect the sight was having on the guests and motioned to the *Au Courant* camera crew to capture that moment of drama.

The harpsichordists were introduced, and then Vitelli, who waited on the edge of the stage dressed in an amazing beige suit of nubby raw silk. His shirt was tied with a flowing Byronic cravat, and his cane was held like a long swagger stick.

The fashion show began. It was called the Venice Collection, in honor of the city, Vitelli announced into his microphone. He would turn the profits from the designs over to the city, to sponsor scholarships for young people talented in handicrafts and design.

One by one the models appeared, wearing elegant Vitelli gowns. There were enchanting dresses and a jeweled *dogaressa*'s cap for evening wear, even a fabulous thin wool coat lavishly embroidered with repeated designs of the lion of Venice done in rich jewel tones.

A hip-length sweater over slim pants had the Campanile of St. Mark's embroidered on one side from hem to shoulder in copper, gold and blue. As a gesture to the sportswear enthusiasts Vitelli had created a fantastic design for tight jeans, across the back pockets of which had been embroidered the outline of a gondola and gondolier. When the model mounted the steps of the stage the gondolier appeared to be rowing. It brought down the house.

Meg saw Maude applauding wildly from the front row. Vitelli was in his element, humorous, waspish and flamboyant. He was whipping his cane like a trainer with his sleek bevy of big cats. Everyone enjoyed it.

At the end, he introduced Franca and her family, telling of their wonderful work and, for Snapper's camera, coming down from the stage to kiss their hands and to make a great show of embracing them. After a long ovation Vitelli handed the microphone back to Marco and retired from the stage.

Marco stepped forward and with a storyteller's sense of drama related the history of the Marco Polo Cup, first in Italian and then in English. Meg knew how much he enjoyed bringing the past to life. The spotlight danced on the gleaming cup standing on its marble pedestal.

"What better way to symbolize this day than to enact the presentation of the cup by Marco Polo to the doge of Venice," Marco ended.

A group of people moved onto the stage wearing medieval dress. At the same time the lights from the chandeliers dimmed, leaving only the flickering candlelight in the tall candelabra. The mirrored room, moody and shadowed, was suddenly taken back to another time.

Marco stepped up to the pedestal, lifted the cover and took out the cup. "I return the cup to the noble Signor Marco Polo," he said and ceremoniously placed it into the hands of the actor playing the role of the famed world traveler. Marco moved back out of the circle of light as another man entered in the grand robes of the doge.

"Dio!" Comandante Biselli hissed, startling Meg from her concentration. "Now I understand! The man playing the part of the doge is Livio Grimani, the nightclub magician. His makeup is clever, but I recognize him!"

"The hypnotist," Meg said. "Ugo's friend." She felt a renewed sense of danger.

The doge moved in stately tread across the stage, his crimson robe flowing over his long fur-edged sleeves. He stopped imperiously before the kneeling figure of Marco Polo, then reached to accept the treasured cup with the deftly graceful hands of a professional magician.

"Now!" Biselli said tensely. "Watch what he does."

Meg saw the fake doge ceremoniously move the cup from one hand to the other, then turn to present it to an older man. "The mayor of our city," the comandante whispered.

A costumed page walked smartly forward carrying a plaque on which was fastened a beribboned document—the parchment deed to the Palazzo Specchiato. He presented it to Marco and held out a feathered quill.

Marco took the pen and signed the document. Then, with well-rehearsed precision, the mayor gave the cup to Marco and in turn signed the paper. Marco handed the cup to the page, who took it back to its place on the pedestal. Marco and the mayor shook hands to the accompaniment of clapping and cheers from the audience, and the lights in the mirrored room went up again.

"It is done, *signorina*," Signor Biselli said. "Young Montevalde and the others will be in custody momentarily. Then, when the room is cleared and the false cup removed, we will play the next part of tonight's drama."

"But what happened?"

"Excellent sleight of hand. The rest we shall find out soon." He guided her away from their vantage point and along the back passages again. Echoes of footsteps and voices filtered through the walls, and Meg knew that people were gathering in the reception hall. She stood at last with Signor Biselli outside the closed door of Marco's office, feeling a growing sense of panic. Signor Biselli's professional imperturbability was a help to her agitated nerves.

After an interminable time the door opened and one of the policemen motioned them to enter. The small office was filled with people. Meg recognized Giulio Prati first, sitting behind Marco's big desk, obviously in charge. Beside him was a tape recorder, and Signor Pelli taking notes. The next thing she saw was the white face of Bette Slocum, staring at her with stricken, incredulous eyes.

Marco stepped forward, led Meg to a chair and sat down next to her. His face told her nothing. Ugo glared at her from across the room, where he was seated between two other guards. On the desk were two identical Marco Polo Cups, side by side.

The air in the office was dense with emotions. This was no time for lies. Meg noticed the magician seated in a corner under guard. He looked sour in his doge's robes. The two men from the kidnapping were there, too, hunched in their chairs and handcuffed to each other.

Giulio Prati smiled almost serenely at Meg. "I regret this necessity, Signorina Brown." His voice was measured. "You were seen entering the hidden passageway yesterday against your will. I must ask for your identification of those persons who abducted you and threatened your life."

Meg hesitated. She no longer felt anger toward the people who sat ashen faced and silent. Signor Prati's voice repeated her name and she raised her eyes. "I was taken from the mirrored room of the Palazzo Specchiato and threatened with death by Bette Slocum and Ugo Montevalde."

Ugo broke in, "How very dramatic! Why don't you tell the truth, Signorina Brown?"

"Silenzio." Signor Prati ordered. "*Signorina*, did either of the suspects mention the substitution of jewels or the Marco Polo Cup?"

"Ugo Montevalde spoke of it to Mrs. Slocum in my presence." Meg felt guided and assured by the formality and impersonality of the proceedings.

"Ah, and can you testify to any mention of stealing art treasures?"

"Yes."

"From whom did you hear this?"

"Ugo Montevalde and Bette Slocum."

He turned slowly to speak to them. "Signorina Brown has already given us a detailed statement. She is alive only because your accomplices took too much time arguing how to kill her." He nodded toward the hand-cuffed men. "They have offered to give testimony, and Signorina Brown's words should finish the case against you both."

Bette Slocum erupted into a fiery tirade. "You take the word of two men who would sell their own mothers to stay out of prison? And that hysterical young woman! Don't you know she has her eyes on the Montevalde fortune herself? She's doing this to spite me! She's in love with Marco Montevalde!"

Meg recoiled from the impact of the wild words. She tried to appear unmoved, but the truth of her love for Marco, shouted in the ugly rasping shrieks of Bette Slocum, shook her.

Bette's voice changed to a rough whisper. "If you thought you could scare me into some confession, you were wrong. I thought this girl would be on the plane back to the United States. That was what I told the men to do. I never thought she would stoop to such an accusation!" She stared malignantly at Meg.

Signor Prati had been contemplating his well-tended fingernails. "It might interest you to know that Ugo Montevalde has already testified to your intention of murder. Before you were brought into the room he wanted it known that it was entirely your idea, that you'd insisted Signorina Brown could not be trusted to keep silent about what she had heard."

Bette rose from her chair, fury in her face. "You imbecile!" She was quickly returned to her place. Ugo smiled in self-satisfaction. There was silence as her words hung in the air.

Signor Prati raised his eyes to Meg. "Thank you, Signorina Brown, for your testimony, which I know was difficult. You will, of course, not speak of this to others not directly involved with the case.'' He rose. ''You have had an extraordinary two days, and the reception is still in progress. Your friends will want to see you. For now, tell them only that you were involved in a criminal investigation and cannot be more specific, except that you aided its solution. They will be proud of you, as we all are.'' Taking her cold hand, he helped her from her chair and escorted her to the door. She looked back at the people in the room. Marco stood impassively, his eyes turned away from hers. He had hardly acknowledged her at all, and yet he must have heard Bette Slocum's screaming words. He must surely have wondered, out of curiosity at least, whether Meg really did love him. Even a man like Marco Montevalde would be curious.

She felt Signor Prati's kiss on her hand, and the door closed behind her.

CHAPTER TWENTY-ONE

THERE HADN'T BEEN A FLICKER OF WARMTH in Marco's eyes, Meg thought as she turned away from the heavy oak door. She looked down at the splendor of her embroidered dress. If there was magic sewn into every stitch, it wasn't working. Magic and romance had nothing more to do with her life; maybe that was good. She could go back to California and get on with the lonely business of reality. She would have to believe that that was best for her.

She started up the worn marble steps that led into the entrance hall. In the crowded room people were circulating or sitting at the many small tables, eating and talking, exactly as she and Teresa had planned. Meg blinked her eyes. This was almost too great a contrast to the somber tension of Marco's office, just a few steps away and yet another world entirely.

Maude spotted her first and sailed through the crowd with open arms to enfold her in a Joy-scented embrace. There were tears in her eyes and her usual hard-bitten expression was very much softened. "I'm so glad to see you!" She planted a kiss on Meg's cheek. "Your uncle and Vitelli finally told me what was happening. I could have killed them for keeping it a secret! Are things okay now?"

Meg nodded.

"What excitement!" Maude crowed. She suddenly leaned closer. "But you're not all right, are you, baby?"

Teresa, Vitelli and Uncle Frank were bearing down on them and Maude said hastily, "We'll talk later. You look like a dream in that dress."

In the next moments Meg was embraced and fussed over by everyone. Her mood couldn't help but lighten under the love and praise showered on her. Reporters and photographers from Italian papers were there, and Vitelli gave Meg the lion's share of credit for the idea of his Venice minicollection. With a practiced hand he whirled her into photogenic poses to show off the embroidered dress for pictures, and Franca and her family were drawn in as well, beaming proudly. Meg started to thank Franca, but the old woman waved aside her words.

The next moment Meg was captured in a bear hug by Roscoe, who was calling her his "little heroine." Rosebud, too. "How awful for you, darlin'," she exclaimed, "but all's well that ends well, I always say. When are we going to have an announcement about you and your precious Marco?"

Fortunately, Meg didn't have to answer, because Rosebud's attention was quickly claimed by members of the Venetian committee.

Meg let herself be moved along on the tides of congratulations and interviews. As she looked around at the people in the room she did feel proud. She had done her part in making this a happy ending for everyone, and the good feeling began to trickle down into some of the empty places inside her.

Giulio Prati, finished with the investigation in the

other room, found her, and told her he had no words that could thank her enough for her help. The authentic Marco Polo Cup was in its guarded case again. "The magician demonstrated his excellent sleight of hand in exchanging the two cups; Signora Slocum will be brought to justice under Italian law and also in the United States, since her crimes were international. Ugo will undoubtedly go to prison for a long time."

"I'm sorry for all of them," Meg said.

"Those were Marco's words exactly. He thinks that in some way he failed in his duty—that he should have seen what was happening earlier and avoided the necessity of this unfortunate ending. Your sympathy will help him, I am sure."

Meg looked him in the eye. "I'm going home with the crew, Giulio. There's a huge amount of work to be done to get out the magazine's Italian issue."

An odd smile quirked his firm lips. "But I am afraid that is impossible, *amica*. You will have to stay here for several more days to give statements. And then there will be the trials—"

"But. . . I've got to leave," she protested. She had to!

"I am serious, my friend. This is not something I am inventing to force you to remain in Venezia. Think about what has happened most carefully. It is not a time to run away, even if you could." He gave her hand a quick squeeze and left her.

Through the long reception formalities Meg observed Marco as he made his rounds, graciously hosting the event. If he had seen her it was not apparent. Finally all of the guests had departed, and Maude and the other *Au Courant* people invited Meg to a late supper at the Regina Hotel. She begged off, pleading fatigue. "It's a little strenuous to be kidnapped," she murmured, to their kindly laughter.

Adella, very heavy with child, was looking tired. "Giulio thinks we should go home," she said. "Do not leave Venezia until we can be together and talk."

Teresa linked arms with Meg. "And you, *cara*—you must rest in your own comfortable bedroom tonight." She laughed. "My mother and your uncle are in the apartment right now. He plans to visit her in Firenze for a week...." She let the thought trail off as they walked up the marble staircase to the second floor.

"They're not...?" Meg's face expressed her surprise.

Teresa smiled. "Your trouble brought them very close together. She gave much sympathy, and she gives it very well, you know. I think your Uncle Frank will never be the same. Come and see."

"And where is Enzo? You should be with him."

"He is with Marco, helping to put the Montevalde jewels under police protection until the trials are over."

"Then they weren't all stolen and replaced with fakes?"

"Only some of them," Teresa said. "But now the real ones will be recovered, *grazie à Dio*. My foolish brother kept a list of the buyers, and Giulio is most pleased to have found it." She grinned up at Meg. "Ugo's fakes did look real. You saw one of them, remember? The missing Empress Earring that mysteriously came back—it was one of Ugo's. I know now that he took one to have it copied, then returned the fake in its place. Maybe no one would have known for a long time if you had not been here and if I had not decided to show you the family treasures."

"We must have surprised him in the middle of the project."

"*Si.* He came back later and exchanged the other real one, also."

Meg paused outside the door to the apartment. "I don't want to see Marco, Teresa. Tell me the truth—is he inside?"

"Of course not. I told you; he is with Enzo." She smiled warmly. "I think Enzo will become like the good cousin that Ugo could not be to Marco."

"I'm so glad."

"*Si.* I must give thanks to San Antonio, my most favorite saint. He is the one who finds things that have been lost." She pulled Meg into a sudden big hug. "I shall burn a candle for Saint Meg—for you, *cara*. Without you we would not be so happy today."

"What about Saint Roscoe and Saint Rosebud?"

"But I shall put candles for them everywhere," Teresa exclaimed. "I love them." She stopped. "Forgive me, *cara*! The sadness in your eyes hurts my heart, and I want you to be joyful as I am . . . *che problema*! Is this a thing not to be solved? Can you not speak of it even to me?"

"I'm . . . too tired, Teresa. Tired to the core."

Teresa opened the door to the apartment. Uncle Frank and Bianca had just moved apart on the couch. He smoothed his thinning white hair and said almost boyishly, "I'm going to run over to Florence with Bianca. If you need me I can get back here *subito* . . . is that the right word?"

Bianca nodded and applauded.

"I've got to learn a little Italian," he said, "because I've fallen in love with Italy."

Bianca lowered her eyes and smiled like an ageless Mona Lisa.

Meg leaned to kiss him. "Don't worry about me. I'm okay, but it's been a long day and I'm very tired."

"That's right, honey." Uncle Frank patted her shoulder. "That Marco has everything under control. He's a man I admire. No fuss, just efficiency." He returned his attention to Bianca, taking her hand in his.

"Oh, I almost forgot," he said brightly. "There's a box on your bed. Bianca and I bought you a little gift. There's nothing like getting something pretty after you've had a hard time. I learned that from Bianca."

"It is *uno regalo d'amore*," Bianca murmured, "a gift of love."

"I think that Vitelli coached them," Teresa said teasingly.

Meg was leery of gifts. She summoned up words of thanks and escaped to her room. In peace and privacy she took off the embroidered dress and hung it away carefully. It was far too beautiful to be wasted on a depressed twenty-five-year-old woman who could barely dredge up the proper gratitude to friends who cared about her.

She looked warily at the ribbon-tied pink box on the bed. She knew it held something to wear, and that much thought had gone into its selection, but she felt strangely stubborn about accepting yet another lovely thing to put over her body.

Finally, dressed in her terry-cloth robe, she sat down next to the box. The ribbon fell away easily, and Meg lifted out a cloud of dusty rose chiffon. The long, full nightgown and its matching peignoir were trimmed with lace, and fragile gold-and-crystal buttons glittered on the low fastening of the robe. Tucked into one corner of the box was a pair of satin slippers with tiny heels—bits of feminine fantasy dyed to match.

She couldn't resist stepping tentatively into the slippers and letting the nightgown float easily down over her head. It settled like a caress against her skin, and she gave a little involuntary shudder. *How like Marco's touch when he was gentle,* she thought. She reached for the robe. It swirled around her like a soft rose cloud. Her eager fingers fastened the tiny sparkling buttons, and she looked at herself in the antique mirror.

Lifting a handful of the chiffon she let it float slowly down again, enjoying the sensual feel of the gossamery fabric against her bare skin.

But she stopped abruptly. What was she doing? She glared at the mirror, and her hands went up to unfasten the buttons.

Just then the intercom by her bed buzzed loudly, and she drew in her breath. Why should she hope it would be Marco? He was probably out somewhere with his friends, celebrating his accomplishments.

Her quiet "hello" was answered by a crackling sound and then, "It's me—Teresa. Are you there, Meg?"

Unreasonably, Meg's spirits sagged. "Yes."

"I need your help in the room of mirrors, *cara*. Someone has left a large pile of papers on the floor. The men were going to dispose of them, but I am not sure if they are yours and should be kept. Invoices and lists of things. The floor polishers will be here early in the morning. I just need you to say keep or throw out."

"But I'm in my nightdress already."

"The one from mother and Uncle Frank? Is it pretty?"

"Yes, it's. . .quite lovely." Meg's suspicions were alerted. "Are you alone? Is anyone around?"

Teresa's tinkling laugh came over the static of the intercom. "Everybody has gone, *cara*. No one will see you but me. Please come, because I want to go to bed. I am just trying to take care of the last things. No need for you to change your clothes just for me."

"Where is Enzo?"

"Starting work already in his studio on his Dante and Beatrice. Isn't that wonderful? And don't ask me about Marco again. He must have gone out."

"I'll be there in a minute."

"Bene!" Teresa said loudly. "Just remember, I love you." The line clicked off.

Meg peered from her bedroom door. The apartment was quiet, deserted. Bianca and Uncle Frank had gone about their own business.

With the soft chiffon flowing around her she ran lightly along the passage that led to the mirrored room. By now she knew the shortcuts in the vast palazzo. Her little heels tapped a soft echoing rhythm in the silence. When she arrived she pushed open the door that led into the mirrored room. There was a dim light in the far corner. One of the tall candelabra was still burning.

The cleanup crew had done wonders. The stage was dismantled and lay neatly in sections, to be removed in the morning. The gilded chairs were gone. She felt a sudden chill as she glanced at the mirrored panel that concealed the secret door. Her own breathing was loud in her ears. "Teresa, where are you?" she called.

From somewhere a slight click startled her to attention. Then a thread of sound began to grow into a soft flow of music—a waltz. "Teresa?" she called again, peering into the darkness. Her heart was pounding with a deep, familiar excitement.

A figure stepped from the ring of deep shadow, and the candlelight made a sudden brilliance of Marco's white silk shirt. The music swirled enticingly around the room, and his moving form reflected itself in the dim mirrors. He was coming toward her, his arms held out. His expression was intense, like a face of destiny.

"Come, *cara*, we must finish our dance." His voice had a rich seductive timbre, a vibrance of command that was the essence of masculine power. "Come," he said again and Meg's feet moved beyond her will. She went toward him slowly, and the music took hold of her, pulling her irresistibly into its rhythm.

Then she was with him, captured by the dark flames in his eyes and held once more in the magic prison of his embrace. Her head found its place against his shoulder, and she felt his cheek rest against her hair. She flowed with him, responsive to every movement of his strong body. They were perfectly in harmony, so that their dance was the dance of one rather than two.

His lips were warm against her eyelids, and she shivered with the intensity of her feelings. What did it matter if this was yet another dream for her? Nothing mattered beyond this moment. Marco was the whole of her world. She felt him pull her even closer, and they kissed in a timeless moment of enchantment. They stood swaying in their paradise while his lips explored hers with an exquisite intimate tenderness, a complete possession that drew her spirit to his. She had no desire to hold anything back.

Finally he raised his head. Her hands, pressed against his chest, felt the deep vibration of his words. "I love you, *diletta mia*. . .I love you!" The words came from everywhere around them—from the mirrors, from the walls—and poured into her heart, to be absorbed into it.

The compelling strength of his eyes made her lift her own wonder-filled gaze to his face. His smile was so overwhelmingly loving that her voice came out in a shaken whisper: "I love you, too, Marco." She paused, realizing what had been said between them. "Oh—I love you!"

"Grazie à Dio!" He swung her with a swift movement into the rhythm of the waltz again. Never in any dream had she danced like this! His strength lifted her and spun her away, and then his skillful hands drew her back to mold her hips close to the energies of his own. It was a dance of triumph and desire and fulfillment. When at last the music stopped, the antique silence of the palazzo reclaimed the room.

Marco's arms released her, and in a single motion he was kneeling before her, his arms wrapped lightly around her thighs and his dark head resting against the gauze folds of her gown. He raised his face, and a glitter of laughter flared in his eyes. "Can you really love an Italian. . .and a blind fool?"

Her hand went out to caress his hair, to touch the firm line of his cheek. Here was the hero who had haunted her heart, the one who had always stood just out of sight in her fantasy of Venice. It was he who had been the tantalizing presence waiting beyond the scenes of *Summertime*. Her breath caught in her throat.

"Will you trust me, my Meg?"

When she nodded, beyond words, he sprang to his feet and swept her into a kiss again, grasping her wrists to press her hands against his heart. The touch of his fingers on the bruises there made her wince. With a remorseful murmur he bent to kiss the darkened marks, and she could feel his tears upon her skin. *"Cara,"* he whispered. "I have hurt you so much—too much—in your heart, and now your sweet body has suffered on my account." He cradled her hands tenderly.

Meg started to protest, but he laid a gentle finger on her lips. "I tell you truthfully, *carissima*, that when you first came here I began to think that I had finally fallen in love. I was tormented by the most compelling yet terrifying feelings of need for you. At the villa you were so sweet and passionate. But, suddenly, you turned cool, making me wonder if I had been swept into a momentary enchantment that had no validity. And then you ran from Venice." He pulled her more tightly against him. "When I found you again you were changed. An elegant career woman had taken the place of the dear and gentle Meg I had known. Here was a sharp intelligent person, capable and very talented. I had to think very much about this—and about the commitments that love demands. You see, I had never truly been in love before."

She kissed his hand, which was stroking her cheek, and waited. His words were the right ones this time. She knew he was being completely honest.

"I would have asked for your love—I would have taken a plane to find you—but you sent my letters back like a slap in the face. My pride is a strong one and I wrestled with it painfully. I thought, have I been wrong? Is she only playing, wanting to hurt a man's pride? How could I have known?"

He leaned forward and kissed her lips tenderly. "But, *cara*, no matter what foolish thoughts fought within me

I was growing deeper and deeper in love. When at last Giulio told me that you had been kidnapped, I thought I would die. I had failed to protect you in my own home. *Per Dio!* And when you came back safely what did I do but try to hide the turmoil of my feelings!" He looked deeply into her eyes, begging for understanding. "But I swear, my Meg, that my heart was breaking with love all that time." With a low groan he pulled her close, his hand searching under the soft chiffon to find her breast.

Meg arched against him. She wanted him, wanted no barriers between them. He felt the shiver of her response as his lips grazed her sensitive ear. "If Vitelli wasn't snoring in my ancestral bed I would take you there right now, curse him!"

"Is that what you want?" she whispered.

He held her away, his fingers digging into her shoulders. "Of course it is what I want! *Dannazione!* I want you, body and soul! I want you for my wife, and I want to make sons with you in the bed of my forefathers!"

The flare died out of his eyes, and he began to laugh, a deep satisfied sound. "I will teach you what I want from you, but not yet, *cara*. I have learned. I will do that only when you are my wife, my beloved. You will never have causc to doubt me again."

Perversely, Meg had a feminine desire to test that noble resolve. She pressed against him, and his response was immediate. There in the silence of the candlelight she let him pull the gown away from her breasts and kiss them until she was helpless with delight. His caressing hands moved freely over her body, and she melted toward him. There were no fears left. With a shy and intimate urgency her hands began to touch him back, to spread the silk of his shirt until she could stroke his taut chest and make his breath come harder.

It wasn't a casual teasing. She needed to feel his strength as something tangible instead of an illusion that would send her reeling back in despair again.

His hands were trembling as much as hers now. Marco took a slow, deep breath and drew the delicate lace over her breasts. "I will not..." he began in a husky passionate whisper, "I will not take what you want to give me tonight. For if I did, you might always wonder. If I do not, you will know that I love you for yourself...."

Filled with her flooding desire, dammed up for so long, Meg stopped his words with a kiss. She opened her lips to him and felt the thrust of his warm tongue against hers. Beneath her searching bold hand the swell of his desire grew hard and hot. He pulled her tight to him and they swayed, together.

Drawing her lower lip between his teeth he bit at it gently, as if it were something of amazing sweetness. Their tongues met and parted, touching and teasing again and again, and then his kiss showed his full intention to possess. An explosion of utter bliss spread like a storm of fire through her body. She was his and she wanted to make herself part of him, so close that nothing would ever sever their union. It didn't matter to her that they would have a hard cool floor for their bed.

Dimly she protested as his lips parted from hers. His arms softened from their tight embrace, but he still held her cradled against him. He lifted her face to his. "Look at me, beloved. It is not right that we make the discovery of our love at this moment and in this place. Who might come in upon us here? When I take you—when we come together in full realization of our passion—I want everything to be perfect for you. Nothing of tension or hiding must be in that first delight when you become completely mine.''

His hand delicately wiped away the tears of love and frustration that slid from her eyes. ''*Cara*, I will not take what I know you would give me now.''

''How would it be wrong?'' she said, barely audibly.

''Because you must understand that I want you for yourself, not as a whim of my uncontrolled physical desires.'' His eyes burned their message into hers. ''I cannot tell you with what joy and honor I feel your need of me.'' She watched as he struggled to say more. His own eyes were wet. ''You must never again wonder about my love, *mia bella*. That sweet girl with her dream of love is still asking me to fulfill her romance. She is mine now, to cherish, and I will give her of my body and spirit.''

His special smile made her heart ache with love.

''But I have found more than that sweet girl. I have found a woman, perceptive and honest and full of courage. She will be a partner in my dreams and plans, and yet be strong and creative in her own being.'' He sealed his words with another kiss, and then smiled down at her. ''Do you know how many times I have been told that I was a fool not to see how extraordinary you were?''

''As many times as they told me I was crazy not to see that you were truly good and kind,'' she said and made a wry face. ''And they were right.''

''Of course, and we *were* fools and crazy, *non è vero*?''

''But not anymore,'' Meg said, laughing. ''I can't

quite believe that there are no walls between us—that I can tell you I love you whenever I wish."

He took her hand and kissed its palm, nibbling at the sensitive center, caressing with the warm tip of his tongue. "And I can do this, and many other things—and love you forever—whenever I wish..."

A sound of hands clapping made them both jump. Marco swung around toward a small side door. François Vitelli stood there, leaning on his cane. He was wearing a velvet brocade dressing gown, and there was a wicked smile on his thin face as he advanced into the room. "How is a man to sleep with music and excessive lovemaking to disturb the vibrations of the night?"

"How long have you been here?" Marco growled. Meg didn't care what he had seen. A swelling pride in Marco's love and her own freely given response took all shame from her.

"Long enough," he laughed in genuine merriment. Meg saw Marco's lips twitch in a slight smile. "Am I to assume that there shall be a happy ending?" Vitelli inquired impishly. "Or must I continue to watch two people whom I admire and hold in friendship act in ways most regrettable, since I am convinced of their love for one another...."

"You will be my witness, François," Marco said in all seriousness. "I will love this woman forever, and I want her to marry me as soon as possible."

"Bravo, *Monsieur le Comte*. Now you act as you appear—a Renaissance prince and not a man who cannot keep track of his treasures...especially the best one of all. And you, *mignonne*—" He fixed his attention on Meg. "Are you happy now? Has the wonderful dream come true?"

Meg nodded, smiling, leaning back in Marco's arms.

"Do not be hasty to agree," Vitelli shot at her. "The dream is only beginning, and there is no happy ending unless you undertake to work upon it for all of your life." He chuckled. "*Alors*—I sound like a philosopher. Am I to end my career as advisor to the sick at heart, the lovelorn? No!" he answered himself. "I will create the most beautiful wedding gown in the world, and I shall call it *Le Miroir d'Amour*. It shall be sewn with tiny, tiny mirrors to catch the light in its skirt, like candlelight chiffon. It shall be a souvenir of love." He moved his free hand in lavish gestures, then drew down his brows.

"But now, I wish for sleep." He approached Marco and gave him the honorary French salute, a kiss on both cheeks. Turning to Meg he pulled her close. "A kiss of congratulation I allow myself, and one more on the wedding day, when you are *ravissement* in the dress I shall make for you." He kissed her gently and expertly and let her go.

"Do not set daggers in the eyes, *mon ami*," he grinned at Marco. "I could not steal your treasure even if I would—because she is so much yours that no one can ever take her away, *n'est-ce pas?* Good night!" He turned dramatically and walked from the room, playing a little waltz rhythm with his cane.

"*Dio mio,*" Marco chuckled. "I feel as if my grandfather had lectured to me. But I will take his advice." He snuffed out the candles and stood with Meg at the great doorway to the hall of mirrors. "This room will remember us, *piccola*, with each of its reflections. The mirrors will show glimpses of our love to our children's children."

On the way back to the apartment Marco confessed to Meg how Teresa had helped him plan, how she had arranged for the music on her cassette recorder. "We know that you would not come if you thought I would be waiting. So she risked your anger to give us happiness."

They found Teresa in the apartment *salotto*, curled up on a couch asleep. Marco wakened her with a little nudge, and when she saw their faces she immediately started laughing and crying.

"Maude promises to make you a special reporter in Europe, Meg," Teresa said. "Isn't that wonderful?"

"How many other people have been trying to help me do what I wanted to do but was too stubborn to try?"

". . . helping *us* to do," Marco corrected.

"Oh—almost everybody," Teresa laughed. "Vitelli was prepared to ask Meg to marry him if that would make you act, Marco. He was even willing to have you hate him for a time. Roscoe and Rosebud were going to call both of you in and talk about love, and that dear friend Snapper wanted to hit you in the nose, my cousin." She was counting the conspirators on her fingers. "And Enzo was planning a man-to-man talk about missing life's best opportunities. He should do that well," she bubbled. "Your Uncle Frank. . . ." She sighed and broke into a broad grin. "There were others, but that is enough for now." She kissed them both impulsively and ran toward her room. "I will sleep tonight, and after I have prayed for Ugo, what good dreams will come!"

Marco held Meg close at the door to her room. "Every year we will celebrate this day, the anniversary of when we opened our eyes. Very soon we will go to the

United States, *piccola*—and Enzo and Teresa. For a time our work will be there with the foundation. Maude will not give you up as easily as Teresa says. But one day she will have to.'' He pressed his lips to her forehead in loving promise.

IT WAS A DOUBLE WEDDING, with both Meg and Teresa radiant in the beautiful gowns designed for them by Vitelli and sewn with love by Franca and her daughters. On the great day Meg rose early and looked out at the pearly glow of Venetian light. How wonderful that this city was now her home! All that longing had perhaps been some vision of this homecoming of her heart.

The ceremony itself was like a dream, with tall candles glowing and the soft light of midday filtering into the old church of Santa Fosca. Marco had insisted on having the wedding on the island of Torcello and on holding the reception at the Locanda Cipriani, where he and Meg had first sipped wine together and kissed. Teresa, wrapped up in a cloud of love, would have agreed to anything. It was Enzo who had proved most surprising. He was completely drawn into the idea of marriage, and with hot desirous eyes he gamboled around his fiancée like a muscular fawn.

As Meg moved up the aisle, holding tightly to Uncle Frank's arm, she recognized many of the faces beaming at her—the Pratis, Vitelli, Franca and her family, her mother and aunt, who had fallen under Marco's spell almost as soon as they got off the plane. But for her the greatest reality was Marco's own face, and his eyes brilliant with love as he watched her come to him.

After the simple double ceremony in the ancient church the wedding party was swept away to Cipriani's for a joyful celebration of hugs, kisses and toasts. It was hours later when Marco took Meg's hand and led her through the crowd toward the exit. Meg's mother wept; Teresa, too, of course. It was Bianca who, leaning possessively on Uncle Frank's arm, caught Meg's bouquet of miniature pink roses. By the time the bridal couple ran for the launch, pursued by showers of rice and rose petals, the evening light was spreading its magic over the waters of the lagoon.

The palazzo was silent as they walked hand in hand down the long halls toward the newly decorated master wing. Marco opened the door to the ancestral bedroom, and Meg gasped in pleasure and surprise. The old Montevalde marriage bed glowed with a new canopy, rich in soft colors and flashes of gold thread. The room was fully furnished now, a picture of intimate delight for the wedding night of a Renaissance prince and his princess. High wardrobes, antique and heavily carved, stood with other priceless pieces of Montevalde furniture.

Beaming, Lucia came in and showed Meg into a charmingly furnished dressing chamber next door. She put away Vitelli's magical wedding gown while Meg once again slipped into her cloud-soft peignoir set. Then the housekeeper kissed her and smiled mistily before walking softly from the room.

Meg felt suddenly shy as she opened the door to the bedchamber. Marco stood at the window, silhouetted against the sunset light, and she paused, half believing that this might all be still a figment of her romantic imagination. But then he was taking her into his arms, and his lips told her that the dream was vital and real. For a long time they kissed, swaying together in the joy of their closeness.

"Must I wait longer?" he whispered. For answer she slid her hands beneath his velvet robe and across his warm bare chest. She could feel the heavy beating of his heart.

He made a soft groaning sound and in turn groped for the ribbon ties of her peignoir. Brushing it off her shoulders, he kissed her again, then with eager fingers began to slip the straps of her nightgown down her arms. The gossamery garment quickly formed a dusty rose puddle on the floor. Lifting Meg effortlessly, Marco carried her swiftly to the great high bed and laid her down gently on the silk sheets. Impatiently he pulled off his own robe.

How beautiful he was! Meg shivered with the force of her love. She felt the heat of his body as he pressed himself to her, the tenderness of his fingers as he caressed her skin. His kisses roamed over her as she reveled in the exquisite sensations he gave her, and his mouth brought her breasts to rosy peaks. He was a marvelous lover, bringing her delight in so many wonderful ways. Meg exulted in his love, returning kiss for kiss, touch for touch until they were each panting with desire, with their need, with their uninhibited exploration of the pleasure they could give each other. When their bodies finally joined it was in a deep healing passion that rocked them both with its magnitude. An explosion of shattering joy sent Meg into a timeless bliss. Marco was hers and she was his, not only in body but in a fusing of their souls as well. Their love was not an ephemeral fantasy; it was forever. It had always been forever.

It seemed like ages afterward that they were silent, holding each other closely and gazing into each other's eyes. Everything was all right at last; there was nothing left to separate them and there never would be. In wonder they touched and kissed and gently touched again. Once more the heady magic of their closeness roused them to passion and completion. This time their lovemaking was a sealing of their promise, a commitment. Never again would they feel loneliness, or doubts that couldn't be resolved.

At last Meg broke the silence with a happy, tremulous sigh. "Oh, Marco, I love you so much! How could I ever have mistaken what's between us for a romantic fantasy?"

From the pillow he shared with her, Marco smiled and traced the line of her lips with a warm and loving finger. He kissed her once, very deeply, then said, "The future will never lose romance, *piccola*, I promise. But it will not be fantasy—it will be reality."

He rose up on an elbow and gave her his special smile, then leaned to kiss her bare shoulder when she nestled against him. "And when stresses come and we need to solve them, you must go to Florian's, and I will come to sit at the next table. Then, like a proper storybook Italian, I will watch you with sexy eyes and try to pick you up—and you will let me!"

About the Author

Catherine Kay is—are—two gifted women whose real names are Catherine Dees and Kay Croissant. Both of them have long-standing love affairs with Venice, Italy. They have each spent many happy hours in that wonderful old city exploring palazzos much like the one in *Interlude*. Italians love romance and are always ready to blow flirtatious kisses, they say with reminiscent laughter.

The authors live across the street from each other in Pasadena, California, a suburb of Los Angeles that's full of trees. They work in an office in Kay's house—the walls of which, Kay says, are held up by books. She is the widow of a college professor of English, who also loved books. Now she lives with Nebi Daniel, the cat she brought from Egypt. Her door is always open to the many friends who roam in and out. Somehow she finds time to keep up with her painting, another art at which she's a professional.

Cathy is a graduate of Stanford and the busy mother of two college-age girls. In her own Spanish-style house she has five cats, two dogs, a parrot and two parakeets. For years she was a high-school English teacher, and she has a deep love of literature as well as of good grammar!

Both women are quite comfortable in their collaboration. We see our characters in the same way, they say, and we've never had an argument about them. They outline their stories in detail, and then each takes sections of the book to work on. Their styles blend easily and well, so that not even their editor can tell which of them has written which chapter. They often go out to lunch together—where, they insist, they get the best ideas for new plots.